REALM OF THE FORGOTTEN

HS SULLIVAN

Overhaul editing by Five Ladies Over Coffee

Hardcover 979-8-9901349-7-3

Paperback 979-8-9901349-6-6

Ebook: 979-8-9901349-8-0

Cover photo: Wolf Quillin

Cover design: HVS

Section headers: HVS

hssullivan.com

Printed by Crocketts Point Press

ALSO BY HS SULLIVAN

Daughters of Legianne

The Unraveling of Covens

For everyone who kept fighting.
I'm happy you're still here.
I love you.

Author's Note

This book contains themes of violence, addiction; religious, physical and emotional traumas; intolerance to sexual orientation, gender, and identity, and politics.

There is on page violence which includes, death, murder, blood, and gore.

Off page reference to murder, sexual assault, and violence.

This book contains explicit intimacy scenes.

Please exercise care for yourself and your boundaries as you read if you choose to continue.

Pronunciation Guide

People
- Róisín - Row-sheen
- Madigan - Mad-ah-gan
- Lina - Lee-na
- Aoife - Ee-fah
- Brenna - Bren-nah
- Shasta - Shass-tah
- Nanette - Nah-net
- Lucius - Lew-shuss
- Matthew - Math-yoo
- Lily - Lih-lee
- Ione - Eye-ohn
- Jessamyn - Jess-AH-min
- Rastead - Rah-steed
- Dionomis - Dee-oh-no-miss
- Marsenna - Mar-sen-nah
- Runa - Roo-nah
- Aja - A-jah
- Anelle - Ah-nell
- Cicile - Siss-EE-l

Fatome - Fah-toe-m

Places/Things
    Legianne - Lee-jhaa-ahn
    Molennius - Ma-lay-nee-us
    Ely - Ee-lie
    Roidon - Roy-dawn
    Alleyette - Ah-lay-ett
    Aunellion - Awn-ell-ee-awn
    Shianshani - Shee-awn-sh-awn-ee
    Talista - Tah-liss-tah
    Briigie - Br-EE-j-EE
    Trifoa - Trih-foe-ah
    Baijiola - Buy-jee-oh-la
    Nianti - Nee-awn-tee
    Locaw - Low-cah
    Nautilanis - Naw-tih-law-niss
    Granier - Gr-ah-n-ee-r

PROLOGUE

TURA'S STOMACH immediately pooled with thick, heavy dread when she stepped through the door of the plane's cabin. Chest tightening, breath quickening, she shuffled along behind the older couple ahead of her.

Everything would be fine. She could find her seat, close her eyes, and then she would be there.

The walls were not *really* trying to suffocate her.

The flight attendant at the head of the aisle greeted her with a smile. "Do you need help finding your seat?"

Tura licked her lips and swallowed the thickness that had filled her throat. "Y-yes, please."

The flight attendant held her hand out expectantly, and it took a moment for Tura to register the intent. Handing her the ticket, she watched as the flight attendant's eyes darted over the printed words and letters.

Tura followed her, feeling helpless, down the narrow aisle to where she stopped and gestured to the middle seat.

"You can just store that adorable bag of yours right up here." She reached an arm up to press the compartment above the seats, its

1

rounded door swinging open. "If you need anything once you get settled, just tap the button."

"Thank you."

Once the plane was in the air, Tura's body settled and the terror of the takeoff faded. She forced herself to stare at the seat-back before her and count her breaths. A quiet part of her was grateful that the seats on either side of her remained empty. It left her with the feeling of some space when the cabin offered very little.

She felt it at the base of her skull first. Just small little tingles and pricks along her hairline. Pulling her eyes from the seat ahead, she cast a weary glance around, taking in the other passengers. No one and nothing stood out to her, so she folded her hands in her lap and brought her focus back to her small little section of the plane.

The tingles and pricks grew and spread until her entire body shivered and pulsed with them.

No.

Her head snapped up and swiveled toward the rear of the plane. Her frantic search was met with silver and gold eyes that were watching her steadily. They had been waiting for her to feel their stare, their burn.

No.

It couldn't be. When she had left home, fled her mother, she had taken care to sever all connections she had to that life. To who she was.

She had used her magic only sparingly, out of fear that it would be a beacon. That she would find her.

Tura quickly turned and brought her chin to her chest. Her vision hazed. Everything growing fuzzy and light. Squeezing her eyes closed, she drew in a deep breath, holding it.

A hand on her shoulder made her jump. She held in the scream that had wanted to explode from her. Trying to pull together her tattered pieces, she lifted her head to find the flight attendant that had helped her find her seat.

"It'll be alright. Just another fifteen minutes and we land in California," she said.

"T-thank you." Tura managed a small smile.

"Flying isn't easy for everyone. You've done well." The flight attendant flashed a quick smile before moving down the aisle.

Tura hadn't been able to get off of the plane fast enough. She had brought only the one small bag with her, which left her able to speed past the baggage claim and toward the parking lot.

Almost there, almost there.

She would be able to finally, truly breathe once she made it to the parking lot.

So close.

The smell of soil, fresh after a spring rain, brought her steps to a jerking, nearly tripping halt.

"How did you find me?" She whispered the words without turning, afraid if she said them too loudly, everything would crumble and disappear around her.

"I know where all of my children are."

Part One

"Hearts will never be practical until they are made unbreakable."
—The Tinman, The Wizard of Oz

ONE
NOW

IT WAS the smell of rot that wound its way through the storeroom of the dingy *Alberto's Curiosities and Atrocities* and tickled her ankles, then creeped along her legs, reaching for her nose. The festering aroma of mold dancing with decay. Róisín McKenna's magic flared to life inside the depths where she had pressed it down. The stone knife formed in her hand as she spun on her heels.

Her blade rested against the throat of the intruder at the same instant their large hand covered her mouth. Panic and rage ignited inside her at the sight of their lips held in a tight line, and nostrils flaring before her. Her side twinged, then flared with heat along the scar across her rib cage.

With her free hand, she reached for her left jacket pocket, feeling the solid weight of the item she had swiped from the glass curio case near the register. With the knowledge she had what she came for, she pulled her magic around her like a blanket and shifted away.

GRIPING THE SIDES OF THE BATHROOM SINK, RÓISÍN GRIT her molars together. Twenty-four hours later, her scar still burned.

7

Squeezing her eyes closed, she let the fresh wave of pain crash over her. As it ebbed, she lifted her sleep shirt.

The long, jagged mark with small punctures at either side had faded quickly. There had been more marks. Ugly, red oozing things. She had been relieved to see them finally heal. Yet... this particular mark still clung to her skin.

Witches didn't scar. At least, that was what she was taught. Until her body had been wrapped in bindings made from osmium. Until an osmium blade had pierced her side. Until her body held the scar it shouldn't.

Before...

It had been just over six years, and nothing was the same. No longer was it just the secrets of her family that left her soul marred and weary when they had been exposed. Everything she had known about witchkind, that her mother, Shasta, Lucius had known... It had all been a lie

The first year had been filled with her hiding, learning what she could about Gea. Just trying to get a grasp on what to do next. How to do it. Staying close to Lina, but far enough that the others wouldn't be able to find her.

Once Lina had the twins, their lack of magic had been enough to have Shasta and Matthew backing off a little, and Róisín finally feeling able to breathe, things slowly falling into place.

Until everything changed. Again.

How different the witches with Earthborn magic were from the witches of the rest of the realms. In them, Róisín could feel that freedom of their untethered magic. So much like her own had become after Caid had brought her to Legianne.

Caid...

She leaned closer to the mirror, studying her face. The scars from her battles, new and old, *those* healed and smoothed over by her magic. Deeper in her heart and soul, scars marred every inch. They were the scars that pushed her forward.

Deeper into the world of Earth's witches. Unbound by rules or laws.

The darkness that was allowed to roam free. Unchecked.

As she stared back at her reflection, the dark shadows that had settled around her turquoise eyes were the only proof of what she had become.

She had fought it, at first.

Then they had come for her.

For Adelia.

Once Róisín was healed enough from that night, she'd tracked Adelia and her family down. Healed her battered body.

Years later, Róisín was haunted by those moments in the bar, the dress shop. After.

Could she have done more for Adelia? For all that Adelia had done for her in the seconds before chaos began, had she done enough to help Adelia in return?

The scar at her side pulsed in time to the beat of her heart.

She dropped her chin to her chest, the sight of her hands still at the sink edge catching her attention. The crimson that covered them as her knuckles bleached white from her grip, stretching the skin. The rivers of it that dripped from her hands, down the porcelain of the sink. Creeping, creeping, creeping toward the drain.

Screams from that night hammered at her senses, making her flinch.

No, it wasn't screaming that she heard. It was shouting. Angry ones in Greek.

Filtering in through the open window of the bedroom behind her, she could hear Mr. Pappas and Mr. Costas arguing over which shop front the bench belonged on. Again.

"Breathe, Róisín," she told herself. "Just. Breathe."

She let her eyes fall closed, then drew a breath in through her nose, holding for a count of ten, before releasing it slowly through her mouth.

The faint smell of musk and freshly cut wood surrounded her. The ghost of lips along her neck tickled up to her jaw, sending her eyes flying open.

Gone were the screams. The blood. The heaviness and hotness of magic in the air.

She was in her small apartment over her tea and trinket shop in Greece. The only noise aside from her heart hammering in her ears was the argument from Mr. Pappas and Mr. Costas across the way.

"We'll just have Rosalie settle it for us then," Mr. Pappas' voice echoed up from the street.

Rosalie. That was who she had become a few short years before.

Not Róisín who had abandoned her family. Who had fled without a backward glance. Róisín who hid in the shadows among those in Earth's realm. More than half of her nights spent laying awake in the latest hours, just before dawn crested the horizon, with the hurt from missing those she left behind clutching her lungs.

She stepped away from the sink and quickly braided her auburn hair. Smoothing her hands down her front, she straightened her dress. Her reflection, her only company, mimicked the movements.

Releasing a heavy sigh, she shook her head to expel the lingering memories and thoughts. She was running late, and her darkness had no place in a day of celebration.

She was late for a wedding.

Two

Róisín lowered herself onto a barstool and motioned for the bartender. With a nod, the bartender turned to the cooler and pulled out a beer. This had been Róisín's routine for the last six weeks. The same bar. The same time every day. That one beer she nursed for the next three hours.

The sigh from the stool next to her had her swinging around.

Adelia waved to the bartender, flashing two fingers.

Róisín lifted a brow. "Long day?"

"You have no idea. The CEO surprised us with a visit this morning, company owners in tow."

Something slivered along her spine, making her straighten.

Róisín had spent hours upon hours scouring the hidden library within the Library of Congress while awaiting the all-clear to return to Maine. Once Lina had the twins and the others returned to their realms.

They learned more about Gea in musty books that had been buried on the bottom shelves, shoved all the way to the back. As though they had been put there to mark who she was as a cautionary tale, but also a hope, an effort to forget she existed at all.

And, they learned about Oathkeepers, their magic. Róisín knew that to find Gea, they needed the knowledge an Oathkeeper held.

Finding them, even just *one*, had been harder. Nearly a year and what felt like millions of dead-ends later, Róisín had been ready to give up. Then, what could only be attributed to Fate doing her a solid, Róisín felt something beckoning her to California.

When she finished stocking the shelves of her small tea shop one day, she wandered a few blocks down to one of the local bars. Adelia had been at the bar, back-to the door, peeling the label off the beer bottle before her. Something deep inside Róisín had sparked to life with such an urgency, she had to cover her mouth to stifle her gasp.

Adelia was an Oathkeeper. A witch born with the gift of knowledge, tasked with being the record keeper of time in Earth's realm. She worked as an archivist for one of the realm's richest, at a privately held firm.

Once Róisín had a plan in place, at six in the evening she began her daily trek to the bar just a few blocks away from where she set up a small herbal shop in Southern California. She always chose the stool three down from where Adelia perched herself every night after work. Slowly, it was Adelia that moved down stools. Until one evening, she was next to Róisín.

At first, Róisín had worried it was because, given the magic, Adelia knew who she was. After a week of regular conversation, Róisín could deduce that her secrets were, at the moment, safe.

Or at least, that was her belief until just a few days ago.

"You're not from this realm, are you?" Adelia asked, before draining the rest of her drink.

Róisín's eyes darted around the bar before settling on Adelia. "No." Her voice came out barely above a whisper. "I fled my home for fear of my safety."

"That's how my family ended up here," Adelia said, an understanding in her pale blue eyes. Her blonde hair tumbled over her shoulders as she yanked the tie that had held it in a tidy bun. "My great-great-great-grandparents left Baijiola at the start of their civil war. We've been here since."

"Unfortunately, Baijiola isn't any different today," Róisín said.

Adelia lifted her gaze from her fresh drink. "You're from there?"

The way the woman's eyes narrowed on her, really taking her in for the first time since they had started talking that first night, made Róisín's magic stir inside her.

She stretched the truth, testing Adelia's magic. "Not from there, but I lived there."

Adelia didn't blink. White had shifted into the blue of her irises. Magic awakening. "I've heard from others Baijiola has found peace."

Had it? What had happened in the years since that day in Talista? Had Troy taken a different path than Henry? He wouldn't even entertain the idea of seeing her when she and Lily had been there. Yet, she had wanted to hope that things, despite Gea, *had* gotten better for the realms.

Adelia's voice broke Róisín from her thoughts and memories. "You should go home, Rose."

"What? Why?" Róisín's magic moved, like a hand, toward her heart. To the space next to it.

"They know." Adelia dropped her voice low. "They followed me here today. They think I don't know, but—" She kept her face toward Róisín. Only her eyes moved across the bar.

The group looked like they had just rolled in from a day in the office. Just like everyone else in the bar. It was the energy pulsing off them that made them different. Even from the other witches that were present. Even from Adelia.

"I've always known who you were, Rose," Adelia said.

"Then why didn't you say anything?" Róisín struggled to keep her attention on the bottle on the bar top before her.

"Because you looked lost. Like you needed a friend. I don't know your story, how you ended up here or what brought you here. I only know your magic. And that group, they're evil." She gave a slight nod toward them. "I'm ashamed to admit that I don't work for good people. But I have a family and the money is good." She reached out and placed one of her hands over Róisín's. "You should go. The stock room at the back has an emergency exit, but it's not alarmed. I'll hang out here for a bit, so it looks like you're just going to the restroom. Get to the alley and shift the hell out of here. Okay?"

Róisín nodded, disappointment rushing over her like a wave. Her shoulders sagged, knowing she would have to start over again. Find another Oathkeeper. Gain their trust to learn how to find Gea. "Are you going to be okay? They won't...?"

"They never approached me for information. They have just been lurking around me all day." She motioned for another drink from the bartender. "Fools forget who I am. I've got an alarm set on my phone to sound like an incoming text. In ten minutes, it'll go off. Hopefully, you're long gone by then. I'll get our tabs because something came up, and you had to go. Then I'll go. I haven't looked their way or acknowledged them, so I can play dumb should something come up tomorrow."

"Adelia, I'm sorry. I should have—"

"You've run from something. You're trying to start new. To heal and find peace. Don't be sorry. Just go. Before they take that chance from you." She gave Róisín a small smile.

"Thank you," Róisín said and slipped from the stool.

She made it three steps before everything went black.

IT WAS A SEARING PAIN AROUND HER CHEST THAT BROUGHT her tumbling back into consciousness. The more she came to, the more the rest of her body hurt. Her shoulders, her wrists. She tried to pull them down to her sides, but they wouldn't move. Her head fell back, hitting something solid, and she pushed her eyelids open. Eyes trailing upward along her arms. She had been bound to a post of some kind.

"Ah, lookie, lookie who's awake," a gruff male voice said.

Her head lolled forward. What was wrong with her? Why couldn't she move? Why couldn't her magic heal her?

"I guess that makes the next bit a little more fun. Our siphon got a little..." The black-haired man that stood before her let his gray eyes wander along her body. "Hung up and is running a tad late."

She moved her lips, trying to speak.

"He prefers his witches knocked out." The man walked around her, hands clasped behind his back. "But we like a show, don't we, boys?"

A hum of agreement chorused around the room they were in.

Róisín squinted, looking around. It was the group from the bar. What had happened? How—

"Adelia tried her best, bless her heart," he said. "She'll be handled however her employer sees fit."

"Don't..." Was the only word Róisín rasped out. She tried to move again. Willed her magic to rise. Again. Each time, something sharp prodded her. Letting her chin fall to her chest, she saw she was wrapped in a barbed material.

"Struggling is pointless against the osmium."

When Róisín lifted her head, she found the man standing almost against her. His mouth curved into a wicked grin. "Look at what it's doing to that pretty skin of yours." His eyes were bright on her face as he stroked a finger over her collarbone, and she fought the urge to shiver. Fought her mind from going back to Madigan's thrall and what he had done to her.

Pressure began building inside her. Pulsing at the base of her spine.

"I thought I told you I didn't want her awake," a new voice snapped out. Their words punctuated by a door slamming closed. A tall man with light brown hair stepped into the light. He studied Róisín with dark eyes as he undid his cufflinks.

The pressure within became more intense, joined now by the feel of fire inside her. Her skin grew tight, and she tried to adjust her position against the feel, only to be filled with blinding pain from her binds.

"And how the hell do we keep a witch *this* powerful knocked out? You're lucky the binds are holding her." The black-haired man stepped aside. "You have little time. Take the magic as she is now, or we're all fucked."

The other man had moved close enough now that Róisín could smell his aftershave and the faint aroma of sex. Her chest heaved and her stomach clenched as she tried to swallow the gag that worked up her throat.

He reached out and hooked a finger under her chin. "This won't hurt. Much."

The slimy touch was met with laughter from the men in the room. Her fear, anger, concern all roiled within her. Reaching its breaking point, the pressure inside her pushed outward. And Róisín's magic exploded.

THREE

NOW

Róisín took the mauve colored bow from the vanity and eyed it.

"Do I have to, Aunt Ro?" Abigail's small face twisted in disgust. "It's so... *ugly*."

"Well, do you want to be in Uncle Wyatt's wedding or not?"

Abigail sighed, her shoulders slumping. "Dammit."

Róisín's brows shot up, and she coughed, hiding a laugh. "Excuse me?"

Abigail was only six, but she was already so much like Lina that Róisín couldn't help the smile that quickly split her face. She was feisty and fierce about everything. While Lina wrestled Sloane, Abigail's brother, into a tuxedo in his bedroom, Róisín had been tasked with helping Abigail do her hair.

Returning to Maine always left her with mixed feelings. Joy, love, heartbreak, and sadness. Grief. It slipped from her heart, down her arm, tugging at her hand, trying to pull her under.

Róisín had given the house to Lina when it had become clear their house on the hill was far too small for a family of four and all that accompanied it. As she twisted the bow in her hand, it was hard to focus as the memories of before nearly broke through the wall she had erected before shifting that morning.

Clearing her throat, she parted Abigail's deep chestnut colored hair into sections for the French braid. "I'll let that one slide."

Abigail's face brightened. "You're the best aunt *ever.*"

"I'm your *only* aunt," Róisín said pointedly.

"How goes it in here?" Lina asked as she whisked Sloane into the room. "Oh, Abby, that dress is adorable on you!"

"I don't want to be *adorable*." She scowled at her mother.

Lina leaned closer so that their noses nearly touched. "You're six, so you will have to suffer being adorable." Then, with her index finger, she tapped Abigail's nose. "Same goes for you," she said over her shoulder to Sloane.

"Is Uncle Wyatt going to be wearing one of these things?" Sloane looked down at the tuxedo. "I don't get why I couldn't just wear my nice Carhartts."

Róisín and Lina looked at one another. Róisín's heart gave a heavy thud in her chest. Lina pulled her lips between her teeth.

It had been a remark that could have easily slipped from Caid's lips. Paired with the fact that Sloane, unlike Abigail, had Lina and Caid's sand-blond hair and hazel eyes. Every day they were reminded of how deep that scar had been carved on their lives.

"Yes, Uncle Wyatt is wearing a tux. So is your dad," Róisín said, stepping in for Lina.

"This is stupid," Sloane said under his breath.

"So stupid." Abigail agreed with a roll of her eyes.

Lina groaned. "It's for barely an hour, you two. After the ceremony, Leslie said you could change if you wanted. Put a change of clothes in the bag on the kitchen counter. That bag will also stay locked inside my car until *after* the ceremony and photos are done. So don't even try it." She squinted her eyes at the twins. "You two need to get going and get to the venue *now*. Your shoes are downstairs. Go put them on, your father is waiting."

With their chins down, the twins stomped down the stairs. Lina turned to Róisín and placed a hand on her forearm.

"You good?" She asked.

"They make it easier." Róisín relaxed her shoulders and tipped her head toward the door.

"They're fun, and absolutely exhausting. How long are you staying?"

"I'll stay for some of the reception, but I have deliveries coming for the shop that I need to sign for."

Lina lifted a brow. "Is that an excuse?"

"No." Her answer came a little too quickly, and she knew it. "I have a delivery, yes." She squeezed her eyes closed. "Dammit, Lina."

"Róisín." Lina sighed loudly, then her arms were around Róisín in a tight embrace. "Have you at least made any progress?"

"I found it." Róisín kept her eyes on Lina and swallowed hard.

Lina held up her hands, her eyes wide. "Oh. Oh, shit. You did? Now what? Are you okay? Did anything happen? Did—"

"Stop." Róisín put her hands on her friend's shoulders and gave them a firm squeeze. "I'm fine. It was an in-and-out thing." Sort of. She hadn't accounted for the visitor. However, *that* would be handled at a different time.

Lina scoffed. "Why do I not believe you?"

Róisín blinked at her.

"I knew it!" Lina threw her hands up.

"I'm *fine*, Lina."

Lina pulled her bottom lip between her teeth, her hazel eyes darting over Róisín's face. She let out a heavy sigh, her shoulder dropping. "Now what?"

"Now, I use the piece to either find her or get a lead on her."

Lina's mouth opened and closed as she struggled for words. Then a loud bark of laughter exploded out of her. "Just like that, huh?"

"In an ideal situation, it'll bring me right to her. But..." Róisín felt defeat settle into her bones. Trying to escape the feeling, she moved toward the door, Lina following.

"Can't we just—" Lina snapped her fingers. The motion caused a spark, then a flame to ignite between the digits.

"Fucking Hells." Róisín stopped and blinked up at the ceiling. "I regret everything I ever taught you once your magic came."

Lina stopped at the top of the stairs and faced her. A wide grin split her face. "No, you don't. But I know you regret teaching Sloane how to shift. As much as *I* regret letting you teach him."

Róisín covered her nose and mouth in time to stifle her snort. "If I'd known he was going to use it to scare the shit out of you and Thomas all the time, I'd have waited. Only a year or two, though."

When Lina's magic had come crashing through her, they had both been terrified it would set off a chain reaction that would bring Helen, along with the others, back to Maine. Two years before, Sloane and Abigail had been wrestling in their treehouse in the backyard, getting too near the stairway where they had forgotten to close the hatch door.

Their fall, Lina's panic at seeing them spill from the treehouse, had been enough to wake the magic in all *three* of them. It took Lina four days to call Róisín and tell her what had happened. She confessed she had waited only because she feared what it would mean for Róisín.

Several months had passed before they settled. Their fear and worry receding when no one arrived.

"We're going to have to move around, aren't we?" Lina asked suddenly.

Róisín hooked an arm around Lina's waist and started down the stairs with her. "You'll be fine here for the kids to finish school. Even for a bit after. If cloaking wasn't so exhausting, I could show you , but that's a lot of magic."

"And magic smells," Lina said.

"Mom! Abby won't give me my shoe back!" Sloane's shouts came from the front of the house.

Lina made a half-choking, half-growling sound. "I did this to myself. I did this to myself."

"But they're *fun*," Róisín reminded her.

"*Sometimes* they're fun. Right now? I'm just praying they don't ruin Wyatt and Leslie's wedding."

"They'll be fine." She patted Lina's shoulder. "Standing on opposite sides of the room from one another."

"Shows how well you know your niece and nephew." Lina rubbed her temples. "They'll find a way, trust me."

The twins found several ways to annoy their mother, while also entertaining the wedding guests. Róisín sat at the back, on Wyatt's side, as close to the aisle as she could get with her hand covering her mouth for most of the service to hide her grin or stifle her chuckles at the antics. To be so young and carefree.

She couldn't help but think of how she would goad Matthew when were children. Her heart gave a sharp beat, and she brought a hand to her chest. So many times she had wanted to reach out to him, to make sure he was okay. To let him know she was okay.

But, to open that door would mean opening the door to everything. And she couldn't go back. Maybe someday, but not yet. She still had to finish this. Whatever *this* was.

The heat of a stare had her lifting her head and shoving down the emotions that had swamped her. She scanned the audience, then the wedding party. All eyes were focused on the bride and groom. Or Abigail, who was currently sticking her tongue out at Sloane.

Thomas reached out and brought his arm around Sloane's shoulders, tucking him against his side. The corner of his mouth moved as he spoke to Sloane. On the other side, Lina was doing the same with Abigail. Abigail's shoulders rose and fell with a shrug, her eyes rolling to the ceiling before she nodded to Lina. An agreement apparently reached between the two.

Before she could lean into the aisle to see Sloane's face, the prodding of eyes tickled the back of her neck again, making her pulse flutter against her neck.

Her heart picked up into a gallop. The magic within her stirred, ready. She needed to get out of there. Catching Lina's eye, she gestured toward the door. Lina's brows furrowed, and she lifted a hand, her thumb pointing upward and her eyes darting across the way to the groom and his party before returning to Lina.

Róisín returned the thumbs up, flashing a quick smile. Then, she slipped from the room.

FOUR

SIX YEARS AGO

EVERY NOISE, every sensation, *everything* was too much. Her body hummed and vibrated, her magic begging, pleading to be released. To try again and make it right. Gritting her teeth, Róisín accepted that the only place she could go was to Legianne.

It would be the place they would least expect her to go.

It would buy her time.

Time to try, just one more time, to heal Caid.

Time to break the connections with the others.

Time to... Rage flared inside of her as she thought of the Goddess and what she had learned.

It all circled back to her own fate, to the fact that Róisín hadn't been meant to live. That she had been destined to be sealed within the darkness with the monsters that dwelled there, thriving off of torturing the vilest witches for eternity.

Sealed within the darkness with *Aoife*. With Madigan.

As she lay Caid's body on a bed in the cottage that was to be her mother's, then hers in Wurbray, just steps from the Coven manor, she thought of Madigan's words. What he had said about the Seer. The Goddess.

Hydrangea de Oro. *Gea*. She hated the way the name tasted in her mouth.

A mere pretender. Hungry for power and control, just as Aoife had been. Mildred. Henry. Frederick. Despite Madigan's words, even he wanted that taste of power as the side dish to revenge and getting the Seer, his parent, freed.

She stroked a hand through Caid's hair, now stiff in places from the dried blood in it. Her fingers brushed his cheek. The absence of his warmth made her entire being shout with violent rage.

Finally, she let her magic free. It flowed through her, caressing her veins and filling her.

She moved her shaking hands, placing one at his broad chest, the other to the mangled skin where his neck met his shoulder. Closing her eyes, she danced with her magic. Felt its warm sunshine fall into step with her. It reached from her fingertips to him. The rest of her magic moved through her to keep the balance, to keep her going.

Life reached deeper and deeper within Caid. Reaching, reaching, reaching, yet finding nothing to grasp hold of.

Tears, fat and hot, rolled down her cheeks, splashing onto his blood-soaked T-shirt. Her breath quaked. Slowly, she opened her eyes, trying to hold on to any sliver of hope she could grasp.

Her magic had knitted his flesh, leaving a scar just above his collarbone.

Yet, his eyes remained closed. His skin was still cold and graying. His chest remained still.

Her eyes burned as she watched it.

"Breathe. Please, *breathe*."

When her vision blurred, she finally blinked, reality stealing her breath until spots danced before her eyes.

She couldn't do it. She couldn't save him. Couldn't bring him back.

A thought wrapped in darkness slammed into her mind. What good was her life magic if it had limits?

Something cold slithered up her spine. It wrapped around her. When it reached her heart, she could only suck in a quiet gasp as a strange calmness settled over her.

Her mind cleared. A small piece of her soul fractured, then disintegrated. Rising from the bed, she straightened her ruined gala dress and smoothed her knotted hair. Simmering beneath the cold calm, something dark with teeth and claws took shape.

And a plan formed.

Róisín crept to the back door of Lina's house. She hadn't dared go to her own. Not only for fear of who may wait there, but the memories it held. The raw pain that would forever cut deep. Pulling her phone from her back pocket, she sent a text.

"I'm in the back. Urgent."

Seconds later, Lina's back door opened.

"Róisín?" Lina whisper shouted. "No lights?"

"No. Please, no lights."

"Then you need to come to me. I'm blind as a bat without my contacts."

Róisín slowly maneuvered around the grill and a chair next to the door. "Thank you."

"For?"

"Your discretion."

"Stop with the formalities. Right now." She snapped her fingers. "Get in here." The door made a scuffing sound as Lina slid it open. "Look, I don't have magic, but I have vibes. Something is screaming *shit, fuck*, this isn't good."

"Lina," Róisín's breath caught in her throat and she couldn't finish.

Lina snapped a lamp on and slapped a hand over her mouth just in time to stifle her scream for what she saw, making Róisín wince.

Róisín had been riding on the new adrenaline rush that had flooded her body and only half thinking rationally. Her mind wouldn't stop chanting to her that Lina needed to know, that Lina needed to be protected.

"Are you okay? Where's Caid? What happened?" Lina put her hands on her stomach and sat.

This was a mistake. I should have waited to come here.

"I... Lina... Caid..." The steel that had formed in place of the cold inside of her cracked. In the slightest of whispers, Róisín managed the words, "Caid's gone."

Lina's eyes grew round. Her hand went back to her mouth just as her chin quivered. "He's?"

Róisín could only nod.

The howl that Lina released broke Róisín all over again. A fresh wave of pain slammed into her with brutal force, leaving her gasping as it rolled and tugged her insides in every direction. She stumbled to where Lina sat and took her in her arms. Together, they rocked and cried.

I'd burn the realms for you, Kincaid McGrath.

"Róisín." Lina gripped her tighter. "What happened? We have to do something. The others? Do they know? Do—"

"They know." She tried to breathe through the words. "But you can't let them know I've been here."

Lina straightened, wiping her face. Beneath her knotted brows, her eyes searched Róisín's face. "What do you mean? What's going on?"

"I..." she lowered her eyes. "After it happened, I left. No. *We* left. And I... I severed my connections with the others."

"Wait. Are you on the lam?" Lina blinked.

Róisín frowned. "Isn't that when you're on the run from the police?"

Lina shrugged.

"I'm not on the run. I-I can't give them anymore. I've lost too much." Róisín chest tightened, and she ground her teeth together. "There are things I need to do now, without them."

"Can't you just say you're done? Come back home to us?"

Come back home to us. Was it still home without Caid?

"It's not that easy, Lina." She scrubbed a hand over her face.

Lina took Róisín's hands, her voice steady even though her face still glistened with tears. "Then what do we do?"

"Oh, no," Róisín shook her head. "No. *We* do nothing. *You* need to focus on the babies. That's the most important thing right now." She lifted her hand to her chest, trying to rub away the heaviness that had settled there. What about her? What exactly did she think she could do on her own?

Burn the realms, a voice whispered inside of her. *Save what's left.*

On her own? Could she?

"Never travel to your destination angry. If you do, you'll never arrive where it is you wish to be," Lucius had told her once when she had come to the manor to train with Brent after a fight with her mother.

She wasn't angry. She was broken. Her heart, her mind, her everything. That had to be different.

No, she could admit she was filled with an anger like she never knew herself capable of. Her elemental magic throbbed at her fingertips. Fire begged to be released, to seek the cause of her brokenness. To avenge.

"I need time," Róisín said finally. She may not care what happens to herself next, but there was Lina, and soon, the twins. Caid would never forgive her for letting something happen to them. She could never forgive herself. "Then I need to figure out how to do what I need to do next."

"I can help if you let me," Lina said.

"Lina."

She groaned and rolled her eyes. "Okay, fine. What do I do when Helen comes back?"

"This—" She pointed to Lina, then herself. "Needs to stay between us." She pulled Lina into her arms, hugging her tightly. "Give me a few days to get things sorted. I'll find a way to communicate with you so we can," she trembled, "with his..."

"I don't like this," Lina whispered into her hair. "You can't do this on your own, Róisín."

Róisín looked around the house. "I have to. At least this part of it. I've already been here too long. Helen will smell my magic when she comes back."

"Then get the hell out of here." Lina waved her toward the door. "I'll dig out all of my candles and open all the windows. Maybe I can smother it and convince her you haven't been here in a while."

Róisín wanted to smile. Her heart wouldn't let her. "I love you, Lina."

"I love you too." She brushed a kiss against her cheek.

RÓISÍN SLIPPED AWAY TO THE ROSE VALLEY FIRST. THE LAST time she had been there, it had been with Caid. His words from that day brushed her ears as she fell to her knees on the dirt between the rose-colored wheat stalks.

"I could see the pain, the sadness when you started telling me about this place. It's not that anymore."

She fell forward, her fingers digging into the soil, her magic demanding release.

Róisín sat back on her heels, freeing the scream that had been building inside her, begging for release before it destroyed her. She screamed until the sound became ragged, hoarse, then faded away to nothing. Collapsing, her chest heaved as her lungs gulped in air.

She gave herself just a moment longer before shifting back to Legianne. In the cottage's kitchen, she closed her eyes and willed her heart to calm. Slowly, a barbed wire wrapped around it, each barb pressing, piercing.

"I think something else was here."

She sucked in a sharp breath, holding it until her lungs protested. Giving the idea time to take shape and grow roots before she released her breath. The barbs slackened their pinch on her heart.

Róisín turned on her heel and walked from the cottage, marching toward the Nianti Field.

The idea would either kill her or change nothing. It could be something else and at that moment, she took that chance in her hands and clung to it.

FIVE

NOW

MATTHEW MCARTHUR had willed his magic to his hands, relieved to feel the heat at them just as the armored bone soldier appeared in the fog, its sword arched high. The blast of fire disintegrated the armor, the skeletal mouth dropping open in a silent shout.

He whirled, his hands wrapped in flames and his anger burning just as hot. They were both going home. He didn't care what Lucius had said. There had to be a way.

"No!" He shouted just as another soldier drove its short sword into Lucius's stomach. "Dad!"

Pushing his legs to move forward, he raced toward where Lucius had dropped to his knees. His blood-covered hands were pressed over the wound.

"Dad!" Matthew shouted again, jerking upright so quickly he toppled his desk chair back, sending himself sprawling across the floor of Lucius's study.

His study now, he had to remind himself as he rolled to his side. The dream, no, memory of his last moments in Aunellion clung tightly to his edges. Covering his face, he slammed his eyes closed. He gasped against his palms, his breath hot and chest heavy as it grew tighter.

Six years. It had been almost a decade since he lost his father.

Then Caid.

Then Róisín.

The wave slammed over him, and he choked out a sob. How had everything changed so much, so quickly? It was as though he had never had a chance. *None* of them had a chance.

His magic brushed the frayed end of the tether that had been forged that day in the ravine behind Róisín's house when they had first faced Madigan. Then it found the twin, the tether Coven leaders held with one another, made when he had inherited the position just hours before she broke it.

Where are you?

It seemed to be a question Matthew asked into the current nothing-ness daily. Where had Róisín gone? How could they truly *not* find her?

Where was his family? The one that he had seen on trips to Earth's realm with his mother.

The boy who barked and splashed in the creeks. Jackson. The boy and place that had not been a hallucination, but a memory. He was sure of it.

How had he and Lily been unable to find them?

It was loneliness that gathered his hands and pulled them from his face, leaving him laying on his side, staring through the tears into the room.

"Matthew?" Lily's voice came from the doorway.

The door had just squeaked closed when he found his voice. "Down here," he said gruffly.

A moment later, Lily was kneeling before him, her amber and gold eyes soft as they darted over his face. "I love you, Matthew. I know you want to find them." She reached out and smoothed his red hair from his face before cupping his cheek. "But you need to take a pause. Just for a bit."

He pushed himself up from the floor, rising to his full height. "I can't, Lily. I need to find them." He looked down at the desk strewn with papers from the files Lucius had hidden away. The files that filled him with more questions with each page he read. "This must have been how she felt. Back when this all started."

"Who?" Lily looked down at the desk. "Your mother?"

"No, Róisín. After she started reading her mother's journals and the books from her family. You could see how it wore at her, bit by bit. After over a century of knowing someone," he shrugged, "you see even the smallest of changes."

"We'll find the Burkes, Matthew. All of them. Not just the ones your mother went to in Earth's realm."

He wanted to believe her. Yet, he had been unable to hold tight to any sliver of hope after so many dead ends.

It hadn't helped that they continued to get pulled away to help with the developing refugee situation stemming from Shianshani.

It never ends. Now that it was started, it will never end.

Matthew pressed a palm to a stack of papers. Something in his gut told him that this was a part of it. If they could just find his damned family, he would have his answers.

He rubbed the back of his neck. "You needed me for something?" He asked quietly.

"What I need from you, Matthew McArthur..." She turned to him and brought her arms around his waist. "Is to come sit at the table with me and eat dinner. Then take a walk with me through the gardens. Maybe rub my feet after?"

His eyes tracked the movement of his hand as it brushed through her strawberry blond strands, sweeping them over her shoulder. "How about instead of rubbing your feet, you join me for an extravagant bubble bath, my lady?"

Her eyes danced with a hint of red and her cheeks turned a light shade of pink.

"Lily." He let his voice drop to a low, deep, near growl when he said her name. "After all that we've done, you still," he brushed the back of his hand over her cheek, "blush when I want our bodies to come together?" He leaned closer, dropping his head so that his lips hovered at her ear. "Is it so hard to believe that I want you, still?"

The sound of her swallow and quickened breath shot straight into him, and he felt his cock stir in his pants.

"I just, oh Hells, I'm ridiculous. Is that what you want to hear?"

His hand settled at the side of her neck, his thumb stroking a lazy line down the center of her throat. "I won't tolerate anyone calling you ridiculous. Even yourself." He pulled his gaze from her throat to her face. "I love you, Lily. You're an amazing, incredible woman who is so endlessly confident with that brain of yours, I wish I could do something so that you'd feel the same about the rest of you."

The way she stroked her hands over his chest, up, then down, his skin lit with euphoric tingles.

"I would be a dangerous woman should I become," her hands hovered at the waistband of his jeans, "*too* confident."

"Never," he whispered, not daring to move.

"I guess we could do that bubble bath," she said. Her index finger drawing a circle around the silver tab button. "However, I'd like to make an adjustment to our evening plans."

"Oh?" The word sounded like it had been strangled out of him, and he suddenly felt fifteen again.

She hummed and slid the tab through the hole, letting the top of his jeans fall open. "Could we start with that bath?"

That was all he needed to hear. He bent and scooped her into his arms, chuckling when she shrieked in surprise. She brought her arms around his neck and rested her head against his shoulder. Her contented sigh filled him with a warmth he'd never get used to. She was his sunrise coming over the horizon to drive out the dark.

Six

LINA WATCHED the white rabbit bounce along the tree line, Abigail hot on its trail.

"I'll beat you someday, *rabbit*," she yelled, pumping her arms faster.

For a moment, Lina's breath caught in her throat.

"And a pompous rabbit, is?"

The memory brushed along her mind and the sound of her brother's smooth, deep voice tickled her ear. An ache in her soul over what had happened was determined to never be soothed. The crack that still ran down the center of her heart as a companion that would always be there.

Shaking the emotions away, she shoved open the patio door and lifted her voice. "Abigail Commons, you leave David alone. Come inside, *all* of you, it's lunchtime!"

Guilt prickled along her spine like nettle on her skin as David hopped behind the twins, making a path for the house. Lina hadn't told Róisín that he had remained. She told Róisín what David had said about her family's Coven and the Jordbrand family. It had seemed helpful at first with Róisín's search. They had used it as a starting point. However, it hadn't taken long for the information to lead them to a dead end.

She set the sandwiches on the table for the twins and placed a bowl of berries on the floor for David.

"I thought I told you to hide when we had company?" Lina asked David, pulling her thoughts away from the jumbled mess of her mind.

He shifted onto his haunches, tilting his head to one side. "I remained in the woods when they were here for the wedding."

"Sitting behind the lowest part of the leaf pile is not the woods, David. You were being nosy." She scolded him like he was one of her own and wanted to giggle at the way he tugged one of his ears between his paws. "Do you have any idea how much shit I'll be in if she sees you? Especially after this long? She thinks you're gone."

"I, I *should* be gone. I shouldn't be able to be here any longer."

Lina straightened, glancing at the twins. They sat across from one another, currently bickering about who was the fastest.

"In the living room, now," she hissed. Once they were away from the kids, she pointed a finger at him. "Tell me everything, now. Why was my brother so pissed off at you that day Shasta had us go to that island?"

"Kincaid was unhappy with me?" The shock in his tone caught Lina off guard. She had been sure that David had known Caid was mad at him. That they had fought or something. She hadn't known why Caid had been ready to skewer David that day, but she saw the anger in his eyes as he had watched him hop toward the house.

"He was ready to have you for stew. Now, I don't know whether he liked you, but I could see it clear as hell that day. He was livid."

David was quiet, his body eerily still.

"David?" She waved a hand before him.

"Perhaps..."

"Perhaps, what?" She snapped harshly.

"That day here with Róisín. She had questions for me. We could not finish our conversation before Kincaid arrived, followed by you."

Lina blinked. The day she had first felt Caid's arrival. Some sort of tugging inside of her that urged her to Róisín's house that day. She had come in, finding Caid standing at the patio door, a look of helplessness and pain etched in the lines of his face.

"She sprinted to the house, I remember." Lina nodded. "What did you two talk about?"

"Róisín asked who sent me here for her, so I told her. I may have also slipped when I confessed I had always known Kincaid wasn't human."

Both of Lina's hands flew up to cover her mouth, quieting the loud gasp that had risen from her before it passed her lips. From behind her hands, she said, "You knew he was a witch?"

"I did," David whispered.

"Did you..." She let her hands fall from her face. "Did you know about me? The kids?"

"No. It was strange. I felt nothing in your presence, and nothing after the children were born."

Resting her elbows on her knees, she held her hand between her hands. She blinked down at the rug at her feet. "Who sent you here?"

"Sister Future. She was the guide to secure Present's loom for Past to preserve for eternity."

Lina closed her eyes and sighed. Riddles. David was talking in riddles. "Can you speak it plain to me?"

"The Sisters of Fate's looms all have different purposes. Sister Future's sees how certain things will impact the present time in all the realms for the witchkind. She is tasked with tracking the"—his ears twitched—"ingredients, so to speak. Should something spoil and cause severe harm to the present, she can then snip it from the loom. It will appear in Past's loom for her to, I guess you would call it *glue* into place so that it cannot be undone."

Lina's body fell back into the cushions, her mind whirring with dozens of thoughts. "Future is a meddler, is what you're saying."

"No. Future may not meddle. She can only guide."

"Wait." Lina shot upright. "If Future snips the threads or whatever from her loom so that something *doesn't* happen — why the fuck didn't she chop the shit out of Madigan's line before things got so out of hand that my brother had his throat ripped out?" When David said nothing, she surged to her feet and drove her hands into her hair.

"The Goddess did not know about Kincaid," David sat.

Slowly, Lina dropped her head to look down at him. She had helped Róisín sort through the stacks of old books, mapping timelines with note after note about Gea de Oro. Magic may still feel foreign to her, but she knew one thing: the Goddess was a twisted bitch bent on doing whatever was needed to hold on to her power. "If she didn't know about him, then how? Shit." Her hands flew to her mouth. "It was supposed to be Róisín, wasn't it? David!" She stomped a foot. "Don't be a piece of shit right now or *I* will cut you to bits and serve you to my family for dinner tonight."

He took a slight hop backward. "Future, she… she tried," his voice broke. "It was never supposed to be this way."

"Mom?" Sloane stood in the doorway, his hazel eyes darting between her to David.

It took Lina several seconds to pull her burning stare from David.

"Can Abby and I go over to the Stanford's house? Casey and Marissa are here this weekend."

Lina wanted to scream, to cry, to punch through a wall. Everything felt too loud and too much. She couldn't tell Róisín anything that David had said, or else she would know. There was no way that Lina could justify the massive secret she had kept over the last six years. Just as she knew that once that trust between her and Róisín was broken…

"Yes," she said to Sloane, then looking beyond him to where Abigail stood chewing her bottom lip. "But the both of you better be home by five for dinner."

With a whoop, Sloane skipped to the front door, followed by Abigail.

"Mom?" Abigail paused halfway through the front door. "Are you okay? Is Aunt Ro okay?"

Lina deflated. Her anger and fear fleeing her body so quickly, she dropped heavily onto the cushion behind her. "We're all alright, honey. But hey, do me a favor? Don't grow up. Being an adult sucks."

Abigail watched her for a moment and then seemed to decide the answer was acceptable. "I don't want to grow up because I don't want to pay bills." Then she was gone.

Lina brought her eyes back to David. "Alright, *rabbit*, I'm seeing why my brother called you pompous that day. Spill your guts about this whole thing, or I'll literally spill your guts. Start with why you said you shouldn't be able to be here anymore."

David's voice was like air when he spoke. "Because Sister Future is missing, and so is her magic."

SEVEN

KING. MARCELO Dionomis had donned the crown for just over one year before being able to toss it aside and be free of the burden. They had been the longest months of his life.

In the aftermath of everything falling apart, the realm had voiced its full backing of change. Everyone, right down to those who benefitted from their positions in court.

His first act, the easiest stone to pull from the pile and break, had been rescinding the dress code laws within the wall.

Everyone had celebrated the moment. Their long outdated clothes demarcating their status piled into a heap and set aflame. As everyone sung songs of freedom and hope, their feet pounded around the courtyard while they danced in their modern attire.

The wall had come next. It had been surprisingly easy. In just two months' time, the innermost part of Talista had been exposed to the life that it had been hidden from for nearly a century. Automobiles, technology, *progress* had been welcomed into the castle with insatiable hunger.

The laws regarding witches, the titles they were allowed, the positions they could hold, who they could hold a relationship with had been considerably easier to shift to equality than it had been for Marcelo to disseminate the laws regarding divorce, and eliminating the laws that dictated who could and couldn't love openly.

However, he had gritted his teeth and dug his heels in. He would not dismantle the monarchy until he had the laws passed, making it so that all his people were truly free.

His resolve and stubbornness proved worthwhile. The people of the realm, the Senate, all voted to support the voiding of the previous standing laws.

With that, he moved to remove the monarchy and put in place a general election for what was more like a president or prime minister. He also enacted term limits, so that there wasn't a chance for a monarchy to slip back into place.

Nolani had expressed concern for the people voting him into the position after what he had accomplished in moving the realm forward. It hadn't been what he wanted, but he prepared himself for that fate.

"It would only be four years," he said, trying to assure himself as much as her.

In the end, it would turn out that the people favored Anthony over Marcelo.

Happily, Marcelo handed the figurative keys to the Shianshani kingdom over, then quietly faded into the background with Nolani.

It had been a relief to be away from it all. The beast inside had awoke on his twenty-fifth birthday and he was filled with a hunger like he had never felt before. It had wanted to consume him. When he fought it, it pushed to drive him to insanity. Anything to find a crack for it to win.

Marcelo fought with every breath and every beat of his heart to keep control of his mind and body.

Aja and Anelle worked alongside the Coven on various spellwork in an attempt to contain it. Each attempt was met with failure.

A failure Marcelo would not accept. He had seen what it had done to his father. What it had done to *Madigan*. One of the darkest, most vile witches in existence.

No. The beast would not consume him. He would not give in to it.

So he fought. Still.

In the years since he had learned that the less he fed it, the less he gave it even just enough to pacify its hunger, he remained in control. Raw meat once every few weeks had been enough. Yet, the nightmares of hurting Nolani nearly drowned him every night.

She had tried to assure him, to ease his worries. "Once we're away from all of this, it will get better. It's the stress. I can see the way it wears at you."

He had taken her in his arms and quietly prayed that she was right.

Now, waking next to her every day, he would shower her body with kisses and tell her how sorry he was for not trusting her.

He could begin eating as he had before the curse took hold of his body. Less he needed something... other.

If only that had been the end of it for them. If only that had been the peace for their realm.

When Anthony's beast woke upon his twenty-fifth, he attacked Cassius. Although Cassius had survived, mostly unharmed, Anthony had broken and snapped.

Everything Marcelo had done was slowly chiseled away, bit by bit.

But only for the witches of the realm.

For almost four years, witches who had yet to find a way out, a safe place, lived in fear of their death. Standing execution orders were in place for any witch within the Shianshani realm.

Orders set in place by Prime Dionomis, the new title Anthony bestowed upon himself.

It had become a mess and, once again, Marcelo's beast was becoming more insistent. His stomach pained from the gnawing sensation of unfulfilled hunger. From where he and Nolani sheltered in the rural North Prindell region of Shianshani, it had prodded at him to hunt.

"You have to go to Matthew," Nolani's voice brought Marcelo from his dazed state, as he stared down at the newspaper before him.

He dragged his ice-blue eyes to her face. "Nolani, he's said no the last two times we've asked."

She rubbed her warm umber-colored hand over her face and shoved it into her deep chestnut hair in a frustrated, jerking movement. "We have to do something. Runa said that Molennius and Ely are overwhelmed. They have no more resources for the refugees."

"What about the others?" He shoved the paper away, but the headline of another public execution in Talista still stared him in the face.

"You'd have to talk to Ione and Shasta about it. I only know that Runa came to Aja this morning asking you to go to Matthew again. We need Legianne. We cannot lose any more people." Her voice cracked and her chin quivered.

He rose from the table and went to her. "Have you heard from your father?"

"No. I've tried." She pressed her face into his chest. "I tried our tether again this morning and there was nothing. I don't know if they made it or not."

"There has to be a way to know if they're just not feeling, what, is it a pull? Something else?" Anelle had been helping Nolani learn and understand the depth of magic and how to use it. It was overwhelming for Marcelo and he couldn't imagine how it felt for Nolani.

"It's a tugging. As they're my family, I can, there's a way to know where they are. I don't know how that part works, but every time I've ever reached for them, there's been a little pull back."

Until now. Her family had finally secured a spot in one of the other realms and had been in the process of fleeing. The raid on their home had happened just as they were set to leave.

"Celo..."

He cradled her head in his hands, tipping it back so that he could see her face. "I'll go talk to Matthew. Come with me. While I'm negotiating the use of Legianne for the refugees, you can check with Lily to see if they made it. I know Ten can do that if she takes me. You need that peace of mind."

She gave him a slight nod. She blinked, sending a tear rolling down her cheek. His throat grew thick and ached. How had everything gone so wrong? Had there been anything he could have done to stop it? He couldn't shake that feeling of guilt that stroked him like a lover, down his arms, across his cheek, whispering in his ear that it was his fault. If he had remained king, this wouldn't be their lives.

The blood of the dead was on his hands.

His body shivered.

The conversation he had with Matthew, Aja and Runa just days before settling heavily over the guilt.

"You know how we end this," Aja said.

"I can't," Marcelo had said insistently, desperately. He had driven his hands into his wheat blond hair and tugged until his scalp shouted.

Seeing the way the tears stained Nolani's face, the pain twisting her features. His heart and mind told him they were right and Marcelo needed to accept what he was going to have to do.

Kill his brother.

EIGHT

SHASTA FIERO thumbed through the stack of papers that had just been delivered to her by Helen, her second in-charge for their Molennius Coven. Her honey-colored eyes scanned the pages of names of Shianshani refugees that had successfully arrived in Molennius that morning.

Ione Wallingsford sat with Runa Lunestran at the kitchen island, their murmurs quiet as they spoke.

After Jessamyn's death, Runa had stepped aside, naming Aja the Coven's leader. Runa and Ione had been with Shasta ever since. Because of that, in a way, the trio had become the initiators and central hub in the Shianshani witch relocation efforts.

"I know, but for right now, babe, we just need to get people there," Ione said. "I don't think they'll care as long as they're safe. We can remodel later."

"We need more than five bathrooms in the castle. You can't put forty people in there and expect that to work."

"Semantics," Ione said. "Fine. We just..." She sighed heavily. "Need to move fast. We need the space *now*."

"I'll have Anelle take care of getting people there to handle it."

Ione with her golden hair and fair skin was a sunrise to Runa's ebony night. Their love for one another had been an echo of what Shasta had been witness to between Róisín and Caid. The kind that would move to the end of time and burn with a fire so hot, no one stood a chance next to them.

When she had returned to Molennius, broken, she had looked at the space where the home she and Evelyn had built once sat. Her heart craved a drink to ease the pain, but her soul urged her away from alcohol, Caid's words of disappointment filling her. Her promise to Lucius to do better, to be better, settling at her shoulders.

Instead, she had rebuilt. Partly for Róisín; should she ever return to them. Shasta would be there for her. A safe place to land, and a room that didn't hold memories of Caid. A haven. Part of her had done it for Lucius, for Caid. For *herself*. Just as she had pushed herself, headlong, into the refugee efforts. Some days, it felt like she was using busyness to keep her demons away, but it was better than losing herself in a bottle again.

Her chestnut-colored finger stopped at a group of names on the list. "Well, shit." She tapped the paper listing the Fatome family names.

Runa lifted his head, his eyes wide. "She who gave *me* shit for saying shit moments ago now says shit?"

Ione chuckled and bit into a slice of pizza.

"When you get lashed for cussing, you stop cussing. Even hundreds of years later, it stays with you." The casual way Shasta said the words left Runa standing with his mouth open and Ione coughing around her mouthful. "Anyway, that's happened. I'm trying to break my habit. You're going to Shianshani to check in with Aja, yes?" She looked at Runa.

He gave her a dip of his head and hummed. "We're supposed to rendezvous at Celo and Nolani's to check his list of the last group against the check-ins around the realms."

"Have Beatrice and Troy sent their numbers?" She asked, shifting her attention to Ione.

"Beatrice sent the full list, names, dates of births. Troy said he'd have his compiled by noon their time today." Ione picked a pepperoni slice from her pizza. Before she could set it on her plate, Runa plucked it from her hand and tossed it into his mouth.

Shasta felt her lips quirking.

"I'm going to Ely later," Ione said.

"For?" Shasta's brows knitted.

"I," her eyes darted up to Runa, who stood eerily still now. His face was a dark storm. "I'm going to see if she'll come with me to talk to our grandmother."

A low growl came from Runa. His stance against this idea was clear. Shasta had to agree with him.

"Do you think that's wise?" Shasta asked. It had been years since she had last seen Nanette, and the meeting hadn't gone well at all. Both women had been deep in their alcohol. Matthew had been missing, and Lily and Ione had fled their home realm of Roidon.

"It's been long enough. Maybe..." Ione frowned.

"She hasn't attempted to connect with you, or Lily," Shasta said.

"She has," Ione whispered.

"What?!" Runa shouted. "Why didn't you say anything?"

Ione pulled her bottom lip between her teeth and rubbed a finger against her chin.

"Lily?" Shasta asked.

"Both of us. She's reached for us through the tether, but we..." Her hand fell to her lap. "We never reached back."

"So you don't know what she wants?" Runa's voice was pitched high with his barely contained frustration.

"I thought at first maybe it was because the Council voted her out as leader and she was looking to hit one of us up for a place to stay, but Lily's right, she's far too prideful for that."

"Well, we know she's still the leader of the Roidon Coven," Shasta pointed out. "I don't think it's a good idea."

"And I agree with Shasta," Runa said with a tight nod. "For once."

"I know. I'm not going into it thinking things will be all sunshine and rainbows. It never was. We need safety for our people. We're working on getting something set up in Alleyette, but I don't know if it'll be enough. An entire realm of witches, Shasta. We're trying to relocate an entire realm of them to places where thousands are already trying to live." She buried her face in her hands and Runa moved to stand behind her, his large hands at her shoulders.

Shasta knew Ione was right. The realms were at a tipping point, and while Molennius and Ely coexisted with humans, there was a very fine line of balance. They couldn't tip it. The tensions in Trifoa and Baijiola were already inching toward too much. They needed more space for the witches.

However, Nanette had drawn the line years before. She would choose her Coven over anything. Even if that meant her Coven remained on their own. Without help.

"I know I can't stop you." Shasta looked at Runa. "And *we* won't. Just... Just be careful, okay? We don't know what she's like after everything. I just know that she was..." Had she broken free of alcohol's hold as Shasta had? Or was she still lost to it?

"We will be. Now" — Ione pointed to the paper Shasta still clutched in her hand —"What's the shit about?"

Shasta handed the paper to Runa. "Take this with you when you go to Aja. Let him know the Fatomes are here, not in Ely, as we'd planned."

Runa's maroon eyes fell on the paper. He frowned. "This isn't all of them. Nolani's brother, Bastian, isn't on the list."

"Has Ely checked in?" Shasta asked.

Ione shook her head. "I was going to grab the list from Brent when I went."

"I can't go to Shianshani with only half the information." Runa waved the paper. "We need to know where he is."

Ione snatched the paper from his hands. "Give me ten seconds," she said before shifting away.

"What's going on in that head of yours, Runa?"

He shrugged his big shoulders and rubbed the back of his neck. "I'm just trying to think of a way to tie her down so she doesn't go to Roidon. The bruises Nanette left on Ione's heart and soul are finally healing. I can't let her land new blows." His jaw flexed. "Family or not."

Shasta pressed her lips together and swallowed. Fighting down the rising tide of sorrow inside, she smiled at him. "That'd go over like tossing a cat into a bathtub full of water."

"I know." He sighed and lowered onto the stool. "Be honest with me, Shasta. Nanette didn't name Lily heir over Ione because she looks like their mother, did she? It's more because Lily is queer, isn't it?"

Shasta's stomach dropped. So much for emotion not swallowing her at that moment. "Yes," she said quietly.

"Nanette doesn't know Ione's with me, does she?"

She reached across the island and laid a hand over one of his larger ones. The second Lunestran daughter, now the second Lunestran son. Runa had told her it was their mother that had performed the spell work to lock the change into place, telling Runa she would rather have a happy child than a dead child. It had left Shasta wondering how in the Hells the Lunestran's had a child like Frederick if they held enough compassion to let Runa be who he truly was.

"Runa—"

"Here!" Ione popped back into the kitchen. "Looks like Bastian is the only one that made it to Ely. I've let Brent know, and he's going to get Bastian brought here so they're all together."

Runa gave Shasta a slight shake of his head, showing the conversation they had started while Ione was gone was finished for the time being. He took the paper from Ione, then reached across the island to grab the others. "I'll get the lists from the others and head to Aja." He turned to Ione and pressed a kiss to her forehead, then brushed another over her lips. "Please be careful."

"You too." She wrapped her arms around him. "It's only a matter of time before Anthony gets daring enough to enter North Prindell."

What a fucking mess this all is.

Madigan had been an easier monster to face than this. Even when he had his magic. The scale of Anthony's chaos reached far wider than Madigan. Hundreds of witches had died at his hands.

Once Runa left, Ione looked at Shasta. "We need to talk."

Shasta's brows rose. Had Ione known what she and Runa had been talking about? "Oh?"

"I think I've *finally* figured out a way."

While relief let go of her lungs, fear grabbed hold of her heart, knowing exactly what Ione was speaking about.

The last visit from Brenna and Stephen from the afterworld a little over six years before had been it. Shasta had tried again and again to call them back through, to reach out for Evelyn, but was met with nothing each time.

She knew it was wrong to not tell the others and wondered if amid all the chaos, they were curious as to why no one was crossing to them. Lucius would have come to Matthew by now, just as she knew Jessamyn would have come to Runa.

Shasta and Ione had been working in secret, trying to figure out what was going on, and the solution they had come up with was that one of them was going to have to cross the other way, into the world of the dead.

She shivered. "I thought we agreed, just one of us?"

"If you go, I go, and I'm certainly not going alone. If the creatures from the darkness are roaming free, I think going in numbers is better than not at all."

Shasta pinched the bridge of her nose. "There's probably a break in the veil where we can cross that'll hold until we return?"

Ione nodded.

"Then we tell Runa. He's the only other one that knows about Bren and Stephen's visit, what's happening. He'll have to make sure nothing slips to our side while we're there."

"I think we should tell Aja, too. If there's two people that have a chance against the creatures, it's them."

"Only Aja. There's enough going on with the situation in Shianshani. We don't need to add to it or take away resources from it."

Indeed, what a fucking *mess.*

NINE

Róisín SHUFFLED along the stone floor of her small shop. She had owned the shop in Greece for two years now, and the simple routines of the store still calmed her. Lifting a hand to turn the open sign, she paused mid-movement.

"What?" She squinted, her eyelids, still heavy with exhaustion, nearly closed over her eyes as she took in the woman's before her, pulling dead flower heads from one of her window boxes. She groaned. "Fucking Hells, Mrs. Svensson. It's too early for this, and you."

She laid her head against the side of the door and gave herself a full thirty seconds to pull herself together, knowing the moment she turned the sign and unlocked the door, the older woman would plow into the shop as she had nearly every day since Róisín had opened.

What would Mrs. Svensson do if she didn't open today?

She could slip back upstairs to the apartment and tuck herself beneath the mountain of blankets upon the bed. Drift away into sleep.

It had taken her most of the night before to work the spell from Brenna's book with the necklace from *Albertos*.

Only to find that the Oathkeeper from Croatia had lied to her. It hadn't been Gea's. Instead, she had been pulled to a small house on Hawaii's big island. A small, bent elderly woman had seen Róisín and asked if she had needed help. When Róisín had shown her the necklace, the woman had become teary, repeating words of gratitude over and over.

Róisín drew in a breath, holding it as she thought of her mother. Everything she had given up, what she had lost all because Sister Future had come to her with Fate's sight.

Everything she knew now about Gea, about Aoife, Madigan... Her mother's death was just a game piece for Fate to move across the board.

Anger simmered in her belly. It was hot, igniting the acid and making it churn.

With a heavy sigh of acceptance, she turned the sign. The lock had barely finished sliding over when Mrs. Svensson's head whipped up, her eyes bright.

"Rosalie!" She greeted her with a kiss on each cheek.

Róisín had learned quickly that she could easily forget her new name if there wasn't some similarity to her given name. She had begun as Maria in a small town in Southeastern France. After six months, she moved and started over, again, in Spain as Rosina, having learned her lesson with "Maria". Now, she was Rosalie.

"Morning, Mrs. Svensson," Róisín mumbled. "The usual?"

"Call me Ana, for Heaven's sake." She waved a hand in the air as though she were waving her married name away. "And, of course, dear. Make it two boxes and throw in some of that nighttime blend as well. I have company coming for two weeks."

Oh, shit. No one was more meddlesome than Ana Svensson. Only a week earlier, she had dragged one of the street cleanup workers into the shop and tried to organize a date between he and Róisín.

"You'd think your landlord would tend to those plants better." Ana scoffed. "All the other shops along this alley are spilling with blooms already. Except for yours. Such a pity."

On cue, a man strolled up to the shop front, carrying a white take-away coffee cup. He eyed the flower boxes, his mouth tightening for a moment. Then he tipped his head back, throat working as he downed his coffee and tossed the cup into the waste bin near the door. Pulling his shoulder length locks away from his face into a bun, he set to work on the plants.

"See?" Róisín said with a forced smile that made her cheeks hurt.

"That's the landlord?" Ana studied the bearded man with interest.

"It's his son. He cares for the properties when he's not at university."

Ana clicked her tongue and turned back to Róisín. "My daughter and her family are coming for a holiday."

The groan rose in Róisín's throat, but she swallowed it before it escaped and instead said, "That's wonderful. From what you've said about her, you two seem very close." Her heart stalled for a moment before giving a heavy thump. The last time Róisín had seen her mother had been when she had crossed her father through the veil with her. Her eyes burned.

"We're very close," Ana said. She lifted a candle and sniffed it. She set it on the counter and gave it a light tap. "I'll take this, too."

"You'll have to be sure to stop in with her. I'd love to meet her."

"Actually..."

Oh, bigger shit.

"She's convinced my eldest, Gregory, to come with. He's just finalized his divorce, and has started dating again."

And there it is.

"Mrs. Sven-Ana, I'm sorry, but I'm just really not in a place to even entertain the idea of dating." The burn in her eyes became more persistent, and an ache grew at the back of her throat.

Ana reached over the counter and took Róisín's hands between hers. "Oh, sweetheart, I know you grieve, but," she patted Róisín's hands, "do you know the way to truly honor the dead is to live?"

"I..."

"I don't know how long it's been for you, but you've been here for almost three years now. You're here every day, but what else are you doing? Have you made friends here? Or are you just talking to your herbs, then going upstairs to sleep?"

If you only knew...

"I lost my husband almost twenty years ago. It took me quite some time to find the ground beneath my feet again and once I did." Her grin split her face wide and she chuckled. "If not my Gregory, why not that chap?" She turned her head toward the window.

"That asshole?" Róisín couldn't stop her brows from shooting up. "I'm pretty sure dictionaries in every language have his image next to rude, grumpy, and jerk."

Ana huffed. "Well then."

Róisín winced. Maybe she'd been harsh in her assessment. Their last interaction still rankled her, even if what he had said *had* been true.

"If not him, maybe just dinner with Gregory. Get your toes wet."

"I don't know, Ana. Can I get back to you on that?"

Pacified, Ana gave her hands another pat before setting her large handbag on the counter to pull out her wallet.

Once she left, Róisín taped a note to the door asking customers to ring the bell as she would be in her stock room, then trudged up the stairs to throw herself onto her bed.

Dating. No, she didn't want to dip her toes back into anything. Gregory could find someone else to entertain over dinner while he was visiting Greece.

TEN

MATTHEW CRACKED his knuckles, Brent's words sounding muffled from across the room.

"She's been at our tether since you came back," Ione said.

Nanette. For years, Lily had hidden that her grandmother had been reaching out to her. And that morning, Ione had arrived in their kitchen to whisk Lily away to her.

His molars creaked as he ground them together.

Lily hadn't told him much about what had happened in the aftermath of his disappearance. Ione had remained tight-lipped, saying it was for Lily to tell him, not her.

But Matthew had learned something about his bonded over their years together. Lily rarely turned to him for comfort, or anyone, for that matter. He saw her pain in the way her eyes would stare unfocused at the wall. Or the way her shoulders inched up to her ears. How she would draw her knees to her chest and tuck her chin in a clear attempt to be small.

Nothing he did could draw her out.

He knew, deep down he knew, it was the consequence of years living under Nanette's demands. *That* part he had managed to get out of her. Nanette's expectations of Lily as the heir to their Coven. Her demand that Lily not train in combat as many other witches did, but remain in her books, learning.

Matthew ran his tongue along the front of his teeth, trying to calm that seething anger that built when he remembered her broken confession. The guilt she carried over what had unfolded when Róisín had gotten hurt by the turned guards in Talista.

"If I had been more like Ione. If I had told my grandmother to fuck off and trained despite her wishes, I could have done *something," Lily said, her voice raw.*

"Maybe we're complicating it," Brent said, yanking Matthew back to Lucius's study and the mess of papers scattered around the room.

"What?" Matthew asked gruffly.

"Where's Lily's list?"

"Lily's list?" He scanned the desktop. For a moment, he had forgotten what they had been doing. Then, he remembered his mother's family. *His* family. They had been combing through records of Aunellion births that they had scavenged from the Alleyette library and the archives there in Ely. "What do you mean?"

"She's a meticulous note taker, Matthew. She and Ione are most definitely list makers. I saw the work they did before. Ione dragged around a white board Lucius had me hunt down."

Matthew had seen the aftermath of the library when they had finally returned to Ely. The stacks of books, papers strewn across every surface, and Ione's frantic scribbles across the double-sided white board. Róisín's familiar scrawl in places.

His heart pinched. Would it ever get easier? He understood. After everything, her disappearance, he understood. It didn't take away how the hole it left in his heart gasped to be whole again.

Why can't we find her?

Because Róisín didn't *want* to be found. Pushed to her limit with nothing left to give anyone anymore, that steel will he knew she had, but doubted herself, had finally surfaced.

Brent held up a hand. "Wait a second." Then he disappeared. Seconds later, Matthew heard the creaking of wheels and the whiteboard was sliding through the doorway. "It worked for them. Why not give it a shot?"

Matthew opened his mouth to answer, but an unfamiliar noise echoed through the house. "What in the Hells is that?" He asked.

"I believe—" The sound cut through the air again. "It's the doorbell."

Matthew blinked. "We have a doorbell?"

Brent hummed and nodded. "However, I cannot remember the last time it has been used."

"Obviously a while. I'll go—"

"The door was open," Marcelo said when he and Nolani stepped into the room. "We rang, but..."

Matthew waved him off. "It took us a second to figure out what the racket was. We," he scratched a fantom itch on the side of his head, "you know."

Nolani pursed her lips before pulling a corner of her bottom lip into her mouth and chewed. "We thought since we're not, that we should... It was polite."

"If only someone would tell that to Ione," Brent muttered next to Matthew.

Matthew snickered, feeling Brent's frustration with Ione's pop-ins. "You received the news about your brother?" He asked Nolani.

She cleared her throat. "My... my brother?"

"We most likely missed Runa," Marcelo clarified.

"Ah." Matthew nodded. "Your family has made it to safety. However, somewhere along the way, they were split up. Your brother arrived here this morning, and the rest of your family is with Shasta in Molennius."

Nolani's body nearly crumpled. Marcelo moved quickly to her side, catching her and bringing her against him. "Thank you."

Silence settled over them. Brent set to work cleaning the board. Matthew wanted to stop him when he reached Róisín's angry, slashing words that read *curse my shitty cheating bonded's new family.*' He filled his lungs with a deep breath, holding it, trying to stop the rush of memories from flooding his senses and taking him down again.

Black crept in, forcing him to his breath before he turned back to Marcelo and Nolani. "Have we figured out Alleyette? Is there enough shelter or will we need to bring hands in to help build?"

"Ione and Runa were working out the details when we last spoke," Marcelo said.

"More like fighting over them." Nolani rolled her eyes.

Beside him, Brent let out a snort. "Be grateful they're in Shasta's hair and not here," he added quietly to Matthew.

He only vaguely remembered interactions with Ione when they had been younger. She had roughly seventy years on him, so they didn't cross paths much. She had always been quiet, watchful, much like Lily. He had trouble reconciling that Ione with the same Ione Brent and Nolani spoke of.

"That's actually why we're here," Marcelo said. He took Nolani's hand in his, then squared himself to Matthew. "We need Legianne, Matthew. If we're to get *every* witch out of Shianshani, even Alleyette won't be enough."

The low buzz began in Matthew's ears.

"The witch population in all realms has nearly doubled. While the humans here and in Molennius may not be concerned yet, the humans in Trifoa and Baijiola *are*. If we were talking about realms where humans were not in control, it would be a non-issue. However," Marcelo's breath was loud in Matthew's ears, "in half the realms, reports are that the humans are prepping new laws."

"Shit," Brent said.

"Lily and Ione have gone to Roidon to speak with Nanette." Matthew's chest grew so tight that for a moment, he could not breathe. "We wait to see what unfolds there. If they're unsuccessful..." They had no choice. They had to save as many witches as they could. They had already lost too many by Anthony's hand. "We use Legianne."

"Earth is always an option too," Brent added.

"No." Nolani shook her head. "It's not. Too many have already said they'd rather risk Shianshani than go to Earth. The humans there, the history, it's all terrifying for witches."

Róisín had grown up in Earth's realm. Brenna had fled Legianne and settled in Ireland, where they lived until Brenna's death. Matthew had spent much of his own life there. While he hadn't experienced issue, he also kept his magic under wraps when he was there. But he understood. What they learned, their history books, it was far too similar a place to what Shianshani had become.

"What about you two?" Matthew asked, trying to push away the walls that were inching closer. "You shouldn't stay there any longer. Especially you," he gave Nolani a pointed look. "And Aja. Anelle, Ten, Cicile... *all* of you."

Marcelo's jaw ticked. "I remain until they're all safe."

Matthew heard the unspoken words, saw them on Marcelo's face. The guilt he carried. "You didn't know. *None* of us knew."

"It doesn't matter. It still falls on me." Marcelo's tone was firm, final.

"We have a plan," Nolani added quietly. "Should things go badly."

"You come here. If things go badly, you come here."

Marcelo and Nolani glanced at one another before looking at him.

"Okay," Marcelo agreed finally. His gaze slid to Nolani, then to Brent. "Do you have a moment?" He asked Matthew.

Brent brought his hands behind his back, clasping them, then approached Nolani. "We'll go to James and Sophie. They'll be able to connect us with your brother."

She gave him a small nod and followed him from the room.

"I thought about what you said in our last conversation." Marcelo paced a few steps toward the window and stopped, turning back to Matthew. "I spoke with Aja and Anelle. We're prepared to face any repercussion."

"Are you sure? Have you talked to Nolani about this?"

Marcelo lifted his palms, moving them back and forth.

"Marcelo." Matthew closed his eyes for a moment. "You could face execution."

"What choice do we have? He's but one man, thankfully. It needs to end, Matthew, and if ending him is how we do it..."

Matthew took a marker from the tray at the bottom of the white-board. He twisted the cap a few times, then tapped it against his hand. Could he do it? Could he be responsible for another life?

Anthony was a monster, yes, but he was just a person, too. Matthew had quickly come to like him. His quick wit, that burning light of hope that shone inside of him. Despite it all, that was who Matthew still saw when he thought of Anthony. Not the monster that was in control now.

He wasn't sure if the whooshing sound he heard in his ears was the blood moving through his veins, or those walls sliding in to crush him finally.

Matthew cleared his throat. "You've confirmed that he has not made others?"

"We still haven't figured out how Madigan accomplished it. And Anthony…" Marcelo let out a deep sigh and frowned. "He wouldn't do that. If he's enacted the decree on witches as punishment for the curse, for what he tried to do to Cassius." His chin fell to his chest. "He wouldn't want anymore like us either."

Matthew drew his hand down his face. His heart hammered in his chest. "Okay." He glanced at the now blank whiteboard. He needed to find his family. Needed those answers. Yet again, he was being pulled away. "We get the next groups out of Shianshani, see what happened in Roidon, and then the four of us meet. Only the four of us."

Marcelo nodded, and the pair said their goodbyes.

Matthew was standing before the board when Brent returned. When he stood next to Matthew, he looked over at him. "What would my father say? How disgusted would he be with me right now?"

"Do not think that Lucius's hands remained clean in his time as Coven leader, or head of the Council."

"I'm not talking about Frederick." Matthew winced at the bite in his words.

"I'm not speaking of Frederick either." His eyes grew dark, his magic turning them a deep green, swirling with black. "You forget." Brent tipped his head to the side. "This is not the first time we've faced a mass exodus of a realm."

Matthew swallowed around the tightness in his throat. "Did you… did you know?"

"No. I had my suspicions." They both turned to the board. "Just as I have my suspicions that there was a reason they kept her birth Coven quiet, and you."

Matthew clenched the marker he still held. "If I ever get the chance to finish this."

Brent held out his hand and waited for Matthew to pass him the marker. "Leave all this to me. Should I need extra eyes, I know who I can trust to bring in if Lily is busy. You need to lead, Matthew. Our Covens need you."

Something akin to a wave rose, then slammed into his chest and made him gasp. "Me?"

"You asked if Lucius would be disgusted with you. I can assure you, he would be far from it, Matthew. Especially if he could see the man you've become these past years. He finished his father's work and made Ely what it was today. A place of safety, of strength. You carry that now, and carry it well."

Matthew realized the noise he was hearing was the sound of his quick breaths. His heart gave a tug, begging for calm.

"If you haven't noticed, you're already in control. Much like Lucius was once he was elected head of the Council. Some leaders are made, but," the smile he gave Matthew was full of pride, "some are born."

Well, shit.

Did he want to lead?

ELEVEN

"N o."

The single word was sandpaper along Tura's throat and across her tongue before it broke hoarsely through her lips. She clutched the small piece of paper in her shaking hands. Her stomach pitched.

"No." The word was a desperate plea.

Her heart hammered against her lungs as she looked from the paper back to the empty building.

This has to be wrong. I'm in the wrong place.

"You're almost five years late," a voice said next to her.

Tura spun. The woman from the airport stood next to her.

"If you would just use your magic, *Sister Future*." She spoke Tura's name as though she had bitten into rotten fruit and was forced to swallow it down. "You could find her far easier."

The blood in Tura's veins thickened and moved slower. Her heart thudded frantically in a panic, trying to move the matter through her body. "I can't. Mother will find me."

The woman looked down her nose at Tura. "Do you not trust me when I say that you are safe here?"

Tura frowned. In the centuries that she and the woman had been together, not once had she given Tura a reason to not trust her. Not

58

even when they had been waiting for what felt like an eternity for fate to do as it had forecast. As it had *promised.*

But the thread... Tura's body shuddered as she recalled stroking the frayed ends of Caid's life thread on her loom.

"The realms are in chaos, child," the woman said.

"Anthony is human. There is nothing I can do about that."

The woman's eyes flared red, and Tura wanted to shrink into the shadows. "The afterworld is barren. Your pets of the darkness have escaped. Your sisters are warded, unable to leave their looms even to rest." The woman crossed her arms over her chest. Her jaw flexed.

"She... she can't do that." Tura lifted a shaking hand to her throat. "My magic, she, no. It's been too long. She can't have any left. How?"

The woman stepped aside for a jogger. "You should know by now that we cannot underestimate her. I did once and look at what happened to me." The woman cast a glance at the storefront. "What she has done to Róisín. The way she has twisted what fate cast."

Tura clasped her hands before her and let her chin fall to her chest.

The woman placed a hand on her shoulder, giving her a light squeeze. "We have been able to send the pets back. Ione is a breath away from the path where she and Shasta should be able to cross through the veil. They're smart enough, determined enough to make progress, but, Tura—" the woman broke off with a sigh. "What happened to that brave, courageous witch that summoned me all of those centuries ago? The one with all those questions and willing to do whatever she needed to do to set things right?"

"I, he, Kincaid... it's my fault. I checked the other looms every day, and his thread, it was never there. Only on mine, as was meant. I don't even know when she..." She swallowed the thickness that was building in her throat just as it had every time she thought of what had happened. "He was *protected.* Not just by Brenna's ward on that silly bond-line inside Róisín that mother's magic creates for them. My magic shielded the fate thread on my loom as well. And he was *here,*"—She threw her arms out and turned—"The *one* realm that remains untouched by her damning magic."

Anger, frustration, and grief hammered at Tura from every direction. Her head throbbed and her stomach was so tight her body wanted to curl in on itself.

"We can still do this," the woman said in a whisper.

Tura chewed her cheek. "How?"

"You need to use your magic, Tura. No." She lifted a hand when Tura opened her mouth. "She's not so far ahead of us we cannot catch her. Even after all this time." She waved a hand toward the empty storefront. "Róisín has learned much here. However, she cannot do it without us. Without the others." She held Tura's stare. "It is time, Tura. Fate has grown weary of waiting when its hand has been full for so long."

"Mother's power. It's slipping. And..." Something bloomed inside of her. Light and fresh. "And it's not just her inability to siphon from me."

"Between what is happening in Shianshani and the chaos rising in the other realms." A wicked smile split the woman's face.

Tura liked it far better when the woman wore the hooded cape that fell over her face, leaving it hidden. She wasn't hideous, no. Despite her unknown age, youth still held her face. Unlined, the rich color of earth after a fresh rain. White brows arched over irises of gold rimmed with silver. Her lips a deep red, always curved in a thoughtful upward tilt. A kind face. It disarmed people. It had disarmed Tura when she had first seen her. To know that face, but to also have seen just what Hecate was truly capable of, made the hair on Tura's neck stand to attention as if it were on guard, preparing.

"Her power is waning," Hecate continued. "Our people are less devoted, unable to justify why their *Goddess* would allow such atrocities to happen to them. Not even the lies she spun about Earth are as awful as what our people are facing now." The woman's eyes glittered with unshed tears, and this time her smile was less wicked, instead filled more with sadness. "Tura, I could set foot on Molennius soil for the first time in almost six centuries It wasn't long, but this morning I assisted in getting my children to safety with a refugee transport. A few mere minutes. But it was enough. Enough to know that Fate demands action. Now."

Tura's eyes burned. The bloom inside grew larger. Hope.

"That's all we need, Tura. They don't have to remember me yet. But the more they doubt and question her, the more I gain back."

Tura's stomach fluttered. "I'm scared."

Hecate stepped closer and brought her arms around her, pulling her against her. "We're at the precipice, Tura. To not be scared would be worrisome. Confidence is one thing, but confidence without fear is dangerous." She stroked a hand over Tura's hair before she stepped back, breaking the embrace. "Because we are so close, we remain together. Come." She held out her hand for Tura. "My magic will get us where we need to go."

Moments later, Tura swallowed down the desperate noise that tried to escape her throat when she found herself staring at yet another empty storefront. No, wait. This wasn't empty. A brightly colored sign that said "*Closed*" in English and Greek greeted them at the door.

The sun against the stark white of the building blinded and Tura lifted her hand to shield her eyes. She turned to the woman and pressed her lips together.

"She's not here right now, but she *is* here," Hecate assured her.

Tura cautiously let some of her magic reach out, stretching, stretching, stretching. "But I can't feel her anywhere. Her magic, she's—"

"Not using it. Or at least only when she needs to. She's doing what she can to remain unseen and safe after all that she's faced here once the witches of Earth learned of her magic."

"It's safe when she does it, but reckless when I do," Tura muttered under her breath.

Hecate put a finger beneath Tura's chin and tipped her face up. "The difference is, if your mother finds you, all she will do is lock you in that horrid cottage as she's done with your sisters."

Tura flinched and tried to look away, but the woman's finger curled and her thumb joined, holding Tura's face tightly.

"And if she finds Róisín," her eyes glanced at the building, "she will kill her. If the witches here don't kill her first."

"You said"—Tura tried to shake her head, but the fingers still gripped her. "You said she couldn't, she wouldn't."

"Nor was she to ever learn of my great-great-grandson." She released Tura with a jerking movement and spun to face the building. Her expression was dark, eyes a storm. "Yet, we saw what she did to him in Shianshani. It's time, Tura, to accept that all of us are in far more danger from her actions than we could ever fathom. She needs to be stopped before there's nothing left and witches become a footnote in history books across all of our realms."

Tura felt her magic stirring inside her. The urge to rip her false face away making that power pulse red, filling her.

Róisín had been their unexpected hope after so long of feeling hopeless. They had known that she would be powerful among witch kind, but the looms had been so wrong. Tura wondered if it had been the power of the magic from Earth that had done it, shielded Róisín's true power from the loom. As it had the fate bond that Hecate had seen burning through the night sky the evening he was born.

TWELVE

Róisín pressed a thumb against one eyelid and her index finger against her other. The groan that had tried to escape five minutes before finally breaking free of her throat.

"Have you thought of a"—Ana bent to inspect a shelf of squid shaped glass trinkets—"book club? A young woman like you should have friends."

Róisín's eyes darted to the clock on the wall. Almost fifteen minutes. She had said she would be ten, and once again, she was staring at a clock that was making her a liar.

"I like my alone time, Mrs. Svensson. Did you want any of this boxed?" She looked down at the array of tea satchels, candles, and figurines.

Ana scoffed and clucked her tongue. "But to be alone *all* the time? And please, sweetheart, call me Ana."

"I'm not alone all the time." In fact, Róisín was late for a birthday party for her two favorite people.

With the twins having winter birthdays, and Maine's winters being known for being cold, and harsh with storms, Lina and Thomas had always held a small, family party on their birthday, then a larger celebration a few months after when the weather warmed and the snow melted. It proved convenient once the twins were older and started having friends come.

The volume of a dozen children could quickly rise to ear splitting levels. It reminded Róisín that she needed to be on top of her game with a few aspirins before she left, so that she could avoid a headache assaulting her before the party was halfway over. If not, she'd have to use more of her magic than she liked to rid herself of it.

Róisín looked up from the counter. She flinched when she saw Ana was eying her with curiosity, a carefully manicured eyebrow high on her forehead. Had she asked something that Róisín had not heard?

Ana looked to the window and back to Róisín. "Am I holding you up, sweetheart?" Ana's eyes now sparkled and her flame red lips curled into a bright smile. "I'll just get out of your hair. Here,"—Ana handed her a credit card. "Elizabeth leaves with the family at the end of the week. I will bring her by so you two can meet. Heaven knows you two hear enough about one another."

Róisín froze, her fingers over the button of the card reading machine. Ana Svensson was a widower. Róisín couldn't deny how often she had witnessed like calling to like in life. That's all it was.

And she wants me to date her son.

"You need to enjoy yourself and your life, Rosalie." Ana winked at her as she collected her bag of purchases. "Live a little."

The moment the door clicked close, Róisín was already locking it and drawing the shades down. After a quick finger comb of her hair, she grabbed the gift bags behind the counter and shifted to Maine.

As she crossed the threshold into the kitchen, Lina was entering from the patio, armed to her chin with plates and pans. "Róisín! You made it." Lina beamed at her.

She reached out and cautiously slipped the stack from Lina's hands. "Don't you have kids for this?"

Lina snorted and shook her head. "Do you really think I can get six-year-olds to take care of dirty dishes on a good day, let alone at their birthday party? I consider myself lucky they can dress themselves." She opened the dishwasher and paused, her eyes dancing over Róisín for a moment before she loaded it. "Something happen?"

"I need to move again. I think. One of my regular customers has spent this past week trying to set me up with her grandson." Róisín pinched the bridge of her nose at the thought. "When she realized that would not happen, she's now determined to play matchmaker between me and the landlord's son."

Lina's eyes widened. "She didn't. Did you tell her he was a raging asshole?"

Róisín glanced through the patio doors to where the twins' birthday party was in full swing. "Yup. She told me his man bun would be fun to run my hands through."

Lina cackled and smacked her thigh. "Shit, I'm sorry for laughing." She snorted and waved a hand in the air. "I can't." She laughed harder. "It sounds so much like something Mrs. Littlefield at the post office would say. Old ladies are wonderful."

"You only say that because you don't have one meddling in your love life." Róisín lifted the gift bags she held. "Have they done presents yet?" She asked, hoping Lina would accept the change in topic.

"They insisted they wait for Aunt Ro." Lina closed the dishwasher and started the washing cycle. When she turned back to Róisín, she froze. "What's wrong? What's happened? Do I—"

"No." Róisín blinked, pulling her attention away from the kitchen table and bringing her mind back to the present. "No. It's not that." Her voice was barely a whisper. "What's happened to me, Lina?"

"What do you mean?"

Róisín ran a hand over her face, letting it rest at the base of her throat.

"Róisín?"

"It's hard to explain," she said roughly.

Lina motioned toward the table. "Sit."

"But the kids are waiting for me to open their presents."

"Yup." Lina nudged a chair out and pointed. "They've waited a few months to have this party, and they can wait a few more minutes for presents. Now sit and tell me what's going on."

Róisín dropped heavily into the chair and shook her head. "I feel like... I don't feel like *me* anymore."

"Well, I wouldn't expect you to stay the same after six years of living.

Róisín. Regardless of what's happened, you're still going to change somehow. It's natural. Hell, *I'm* not the same person I was six years ago, either."

"You seem to be mostly the same."

Lina's eyes narrowed. "That's not completely a compliment."

"It wasn't meant to be." She shook her head. "What I mean is, you've changed because you've grown, become a mom. You're not... Someone completely different." Róisín brought her hands together, weaving her fingers together before clasping them. She watched the skin on her knuckles tighten to the point of turning white. "It's almost like I've shut off. In my head, in my heart, everywhere. The things I've done the past few years—" Lina's hand appeared over hers and she stopped.

"You can't blame yourself for what you've done to those smarmy ass witches. We'd be mourning *you* if you hadn't."

"It's not the same, Lina. Even in Shianshani, facing those guards. I was doing it to save myself, to save others, but there was still something in here." She brought a hand to her chest. "I *felt* remorse for it, even in a small way, because a life is a life."

"They were monsters trying to eat you, Róisín."

"They were *people* before they were monsters. I've killed monsters. Shianshani was different."

Lina sighed and leaned back in her chair. "I won't sit here and lie to you that you've gotten a little rougher around the edges, because you have. You're a little grittier than before, your voice a little darker sometimes. It's a bit spooky," she added offhandedly. "But you're still *you*, Róisín. You haven't lost yourself, you're not becoming some villain in your life story. That woman is a lie. You were all so gaslit into believing otherwise. I wouldn't be surprised if it were some deeply internalized thing in you that's telling you that what you're doing is wrong. *Ignore it.* It's a lie. What you're doing is *right*. Think of how many lives have been ruined by her fucking with them."

The tightness that had been building in Róisín's chest eased enough for her to breathe, and she nodded.

"Stay the course, Róisín. Don't let that voice convince you otherwise. I'd hate to kick your ass."

Róisín lifted her eyebrows and watched Lina rise from the table.

"Now, the food is probably almost done on the grill. Let's go stuff our faces with snacks and rally everyone for presents before one of my kids breaks their neck."

THIRTEEN

S HASTA DROPPED her forehead to rest on the back of the hands laying on the hood of the old, rusted Jeep that still sat tucked off to the side of the yard at Róisín and Caid's cottage in Ireland. It had been months since she had been to this place. She had once come regularly. Weekly, then monthly. Hoping to feel Róisín's magic present, even just a trace of her passing through.

Her shoulders shook with the first quiet sob. She pushed herself upright and walked toward the cottage.

"I fucked up, Bren," she said to the face of the cottage, her words thick. "I really fucked up," she added in a whisper.

She had just gotten Róisín back, and now she was gone. What had Shasta done to help her? To stop her? Nothing.

Shasta had been so entangled with the demons she let grab hold of her after the house had locked her inside that she couldn't even bring herself to be there for the one person she had still loved more than anything in any realm.

She had failed Róisín. Every time she had downed a bottle of bourbon or whiskey. Every time she reached for another beer. She had failed her.

Before that day in Shianshani, when had the last time she had seen Róisín been? When they'd made the plans for the gala? Sooner?

Shasta rubbed at her face aggressively, lowering onto the top step of the small porch. She ran her tongue along her teeth before grinding her molars together.

"Hey, mom? Don't die."

Her head fell back, and she closed her eyes. She had loved Caid too, just like he had been hers. Had she ever told him how much he had begun to mean to her in such a short time? Not just because of who he had been for Róisín, but for who *he* was.

"Fuck!" Her shout echoed across the glen.

A drink. I need a drink. It'll quiet the noise. It'll quiet the pain.

She gripped her middle, folding over her legs. Her chest squeezed and her stomach grew heavy. No, she couldn't. She wouldn't. Every day had been a battle, but she was doing it.

For Róisín.

For Caid.

For Lucius and all the promises she had made to him before he had left for Aunellion to save Matthew. Lucius, her brother, one of her best friends.

Shasta wrapped her arms tighter around herself. She rocked back and forth, trying to ease the pain that pricked against her every fiber.

She had become the ghost that lurked in the background of their story. The 'what ifs' hammered at her every single day since. Regret filled her, one heavy stone at a time.

If she could have held herself together, had faced her grief, her fears, everyone would still be together. They would be whole, this family they had created.

Instead, Lucius and Caid were gone.

And Róisín... would she ever return? Would Shasta ever get the chance to hold her tightly again? Tell her how much she loved her?

To tell her how sorry she was for all the mistakes she had made?

What would happen once they could get through the veil? How would she tell Brenna and Stephen? How could she face any of them again?

She shoved to her feet and flexed her hands, trying to grip what bit of calm she could manage. Ione would be returning from Roidon soon and Shasta would need to be as clear-headed as she could manage if they were going to cross into the afterworld.

There wouldn't be any more mistakes. She would lose *no one else*.

Fourteen

MATTHEW STEPPED into the kitchen just as Lily and Ione shifted in. Runa, seconds behind, quickly whisking Ione into his arms.

Ione gasped against his broad chest. "Babe, you're crushing every organ."

"I don't care." He pressed his lips into her hair. "We're not bonded, but I could *feel* that. Shit. I'm so sorry."

Matthew cleared his throat. "Ione, you still have your room upstairs if you, uh, need it."

Runa released her and when she turned to Lily and Matthew, her eyes were bright and cheeks pink. "We're actually going to head back to Molennius. I'm supposed to check in with Shasta when I get back."

"Everything okay?" Lily asked. Her eyes remained on the couple. She had yet to look at him.

"Everything's fine." Ione waved a dismissive hand. "Just helping her with some fine tuning of the wards on the house. She said something still didn't feel right."

Lily pursed her lips, studying her sister. "If you need help, let me know."

Ione leaned against Runa and gave her a small smile. "Thank you, Lily."

"You deserve this, Ione. Don't let her take that from you," she said quietly.

Ione dashed away an escaping tear with the back of her hand and nodded before the pair shifted away.

"Lily." Matthew waited for her to turn to him. Instead, she remained, staring at the space her sister had just occupied. "Lily."

She turned to the refrigerator and began pulling out items. That had been something else he had noticed. Lily baked when something was bothering her. He'd come into the kitchen countless times to find mounds of muffins, racks and racks of cooling cupcakes. Sometimes, his steps would falter and he'd be brought back to Aunellion and his hallucinations.

Except, how much was truly hallucinations? How much was something else? If that were the case, what *had* been happening to him in Aunellion? They still hadn't even explored the possibilities. Everything was still settling before it had all been tossed back into the air.

How did Lucius do it? How did Lucius hold leadership over not just their Coven, but all Covens? And how did he do it, while also being his father? Being all that he was to Clarissa?

I'm failing...

He was a shitty mate to Lily. He was a mess of a leader to his people and couldn't even find his family.

Swallowing it down, he moved toward her and smoothed a hand over her back before hooking his arm around her waist. "You good?" He drew her against him.

She laid her head against his shoulder, her body leaning into his. "We've got Roidon on the list now."

"Marcelo came."

She stepped back. "Are they? Have they gotten out too?"

"He refuses. He won't leave until the last witch is out of Shianshani. And if he stays, we know Nolani will stay."

"It's too dangerous for her, for them. Matthew, you've got to talk sense into them!"

He rubbed the back of his neck, his eyes on the floor in front of him.

"I've tried, Lily. Every time he comes, I've tried. He blames himself because if he hadn't changed the laws and stepped down as King, Anthony wouldn't have the power he has right now. The witches would be safe."

"We don't know what Anthony would have felt compelled to do if he was powerless." She rubbed at the skin along the base of her neck. It turned red, but she continued to rub, the skin wrinkling in the wake of her fingers. "You know I'm right, Matthew. Look at what's happened. Aoife, Madigan, the others? Look at what they all did in that quest to put themselves where the Goddess is."

His shoulders slumped. He lifted his head and tipped it to one side, then the other, before he let out a heavy sigh. "We know well enough, Lily, that there's plenty of ifs that come into play."

"Tell me why you seem to be relieved Nanette will take in refugees," she said.

He blinked as though her abrupt redirect of the conversation had been a physical hit. Deflecting. He knew what she was doing. It was spread out before them in what looked like a doomsday prep of bread making about to take place in the kitchen. He wanted to demand she tell him what Nanette had said to them, to her. Instead, he pressed his lips together. He knew that wasn't how to show her he was her safe place, her shelter.

How much longer before she realized that and actually came to him when she needed someone? How long before she stopped doing this?

Why couldn't he just tell her he knew? Knew every single one of her tells instead of letting her draw inward and hiding from him?

Matthew ran a hand over his face and sighed. "That was why Marcelo came. He asked again about Legianne."

She sucked in a sharp breath.

"I told him we would wait to see what you and Ione could work out with Nanette." He shoved his hands into his hair and shook his head. "Why can't I let them? Why can't I just say yes? Even if she comes back, she..." His voice broke. "She fucking hates Legianne. Hates what it represents for her family, for her. She wouldn't give a shit if we used it."

Lily took a slight step toward him. "I miss her."

The crack in her voice, the small confession, had him pulling her against him again, hard. A small gasp of surprise bursting out of her as they collided. It was a small fruit on a low branch she had offered him, but he would take it.

"Me too," he said against her hair.

Her arms came around him, her hands grasping at the material of his shirt.

Talk to me, he wanted to say. *Let me help you the way you help me.*

Unable to find his voice and afraid to push her away, he bent his head and kissed her temple. "You know I'm always there for you, right?"

"Of course," she said. She tipped her head back to look up at him.

He studied her face for a moment. The gold of her eyes with the small flecks of brown around her pupils. The lines that were appearing between her brows from the way she was always knotting them together when she thought no one was looking.

"I love you, Lily." He brushed his lips over hers. "Always." He kissed her jaw. "Forever." His tongue skimmed along the column of her throat when she tipped her head further. "Even from the afterworld." He nipped her collarbone, and she sighed. "No matter what."

Her body tensed, and he wanted to grin. She knew he was onto her. Now he just needed to figure out how to coax it all out.

Before...

R ÓISÍN RELEASED *a soft hum as lips skimmed along the inside of one of her thighs.*

"Magic," Caid murmured against her skin. "You have literal magic."

The awe in his voice was a palpable weight on her heart. "You're okay with that?" He had only known for just a few hours, and after she had cried all of her tears, she felt as though she had been waiting for the door to close. For him to realize everything she had confessed to him, the danger she faced against Madigan, and decide that it was too much.

His head snapped up, heated hazel eyes landing on her. They narrowed briefly, before the knot formed between his brows. "Why wouldn't I be?"

She remained silent, unable to find her words. Inside, one half of her was battling against the other. Her doubts and insecurities doubling down, trying to fend off the parts of her that dared to still hope, to dream.

"What would I do? Run through the streets of Greens Glen screaming that witches are real, and try to convince everyone to tie you to a pyre?"

Róisín pressed her lips together.

"If anything, the moment someone found out you were and came pounding on your door, they'd have to get through me first." He kissed her

hip. *"There isn't anything that can keep me from being right here with you."*

"But, I'm not..." She swallowed. Her throat thick and tears threatening. *"Human,"* she said quietly.

He shifted his weight and crawled up her body. Resting his forearms on either side of her head, he bent his head until their noses touched. *"So?"*

She blinked rapidly. The burn behind her eyes becoming too much.

"I love you, Róisín." He kissed her nose, then brushed his lips across her cheek. *"Does you living for, well, ever, and having magic change what our days ahead look like?"* He shrugged a shoulder. *"I can't lie and say no."*

Róisín moved her hands to push against his chest, trying to create space so that she could move. He slipped his arms behind her and rolled so that she was atop, then moved his arms, banding them around her.

"Caid."

"My future doesn't have a day without you in it, Róisín. If it's unchartered waters I'm heading into, you're the one I'm going into them with. You need to understand that. I don't know the right words to say, or what to do to show you that." His chest pressed against hers with his deep breath.

She relented her struggle, opening her eyes.

"We'll take on each storm as it comes." He lifted one of his hands to tuck her hair behind her ear. *"Together."*

"Are you sure?"

"It's the one thing I'm absolutely sure of."

Her smile was small, hesitant. Her heart still thudded heavily against her chest. Wiggling, she freed one hand that had become pinned between them when he rolled them over. Her fingers danced along his jaw, stopping at his chin. *"I love you."*

He grinned at her.

"What?"

In a blur, she was on her back again. His arms were slipping from around her and he was again moving down her body. His warm kisses leaving a trail over her skin.

"Caid?"

"Now that we've got all of this settled, shh. Let me taste you..."

Sixteen

Róisín was greeted by an assault of sounds when she stepped into the backyard and the twins' party. Conversations between the adults struggled to be heard over the shouts of the kids and the revving engine rounding the house.

Sloane zipped by, heading for a lap around the pool on a small green and white dirt bike. A dozen kids, including Abigail, trailed behind him, their fists thrusting into the air as they whooped in delight when he lifted the front end of the bike off the ground.

"Faster!" One of them shouted.

"No. Dear God, no," Lina practically pleaded. She cast a glance toward the grill, shaking her head and letting out a heavy sigh before stalking off toward the cupcakes.

"They'll be fine," Thomas called from where he stood, placing the burger buns on the top rack of the grill.

"Says the one who won't have to deal with a kid in a cast during *summer*," Lina grumbled around a mouthful of chocolate cupcake.

Róisín watched the front tire slam to the ground, sending Sloane bouncing and laughing before he took off around the house. A spray of dirt and grass kicking up as he turned. She slowly turned her head toward the grill and cocked an eyebrow up at the men standing there. "A dirt bike? Really?"

Caid flashed her a sheepish smile and shrugged. "Why not? We had them at that age." He gestured between him and Thomas.

She tried her best to give him her annoyed glare, but failed. "I don't know why you wasted Lina's time asking what her approved gift list was if you were just going to be a typical uncle about it."

"Made it all that more fun when I unloaded it this morning." He passed the metal spatula to Thomas and stalked toward her. "And yes, I bought two. Abby broke hers already jumping off the rock wall. I told her I'd look at it after presents."

As though on cue, Abigail's voice pitched over the ruckus of the backyard. "Uncle Caid is gonna suck on Aunt Ro's face again!"

"They do that a lot, sweetheart. Just look the other way." Lina nudged Róisín with her elbow as she passed on her way to the present table. "Keep it PG please."

"Who said anything about sucking face?" Caid asked. His hazel eyes flashed with mischief.

"Oh." Róisín lifted her hands. "No." She took a step back, bumping into the table with platters of food. "Don't you dare."

Lina, realizing what was happening, said, "I'll go grab some towels."

"It's freezing, Caid. Stop—" She shrieked as her world tipped upside down and she was suddenly facing his back. "Kincaid James McGrath, put me down!"

"Put you down?" His playful tone made her squirm harder, trying to free herself. "Alright."

With a splash, her world was suddenly ice cold. When she surfaced, the adults were sharing a chuckle while the kids cheered for Caid. His eyes danced with browns and greens, his magic flaring as he stood with his arms folded on the rail of the pool wall. "Need me to warm you up, Mrs. McGrath?"

She swam over to him, her teeth chattering. "You think you're hilarious," she stuttered. "Don't you?" Instead of letting him answer, she ducked beneath the surface. With a surge aided by a touch of her magic, she sprung up, grabbed him by the shirtfront and pulled him into the water with her.

His shoulder length hair had freed itself from the messy bun it had been carelessly tossed into and was plastered to his face when he surfaced, making her laugh. As he shoved it from his face, she swam closer. Her voice low and coy, she asked, "Need me to warm you up, *Mr. McGrath*?"

Caid lowered himself so that his shoulders were beneath the water. The movement brought him eye level with her. "Just wait until we get home." He reached one of his arms out. "The *landlord's son* has plans that will take all"—he hooked a finger into the waistband of her jeans— "Night..." He tugged her closer. "Long." He gave her a light, audience friendly kiss.

"Let him know that I'm going to hold him to that." She let her hands smooth over his chest before trailing down. She pressed her palm against his rock hard length. "For now, you should probably turn the magic off before you get out. You know..." She rubbed against the fabric, making him hiss out a curse. "Cool yourself down." She pulled her bottom lip between her teeth. "A bit."

A low growl vibrated from his chest. "You should probably turn yours *on*." She looked down to where his eyes were locked and saw that her nipples were pressing against the fabric of her shirt.

"Alright everyone!" Lina clapped her hands. "Time for presents!"

SEVENTEEN
SIX YEARS AGO

Darkness.

It surrounded Caid like a cold, heavy blanket.

He reached out, trying to grasp onto Róisín. He couldn't leave, not yet. Not without her. He had promised her.

Together...

His body was jostled. He fought to lift his eyelids, but they refused. He tried to draw in a breath; his lungs remaining frozen in place after his last jagged exhale.

Róisín's name had been a broken whisper from his lips.

Warm hands pressed on his neck, his face. He knew it was her. Knew that the wetness that splashed onto his cheeks, his forehead were her tears. The dark may have been pulling him deeper, deeper, but somehow, he knew.

His promise of together had become a lie.

He had failed her. Failed them.

He had broken her heart.

If his still beat, it would know a pain so vicious and brutal, that *it* would be enough to stop the organ from pulsing in his chest.

Had he told her he loved her?

Was Madigan truly dead?

Would she be safe from the fate they feared she had been given?

No.

He wanted to roar, to shout. He wanted to wrestle away from this abyss he had fallen into. Fight his way back to her.

The scream shattered the surrounding blackness. A raw, desperate sound.

Other noises rose with it. Shouts.

Then, silence.

Róisín.

Róisín.

Róisín.

CAID'S BREATH CAME IN A SHARP GASP, DRIVING HIM UP INTO a sitting position. The room he was in was dark, unfamiliar.

He lifted his hand to his neck, feeling the flesh there. Near his collarbone was a raised, jagged mark. The only sign that what had happened hadn't been a nightmare.

"Róisín!" He pushed himself off the bed, moving toward the door. When he stepped into the hall, he looked left, then right.

Where the fuck am I?

"Róisín!"

His heart begged him to slow, begged for calm. Its sharp beat shouting at him that only moments ago it had been *still* in his chest. His lungs echoed the sentiment. Caid's breaths coming in pants.

It didn't matter. He needed to find her.

"Róisín!"

He pushed his tired and weak body toward the stairs, gripping the banister. It was then that he recognized where he was. The cottage in Wurbray. It had been only months since they had been there, when Brenna had told them everything she knew. Or maybe it had been weeks. Caid wasn't sure around the pounding in his head. He still hadn't grasped how time moved when they weren't in just one realm.

Caid's knuckles tightened around the banister. His muscles fighting the command to hold still, be silent, as he listened to the sounds around him.

A soft scrape from the direction of the kitchen carried through the house.

"Róisín?"

A shriek followed by a clatter were the response he received.

Then, "Caid?" The tremble in her voice clear from where he stood.

His body shot forward, sending him stumbling down the stairs, then crashing against the wall. Using it as a crutch, he hurried toward the kitchen. When he shoved the door open, he found her standing in the middle of the room. The light overhead dim, casting shadows across her face.

Róisín had one arm out of a coat sleeve, the other frozen in mid-movement. Her auburn hair, that always reminded him of mid-autumn in Maine, was a mass of tangles around her face. A face that was covered in dirt, dried blood, and littered with cuts and bruises. And her eyes, those bright, Caribbean water turquoise eyes of hers, were wide and unblinking. A rainbow of colors beginning to swim in them.

A sound between a gasp and a sob burst from her before she wrestled herself free of her coat, cursing when she finally got her arm out. Then she threw herself at him.

"Caid." She buried her face in his chest.

Welcoming the pain that flared through his body when her nails bit into his skin, he banded his arms around her, drawing her even tighter against him. Her body shook violently as her sobs crashed against his chest like thunderclaps.

Slowly, he felt himself breaking. The warmth of his tears spilling from his eyes, flooding down his cheeks. The shaking, gasping breaths of his sobs.

So close. Too fucking close.

Too fucking close.

Her body tensed against him, and like a switch, she abruptly quieted.

"Róisín?" He brought his hands to her face, his knees nearly buckling at the feel of her skin, its warmth, beneath his calloused palms.

"Lina," she breathed. "I need to—" She made to pull away from him, but he wouldn't release her. "Caid, I need to go home, I need to—"

"Where have you been? What have you done?" The smell of sulfur stung his nose. Sulfur and something familiar he could not place.

It'll consume her.

The memory of the voice within skittered along his spine to the base of his skull, lifting the tiny hairs at the back of his neck.

"No. Tell me you—" He swallowed the rest, unable to say the words.

Fresh tears splashed onto her cheeks. She cast her eyes downward. "I tried. I went back—"

"Are you fucking insane? *Alone?*"

"You were dead, Caid. Fucking *dead*! I tried... I tried everything." Her last word dropping off into a whisper. "I tried everything, and you were still so... cold. And in here"—She slapped both of her hands hard against her chest—"It was fire, and blades, and, and explosions. Everything that was *in* was being pulled *out*. I couldn't." She pressed her trembling lips together and shook her head. "After I got back from Maine, I couldn't leave you. I had to try. Whatever it was that day, if it was still there, maybe it could help me." She sniffed. "Even the well spring was quiet this time. Like it never existed."

Fear gave way to relief, and Caid struggled to remain upright. He grasped around behind him, finding the edge of the counter. Leaning against it for support, he wanted to yell, to rage. Tell her she was foolish for what she had done. That she was lucky whatever had been there was there no longer. Yet, he knew. He knew that feeling she felt. Understood that desperation she felt because he had been there himself once before.

He had bargained anything and everything that day he held her lifeless body in his arms.

"I need to tell Lina," she said quietly. "We, she, I, fuck." She pinched her lips together, closing in a sound of frustration. "I don't know if Helen's gone to her though. By now, I don't know..."

He reached a hand out to her, catching just the tips of her fingers with his. "Róisín, what happened?" He asked softly.

"Madigan, he told me things about his family just as everything was going crazy in Talista. When you"—Her face twisted and she squeezed her eyes closed—"I didn't think. I just acted. It all slammed into me so fast. Knowing I needed to *go*. To get out of there with you and leave the others behind. When I got here, I just—" She wrapped her arms around her stomach. "I let my magic burn away everything. Every connection to the others, my life, all of it."

Caid pushed off from the counter. Linking their fingers together, he lifted his other hand to brush the hair from her face. He cupped her cheek, then pressed his lips to hers. His eyes burned with fresh tears at the feel of her lips beneath his. "Go get Lina. Please. I don't want to scare her. I think I would if I was the one that went." He kissed her again. "Be careful. The both of you. I'm still trying to grasp all of this, sort out everything. But right now, my sister and I..."

Róisín tucked her head beneath his chin. The feel of her lips brushing over his collarbone, over the scar that was there, had his body trembling and his chin quaking.

"I'll be right back," she said against his skin.

Once she was gone, he drove his hands into his hair and tugged. Then he did the one thing he had wanted to do most after seeing Róisín's broken, pain etched in across her face when he had walked into the kitchen. He let out a roar that shook him from his core outward.

"...a fucking *trip*. That's what—" Lina broke off into a blood-curdling scream filled with terror that rattled Caid right down to his marrow. "What. The. Fuck?! What the fuck?!"

He wanted to go to her, to scoop her into his arms. Hug her, sway with her as they always did when they hugged. Instead, he shoved his hands into the front pockets of his tattered, blood-covered jeans, and stood frozen while she stared at him.

"Róisín." Lina kept her eyes on him and groped for Róisín. "What the hell is going on? How?"

Róisín took Lina's reaching hand between hers, then moved closer to her. "Before I came to you, I tried one more time to heal him." She looked at Caid. "I hadn't been able to do more than repair the wound at his neck. Or," she turned back to Lina, "at least that's what I thought. When I came back, he was... alive."

Lina took a slow step forward. She kept her hand tight in Róisín's, but lifted her other, reaching for him. She hesitated, stopping and pulling back slightly. Unable to stand it any longer, Caid closed the gap, pressing his chest against her hand.

Her lids fluttered as she blinked quickly. "You're real."

"I am Leen." He covered her hand with one of his.

She frowned at him. "You sound different, though. Your sleepy voice you have when I pound on your door because my coffee machine's broken again and I'm desperate."

"I did just take a nap." He tried for a joke, but when both women only remained frowning at him, his shoulders rounded.

Róisín's attention was on his neck, eyes narrowed on the scar. "It could just be temporary," she said, more to him than to Lina.

Lina looked over her shoulder to Róisín, then back to him, her brows in a tight knot. He sucked in a breath, holding it as her eyes lowered, her pupils becoming small little dots in the hazel.

"One of you needs to tell me right now what exactly happened," she demanded.

"Leen—"

She slapped a hand over his mouth, her nostrils flaring wide. "No. You don't just get to go *fucking die* on me, Kincaid James McGrath. Die on me and then you!" She whirled to Róisín. "You show up at my house looking like Uma Thurman in Kill Bill. Then, *then!*" She threw her hands up and shook them wildly. "You come back, whisk me away to an entirely different world from my own, expect me to stand before my *not dead* brother and move on with my merry fucking life like none of that just happened." She stepped back, so that she was no longer standing between them. "Especially because I can guarantee whatever you started planning at my house, you're still planning."

Caid's head snapped up to where Róisín stood, her bottom lip snared between her teeth. "Róisín."

"I didn't lie when I said I'd burn the realms for you."

His heart dropped into his stomach. Her jaw flexed and her eyes became a storm of dark blues and grays. He didn't come back from the dead to lose her. Not again. But she was determined. Whatever she had learned earlier that night, whatever had been festering within her over the past several weeks, then his death, she was determined. Which meant so was he.

"Fates be damned," he said.

"Wh-what's happening?" Lina's head turned back and forth, watching them stare one another down.

"You are going home, Leen. But first—" He was at her in one step, wrapping her in the best bear hug he could manage without squishing her too tightly. Her arms came around his neck and she buried her face there.

"Don't die on me again, please. I can't." She sniffed. "It was enough. Today was enough. No more, okay?"

"Okay." He swayed a little with her, stroking a hand up and down her back. "I love you so much, Leen."

"I love you, too." She pressed her face tighter against his skin. "Asshole."

The laughter rumbled out of him. It was a light chuckle at first, feeling off in that moment of darkness in the kitchen. But then Lina snorted and then the siblings were nearly howling with laughter.

Caid dropped his forehead to hers. "I'm sorry."

"Just don't do it again." She lightly slapped his chest.

"And whatever it is you think you're doing with all of this"—He gestured around the kitchen—"Forget about it."

Lina huffed and rolled her eyes. "I don't think so. I'm *in* this now. If I've gotta zip my lips around Helen and whomever else comes knocking about you two, especially you." She pointed at him. "Then I don't think so. I don't know what help I can be, but I'll try. *Planning*, we all know I'm a fucking pro at that. You two can't do whatever this is on your own."

"She's not wrong, Caid," Róisín said quietly.

He drew a hand down his face and sighed. "We'll figure it out as we go." He leveled his glare at Lina. "For now, you go home and just do the pregnant thing. Have the babies. With any luck, you won't have magic and then everyone will go home, so *we* can go home, too."

"Until then?" Lina asked.

Caid looked around the kitchen, knowing Róisín had hated Legianne and Wurbray. "We'll figure it out as we go," he repeated.

"I hate this," Lina mumbled.

"We all do, Leen. We all do."

Eighteen

Now

Róisín settled a hand on Caid's thigh. The warmth of him radiated through his worn jeans. Her nightmares were still plagued by his cold, lifeless body. His stilled chest. She spent every waking moment she was near him, touching him. A reminder that he was there. He was with her.

That they were still in this, together.

Caid brought one hand away from the wooden embossed steering wheel of the old, square bodied Chevrolet truck he drove when they were in Maine and laid it over hers at his thigh.

"You ready to talk about it?" His voice still held those gravelly, sleep roughened tones.

"I guess that's what happens when your throat gets ripped out," he had said when Lina noticed it. Róisín had winced at the briskness of his reply, despite knowing that it was merely his way of trying to look at what happened with a sense of dark humor.

She listened to the soft tune of a country song that was coming through the speakers of the metal doors for a moment, then cleared her throat. "Talk about what? I will not apologize for telling Mrs. Svensson you're an asshole. Because you *are*, Caid. You were being and still are being ridiculous over me—*What*?"

He had pulled up in front of their log cabin tucked in the woods twenty minutes north of Greens Glens. The dim lights from the truck illuminated the small porch littered with empty plant pots that Róisín had yet to seed for the spring growing season. Once the days of the *after* had taken shape, Caid, who had known about the empty cabin for years, located the owner and convinced him to sell. Remodeling it had been a way for him to stay busy, he said. Róisín knew it was his way of being close to Lina, but out of sight still should anyone show up in Greens Glen looking for Róisín.

Inside the cab of the truck, the dash lit Caid's face. He was staring down at her with his signature *I smell bullshit* expression. One eyebrow arched and the opposite corner of his lip tipped in a smirk.

Slowly, he turned so that his back was against his door.

"Caid."

"I'm not talking about that. Although, that you waited until I went to work before sneaking off, which you should know you can't do anymore with the way we're connected now, on your little *mission* is something we're definitely going to talk about."

"It was an errand. A quick one." She crossed her arms over her chest. "And fuck, Caid. I almost *stabbed* you. You don't sneak up on people like that!"

He scoffed and shook his head. "You knew it was me. Know how I know? Because you *didn't* stab me."

The cab of the truck grew hotter. With a groan of frustration, she scooted away from him, across the bench seat to mirror him against the passenger door.

"Besides, that's not what I'm talking about. I'm talking about,"— He jabbed a thumb toward the cabin—"What's inside."

Of course, he'd gone inside when he'd shifted there earlier. He wouldn't just load the bikes he must have had stashed in the small shed and go.

"Caid—"

"How much more?"

The dim glow from the dash did little to reveal his expression clearly, but she felt the heat of his stare despite the darkness in the cab of the truck.

"How much more?" His voice cracked when he repeated the question. He ran a hand over his face.

She drew her knees up to her chest and wrapped her arms around them. She couldn't deny him his anger or frustration. Every stone she unturned in her search for Gea instead revealed someone lying in wait to take her magic. To make it harder, her magic had been ever changing since they had gone to the well source in Legianne. It was louder, heavier inside of her. Then there was the way it built inside, pressure pushing, pushing, pushing, until—

"Maybe it's time we bring in help." Caid glanced to the cabin, then back to her.

She loosed a growl. On the surface, she could say that it wasn't safe, she was protecting them. This was *hers* to shoulder and hers alone. Yet, deep down, it was because she was scared. She had severed her ties with them, then fled without a backward glance. To face them after that, she couldn't bear to see the anger on their faces or hear it in their voices as they turned down her apologies. She'd abandoned them.

"Dammit, Róisín. Then what do we do?" He lifted his hands, then dropped his head back to rest on the glass. "Just at least think about it, okay?"

Her attention trailed down the column on this throat, down, down, and rested at the jagged scar peeking out around the flannel shirt he wore. *I'd burn the realms for you...* "Okay," she said finally.

"Thank fucking Christ," he said to the metal cab roof. She let out a squeal when his hand gripped her calf and he pulled her to him. "Now come here."

"I can walk inside, Caid."

He laughed. "Oh, honey." He shook his head. "We're not going inside."

Her breath caught as his hand moved up her calf, along the inside of her thigh. His thumb brushed the seam of her jeans up her zipper, then his fingers were wrapping around the waistband. He gripped tightly, then effortlessly pulled her into his lap.

"Show off," she said against his mouth.

He grinned. His fingers danced down her throat to her chest, where he smoothed his large hand along the skin until reaching one of her breasts. "You like it."

"Does this mean the landlord will knock off a few notes from next month's rent?"

Caid hummed. "Maybe if you retract that asshole statement. I'd hate to have Mrs. Svensson think of me like that."

Róisín rolled her hips, rocking over where his cock strained against the fabric of his jeans. "She told me it would be fun to run my hands through these locks." She tugged the elastic free. His still damp sand colored hair tumbled in loose curls to his shoulders.

"Did she?" He tugged the zipper of her hoodie down and nudged it over her shoulder. His lips were warm against the skin over her heart. His beard, rough against her skin, sent a jolt right to her core, and she couldn't contain the moan that slipped out.

She danced her fingers through his hair. "I told her I preferred short hair." She rocked again, satisfaction filling her when he released a groan. His teeth grazed her breast just above her nipple.

"Is this your way of saying you want me to cut it?" He sucked the nipple into his mouth, stroking his tongue over it once, twice before circling it.

Róisín gripped his hair tighter. Her hips sought that just-right pace that gave her that friction she needed to soothe the ache building between her thighs. "Caid."

He released her and pulled back. "You didn't answer my question."

She tugged at his hair, tipping his head back. "You could let it grow to your knees." She tugged again before releasing it. Moving her hands down, she stroked his beard. "This too, and I wouldn't care. As long as I have you, I don't fucking care. I just want you. Any way I can have you."

His response was a low growl before he crushed his mouth to hers. With their lips still tangled, their teeth clashing, she wrestled free of her hoodie, hitting the horn. She bumped it again with her ass when she lifted off him to get the space to nudge her jeans over her hips.

"Maybe we *should* go inside," he said. "Neighbors are only a few acres away. If they hear the horn at this hour…"

"No way." She laid across the bench, tipping a knee out to rest it on the dash. "I don't have the patience for those nineteen steps."

He reached for the back of his shirts and pulled them over his head. "Oh?" He traced a line down her chest and rested his palm over her stomach. "Tell me what you want, Róisín."

She lifted the leg that was resting against the seat and placed it over his shoulder. "Say my name again."

"Róisín."

The muscles of her stomach quivered beneath his hand. "Again," she breathed.

He hummed her name and moved his hand lower. "Róisín," he murmured and stroked along her folds. "Róisín." He drew circles with his thumb over her clit. Her hips bucked beneath his touches. "Róisín." He bent, lowering his mouth to her. The next time he said her name, it hummed along her clit and her hips rocked against his mouth.

When he closed his mouth over her, she cried out and gripped his hair with one hand. Her back arched and her body lit, muscles growing tighter with the heat exploding through her when he pressed one finger into her, then another. The euphoric tingles left her feeling weightless as he stroked, sucked, and licked. Her name whispered over her most sensitive parts, over and over. Faster and faster, her breaths came. That fire inside her burning hotter, inching closer to the sparks.

He shifted over her more, spreading her wider, pushing his fingers in deeper, curling them inside her. It was enough to send her over the edge. Her vision danced with spots, hazing around the edges until her body tumbled into the pool of ecstasy his touch had thrown her into.

Caid's fingers continued stroking as he lined himself up, gripping his cock in his free hand. When his fingers pulled out, his cock pushed in. His thrusts slow, rolling, as he brought her down from the high of her orgasm.

When her hips slowed and her back settled against the seat, he lowered over her, his forearms resting next to her head. He nudged her nose with his and brushed his lips over hers. His smell was fresh cut wood, musk, and *her*. Her walls clenched around him, and he grinned down at her.

"I've been wanting to do this since the day I bought this thing," he said.

"We could have in your old one." She brought her hips to meet his as they worked to create a new pace with their bodies.

"We could have." He nipped her jaw, then peppered her neck with kisses. "Getting to have you sprawled out beneath me like this, though?" He thrust into her hard. Her head bumped the armrest on the door. "Shit, sorry." He moved a hand to the top of her head. "Maybe we're too tall for this."

She wrapped her legs around him, hooking her heels at his back. "Scoot me down a bit. I'll be fine."

He moved their joined bodies away from the door and resumed his leisurely pace.

"See? It's—" She moaned, her core fluttering as she tightened around him once more.

"Faster?"

It took her a moment to find her answer, lost to the sensations and trying to catch her breath. "No. This." Her body quivered and made her breath shake. "This."

He groaned his agreement. "Róisín."

Her body burned and throbbed. Electric tingles raced across her skin, burrowing deeper with each pass until they sunk into her core and her muscles coiled tight.

"I'm going to–Caid," she tried to speak around her pants. Everything snapped free inside her. The muscles in her body fluttering, then tightening around him, gripping him. She was still shattering around him when he came. His warmth spreading up and through her.

When their bodies had stilled, she drew a hand over his back. "I'm happy you bought this truck."

"Me too." His breath was hot against her neck. "Gimme a second and I'll stop crushing you."

She wanted to tell him to stay, to lie on her longer. She didn't care that his weight atop her chest left her only able to take half-breaths. Having him draped over her like this, body warm, breathing, *alive,* was everything to her. Instead, she said, "Can we do the next round inside, though? I think I've got a cramp in my foot."

His body shook over her as he rumbled with laughter. She held him a little tighter, closing her eyes and soaking in the moment. Soaking in every vibration his voice created against her skin. How every breath made his chest hair tickle against her.

Her reminder that he *was* there. He was still hers.

NINETEEN

ATTHEW'S EYES shifted from one sheet of paper to the other, the index finger on one hand trailing along the written names of refugees on one, while his other hand marked the arrived box next to the same name on the other. His head had started to throb with the headache hours before, but he ground his teeth together and pressed on.

Grateful, he had to remind himself. He was grateful that Roidon had opened its doors to the Shianshani witches. Despite that they refused to do the list checks, handing all the paperwork to James that morning when he shifted there to collect the confirmed names list to bring to Aja and Marcelo.

Lily still hadn't opened up to him about what else had been said, but the tension pulsed off her and Ione in the hallway when they had returned. He could only guess that it had come down to both his bond with Lily, and Nanette's ongoing vilification of Ione.

"Wait," Lily's voice cut into his thoughts. He lifted his head and squinted in her direction. She and Brent were on the far side of the study, scribbling and drawing lines across the white boards that now formed a wall in the room.

"No." Brent pointed to a scribble. "This date is wrong. These Burkes have only been here for a few decades."

"That sucks." Lily's marker made a squeak and thunk with her angry dashes through the numbers. "But wait. No." She hopped on the balls of her feet and waved a paper. "Right here!"

Matthew's heart skipped in his chest and he leaned forward.

Brent bent his head closer to Lily's. "Montana?" He straightened, his head turning to the left, then the right as he took in their information.

"Montana." Matthew shot to his feet.

The pair whirled to face him.

Fishing with Lucius and the barking boy. "Give me a second." He waved them off. "Just..." He had to slow his thoughts down, catch his breath. "A second."

"Matthew, are you alright?" Lily asked. She cast a nervous glance at Brent that had him stepping forward and bracing his body like he would need to catch Matthew.

Maybe the weakness that seized his body everywhere except his feet, which felt like bricks, meant it wasn't just him imagining that the blood had pooled there.

"M-Matthew?" Lily moved closer.

"I'm fine," he managed. There was so much noise inside of him. His feet scuffed along the floor, and he stumbled.

"I've got you," Brent said. "Here." He nudged a chair with his foot. "Sit. You've gone whiter than a clean board, so that second you need should perhaps be spent sitting."

Matthew's body hit the chair with such force, the chair tipped back slightly. When the front legs slammed down, he was momentarily catapulted back into the dream in which he was confronted by Nanette and Lucius over his bond with Lily and found out that Madigan was with the Seer.

He pressed his fingers against his eyelids and reached deep, deep down to find a semblance of calm.

Montana. Fishing at the creek. Lucius's constant change of Matthew's hand on the fishing rod. The barking boy he had hiked with once before when he'd been called to babysit so his mother and the barking boy's mother could have privacy. Matthew had been right. *Memories.*

"Jackson," Matthew said. "Jackson Burke."

Lily's eyes fell on the paper she had in her hand. "Mother is Marion Burke."

"Marion," Matthew whispered. His heart galloped in his chest, crashing wildly into his ribcage, then his lungs.

"Matthew, have you met your mother's brother and his family before?" Brent asked.

"I didn't know who they were. She said they were family, but she was so—" Frustration began to build a home inside of him. "She was vague about it. About it all. She said I needed to know them. She was helping Marion with something. Jackson was just a boy, maybe around thirteen?"

Lily knelt in front of him and handed him the paper. She placed a hand on his knee, giving it a light squeeze. "I think we found a match."

His brain consumed all the information on the page before him. Hungry for more, needing more. "They're still there?"

Brent crossed over to the table he and Lily had set up on one side of the line of boards. After a few seconds of rifling through papers, he returned. "It looks like Declan passed recently. Around seven years ago. Marion is still there."

Hope readied its large steel ball, preparing to knock down that home frustration was racing to finish. "Jackson?"

Brent's finger skimmed down the page. "It looks like he took over ownership of Marion's sister's home around five months ago."

"Declan was his father?" Lily stood and looked over Brent's arm.

"Yes. He was Clarissa's older brother. It would appear when the family resettled after coming here during the last refugee wave from Aunellion, he too split off and went his own way. Most of them resettled in Roidon and Molennius. It looks like most of the Burkes resettled to Earth."

Lily's eyes were wide when they found Matthew's. "Roidon? Are they..." she made her way toward the table, but Brent stopped her.

"The Burkes on Roidon are all on the deceased record books."

Hoping his legs would hold him, Matthew rose. "How? How have so many people from my mother's family died? How much older than my mother was Declan?"

"Thirty-seven years."

"So young," Lily whispered.

"Make it make sense, please," Matthew said thickly to Brent.

"I..." He waved the papers. "I wish I could. Even I don't understand it."

"Where is Jackson now? You said he took his aunt's house," Lily said. "Maybe he and Marion can help. You said Clarissa and Marion were doing something together."

Matthew pinched the bridge of his nose. "Why didn't I have a tether to them?" When Brent only pursed his lips, a powerful gust of wind blew through him, whipping the wrecking ball away from the house. "What do you know?"

"Not much." His admission was followed with a frown. "I know Lucius and Clarissa were searching for something before she got too sick to travel."

"That doesn't answer my question about the familial bond. Lucius." Matthew's stomach sank. "He said our tether was because he accepted me into his Coven. It was *our* familial bond, wasn't it?"

Brent nodded. "That is the only thing it could be. Adopted witches never receive a Coven line." He frowned when Matthew could only stare back at him. "He never spoke to me about your bond. I'm sorry."

"No. It's okay. I just..." Matthew rubbed the back of his neck. "It circles back to wanting to know why."

Lily came up to Matthew's side. Her hand slid down his forearm to grasp his hand. It took every ounce of strength to not lean into her.

"And why would I have that with only him and my mother, but not the rest of my family?" Matthew watched the way Brent's eyes darkened. He had rarely, in his one-hundred-thirty-three years, seen Brent's magic surface in the way it had other witches. To see it stir now had him braced for what came next.

"When Clarissa returned to Ely, with-child, she made the choice to sever her own tie with her family."

"But why?" The alarm in Lily's voice was clear.

Brent's eyes didn't move away from Matthew's. "To protect you."

"From?" The one word felt impossible to Matthew. His body so tense, so tight and still squeezing, he was unsure how he remained conscious.

Brent extended his hand, holding the papers. "That's not an answer that I have. Your aunt and cousin? I can bet they do."

Matthew looked at the copy of the deed to the house Brent had said Jackson took ownership of, reading the address in Earth's realm.

Maine.

"I need to"—He groped for the chair he had been in—"I need to sit."

He hadn't been to Maine since he and Shasta had gone, knowing that they would be the best ones from their ever-shrinking group, to relay the news of Caid's death to Lina. He knew that Shasta had returned several times after helping Lina with the pregnancy and later the birth of her twins. He hadn't been able to go back. Hadn't been able to face the memories. Hadn't been able to deal with the pain and the grief.

It looked like he was going to have to face those demons if he wanted answers to the ever-growing list of questions forming around his family.

TWENTY

Lina rolled and pressed her face against the warm back next to her.

"Happy Mother's Day," Thomas said, his voice still thick from sleep.

"Shh, lower your voice." She slid a hand over his side and down his abdomen. "The kids will know we're awake and the chaos will start."

"You're doing that and expect me to be quiet?"

Her hand moved lower, teasing. "Maybe it's to make up for the hand you put over my mouth last night."

When her hand moved lower, stroking his cock, he groaned. He flipped to his back and pulled her over him, then stilled. His brown eyes widened. "Is something burning?"

Lina sniffed the air. Her senses were met with the smell of burned toast. "Dammit." She dropped her head to his chest. "Why'd we have kids again? Not only did we have one, but were crazy and went for two."

His chest shook beneath her when he chuckled. "I know how much you like a bargain, so the two for one made the most sense."

She sighed and closed her eyes. "We should've sent them off with their uncle and aunt before they left last week. Could've been their place the twins were trying to burn down. Not ours." She lifted her head enough to give her space to lick a line up Thomas's chest. "Then we could've made all the noise we wanted."

"They did offer," he reminded her.

"I know. I also saw the way they were looking at each other across the yard. It seemed smarter to send them off to go, what did Abby call it? Suck face." Resigned to the fact that they needed to go make sure their house wasn't actually on fire, she rolled off him and collected the pair of joggers and t-shirt she had hastily discarded as they had tumbled into bed the night before. "Between us, and Caid and Ro—" She tugged the joggers over her legs. "Well, and Wyatt and Leslie, too, it's not all too much, is it? Should we try to get them to tone it down? Should *we* tone it down?"

Thomas moved to the side of the bed and stood. "None of us are grinding all over one another." He bent and pressed a soft kiss to her cheek. "Or actually sucking each other's faces—"

"Or sucking anything," she added offhandedly.

He snorted. "All the kids are just seeing healthy adult relationships. People in love."

A small part of that growing anxiety settled. The McGrath kids hadn't had the best role models growing up. It hadn't just been that their parents didn't want children, yet had them anyway. Their relationship had been cold and unwelcoming. As Lina had gotten older and began losing herself in books, she often wondered if her parents had married out of some outdated obligation or their parents had arranged it. She would ask, but the last time she had talked to either parent had been just after she had the twins. She had seen her father in the post office. Two days later she'd seen their mother in deli of the town's little local grocery store.

"I hope you expect nothing from us. You have your brother, that's all you're getting." Her mother had said. The words still clung to the most tender spot in Lina's heart.

It had taken everything she had to not break in the middle of the store when their mother turned her back and walked away. No one in town had known about Caid. Shasta and Matthew had come and had given her the child-rated version of what had happened. She must have played her part well, because Matthew left, and Shasta only continued to return until the babies had been born. When there were no signs of magic after those first six months, Shasta's visits stopped and she had been alone.

"Sloane!" Abigail shrieked. "That's the third egg you've dropped. Mom's gonna hang you from the ceiling fan."

Lina rolled her eyes skyward.

"Hey." Thomas stepped closer and cupped her face. "You've got this. You're an amazing mother, Lina. Don't let her take that from you. You've broken that cycle. Both you and Caid have."

Her eyes stung, and before the first tear could spill, she leaned into him. "I love you, Thomas Commons. Now, if you'll excuse me—"

"Lina Marie McGrath-Commons." Róisín's voice was tight, rich with anger, and Lina's brain churned, fear?

Shit. David.

Lina yanked her T-shirt over her head and pushed by Thomas heading toward the sounds of Caid and Róisín's voices, bickering and cussing at one another.

"Mom!" Abigail met her at the bottom of the stairs. Her hair was a mess of brown curls in a bun atop her head. There was a flour hand-print on one side of her face and a dark smudge on the other. "Go back to bed. We have a present for you and you're supposed to have it in bed."

Lina eyed the dark mark. "Is that—" She pressed a finger against it.

Please be chocolate.

"Pancakes!" Sloane announced, shifting between them with a plate heaped with... something that certainly did not look like pancakes.

Lina yelped and fell backwards, her bottom slamming hard against the stair tread behind her.

"Surprise!" The twins shouted in unison.

Lina held her breath and dragged a hand through her hair.

She cleared her throat and glanced from the burnt pancakes to Sloane, then to Abigail. "Thank you, my sweet babies. Why don't you, uh,"—She nodded toward the kitchen—"Go set those on the table. Then grab plates, cups, and whatnot to set the table. Where did Aunt Ro go?"

Abigail pointed to the front door. "Uncle Caid came stomping in and dragged her out saying something about her sitting her *fucking ass* in the truck because he gets to kill that *damned* rabbit."

Sloane covered his mouth too late to hide his snicker. "You're in trouble,"

"No." Lina got to her feet. "She's not." The sigh she released had been meant to lighten her. Instead, it only left her feeling heavier. "She gets a pass, for that only," she added, looking pointedly at Abigail. "Go set the table, please."

Sloane and his plate of questionable pancakes shifted away, leaving Lina standing with Abigail.

She took her bottom lip between her thumb and finger, her eyes sad when she pulled them away from the front door. "Is Uncle Caid really gonna kill David?"

"Honestly? If I don't stop them, yes." She reached out to Abigail and brushed the flour from her cheek. "A lot happened while you two were in my belly, playing soccer with my bladder. A lot that's hard to move forward from." There was a shout from the front yard and Lina spun Abigail toward the kitchen. "Keep David inside, please."

"He's in the pantry," Abigail said over her shoulder.

Rubbing her eyes with the heels of her palms, Lina braced herself for what she was about to walk out to. She not only needed to save her friendship with Róisín, but she needed to keep her rabbit alive, too.

And convince both Róisín and her brother to calm down enough to listen to what David had told her the week before.

Her hand had just closed around the door handle when a crash sounded in the kitchen, followed by a curse from Sloane.

"You're not supposed to use your magic that way, dumbass!" Abigail scolded him.

"You can't tell me what to do," he said.

"Hey! Put me down, right now," Abigail's voice rose.

"I got them," Thomas said, racing past her. "You go take care of *them*." He pointed to where Caid was walking in long strides across the yard toward his truck with a shouting, cursing, Róisín slung over his shoulder, also shouting and cursing.

Lina pulled open the front door and marched out onto the porch.

"Kincaid James McGrath, put her down right now. Then, the both of you shut the hell up and listen to me."

Caid froze with the door to his truck half open. Slowly, he set Róisín down and turned to face her.

Why can't my mom voice work on my damned kids this well?

"Yes, I still have David. Shut up." She pointed a finger at Caid when he opened his mouth to speak. "Both of you." She shot Róisín a glare. "You two will come out back and *behave* while David tells you what he knows. You're going to need to hear it."

Caid and Róisín exchanged a wary look. Róisín's shoulders dropped and her body seemed to deflate.

"Fine. But after, that rabbit is mine," Caid said.

TWENTY-ONE

I T TOOK every ounce of strength Caid had to keep himself rooted to the chair he sat in. The two most important women in his life stood before him, their emotions flooding him.

From Lina, he felt her shame, and her fear. Through Róisín, it was betrayal woven with fear.

Lina's lips pressed into a thin line and her eyes blinked rapidly as she waited, watching Róisín who stood with her arms crossed and jaw clenched.

They had been instant friends when Róisín moved to Greens Glen, but something had changed that day six years ago. They had become something *more* in the wake of his death. A hardened and darkened side of Róisín and Lina had been revealed. He had to wonder if he would have ever seen it if that day had ended differently.

He had almost lost everything. Not just Róisín, but Lina, the twins, Thomas and Wyatt.

The patio door slid open and Abigail appeared with David clutched in her arms. Her soft brown eyes were shining with tears, near spilling, when she looked at Caid questionably as she passed by him. His heart squeezed, and he immediately regretted the things he said just moments ago.

He knew Sloane was behind him, face pressed to the window. His small heart hammering as he waited to see what happened next.

That had been a distinct feeling. The line, that rope-like connection he held with Róisín before, was gone. Nothing remained of it. Instead, they were connected in a more whole bodied way, in this after. He could sense her in different ways, and sometimes that connection between them was involuntary. As it was now when her fear kicked up a notch, coming at him in waves instead of ripples, at the sight of David.

When Lina, Abigail, and Sloane came into their magic, the connection had been the same. Róisín couldn't explain how or why when he had questioned it. Questioned why, when he had come back, their bond tether hadn't tied back together as it had when *he* had saved *her.*

"Uncle Caid?" Abigail's voice was tiny. She had set David down on the patio and now wrung her hands before her. "He's a good friend to mom. And us. He doesn't mean to hurt you and Aunt Ro."

He swallowed down the thickness trying to choke him and waved her closer. He waited until she was close enough to tug into his lap and draw her against his chest. Pressing a kiss to her hair, he said, "I talk a big game, kiddo, but I'm not going to do anything to David."

She wrapped her arms around his neck and squeezed. "Promise?"

"Cross my heart. We just need to figure out what's going on. Talk some adult stuff out. It'll be okay."

She glanced nervously at Róisín. "Aunt Ro and mom?"

"They'll be okay too. Little speed bumps in life." He felt like he was trying more to assure himself, not Abigail. "Why don't you go in and help your dad and brother finish brunch?"

Abigail hesitated a moment before releasing him. She gave him a quick kiss on his cheek and darted inside.

David's ears twitched, and he hopped so he was facing Caid. He wouldn't kill the rabbit, no. But he didn't trust him. Trust had been lost the moment he had revealed to Róisín that he had always known of Caid's magic. To have David still there could mean that Gea was still watching Róisín.

That woke the smokey, sludgy side of his magic. The part that spoke to him in that gravelly, hissing voice.

Róisín looked at Caid, her lips pressed in a way that he could tell she was trying to hold herself together. To keep the words in, keep away the tears. To keep herself there and not flee. He reached out to her with his magic, lifting the fire of his elemental magic up, up, up, and wrapping her in a warm hug. He gave her a slight nod, his way of letting her know she could lead this moment.

If she wanted to go, even if it was his family, he would go with her.

They had already had two close calls. Caid was a believer that things came in threes. Three jobs for him to find that carpentry was where he thrived. Three homes to find the one that fit that space that craved comfort inside of him. Róisín had been his third adult, mature relationship.

His old Chevy was his third truck and, as his mind wandered back to the night before, Róisín sprawled beneath him on the bench seat, was his most favorite of all of them. The memory had him shifting in his chair.

Róisín made a light coughing noise. When he glanced at her, she lifted a brow at him before dropping her attention to where he strained against his jeans. He shrugged and grinned at her. If that was what brought her from the edge of that ledge she'd perched herself on the moment they'd come into the house to find David in the kitchen with the kids, so be it.

"Sloane—" Thomas's shout was cut off by a crash that was followed by Abigail's giggle.

Lina winced and cast a glance toward the house.

"How about a ban on magic today?" Thomas asked.

"Daaaaaad," the twins cried out in unison.

"Nope. It's Mother's Day. No magic. You two have almost burned the house down. Now you've broken your mother's favorite salad bowl."

"Oh no," Lina said sadly, her eyes back on the house.

"Thomas has it under control," Caid said. "Let's get this"—He pointed at David—"Conversation going. Prolonging it doesn't make it better."

Lina sighed and tipped her head back to blink at the sky. "I'm really sorry. I want to say I didn't lie, because it never came to a 'Where's David?' Or a 'Is David still here?' But... I did lie by omission. For that"

—she frowned at Róisín. "I cannot be any more sorry. I'll do whatever it takes to fix this."

In a jerking motion, Róisín dashed away a tear that had escaped to roll down her cheek. "Why are you still here?" She asked David. "You said Future asked you to be here, but you also said you were a charge of *her.*"

"Better question," Caid began, sitting forward, narrowing his eyes on David. "Does she know Róisín is here, or that my sister and the kids have magic?"

Lina sucked in a loud breath and cursed.

"She knows nothing," David said. He shifted so that he sat on his haunches. "Earth's realm has always been difficult for her. For what reason, I'm afraid, I do not have the answer. Only our Creator would know."

"Creator?" Lina and Róisín asked together.

"I'd wondered..." Lina chewed on the corner of her lip. "Like you said that time, Róisín. The well sources couldn't have just... *formed* on their own. Somehow, someway, they were given the magic that fed the Covens."

Róisín pursed her lips. "If there is someone else, how could they let Gea do all of this, though? She's messed with the lives of witches for who knows how long. To let her do it without consequence makes them just as awful as she is."

Three pairs of eyes dropped to where David was stroking an ear between his paws.

"Talk, rabbit," Caid said roughly.

"I, I don't know our Creator, I'm afraid. I know not who or what they are, where they are. I don't know if any of us do," he confessed.

"Are they...?" Her throat bobbed with her swallow. "Could she have?" Róisín asked, gliding a finger along her neck before her eyes flared wide when she looked at Caid. "It would make sense how this could happen."

David cleared his throat, his next words stopping her spiral, but doing nothing to calm the storm building inside of Caid. "We do not know what has happened to the Creator."

Róisín let out a loud sigh and knelt on the patio. "What *do* you know, David? Tell us that much. Because from where I stand right now, I still can't trust that she's not somehow tied to you and has known every single thing I've done these past years. My life being at risk is one thing." She reached out and batted his paws away from his ear. "Their lives are not for her to use in this fucked up game she's playing."

Lina brought a hand to her mouth and wrapped her other arm around herself. Róisín's words were the sign that she had been forgiven for her indiscretion.

"I know she is tearing through the other realms looking for Future. She's caused disturbances among the other spirits in her search."

Róisín rose slowly. "What do you mean, 'looking for Future?' Where could she have gone?"

"Sister Future disappeared the night you died." David's small, black eyes were on Caid. "When she disappeared, so did her magic."

Caid stood and turned to Róisín. "What does that mean? Is fate like, broken or something?"

"I..." Róisín's throat bobbed with her audible swallow. "I don't know." She rubbed her temples. "I know this can't be good, though. Gea was already volatile. That's clear in what she did to the Seer. What we can still only assume she planned for me. Some, or maybe all of her power, has to be tied to the Sisters. They're Fates."

"We're totally fucked, aren't we?" Lina asked.

Róisín hooked her pinky around Caid's. The racing, skittering ants of her anxiety filled him. He twisted his hand so that he held hers fully and gave it a light squeeze.

"You need more than us, Róisín," he said softly.

Her sad *no* came on her exhale.

"More what?" Lina asked.

"Help. Brains. Magic. We need..." Caid closed his eyes and said, "The others."

"Oh." Lina's eyes widened. "Oh." She came forward and wrapped Róisín in her arms, swaying with her as she always did Caid.

Caid stepped back to give them room. Chest was heavy and his heart pinched, he was relieved to also have some space for himself. When he turned to the house, sensing eyes on them, he saw from the master bathroom a set of hazel eyes and another of brown.

"We have to ward them," he said suddenly.

"What? Who?" Lina sniffed.

"Them." He pointed upward.

"Shit," Róisín said. "They would. They would follow us wherever we went."

"We can do it, though, right?" Caid asked.

Róisín's eyes glinted with mischief as she smiled at the bathroom window, waving. "Oh, we can."

Lina leaned around Róisín and lifted a brow at Caid. "I feel there's a story here."

Róisín's laughter was full and warm. "It was the only way to get Matthew to stop trying to steal my first girlfriend."

Lina snorted.

At the mention of Matthew, Caid's heart released, shifting in his chest, painfully. Two false starts the men had gotten. What would their relationship be like if they did all come back together again? Life didn't come with a map. A life with magic, and the roads they had all traveled on, were far more confusing and twisting. He could accept not being forgiven by everyone, but he wasn't sure what he would do if they turned their back on Róisín.

"Hey." Róisín's hands were at his chest. He realized that it was just them on the patio now. David and Lina had disappeared, presumably inside. "Where'd you go?"

He brought her close and bent to bury his face against her neck. He hadn't told her he, too, needed that physical reassurance that she was there. A confession she had given him in the months after, when he had woken up one morning and she had been sprawled over him, clinging to him tightly.

It had been a struggle, before. Those times after Alleyette when they had been separated had given his mind chances to doubt that she was still there with him after the day in the ravine. But he had managed.

Since Shianshani, those moments that he wasn't in her presence felt impossible. Dark edged up, wanting to swallow him as it had that day, pulling him down, down, down. Whispering in his ear until he was nearly convinced that his chest had stilled and his heart no longer beat.

Sensing the emotions swamping him, she wrapped her arms around him, her fists clutching the back of his shirt.

"Caid." His name a broken whisper from her lips.

"We're here. We're together." He kissed her neck. "We're here together."

She moved and took his face with her hands, bringing his mouth to hers.

He wanted to lean into another kiss, to sit and hold her in his arms forever, but David's information had urgency taking him over again. "We should go in."

"One more second." She pressed her face against his chest. "If I'm going to go become the bad aunt to those two, I need just one more second."

Caid couldn't help but think that for how much everything had changed, it was still the same.

TWENTY-TWO

TURA SAT before the false loom, her fingers gently tracing along the lines and patterns that had her brows drawn and her bottom lip caught between her teeth.

The true loom of Fate's future path had been destroyed. She had left it splintered and torn in her equally destroyed room. Before she escaped, she created a false loom to bring with her. She may have been able to quiet her magic to hide where she was going or what had truly happened in that room, but she could not leave behind her duty to Fate.

Her choice to leave behind the chaos of her room had been more of a knee jerk reaction, an impulse. Her rage drove her to hurl a vase at her window. The rest happened from there. She only halted when she found herself before her loom, ready to tear it to shreds. Her chest had been heaving, her breaths loud by that point. There was thunder roaring in her ears, and her eyes were still blinded by her tears.

With swift hands, she crafted the false loom, then set to work destroying her loom that had danced with threads before her eyes for centuries. It had hurt her heart to do it, but she could no longer trust her mother. Not after what she had done.

The tattered room had been her message to her mother.

However, fearing retaliation against her sisters, Tura had left a few drops of blood on the floor. A few shreds of her nightgown to make it appear as though there had been a struggle.

The sounds of her sisters stirring had snapped her back to her task at hand and she quickly bundled what little else she needed, then fled.

After she found a quiet space and pulled the false loom up before her, she had cried out loudly when she saw the green and gold thread slowly pulsing back to life in the way it grew thicker from its once frayed ends alongside the burgundy one.

Caid and Róisín.

Hope.

Now, standing before the loom next to Hecate, it was her mother's thread she watched. It cut in and out of the loom, never truly creating a pattern. In some places, it disappeared entirely.

"What could it mean?" Tura asked quietly.

Hecate leaned forward and squinted her eyes. "Your mother's I assume?"

"Yes." Tura nodded and lifted her hand. "See here? It would only cut in and out like this if her life was literally going in and out of existence." From the corner of her eye, she saw Hecate's lips turn downward.

"It could be possible the loom is showing us that she will find the way through the veil in search of you. Without the presence of your magic coupled with being here in Earth's realm, she could not feel that maternal link with you. She would assume that you've moved on."

Tura focused on the loom again. "She doesn't have any of my magic left for the veil."

Hecate rested a hand on her shoulder. "We've seen your mother's ambitions, Tura. We cannot discount that she would not find the same way through that Shasta and Ione now have in their hands." She turned to Tura. "It is time. Everything we've done. All that Fate has given us. The end begins now."

Tura's stomach slammed down into her toes and a knot tightened at the center of her chest. Once her magic was released, the astronomical skies across the realms would ignite and Gea would know.

"Shouldn't we wait until they're ready? He doesn't even know who you are, to him, to us. They don't know why or what they need to sacrifice." Tura's breath quickened. "We'll only have hours, at most, once I do."

"Time has never been our friend, my sweet child." Hecate cupped her face. "It's a good thing I know how to talk fast when I need to."

Tura wrinkled her nose.

"We know Kincaid and Róisín will return shortly. That path directed itself." Hecate's thumbs were soft as they stroked over Tura's cheeks. "I need you for the others."

Tura looked down at the loom.

"Bring Matthew and Jackson together, Tura. It's the ball at the head of the pendulum. The rest will follow suit." She leaned closer, her mouth at Tura's ear. "It's time to set the table."

Tura swallowed hard. They were really doing this. "I hope you have a plan, Fate," she said into the sky with a whisper.

"Oh, it does." Hecate chuckled.

Twenty-Three

Róisín turned the sign over on the door to the tea shop and began opening the blinds for the day. She was exhausted. It had been days since she had last slept, David's words running on a loop in her head.

She closed her eyes and pressed her fingers against her eyelids until spots danced across the dark.

The pressure that had been building at the base of her skull was a familiar feeling that she had hoped to never feel again. The push of time. The push of panic. Of fear.

It had been absent. Something cold and dark settling deep into the places those feelings lived before Talista. Now, as that panic and fear crept back in, she doubted herself. Again. Had she done the right thing, leaving everyone behind? Had every single life she had taken in the last five years been hers to take? Why was she still figuring things out? Why hadn't she been able to act on Gea yet?

Clenching her jaw, she shoved each doubt down as quick as it rose. She was biding her time. It had to be perfect, she reminded herself. Once they found Gea, once they showed their hand... Time would not be on their side. They'd have to be ready. More ready than they'd been in Talista.

Or at least, more ready than they had convinced themselves they were that day.

She wasn't risking Lina, and she wouldn't lose Caid, again.

The door to the tea shop opened, sending the bell overhead jingling and her thoughts scattering.

"What a beautiful morning!" Mr. Pappas greeted in Greek as he breezed in. "Will we be seeing you at the neighborhood party this evening?"

She stepped behind the counter and offered him a warm smile. "Of course, Mr. Pappas. I told Mrs. Pappas yesterday when she stopped in that I wouldn't miss it for the world."

He beamed at her. "Excellent. Just like that clementine and chamomile tea my lovely Eileen brought home yesterday. Do you have more?"

Róisín walked over to a shelf of loose tea displayed in jars. "Do you want it loose, or should I bag it individually for serving?"

"Oh." He tapped his chin and studied the jar she held. The bell jingled again, Ana coming in with a younger woman trailing behind her.

"Don't mind us," she said to Róisín.

"Perhaps bagging it?" Mr. Pappas said, sounding uncertain. "I have never made tea much on my own. I know we have these"—he made a dunking motion—"metal, with the handle. But I would overfill it and run out so quickly."

"Bagged, it is. Are twenty bags alright? Or would you like more?"

"Twenty will do," he said with a nod.

Róisín moved to her prep station behind the checkout counter. While she weighed and closed the bags, a chill settled into her bones, making her body tremble. Glancing over her shoulder, she saw Mr. Pappas standing with Ana and the young woman, chatting. Ana was animated as usual, her hands flying, brows rising and falling as she spoke, translating rapidly to English for the woman with her.

No one else was in the shop and she knew Caid had been running a few for her errands that morning.

Sealing the last bag, she packed the small tea box with her shop logo on it and tied a ribbon neatly around it. Turning back to the register, the faint electric smell of magic tickled her nose, making her magic stir and try to rise within her.

No. Please. Just stay hidden. We're okay.

She said it more for herself, but was relieved when her magic tucked away into a hidden place inside.

After she handed Mr. Pappas his order and he had left, she focused on Ana and the young woman. The quicker she could clear them out, the better. The cold seeped deeper, freezing her lungs, her heart.

Breathe, Róisín.

"Rosalie, this is my daughter, Elizabeth." Ana motioned to the young woman. "She leaves tomorrow, so I wanted to make sure she went home with the best teas."

"It's a pleasure to meet you." Róisín extended her hand. "I've heard so much about you."

Elizabeth smiled shyly. "It's a pleasure to meet you as well."

The moment their hands touched, the air became trapped in Róisín's lungs. Confused, she looked down at their joined hands and back at Elizabeth's face.

The bell chimed, and the trio turned toward the door. Caid entered looking like *Caid* again. His face clean shaven, hair cropped close to the sides of his head and trimmed at the top, leaving it to curl slightly over his forehead. Her reaction of surprise came from the box he held in his hands. The same box she had accepted in a delivery that morning before opening and had placed in the back storeroom.

"It was blocking the walkway," he said. He caught her eye as he walked by them, and she saw the unasked question there. The question that his magic tried to ask her, but the way his jaw flared with the audible grinding of his molars told her he was trying to hold it down. Keep it hidden.

Her magic stretched its fingers to reach out to him, but thankfully, remained quiet. She hesitated a moment before giving him a slight dip of the head.

"This is excellent," Ana said brightly.

Oh, shit. Not this right now.

Róisín turned back to her. "Mrs. Svensson, Ana," she corrected herself under Ana's glare, "it's not—"

Ana waved a dismissive hand, sending a warmth through the air with the gesture. "Róisín and Kincaid, we no longer have time for these dalliances. You two need to take a seat so we can all have a little chat."

Now both her and Caid's magic rose. Rose with such speed, such fury that she gasped and she could hear the way Caid's teeth snapped together.

Before she could question who Ana was, how she knew who they were, the door opened and two women walked in.

"Wonderful, we're all present this morning," the first woman who entered said.

Róisín only half heard her, for her eyes were on the other woman dressed in a pair of lilac linen pants and a loose t-shirt the color of a sunflower.

"Sister Future," she said on a breath as she fought to remain upright.

"Please, call me Tura," the woman said.

What was going on? David had said Future was missing. Yet, here she was, her violet-colored eyes filled with relief when she looked at Róisín, then to Caid.

Breathe, Róisín, breathe.

Róisín did breathe then. Faster and faster. Caid came to stand at her back. A tower to protect her from a storm. His magic's voice whispering along her spine promises of that protection and safety.

The woman in the green dress stepped forward, her magic's power pulsing in heavy waves around the room. She was powerful, whoever she was. But... Róisín straightened and tipped her head to one side. She wasn't here to cause harm. To any of them. Róisín felt something shifting around her, wrapping around her softly. She couldn't explain it. Her magic calmed, and her heart steadied.

"Wh-who are you?" Róisín managed.

"I'm Hecate." She sketched a slight bow before rising and flashing a warm, genuine smile. Then she gestured in Caid's direction. "His great-great-grandmother."

TWENTY-FOUR

"I DON'T like this," Aja's rumbling voice filled Shasta's kitchen when he entered.

His proclamation was punctuated by a thump overhead and a giggle.

Shasta sighed. "Just be happy they don't live with you. I ask them every time they disappear, but..." She motioned to the ceiling.

Aja squinted at it, then his lips moved with a few whispered words and the kitchen fell silent again.

"Thank you," Shasta said. "I don't have it in me to cast one, again."

He lowered himself onto a stool and studied her beneath lowered brows. "As much as I am grateful it's you that has to deal with that." He pointed upward. "That's not what I'm speaking of."

She set the towel down she had been using to dry dishes. Despite the new kitchen, for just a moment when she faced him across the island, she couldn't help seeing Caid there years before. They had shared the space of her old kitchen enough times that it had become a part of their growing relationship. Her lungs gave a tight squeeze, and she shook her head to bring her focus back to Aja.

"You two are really going to attempt to cross the veil?"

Shasta scratched the top of her head and shrugged. "It seems that way."

"Why was nothing said to us before?"

"Well..." She drummed her fingers on the surface of the countertop. "We were sort of in the middle of a bunch of other things. It seemed like something we could handle once we crossed a few of those things off the list. Except—" She frowned and her shoulders dropped. "The fates fucked things up."

Aja grunted in agreement.

"She knew, didn't she?" Shasta asked softly.

He rubbed a hand over his face and nodded. "She'd known for nearly a century what her fate was. Yet, she continued to plan, to act, and once Frederick was gone, she grabbed the reins and raced to do as much as she could with the time she had left."

"You loved her." It wasn't a question, but a statement.

"She and Diana were my world."

Shasta's eyes stung and the bridge of her nose burned. "If we don't find out what is happening, she'll never be able to cross over. None of them will."

He scratched his jaw, his dark eyes lifting to hers. "Would you be able to find Diana? She never—" He cleared his throat. "She never crossed over after her death. But for her to not be in the afterworld makes no sense."

There were a lot of things that had stopped making sense to Shasta. Even before Brenna began assembling the pieces that needed to be brought together for Róisín. Then Evelyn's last visits.

"It could be that she was one of the ones that hasn't been able to leave longer than the others. Stephen had learned that some had trouble for decades, while most seemed to begin to struggle around eleven or twelve years ago."

"And six years ago, absolutely no one could get out."

She nodded. "That was what he and Brenna said the last time they could cross. Given that I haven't seen either of them since, I can only deduce that they too are now beholden to the afterworld."

He crossed his arms over his broad chest. "I repeat, I don't like this. But"—He lifted a hand to stop her—"We need to do this. If something is happening to our people on the other side of the veil, we need to know. We need to remedy whatever it is."

She let out the breath that had been weighing her chest down. "The question is, are *we* ready to face whatever it is we may find there?"

The sound of footsteps racing down the stairs had him standing from the stool. "We don't have a choice. For our people, our loved ones, *we* have to do whatever it takes."

"No, don't. Don't even think about it," Runa said from behind where Shasta and Ione stood.

Shasta turned to see that Aja was standing next to Runa and Runa's arm was extended, palm against Aja's chest. Aja's head was turned to Runa, his forehead and brow lined with the marks from his scowl.

"I'm serious." Runa's tone was warning. "We heard enough of it at the house. We get it. You don't like it."

Ione groaned and Shasta could only roll her eyes and sigh. They had come to the desert that spanned Molennius's South Pole. Far from any humans or witches, isolating the risk should something that had escaped the darkness into the afterworld slip through the veil once they opened it.

"I was only going to tell them both to be careful, and thirty minutes, as we agreed. Or else we pull them and seal the veil," Aja said tightly.

Runa's body relaxed, and he dropped his arm. "Oh."

"Are you ready?" Shasta asked Ione.

"I don't know if I'll ever be ready to *willingly* go to the afterworld," she said. She lifted a hand to her chest, rubbing at the base of her throat. Something Shasta noticed Lily did as well when she was nervous.

Shasta moved closer and clutched the hand between hers. "This is just to see if it works. We're in and out. If it works, then we figure out the rest."

"If it works, we go with you next time," Aja said. Runa nodded in agreement.

"If it works, we have an army of witches waiting on this side and bring an army in with us," Shasta said.

"I can get behind that plan." Aja pulled his shoulders back, stretching out his chest as he tipped his head from one side to the other.

"And we figure out why our people are trapped," Ione added.

"That too," Shasta agreed.

"It'd be nice to see Jes again. Make sure she's okay." Runa's voice was quiet, filled with grief for his sister.

"Okay." Shasta blew out a deep breath. "Enough chatting." She brought her hand up and Ione dropped one of hers onto it.

As the pair whispered the words that would join their magic and its power together, the wind kicked up around them, lifting grains of sand to shape a funnel around them. Electricity charged hotly through Shasta's body, raising the hairs across her skin.

"What the fuck?" Runa's voice sounded from somewhere distant.

"Grab them," Aja shouted. "Quick!"

But it was too late. It was the silence Shasta noticed first. Then it was the chill in the air.

"Where are we? Is this? This can't be the afterworld," Ione said next to her.

Shasta slowly opened her eyes and took in her surroundings. Something wasn't right. This *was* the afterworld. She could feel it deep in her marrow that this was their resting place. Where they existed *after*. But something was different.

"It worked," she whispered.

"I don't want to die. Not if this is where we go. Mother made it sound so calm, and beautiful," Ione said.

"We create the world we are to spend eternity in once we're here. Maybe..." Shasta spun in a circle, taking in everything. "Maybe this is just what's outside of those worlds?"

"Where is Tura?!" A shrill voice broke the silence. "What have you done with her?"

"Shasta." Ione gripped her arm tightly.

Shasta rested a hand over Ione's and together they took a step back. A figure wearing a billowing blue cloak was barreling toward them. Golden locks peaked from beneath the hood.

"Where is she?" The figure demanded.

"Who is that?" Ione asked with a whisper.

"I don't—" Shasta shook her head. Something in the distance grabbed her attention, and she dragged her eyes away from the figure that getting alarmingly closer with every second they let pass. When she focused, she realized what she saw was a second figure sprinting toward them. Recognition was instant. Stephen. Róisín's father.

He was silent, his hands waving frantically. No, Shasta squinted. Was he silent? His mouth was moving, one word, over and over.

"Go!"

Her attention darted back to the cloaked figure. Like the tumbler to a lock, understanding clicked into place. "It's—" She began.

"Where is Tura?!" The cloaked figure was before them now and Shasta could see their face.

"—the Goddess."

Tura? Who was Tura?

Realization slammed into Shasta, stealing her breath. She gripped Ione's hand tighter, her magic flaring.

"Now, Ione. Now!"

Not even a second later, they were sprawled on the sand of the Molennius desert. Aja and Runa instantly at their sides, pulling them to their feet.

"What? What is it?" Runa began frantically patting down Ione. "What happened?"

"I don't know." Ione batted his hands away. "Give me some space." He took a startled step back, looking like a wounded animal. Ione pushed her hair from her face, then leaned into him. "Okay. Now you can hold me. Shasta?"

"We need to get everyone together," she said. She had been shocked at how level her own voice sounded as she spoke, given that her heart was hammering against her throat.

"What did you see?" Aja asked.

"Stephen was there." She looked at each of them, making sure she had their attention, "And the Goddess."

"The Goddess?" They questioned in unison.

"*That* is who the screaming person was?" Ione's eyes were wide and she tried to burrow closer to Runa. "I expected a babe, not someone who looks like they just crawled from a sewer pipe."

Shasta nodded. "She was coming after Ione and I. That's not all. She was demanding to know what we did with Tura, where she was."

Aja's body snapped up straight. "Sister Future."

"It took me a second to realize that's who she meant. I haven't heard Sister Future referred to as Tura in centuries." Shasta tugged at the collar of her shirt that suddenly felt too tight and close to her throat.

"If she's looking for Tura in the afterworld," Runa trailed off, his ebony face going ash gray.

"Runa and Aja, go to Marcelo and Nolani. Tell them of what's happened with the afterworld, but say nothing about Future *or* the Goddess just yet. Ione and I will go to Matthew and Lily. Then we'll meet at my house tomorrow morning. We can discuss it all then, and try to figure out what in the Hells just happened."

"What about the refugees?" Ione asked.

"I'll have Matthew put Brent in charge on our ends. Cassius and Marsenna both have it handled solidly enough for Baijiola and Trifoa. The less they all know right now, the better."

Shasta brushed the sand from her clothes and tried to shake what she could from her hair. She hadn't known what to expect if they got through the veil. But she knew with all certainty it hadn't been the Goddess.

At least Stephen is still there. Which meant that hopefully, the others were too.

TWENTY-FIVE

As Matthew maneuvered the sleek, black Audi sedan around the winding coastal roads, he let the smell of the salty ocean air sooth his senses.

He found his family. Answers were finally within reach.

Matthew had wanted Lily to come with him, but she insisted this first visit should be just him and Jackson. She would stay and help Brent with the refugees.

Even when he had begged her to come.

"It's a few days, Matthew," Lily said as she peppered his face, his throat, his chest with kisses that morning before he had left. "Take this time to be with your family."

He had rolled them so she was tucked beneath him. "If I can put a pause on it all"—He stroked a hand up her side and palmed her breast—"I can think of far more exciting ways to use my time."

After that, it was her giggles, soft sighs and whispers of his name as they brought their bodies together and made love.

With thoughts of Lily strengthening him, he eased the car over the packed rock of a narrow peninsula lined with the parked cars of people enjoying a late-spring day on the water. Jackson's house perched on the point just beyond, facing the harbor of the town of Eagle Head.

When he turned the car off, he let his head fall back against the headrest and closed his eyes. The last time he had seen Jackson had been the time at the creek when Lucius had taken them fishing. The day he asked Lucius why Jackson called him Uncle Lucius.

Matthew dragged a hand over his face, cursing softly. Pushing out of the car, he studied the house like it was the answer to everything. What would Jackson know, if anything?

Would he know why Clarissa, being Aunellion, had been shielded from not just him, her own son, but everyone? Not even Shasta had known. Just as no one had known that Lucius was his real father.

Why?

"I'm not going to get answers standing here, am I?" Matthew muttered to himself. He ran a hand through his hair and made his way along the stone pathway that led to a large oak door. He had just lifted his hand to knock when the door flew open and a tornado with pale blonde hair appeared.

"Shit!" The woman's blue eyes flew wide. She placed a hand on her heaving chest, her fingers patting it as though to calm herself. "I'm so sorry. I was just leaving and..."

Matthew blinked down at her. "Is..." He lifted his gaze and looked into the house. "Is Jackson home?"

She shifted her weight so that one hip popped out and she rested her free hand on it. "Depends. Who are you?"

"His cousin, Matthew," he answered right as her scent hit him. It wasn't magic, no, but it was familiar. It reminded him of... "You're a Trifoan mer."

She flashed him a wide grin. The sides of her face shimmered briefly with iridescent scales. "You've got a pretty keen sense." She stepped back and swept her arm toward the inside of the house to gesture him in.

"Nadia? Did you for—" A tall, copper haired male came to a halt in the living room just beyond the entrance. "Matthew."

Matthew's heart raced and his palms grew sweaty, but he gave him a slight nod. "Jackson."

"Holy shit." Jackson changed direction and hurried toward him. "I didn't think I'd ever see you again."

Matthew tensed when Jackson's arms came up. Then, Jackson drew him into a hug, giving his back a few firm pats. Matthew brought his arms around the man. "You've grown a bit since the last time I saw you."

Jackson stepped back and gave a light chuckle. "That sort of happens in the span of forty or so years."

"Do you still bark?" Matthew asked.

"Uh." Jackson winced and rubbed the back of his neck as Nadia, still holding the door, her attention bouncing between them, let out a quiet snort. "About that..."

"I'm gonna go grab Parker," Nadia said.

"Ah, shit." Jackson motioned toward her. "Matthew, this is my girlfriend, Nadia. Nadia, this is—"

"Your cousin, Matthew." Nadia ducked around Matthew to press a kiss to Jackson's cheek. "We met when I almost plowed into him running to the car to get Park."

Jackson looped an arm around her waist. "We can still catch that movie later if he wants," Jackson said.

She stepped closer and laid a hand on his chest. "We can raincheck. Beau was coming by with the kids later, which means a fire will get going, eventually. Which *also* means s'mores. You know Park and his s'mores."

The way Jackson's eye lit, and their corners crinkled with his smile, Matthew could guess that Jackson knew exactly how much Parker liked s'mores and that Jackson liked them too.

"If you're sure," Jackson said. "Tell him we can add ice cream to the date. I think Dorman's opened last week."

"He's already in love with you, Jackson." She let out a soft laugh and shook her head. "You don't have to keep trying to seal the deal."

Jackson's cheeks turned light pink, and he shrugged. "Can't help it. I love the kid. Just like I love his mom."

It was Nadia's cheeks that heated now, flaring a deep red. She leaned closer to Jackson's ear and Matthew heard her whisper, "He knows what I am. So, you don't have to worry about that."

Jackson's expression turned sober quickly and his eyes locked onto Matthew's. "How? It wasn't until she was in the water, full fin on display that I knew."

The memories of the trips to Trifoa's burgundy sand beaches hurt triple fold. How many times had he gone with his mother? With Brenna and Róisín?

"I used to go to Trifoa with my mother a lot," Matthew's answer came roughly. "I recognized the scent."

Nadia's face paled. "I hope it's a good one."

"Excuse me?" Jackson choked out.

"Not that way, dummy." She slapped playfully at his chest. "Do you want to go around smelling like rotten seaweed?" When he shook his head, she gave a satisfied nod. "Exactly."

Matthew smiled at her. "No, it's not anything rotten. The only way I can describe it is a palm trees, sun, and salt-tinged breeze riding on an electric current in the air."

Nadia pursed her lips and tipped her head to one side. "I like that. Alright, I need to get going. They're probably wondering where the hell I am."

Jackson grinned, his eyes dropping to the mark on Nadia's shoulder. "I think they'll know when you get there."

"Such an animal." Nadia sighed and rolled her eyes.

The noise that escaped Jackson's throat when the pair's lips touched on a parting kiss was far from human and had Matthew straightening.

Jackson waited until the front door clicked closed before he gestured for Matthew to follow. "You're definitely going to want a drink."

A knot formed in both his stomach and his chest. "I am?"

"Yup," he said. He approached a cabinet and began pulling out unopened bottles of liquor and setting them on a nearby bartop. He turned to Matthew, a bottle of whiskey gripped in each hand. "You asked if I still bark."

Matthew rolled his neck and cleared his throat. "I did. Thank you," he added when Jackson handed him a glass of amber liquid.

"I do a lot more than barking now." Jackson kept his eyes on Matthew as he tossed back his own glass of liquor.

Matthew drew his brows together.

Jackson lifted a hand and wiggled his fingers. "Normal, right?"

Matthew nodded. A whirring sound had grown louder somewhere distant inside of him.

Slowly, Jackson's fingers lengthened. His nails blackened as they grew jagged. The skin of his hand thickened, then turned gray. He flipped the changed hand back and forth for Matthew to see.

"It gets better than that monstrosity," Jackson said gruffly.

When Matthew could pull his focus away from the hand, he was met with the face of a monster. Not an entirely unfamiliar one, either.

"What the fuck?" Matthew gasped and took a step back. He couldn't take his eyes away from the face so much like the ones he had seen that day in Talista.

"It's the curse," Jackson explained.

"Curse?" Matthew croaked.

Jackson nodded. His face had returned to normal and a quick glance at his hand showed Matthew that it, too, had changed back.

"Frederick's curse has..."

"I don't know a Frederick," Jackson said. "But this? This is Cronan Milsenett's doing."

Matthew's thoughts were moving too fast. He couldn't catch any of them. "Cronan? You mean Madigan's father?"

"The one and only. You should sit." Jackson pointed to a chair just behind Matthew.

Matthew dropped heavily into it and immediately buried his face in his hands. "I... Shit. This only gives me more questions."

"Why don't I tell you what I know and we go from there? I know you weren't told much. If anything." There was sympathy, and understanding, in Jackson's tone.

"Why?" The word was a broken whisper that hurt when he spoke it.

"My mother would best be able to explain that." Jackson sat on the table before him. "Here, have another."

Matthew downed the contents. The bourbon warming his throat and burning his stomach.

"And speaking of my fabulous mother." He flashed a quick, boyish grin. "The way she tells it is probably the best way to tell it. When that bitch Gea de Oro took the Seer from us, Cronan lost all his marbles. Or at least what he had left of them in that already depraved mind of his."

Matthew lifted a brow.

"Cronan nor Gea have a very large fan base among Aunellions."

Jackson shrugged. *"Anyway...* One mass exodus of witches got off-realm before Cronan went nuclear. He used that awful little spell work book of his, said some words from it, then disappeared completely."

"Died, you mean."

"Sure. Whatever. Given Madigan eventually inherited, it's pretty safe to assume that's what happened."

A puzzle piece clicked into place and Matthew lifted his head. "Frederick's curse on the Shianshani King's lineage, that came from Aunellion."

"What was this curse like?"

Matthew studied Jackson, the open curiosity there. "Have you ever left Earth's realm?"

"Never. For the longest time, it was forbidden by my parents. We never had the desire, we were happy here. After my father died, I took over our business and that became a distraction that stopped me from ever wondering about"—he looked toward the harbor through the patio doors—"out there. My mother shipped me here because apparently I was acting like an asshole. This was my aunt's house. Not Clarissa's," he clarified. "My mother's sister, Sheridy. She left this place to me, and my mother felt it was the perfect time to kick my ass out of Montana."

"You don't seem too upset to be away from there," Matthew noted.

Jackson's smile was quick and shifted his entire face into something light and hopeful. "Nadia and her son were an unexpected surprise."

He knew how Jackson felt. It was how he had felt about Lily all those years before.

"The curse on the King's family, I'm not really sure," Matthew confessed. "I was sort of, uh, in the middle of something when that came to a head. I came into it at the tail end of everything. Well, what we'd *thought* was the tail end of shit."

Jackson lifted a brow. "Let me call for delivery. Something tells me this is going to be a long, long night for the both of us."

TWENTY-SIX

R ÓISÍN HAD been taken over by an onslaught of feelings. As she tried to keep her breathing slow and even and her heart from pounding out of her chest, her magic cried out, prompting Caid's magic to rise.

The sludge and shadows of it wove around her, stroking, soothing. Caid's rough hand squeezed hers before tugging her closer to where he sat on the window seat at the back of the tea shop.

Hecate was their true Goddess. Their creator. Not just witches, but it was Hecate that birthed magic into the realms. Gave each their own well source to feed the magic and keep the witches strong.

And she was Caid's grandmother. *No.* Caid's great-great grandmother.

For centuries, she has been working with Sister Future, to restore the power that Gea had taken and reclaim her place in the surrounding realms. Every act that Brenna had taken had been at the instruction of Tura, guided by the loom.

"So, you've been following us?" Caid's eyes were on Ana.

"I wouldn't say following." Ana's smile wasn't malicious. It was pure mischief when her lips split before she said, "I've just always... been there."

When her glamour fell away, Caid's facade cracked. His jaw fell open, eyes growing round. "Grace Littlefield? The postmaster?!"

Ana's smile was blinding. "I've been with your family since the beginning." She pat Hecate's hand.

"H-how?" Róisín asked roughly. "I'm trying to follow all of..." She waved her free hand. "This. But, if you are the one that created magic, can't you just... take back the realms? What do you mean you can't *go* there? You're here."

Hecate's smile didn't reach her eyes. "Unfortunately, I learned the hard way that none of us are untouchable. Not even I. By the time I realized what Gea was doing, my power in the realms was too weak to stop it." She pushed to her feet and walked toward a display case of hand painted coasters. "I set down roots here, in Earth's realm. When my Elspeth decided she wanted a family of her own, this is where she chose. Our magic is strongest here because of the belief not just among our people, but among the humans as well. You see, there are many religions that recognize some form of a goddess of witchcraft or the earth's arts."

"Earth's arts?" Caid asked.

"Fancy way of saying spell users." Ana winked at him.

"I became comfortable in the routine of it all, and therefore complacent. And—" The frown that turned down the corner of her mouth mirrored the frown of the storm cloud on the coaster she examined. "I was too trusting."

"It still doesn't explain how." Róisín's patience was wearing thin. Not only were old wounds about all that her mother had done and sacrificed reopened, but she found herself on the precipice of the next steps.

"Seed magic," Sister Future spoke up.

"Seed magic? What the Hells is *seed* magic? Sorry, Sister Future." Róisín quickly bowed her head in apology.

"Call me Tura, please." Tura reached behind her and took a tea tin from the shelf. She opened it and tipped some of its contents into her hand. "Seed magic is as it sounds. Say these are corn seeds that are to be planted for the annual harvest. If there is something that you want to... *imbed* for lack of a better word, you can cast that spell work on the seeds—"

131

"Then the corn will hold that magic, which will then be consumed by a person," Róisín said.

"And passed on to those who come after, yes. Seed magic becomes a part of a person's very being," Tura said. "Then it is passed on through generations."

Róisín pointed at Hecate. "That still doesn't explain how it took her power away from the realms."

"Fate has checks and balances." It was Elizabeth, Ana's daughter, that spoke now. "One of those checks and balances was to keep Hecate from becoming consumed by her power to create magic and people who wield it. That was done through the power of belief."

"Church?" Caid asked.

"In a way, yes." Elizabeth nodded. "A base level of belief in Hecate as our true creator had been retained around the realms for well over a millennium."

"I wasn't a very active member in the lives of those I created," Hecate said from where she stood at the window. In the glass's reflection, Róisín watched her eyes track the people milling around the alley between hers, Mr. Pappas', and Mr. Costas' shops. "I believe everyone has a right to their own choices and consequences of their actions. I never stepped in unless Fate absolutely insisted I did."

"And Fate insisted you did, when? When my grandmother decided to murder our Coven? Or was it when my mother killed herself so that her magic would go to me, and not my grandmother? What about Lucius?" Róisín was at her feet, tears streaming down her face. "What was it that Fate found so important that you finally needed to step in?" She was shouting now, but she didn't care. The rage that burned inside of her even pushed back Caid's magic, sending it away with a hiss.

Hecate turned away from the window. "Although I've been working with Tura since the night the sky cast among the stars the story of your fate—" She looked at Caid. "And his," —she brought her eyes back to Róisín, and her next words stopped Róisín's heart—"it was Gea pulling his thread from the loom that brought the full force of Fate into action."

TWENTY-SEVEN

T HE TRUCK jerked and sputtered as Nolani shouted to Marcelo variations of *gas, clutch,* and *brake, BRAKE!* She let out a shriek and gripped the handle on the dashboard just before the truck shot forward, then completely stalled out.

"Why in all the Realms did you get one of these?" Her tone was angry and clipped. She jabbed a finger at the shifting knob. "You can barely drive an automatic, Celo."

"Oh, road trip! Where are we going?" Runa asked from the back-seat, making them both jump.

Nolani whirled to face him. "What the fuck, Runa?"

Runa ignored her and stroked a finger over his chin in thought. "What do you think, Aja? Could we shift an entire vehicle to a different realm?"

Aja leaned forward, materializing from the shadowed back seat. "Nothing is impossible."

"What can I do to convince you to wear a reflective vest of some type?" Marcelo asked. The number of times the man had appeared from a darkened corner was startling. Although Marcelo was sure that even if his skin were not the color of night, he could still successfully steal away into the shadows.

"We need to talk. I'll gather Anelle, Ten, and Cicile. We'll meet at the house in thirty minutes."

"What's—never mind," Marcelo mumbled when Aja shifted.

"Can't drive a stick shift, huh?" Runa smirked at him.

"I can too," Marcelo replied defensively.

Runa hummed, his eyes dancing with mischief. "Get out of the driver's seat. I'll drive us back."

"Oh, I can get us back," Nolani said.

"No, no." Runa shook his head and pulled Marcelo over the armrest and into the back seat with him. "I haven't driven in ages. Ione prefers the shifting mode of travel, and I've yet to convince her of the fun local travel is by car."

Nolani arched a brow. "Can *you* drive a stick?"

A deep, dangerous chuckle broke free as he hopped into the driver's seat. He wiggled the shifter and turned the key back, then forward again. The engine roared to life and Runa let out another chuckle.

Marcelo found Nolani's eyes as he groped blindly for the seatbelt. "If we die today, know that I only ever loved you."

She rolled her eyes and buckled her own seatbelt. "So dramatic."

"Let's just hope that he gets us there alive. I've got a feeling this is important."

"Oh." Runa shoved the truck into first gear. "It is." The tires of the truck screamed against the asphalt as the truck sped forward. "The veil is somehow warded so no one can cross to the living side. The Goddess is in the afterworld looking for Tura. Sorry," he sighed dramatically, pushing the shifter into second gear. "Sister Future. And shit. I wasn't supposed to say most of that."

"Sister Future is..." Nolani's eyes rounded. "Dead?!"

"No, not dead," Aja said, dropping a book on the coffee table in front of Nolani. "Between Shasta and Ione, we can deduce that she's among the living. However, she *is* missing."

Ten's eyes were focused on the book, her eyes lined with tears. "You think she's...?"

"No." Aja dropped into a chair across from where all the others had crammed onto the sofa. "This isn't Hecate. Hecate and Tura have been working together since Tura learned of what Gea had been doing. Something tells me this circles back to something Gea has done."

"Hold on. Slow down. I can't keep this all straight." Marcelo waved his hands to halt the conversation around him. "Who is Hecate? Why does that sound familiar? And who is Gea?"

"I've seen a book like this before." Nolani brushed her fingers over the cover. Her voice was low when she said, "Your mother carried one with her, Celo."

Marcelo gingerly thumbed the book open. He studied the first few pages. Yes, his mother had, and most likely still did, carry a similar book. There had been many times he had found her in her gardens with her tea reading it. He used to tease her, asking how she hadn't had it memorized yet. "Jessamyn gave it to her." He swallowed. "That's where I know the name Hecate. She was another witch, right?" He looked at Aja for confirmation.

"She *is* way more than a witch," Runa answered.

"Hecate is our creator," Aja added. "Gea is a created daughter of Hecate's, and also the mother of the Sisters, Senna, Alina, and Tura."

"Senna, Alina, and Tura?" Nolani's nose wrinkled. "They're the Sisters? Why have I never been taught this? Or that the Goddess is their true mother?"

Marcelo placed a hand on her thigh, just above her knee. "Jessamyn was never a child of the Goddess, was she?"

Anelle cleared her throat. "None of us are."

Her confession fell like a heavy blanket over the room, silencing even the soft whir of the refrigerator.

"Nolani," Marcelo whispered. "Are you alright?" He needn't have magic to feel the way her energy flared or her body tensed next to his.

"I—" She snatched her hand away from the book as though it had burned her. "I need a moment."

Marcelo watched, helplessness pulling at his body, as she darted from the room. He gave her five seconds before he was moving to his feet. "She should have known this."

"Over the centuries, fewer Covens held belief in, or made offerings to, Hecate. Gea became the one placed upon altars." Aja rubbed a hand over his head. "After enough time, it became dangerous for families to openly believe in a power other than Gea. Reports of witches losing their power became more frequent. Many took it as a sign from Fate that they were being struck down for not believing Gea to be the Goddess and our creator."

Marcelo glanced over his shoulder. Nolani sat behind the house on a small wrought iron lounger with her elbows on her thighs, head between her hands. "If Hecate has been all but forgotten, how do you know so much? How did my mother have a book about her?"

"Shianshani witches have always been the outliers. Pair that with Jessamyn's undying quest for answers... one thing led to another during a trip to the Coven's well source a few centuries ago..."

"And that's how Jessamyn learned the truth," Marcelo deduced.

"In a way." Aja nodded, but Marcelo felt there was more to the story. Especially after the look of respect and appreciation Runa cast Aja's way. However, something told Marcelo that it added nothing to their situation at hand.

"So, what do we do now? Find this Tura?" Marcelo asked. "How in the Hells do we even find one of the Sisters of Fate? That has to be like a needle in a haystack."

"And something tells me if a Sister doesn't want to be found, she will not be," Anelle said.

"That, too," Marcelo said.

"To be honest, I don't know what we do now." Aja slumped against the seat. "We don't know what any of this means other than what Ione and Shasta saw across the veil."

Marcelo shoved his hands into his hair. He wanted to welcome the distraction from his brother. It could give him a chance to put distance between them, what was happening. Allow him to catch his breath. Looking back to Nolani, seeing the way her slender shoulders shook, he grit his teeth.

There would never be a break.

Not until it was *all* finished.

If that meant he needed to hunt a Sister, restore a Goddess, *and* slay his own brother?

He would. So he and the woman he watched straighten her shoulders and dry her cheeks before rising to her feet, could finally have that life together that he promised them all of those years ago.

Nolani froze with her hand on the door handle when she saw him staring at her. *"Are you okay?"* She mouthed to him.

He nodded and turned back to Aja. "If we can get Hecate back into her power, what does that mean for the rest of us?"

"Freedom," Aja said.

Twenty-Eight

Róisín stumbled backward as though she had been struck. One of Caid's arms banded around her waist, pulling her against his solid frame. His warmth anchoring her. At her ear, she could hear the steady in and out of his breaths. Against her back, however, his heart was a jackhammer.

"Check and balances," Elizabeth said. Her tone was soft and motherly. "Fate can be guided to its destination. However, it cannot be redirected." She paused for a moment before adding, "In any way."

"It is the first time that such a drastic measure has been taken against Fate," Hecate said.

He's here. He's with me. That's all that matters. Forget what's happened, Róisín. Focus on the now. Focus on what you need to do.

She closed her eyes and willed her body to still. Everything, even the hairs along her arms, felt as though they were racing.

"You two were gone before Tura could get me to Legianne," Hecate continued. "I wanted to... I would have told you both, then. But..."

Róisín pulled her lips between her teeth. A scream hammering up her throat, growing nails as it rose, trying to claw its way free. Caid's warm lips at the back of her neck had her body stilling, her shoulders dropping.

"It's not..." She swallowed hard. Her eyes burned as the fear of putting the words to her question made her pulse quicken. "He's here, right? Fate won't.... It won't take it back when she's gone?"

Caid's arm tightened around her. "I'm right here," he whispered against her skin. "I'm not going anywhere."

Hecate leaned forward and slipped one of Róisín's hands into hers. "It wasn't his time, Róisín." She looked beyond Róisín to Caid. "This isn't a second chance because you never lost your first one."

"Why can't you just kill her?" Róisín asked. "If you've made us, you can unmake us."

"It's not that easy, unfortunately," Hecate said.

"Checks and balances," Elizabeth repeated.

Róisín narrowed her eyes at her. "I got that part already."

Ana reached over and laid one of her hands on Elizabeth's thighs. "What Lizzie means to say is, our lives cannot be ended without due cause if it is to happen outside of age. It's, unfortunately, how Madigan was allowed his reign of terror in the realms."

Róisín straightened. "Was any of that true?"

"What do you mean?" Hecate asked. "Was any of what true? Madigan was very real."

"That it was supposed to be me to end him," Róisín said. "That it was supposed to be me for all of it. Or was I right, and it was all just a ploy for Gea to wear me down?"

Hecate's face turned to stone. "Who told you that?" She looked over at Tura, who shook her head. "Róisín, what did Gea tell you?"

"That night, in the Dead Forest, after I killed Aoife and Madigan, she told me she had placed my mother in the afterworld," Róisín said.

"What a crock of bullshit," Elizabeth muttered. "That wasn't her."

Róisín shifted to face her.

"We did that." She waved her index finger from Ana to herself and back. "*And* got your father there as a bonus. It would have happened sooner, but she kept letting the darkness's little pets loose after us." She winced. "Sorry, Tura."

Tura waved her off. "They're not kind. This, I know."

Róisín studied Tura for a moment. The way she sat ramrod straight in her chair. Her hands clasped in her lap. Why had Elizabeth apologized?

"What else?" Hecate encouraged.

"She said a lot of things. She wouldn't shut up, actually." That should have been the first sign that something wasn't right, Róisín realized. "She told me I needed to unite the Covens. For what reason, she didn't say. Just that I was to bring everyone together."

Laughter burst from Hecate. She quickly covered her mouth, her eyes growing wide. "I am so deeply sorry for that. While I'm quite sure she had a different means for that task, Fate did not" Hecate scooted forward in her seat, her eyes alight with mischief. "The night you were born, the astronomical fate across the realms showed that there would be a child so loved by many that the Covens would unite under a new future."

"And we're supposed to solve that riddle?" Caid asked.

"It's not a riddle, Kincaid. Think about it." She tipped her head to Róisín. "Her mother is from Legianne. Shasta, Brenna's closest friend, of Molennius. Lucius of Ely, Jessamyn of Shianshani, and Lily of Roidon. And you,"—She grinned at him—"of Earth."

He lifted a brow. "So, we're like the Power Rangers?"

Hecate laughed again. "Whatever that is, no. But you all have a part in this." She took Róisín's hand again. "And you were never meant to do this alone."

For the first time in what felt like hours, a sense of calm settled over Róisín. "If there're this checks and balances thing, is that why she hasn't been able to kill you and doom us all?"

Hecate leaned back in her seat. "Gea cannot kill me because the only thing that can send me across the veil to the afterworld is death's magic."

This time, when the world dropped from beneath Róisín, she wasn't sure she was going to stop falling.

TWENTY-NINE

C AID STOOD with his arms folded over his chest before the
window of their apartment facing the alleyway and street in front
of the tea shop.

Every one of Róisín's fears had been confirmed. He had been unable
to form words. Instead, he sunk deeper into the sludge of his magic.
Letting it swallow him. Let it feed that darkest part of him.

Gea had always wanted Róisín's life. It was the only way she could
take that magic from her.

The magic she needed to kill Hecate.

To have complete control.

Ana, Elizabeth, Hecate, and Sister Future — no, *Tura*, had left
hours before. Róisín would have pushed on through the night, taking
any information the quartet would give. But he had seen the way the
bruises had surfaced and grown beneath her eyes. The way her eyes
struggled to stay focused. Thankfully, Hecate had seen it as well and
ushered the others out of the shop.

"Let's go dance," Róisín said, melting against him once the door to
the upstairs apartment clicked closed.

"Mm, no." He wrapped his arms around her, swaying them gently in the living room. "How about let's go to bed? It's been a long day. A very *long* day. You need rest."

"Just for a bit. Please?" She buried her face in his chest. "If we don't, you know Mr. Pappas will hammer on our door in a half-hour."

He slipped one of his hands into hers, and taking a step away from her, spun her around. As much as he hated to admit it, she was right. Of all the places they had lived in the years since, this little neighborhood in Greece had been most like Greens Glen. When Mr. Pappas teamed up with Mr. Costas to attempt to play matchmakers, pairing the landlord's son with the tea shop owner, he felt that sense of community settle over him.

"Go get changed." He waved her toward the bedroom.

She gave him a sleepy grin, then darted into the bedroom.

While he waited, he watched two children, near Sloane and Abigail's age, dancing with their parents along the walkway. Their peals of laughter floated up through their open windows.

The twins were safe. Hecate had guaranteed it.

"Earth's witches are under my full protection," she said.

She hadn't explained how, but her curt tone had settled the riot building in Caid's stomach.

He was grateful for it. It gave Lina and the twins safety. The chance to live their lives without the chaos and terror Caid had been witness to.

If they didn't find Gea, if they didn't kill her, would she eventually figure out there *were* witches in this realm? What then?

"We won't let her," Róisín said from the bedroom doorway.

He spun to face her. The sight of her in the strappy, sunflower printed sundress that hit mid-thigh, her autumn-colored hair neatly coiled atop her head, stole his breath.

"Her time is over, Caid." She walked across the room, stopping in front of him. "She won't win. I won't let her, and I know you won't let me do this alone."

Caid brought up a hand to cup her cheek. "Damn right I won't." He brushed his lips over hers before wrapping his arms around her, pulling her tightly against his chest. There were no words that could soothe this for either of them. Instead, he held her and buried his face in her neck.

"She'll die, Róisín," he said. "We won't let her live."

Her body stilled, and she pulled back slightly. Her eyes swam with blues, danced with specks of red and green.

"For all she's done, she'll pay," he promised. "If we have to go with her, we go with her."

She stared at him, unblinking for a moment. "Us against the realms."

"Always."

Smoothing her hands over his chest, she let one hand rest over his heart. "Take me dancing, Mr. McGrath."

He covered the hand on his heart with his own. "The pleasure would be all mine, Mrs. McGrath."

MR. PAPPAS GREETED THEM AT THE EDGE OF THE DANCING crowd. He smiled and winked at them as he spun Mrs. Pappas around with such a flare that her skirt floated up and around her waist. She let out a hearty laugh and cast a wink of her own in their direction.

"We need to tell the others," Róisín said next to him.

Caid gave Róisín's hand a squeeze. "Are you sure?"

She surveyed the crowd before them. "We could go to Ely tonight."

He couldn't stop the way his body jerked, and he pulled her against his side.

"Caid."

"Sorry. I... Shit. It all sounded like a really fucking fantastic idea to find everyone else, but now, I don't know. Knowing we're good here; that right now she can't get us on Earth."

"Then we get everyone here. Somehow. Where we know they'll be safe. It'll make it easier to find the rest of the information we need."

He nodded. "It makes the most sense. But how?" From the corner of his eye, he spotted Ana and Elizabeth moving toward them and tensed.

"Why are you two not dancing?" Ana took Róisín's hands in hers and tugged her away from Caid. "Tonight, we pretend everything is glorious and full of joy. Happy endings."

Elizabeth rolled her eyes. "Mother. You sound like you have us all condemned to death. We still can have that happy ending. And"—She motioned to the faces wide with smiles around them—"If you haven't noticed, there's plenty of joy around."

Ana waved her off. "Best to be prepared for anything."

Caid felt one of his eyebrows crawling up his forehead. He had to agree with Ana. Prepare for anything and expect the worst. They'd failed to do that before. They hadn't been fully prepared. They hadn't had the *time* to be.

"See?" Ana pointed to him. "He gets it."

Róisín gave him a questioning look.

"She's not wrong," he admitted.

Elizabeth let out a dramatic sigh. "Great, now there's two of them."

"Always the optimist." Ana slipped an arm around Elizabeth's waist. "Just like your father. Just because Kincaid and I prefer to be realistic about things..." She gave a slight shrug. "But hold on to that optimism. We'll need it. And you." Her head swiveled to Róisín. "You're the pessimistic one. None of that nonsense. It'll eat you alive and keep you awake at night."

Róisín jaw dropped and Caid smirked.

"I am not a pessimist," she said stubbornly.

"You're adorable," Caid said. "Come on, let's dance."

She let him sweep her up into the tempo of the song the band was playing. They swayed and spun for a moment before she pouted at him.

"I'm *not* a pessimist."

He dipped her low and brushed his nose along her collarbone, drawing in her scent. "I wouldn't call it pessimism."

Her eyes narrowed as she remained suspended in the dip.

"What?" He grinned at her before giving the tip of her nose a quick kiss.

"Then what would you call it?" She asked, the last word pitching high as he jerked her upright and crushed her body against his, spinning them around.

"I don't know if there's a word for it." He flexed the hand he had at her lower back. He remembered how shy she had been the night he had met her. How unsure she had been when she first faced Madigan, when they had been pulled out of the ravine.

"Kincaid James McGrath," she said against his chest, tugging him from his memories.

"Róisín McKenna McGrath. Oh." He chuckled when she tried to move closer to him. "You like that huh?"

"Dammit," she mumbled. "I hate you."

He swayed-stepped them away from where they had been surrounded by people, slowing his movements when they reached a place more private. "You absolutely do *not* hate me."

"No," she shook her head against him. "No, I don't. Stop deflecting." She tipped her head back, looking up at him beneath her lashes. "It doesn't matter what Ana thinks I am. But you, I need to know."

He pressed a kiss to her forehead. "You're not the woman I met seven years ago."

Róisín tried to push away from him. "I knew it. I knew Lina was lying to me."

"Would you let me finish?" He held her tighter. "When we met, you had pretty much just stepped into the world on your own, or, I guess you could say, realms, right? But you were... you were free."

She chewed on her bottom lip, brows knitted together.

"Anyway." He tucked a tendril of hair that escaped her bun behind her ear and gave her a soft smile. "*That* Róisín was probably a pessimist. Glass half-empty, I can't do it, it's all going to go to shit and all that."

She tipped her head to the side, the fire that had been simmering in her eyes fading. "And now?" She asked in a whisper.

"I've watched you find yourself." He cupped her face. "Not just who you are, but what you are."

Her question came out almost breathlessly. "Who is that?"

"You're strong." He kissed her left cheek. "Smart as hell." He kissed her right cheek. "You're compassionate." Her nose. "Kind." His lips brushed the left side of her temple before he brought his mouth to her ear. "You're so incredibly fierce." He nipped her ear lobe. "A powerhouse."

Her body trembled in his arms.

Caid stroked a hand down her back. "*That's* what I mean by you're not the woman I met. You've grown and become so much more. Not afraid to stand tall, even when you're scared shitless." His lips ghosted the shell of her ear. "You've become a force to be reckoned with."

Her cheeks flared pink. "Let's get out of here."

"Finally." He scooped her into her arms, laughing when a small shriek of surprise escaped her. With her arms wrapped around his neck, her head resting against his shoulder, he made his way through the thinning crowd toward the shop and their apartment, where they began stripping each other's clothes off before the door even clicked shut.

Part Two

"The way you stop time is by stopping being ruled by it."
—Matt Haig, How to Stop Time

THIRTY

FIVE YEARS AGO

C AID LAID out the cash on the table, adding extra for the server's tip. He had signaled for his check the moment he felt Róisín's heart begin to race.

As he stood from the table, her magic reached out to his. Desperate. Its claws scraping as it grasped his, causing him to nearly trip over the threshold of the restaurant as he pushed through the door.

Something was wrong.

Something had been wrong before they had even left their small house that morning.

Róisín had been meeting with the Oathkeeper she'd found, Adelia, for weeks. Returning home each night, radiating a little more confidence than she'd had when she'd left.

She was working on building Adelia's trust before she asked anything about Gea, and the wait had Caid on edge.

He went to work with Wyatt every day, tried to push it from his mind. By the end of the day, he was exhausted. Physically, mentally, and deep, deep inside of something he didn't have a name for.

He hadn't hesitated when she asked him to come with her that evening. He was grateful that the moment she sensed something wrong, something off, she didn't push to keep doing it alone.

Caid stood on the sidewalk between the bar and restaurant, scanning the surroundings with his eyes, while his magic reached and probed. Searching for Róisín.

There. At the very end of the street sat a low brick building with what appeared to be two formal wear shops. Turning on his heels, he made his way toward it.

His magic urged him to move faster, making it harder for him to keep the casual appearance and pace. He didn't want to draw any attention to himself. He didn't have time for it.

The shops were dark with the late hour, closed for the day, so he ducked down the alley to the left of the building, in search of a rear door.

When he found the steel security door at the back, his magic coiled down his arm.

"No. We shift in," he said to it. "Shift in, get my wife, and get the fuck out. I can't land on the ten o'clock news, given I'm supposed to be dead."

His magic expanded inside of him, then deflated quickly.

Did his magic just... *sigh?*

Caid shifted into the building and into what felt like an inferno. A wall of heat blasted him. Instinct had him throwing his arms up to protect his face, his magic wrapping around him at the same time.

Róisín's scream pierced the air, sending him diving into the heat in search of her.

He found her in a back room, one arm attached to a post from an industrial storage shelving unit. The other dangled limply at her side covered in blood. Her head was hanging down. When he stepped closer, he stumbled over something on the floor.

Looking down, it took him a moment to register what he was seeing. A leg.

He took in the room as he made his way toward her. Limbs. *Everywhere.*

What had happened?

"Róisín," he whispered her name. Cupping his hand under her chin, he lifted her face to his. "Róisín, baby, wake up."

A broken moan sounded from her throat.

He reached up to free her wrist, hissing in pain when his fingers contacted her binds.

"It's... warded..." she said hoarsely. "I can't... I can't shift."

"I've got you." He ground his molars together and reached again for the bind. Expecting the burn this time, he braced for it. In two tugs, he had her free. Her arm tumbled down, landing on his shoulder. After a few seconds, he had what was left of the binds off and her body collapsed against him.

"Caid..."

"I've got you," he repeated.

"What... Oh—" Her body shook as she convulsed. "I did that. I..."

"Don't look." He turned her head, so that she was tucked against his neck. Then he swung her up, as gently as he could, into his arms.

"Caid, I—" Her body shook in his hold.

"Shh. Let's go home. I'll get you cleaned up, and your magic can heal you. We'll figure it out." He kissed the top of her head.

Although he wouldn't admit it to her, for the first time in a year, he was questioning whether they could do this on their own.

THIRTY-ONE
NOW

MATTHEW ROLLED over and promptly crashed against something solid. Groaning, he rubbed his forehead and blinked his eyes open. He stared at the light gray wall for nearly a minute before everything came crashing back around him making his head throb.

He and Jackson had spent the better part of the last three days together, deep in bottles of liquor, filling one another in on their lives, what they knew, and trying to figure out the parts they didn't.

On Matthew's end, he told Jackson of Madigan, what had been learned of the Seer. What had happened on Alleyette and how he found himself trapped in the Fog Fields in Aunellion.

What Lucius had sacrificed to get him home to the others.

Then, what he had come home to. Monsters. Death. Losing nearly everything.

When he had finished, Jackson told him everything he knew of Cronan Milsenett and the curse he placed on the remaining Aunellion witches. How his mother, Marion, had been trying to figure out how to break it in the centuries since. So few of them remained, each of them touched by the curse differently. None, however, as Madigan had been when he'd taken over the King's body.

Jackson deduced it had to have been the way Frederick used it.

"They seemed to believe that it was Frederick's way of gaining ultimate control over Shianshani," Matthew confided. "I don't have a thought either way." He rubbed aggressively at the back of his neck. "I was sort of stuck in a field, dying."

"That wasn't by chance, Matthew," Jackson said in a low voice. His speech had been slightly slurred, as both men, by that point, hovered just before the line of full drunkenness. The sound of the waves cresting the rocks just beyond the house was the only noise aside from their voices.

"What do you mean?" Matthew tipped the bottle of whiskey upside down, three lonely drops splashing into his glass.

Jackson's deep copper-colored eyes leveled him with a stare. "You're either drunker than you're letting on, or you're denser than a pile of bricks."

Matthew had rubbed a hand over his face, pressing his fingers into his eyes. "It doesn't help that this"—He waved his other hand out and away—"Is something I'm only just learning. My *parents* weren't exactly forthcoming about it all. You seem to know far more than I do. Which, to be frank, fucking pisses me off."

"She had her reasons, Matthew. Who she was, what she inherited, it was going to you once she passed."

Matthew's hands had fallen from his face, and he had tried to focus on Jackson's blurry figure. "What the fuck are you talking about?"

"The Burkes are descendants of the Seer."

"That's no secret. My mother told me that long ago."

"*Think* about it, Matthew."

He ground his molars together to stop from shouting at Jackson. He was done will all of the talking in riddles.

"Clarissa was the only Burke to inherit sight. Which means *you* inherited that same magic from. Those weren't hallucinations, Matthew. Which is very dangerous for *you*."

Matthew shoved to his feet and stalked toward Jackson. He bent, so that he was nearly nose to nose with him. "What does that *mean?*" He whisper shouted at him. "Because I *didn't* inherit my mother's sight when she died. I got some of her elemental magic, and that's all."

"She hadn't known that then," Jackson said softly. "She only knew that there was a possibility. I can imagine as a parent that would be all it would take. I know if it were Parker, I would do whatever I had to in order to keep him safe. Even if it meant I would leave out parts of who I was. Not all lies are bad."

Matthew's legs had grown weak as reality clamped down hard on his shoulders, the weight unbearable. He had fallen to his knees before Jackson, nausea roiling his stomach. Then, the alcohol took him and everything went dark.

Now, greeted by the sweet smell of maple and something he couldn't quite put his finger on, embarrassment filled him. He had drunk himself into a stupor and made an ass out of himself.

That, however, paled compared to everything he had learned here in this house in Maine. Every ache he had thought he was moving beyond felt raw.

His body screamed in protest as he rolled away from the wall and brought his feet to the floor.

A light knock at his door sounded more like elephants trampling through his head. "You up? Nadia made breakfast. Plenty to share."

Shit. The last thing Matthew wanted was to stumble into the kitchen with Jackson's girlfriend there.

"What the fuck is going on?" He mumbled.

The Goddess took the Seer? Locked them away? That couldn't be right.

Were the things he saw in Aunellion visions? Or were they truly just hallucinations? He had known his mother was a descendant of the Seer and would occasionally have a vision. But it was rare, and she said they were like looking through dirty water when she saw them.

Everything he saw had depth, sound, and vibrant color. He had seen the flecks of gold in Lily's eyes and the way they had danced and shone when the light caught them just right.

His mind raced to recall the possibility of other times, and around the ache jackhammering his temples, the faded edges of the dream when Nanette and Lucius had confronted him about his bond with Lily surfaced. The night they found Madigan with the Seer.

But they didn't confront him.

And in their final moments together, Lucius had supported Matthew's future with Lily.

Why had he never had them sooner when he had inherited her magic after her passing?

For every one question answered upon his arrival in Maine, Matthew had accumulated fifty more that made his head throb.

"You alive in there?" Jackson nudged the door open.

"I'm hungover as shit," Matthew said with a groan as he fell back onto the bed.

"Here." A glass appeared over him. "Drink this. She may not be a witch like us, but my lady knows how to make magic in her drinks."

Matthew struggled back up into the sitting position. He eyed the glass that Jackson now waggled lightly in front of him.

"Trust me."

Matthew found he *did* trust him. Completely. In a way that he had only ever trusted one other person in his life. He took the drink and downed it in one go. "What are your plans for today?"

"Nadia has to work, which means I usually mope around here until she's done and she and Park come over for the night."

Matthew snorted. "You're so gone for her, aren't you?"

"Obviously. I showed her the monster I am, then she showed me her fins, so..." He shrugged. "I guess it means the feeling's mutual."

"You're not a monster."

Jackson let out a snort this time. "*You're* not a monster. But yeah, I definitely am."

"Why am I not, you know, cursed too? If my mother was Aunellion..."

"The only conclusion they kept circling back to was that Lucius's Coven was older than ours. The power in his bloodline was stronger, so it outweighed anything the Milsenetts could do."

Matthew nodded, accepting the answer as the only reasonable one at that moment. "How far is it from here to Greens Glen?"

Jackson's brows flew up. "Like out near Moosehead?"

"I have no idea what that is."

"Probably a good four-hour drive? We could shift in a blink, though."

"No." He rose from the bed. "I need to drive. There's a lot of shit going on up here—" He tapped the side of his head. "With everything we've talked about and things going on back home, I need some time to sort through it."

"Alright then." Jackson gave him a quick nod. "We can head out after Nadia leaves for work. I'll let her know I won't be back until late tonight."

After Jackson left the room, Matthew walked over to the window that took up nearly the entire wall. He watched as lobster boats bobbed out in the harbor, pulling in their traps for the day. He should go to Lily, tell her he was going to stay in Maine a little longer. Tell her he was going to find Róisín. Something inside of him had pushed him harder to do so that morning. He needed to find her.

Was she in trouble? Was that why? They had been a unit for so long that he wouldn't question that some type of natural connection had formed between them. Maybe in the haze of his drunkenness he had accessed it.

He sighed and turned away from the window and the early summer scene that had been spread before him.

"Isn't this cozy?" Jackson said from the passenger seat as they slowed coming into the small village area of Greens Glen. "Nadia would *love* this."

Matthew could see from the corner of his eye Jackson's head swiveling back and forth, taking in the town.

"What exactly are we doing here again?" He asked, bringing his attention back to Matthew.

"Hoping to catch someone on a good day."

"Uh..."

"It's sort of complicated. I haven't been here in several years, which" —He lifted a hand to stop any interruption—"Is my fault. I thought it was the right thing to do, but now..." He blew out a sharp breath. "I'm realizing that was probably a mistake."

"Old girlfriend?"

Matthew's chuckle came quickly, catching him off guard. "Ah, no. Or, well—" He winced and slid a quick glance at Jackson, who was watching him with a smirk. "No."

"Oh, this just got *good*."

"Alright. So—" Matthew took a hand from the steering wheel and shoved it in his hair, giving it a quick tug. "Today I'm hoping to catch Lina in a good mood so that maybe she'll dangle a lead in front of me on where Róisín is. Because there's no damned way those two haven't talked at all in the last sixish years. I don't know if it's being here in Maine or something else, but it's right under my skin, this nagging itch telling me I need to find her. *Now*."

"And Róisín is?"

"Sort of like a sister to me. Brenna, her mother, was really close to mine. And when Stephen, Róisín's father, died, Lucius took her under his wing and treated her as his own."

Jackson clucked his tongue. "Care to elaborate on the 'Or, well?'"

Matthew felt his face heat. "Nope. It was one time, fucked it all up. It's in the past."

"Gotcha. Lina?"

"Róisín's best friend and Caid's younger sister." Matthew's grip on the steering wheel tightened and his lungs pinched.

"Caid is?"

"Caid was Róisín's bonded."

"Fuck." Jackson's one whispered word was loaded with understanding and emotion.

Silence fell over the rest of the ride to Lina's house. Except, the moment Matthew pulled to a stop out front, he knew something was off.

"What's up?" Jackson peered up at the house that perched tidily atop the hill.

"Shit. They don't live here anymore." Matthew's heart had jumped from his chest and lodged itself into his throat.

"She left town?"

No. Lina wouldn't leave Greens Glen. She had fought too hard to get Madigan out when he was posing as Stewart Munson. Of course, Caid had still been alive then.

Matthew slowly pulled away from the curb and drove aimlessly through the town along the maze of side streets. Before he knew it, he was at the entrance of Róisín's old cul-de-sac. On a hunch, he turned down the road, parked in front of the farmhouse, then climbed out of the car.

Jackson leaned over the center console and peered up at Matthew through the open window. "Want me to wait in the car?"

Matthew looked over the roof of his rental car and studied the house. Not much had changed since he had last been there. At least what he could see in the front yard. A grey four-door sedan was parked in front of the single-car garage, and a flame red SUV the size of a house was parked next to it. It *had* to be Lina's. Which meant he was right. She and Róisín had remained in contact, and Róisín had given her the house.

He rubbed at the spot just over his heart as he made his way toward the front door. Jackson quietly fell into step beside him as they walked up the steps of the porch.

A shout sounded from the other side of the door, followed by the thunder of feet. He had just lifted his hand to knock when the door flew open and he was greeted by a young girl with brunette hair and mischievous brown eyes.

"Who are you?" She demanded.

"Step away from my sister, mister," came a voice behind them.

Matthew stepped so that he was standing sideways and glanced down the stairs, immediately losing the ability to breathe. The young boy with a slingshot in hand, aimed at him, was lanky and clearly the same age as the girl who had opened the door. But it was the sand-colored hair and hazel eyes that had stolen his breath.

"Are you okay?" Jackson whispered.

"I'm—"

"Matthew?" A familiar voice asked.

He turned back to the door and came face to face with Lina and the overwhelming smell of magic hitting his nose.

Thirty-Two

T HERE WAS exactly ten seconds of peacefulness in the backyard. Ten seconds in which Lina got to soak in the warmth and smell of her husband.

"You can't use magic! That's cheating!" Abigail shrieked from the treehouse.

"Dammit, Abby!" Sloane yelled back. "That hurts when you use the wind like that."

"Then don't soak me with your rain balls!"

"It's not too late for boarding school," Thomas murmured into her hair.

She let out a deep sigh and buried her face in the crux of his arm. "We can't take that risk. They'd show their new classmates their tricks to fit in and it'd be a disaster."

"Maybe Róisín can figure out a way to spell their magic into a deep, deep, *really* deep sleep?"

Lina laughed so hard that a soft snort slipped out. "Oh, wouldn't that be a dream." She pushed herself up and climbed off the chaise they were snuggled on.

"*Abbyyyyyyy!*" Sloane wailed.

Lina and Thomas both winced.

"Could we do it now?" His brown eyes tracked Abigail's descent from the tree house ladder. Her feet had just touched the grass below when she was lifted into the air and spun around.

"It's so very tempting." Lina pinched the bridge of her nose. "Sloane, put your sister down."

"She started it!" He cried out.

"I don't care who started it. It's getting out of hand and the last thing we need is for someone to see you tossing your sister around inside a freaking tiny *tornado* in our backyard."

He looked from Lina to Thomas, then side-eyed the cyclone he had trapped his sister in. "Fine."

"Your brother and Róisín are coming next week for the entire week, right?" Thomas came to stand next to her.

"You're thinking the same thing I am, aren't you?"

"They love taking them on adventures. Maybe they can go camping or something."

Lina leaned into him, using his steadiness to steady herself. There wasn't anyone else in the world she would want to do life with, even if they were going to have to say their goodbyes while she still had centuries of time left. Once in a while, that fact crept up behind her and grabbed hold of her, clutching so tightly it left her breathless.

It was just edging up when Abigail shouted that Sloane was it and took off in a dash toward the house, racing past where they stood.

"Yep. They can go with their aunt and uncle for the week," Lina said decisively.

"Let me take you somewhere." He turned her to face him. "When was the last time we went somewhere, just you and I?"

"Not that long... Oh. Wow. Things happened with Madigan, then Caid's magic." She rubbed her temples. "And now the twins. When they're at school, I'm doing town stuff and trying to help Róisín and Caid as much as I can from here."

"Exactly." He put his hands on her shoulders and guided her closer. He had just bent his head to kiss her when her body tensed. "What is it?"

"I don't know," she whispered. "But please, stay here." Before he could argue, she was racing into the house.

"Step away from my sister, mister," Sloane's threat floated through the open front door.

Lina lifted her magic so that it embraced her, just beneath her skin, ready at her beck and call, but still deep enough inside that the glow that she had yet to learn how to mask remained hidden. When she saw who stood in the doorway before Abigail, his face pale and eyes glassy, her pulse raced at the side of her throat.

"Matthew?"

His face immediately twisted into confusion. His brows drawing together tightly and his lips slightly pursing. His nostrils flared as he studied her. "When?" His question was gruff.

"A couple years ago," she answered quietly.

His eyes dropped to Abigail, then lifted back to Lina, and she saw the question there.

She nodded. "Same time."

"You didn't reach out."

"Shasta didn't exactly leave directions on how to do that should it happen later down the road when you all weren't here. Everyone couldn't get away from here fast enough once I had the twins and none of us showed any signs of magic." She hadn't meant for there to be so much bite to her words. Guilt flooded her when he winced and looked at his feet.

"Mom." Abigail turned to her and the wide-eyed, nervous look on her face made Lina's stomach drop. "I'm sorry. I opened the door, and they were there. They smelled funny and I—" Her throat bobbed with her swallow. "I panicked."

Shit.

Matthew cursed lightly, his hand flying up to the back of his head. The copper haired man next to him quickly covered his mouth to stifle his laughter.

When the small pebble pinged against the doorframe, Lina knew what had happened. She tipped her head back and blinked up at the ceiling.

Plink, went another pebble, then, "Hey! I'm just an innocent bystander," the man exclaimed.

"Guilty because you know him," Sloane said. *Plink.*

The slingshot was Caid's fault. Given what Abigail had just said, Róisín would be there momentarily, *with Caid.*

Who, to Matthew's knowledge, was dead.

Shit, shit, shit.

"Abby, grab your brother and go out back, please. I need to have a quick word with these gentlemen."

Abigail chewed her lip, hesitating. "I'm not in trouble?"

Lina cupped her cheek and kissed the top of her head. "No, you're not. You only did what you thought you had to do. It was the right thing." She glanced toward Matthew. "It couldn't last forever," she added solemnly, causing Matthew's brow to wrinkle. She waited until she heard the patio door close before facing both men square on. "Who are you?"

"Jackson Burke, ma'am. Matthew's cousin." He held out his hand. Cautiously, she accepted it and his firm shake. "I, uh, take it we did not, in fact, catch you on a good day."

She pressed her lips into a line, knowing full well she was scowling at Matthew. "No. But he's about to get exactly what he wants, anyway. I just hope he's ready for it, because she's going to be *pissed.*"

"What do you mean?" Matthew straightened.

"She was getting ready to come to *you.* All of you. Under her terms. Not all of yours."

"I'm not"—He shook his head—"This is me. I'm here on my own. I didn't expect..."

"No." She shook her head and put her hands on her hips. Her anger for her best friend, her sister-in-law, rising. If she only knew how to magic the two men before her away. To protect Róisín. To give her more time. "No, you didn't, did you?"

"I'd just hoped, fuck." His shoulders dropped and his chin fell to his chest. "I don't know what I hoped. I learned some really damning shit about my family, Aunellion." He tipped his head toward Jackson. "And I *think* the Goddess."

Lina barked out a laugh. Matthew and Jackson flinched. "And you what? Wanted to draw her back in? Hasn't she lost enough?"

She felt someone approaching her from behind and braced herself.

"I want to keep her *away* from it. I can't explain it." His hand went to his stomach. "Something feels off, and it doesn't..." He dropped his voice lower. "I don't think it's safe for her."

The figure stepped from behind Lina and stole Matthew's breath away, leaving his mouth to fall open.

"That's because your Goddess wants me dead," Róisín said.

THIRTY-THREE

S HASTA APPROACHED the middle-aged woman with silver streaks
peppered through her nearly black hair. The woman kept her eyes
downcast as she tapped on her phone screen, a small laugh passing
through her lips.

Shasta cleared her throat. "Excuse me?"

"I'll be with you in just a moment, ma'am," she replied. A deep
burgundy colored nail dragged along the screen, rolling up the Instagram feed on the phone.

"I'd like to rent a car." Shasta watched her continue scrolling.
"Preferably today. Before noon." *Scroll.* "Is there a manager around?"

That got the woman's attention. The phone dropped like a hotcake
next to the computer's keyboard. "Are you looking for compact, mid-
sized, convertible, or?"

"A plain sedan is fine. I only need it for two days at most."

She shifted her attention to the computer screen. After a few taps of
the keyboard, and a few more of her nails on the mouse, she turned back
to Shasta. "I've got a silver Toyota Camry if that works."

"Perfect." Shasta pulled her card from her wallet and handed it to
her, then slid her an identification card. She'd last used it seven years
earlier and hoped it was still passable.

Watching the woman enter the information, Shasta chewed her cheek. She should have made sure it was updated. Or, better yet, she should have just shifted to the location closest to Matthew. If he was with his cousin, who was also a witch, what would the harm in that be?

"Alright, ma'am." The woman rose and handed Shasta back the cards. She reached over to the printer and snagged the two sheets of paper waiting there. "If you could just sign and date the bottom of these while I grab those keys for you."

Shasta skimmed over the wording of the first page, the agreement and fees, before signing, then added her signature to the payment printout.

"The fee charged today covers two full days and added insurance. If you need it longer, just give us a call. As long as we don't have a reservation for it, it will be easy enough to charge the card for the added days."

Shasta took the keys from the woman. "Thank you."

Once in the car, she dug through her handbag for the cell phone she brought and punched the address she'd gotten from Brent into the map feature. When the directions popped up on the screen, including the distance and estimated arrival time, her chuckle filled the small cab of the car.

The rental business was only a five-minute drive from her destination.

"I should have just shifted," she said with a sigh and placed the phone into the cupholder near the gearshift.

Her head was still pounding from Ione and Lily's argument when they had arrived in Ely. Lily had always been a small, quiet mouse of a girl and grown into a similar type of woman. Shasta had noticed how she always shrank into the background at the group gatherings and said very little. Not that she wasn't observant. Lily was a sponge, soaking everything around her in.

Ione was a wrecking ball.

Something had been simmering between the sisters that gave that wrecking ball a target and the momentum to swing it.

Shasta had been caught in the debris. She had been unsure how to ease the tension enough to get Ione to focus on what needed to be done, or give even a temporary solution.

Lily had been young when Moira passed. Ione was already nearing her first century in age. She was loud, loved fiercely, and had an independent streak as stubborn as Moira's. Nanette had tried to rein her in, but failed. So, instead, she focused on Lily. Young, impressionable Lily. Directed everything from her studies to her social life.

As she watched Lily's small hands furiously shape and pat loaves of bread with tears streaming down her face while she and Ione slung insults at one another, Shasta couldn't help but wonder how much damage Nanette had done trying to hold on to the girls in the only way she knew how.

Shasta got Ione off to Molennius, and Lily sorted with her baking, then shifted to Earth in search of Matthew.

Had he known the tumult the sisters were facing? Was Lily on her own?

With a sigh, Shasta pulled her car to a stop before a house perched at the end of a narrow peninsula. The day was warm and cloudless, the ocean just beyond the house beckoning. If Molennius's oceans were not so tempestuous, Shasta would have opted to build near one. While water was one element she only bore a bit of magic for, it had always been the one elemental and nature comfort that truly soothed her to the soul.

She rang the doorbell twice and after waiting several minutes, the door finally creaked open. The woman who had answered the door was a petite thing with light blue eyes and pale blond hair that reminded Shasta of moonlight.

"Hi, my name is Shasta Fiero. I'm looking for Matthew McArthur and Jackson Burke?"

"Matthew's aunt? Right? He mentioned you this morning at breakfast." The woman studied Shasta for a moment before offering her hand. "I'm Nadia Copeland, Jackson's girlfriend. They've just stepped out, but you're more than welcome to come in and wait if you'd like. It's only the end of May, but damn, is it hot out there."

Shasta smiled at her. "Did they say how long they'd be gone for?"

"No. Jackson just said they may be late getting back. They left in Matthew's car."

"You're Trifoan," Shasta realized with a slight gasp.

"I am." She nodded. "My family left a little over two hundred years ago when Mildred passed the Waterlife Act that prohibited us from ocean waters."

And a mermaid without their salt-watered homes was a dead mermaid. Trifoa still had mermaids, but very few and they were rarely seen.

Shasta's smile turned into a wide grin. "It's truly an honor to grace your presence, Nadia."

Her cheeks turned pink, and she blinked quickly. "Oh, gosh, thank you? I think?"

"It is very much a compliment. Your people, the Trifoan Mermaids, were revered, and still are in many of the realms. With Mildred's passing and Beatrice's leadership, I hope that many of your people can return home."

She pulled her bottom lip between her teeth. "Do you think that'd be possible? Some day?"

"Beatrice has already proven to be a much more fair and progressive leader than Mildred was. Trifoa's landscape has changed immensely in less than a decade. For the better."

Nadia's eyes shone with unshed tears. "My parents will be happy to know that. I don't think I could ever go. Not just because of Jackson, or my son, but..." She looked across the yard to the ocean and the small strip of beach that lined the peninsula. "This is my home."

"Understandable." Shasta nodded. "It's a beautiful home, too. If they're not returning until late, I would hate to occupy any more of your time. I'm sure you have things to do, especially having a son." She winked at her. "I'll just pop by later, or first thing in the morning."

"Are you sure?" She glanced over her shoulder. "There's books. Magazines. I'm sure you could find plenty to pass the time until they returned."

"That's a very kind offer, but I'm fine. Thank you."

After she climbed back into the car, Shasta's head fell against the headrest as she fought back the urge to scream. She squeezed her eyes shut, her body shuddering, begging for just a drop of alcohol. Only one sip.

Instead, she turned the key, listening to the engine of the hybrid car's soft rev as it started.

She could return to Ely, have Lily reach through the connection she and Matthew had. But, no. She had to figure this out herself. There was still a bit of time left, and this was her task to handle. Everyone else had enough on their plates.

Slowly, as she churned that thought over and over in her mind, the urge to drink it all away lessened. It had been the one thing that kept her feet on the ground and the glass out of her hand since Caid's words in the cottage's kitchen that day, and the heartbreak on Lucius's face when he finally cracked open about Clarissa's last moments. When Shasta wasn't there, because she was in her atrium, three bottles of bourbon deep.

I can do this. I made promises. I need to feel, even when it's ugly. Even when it hurts.

Instead of giving into the urge to drink, she drove. Town limit signs blinked by her as she drove and drove, something in her gut tugging her along, guiding her.

Until she realized where she was heading and quickly pulled to the side of the road. Her heart racing and unable to catch her breath, she lay her forehead against the steering wheel.

"She's not there, Shasta," she scolded herself aloud.

In the years that passed, she had kept track of the property deeds in the Greens Glen area. She had seen when Caid's house had sold to a couple from southern Maine seven months after Helen returned to Molennius. When Bill Smithfield's house was sold to a family from Idaho. When Wyatt added his longtime girlfriend's name to the deed to his property. She knew Lina and Thomas remained in the home on the hill, and Róisín still held the deed to the farmhouse in the cul-de-sac. Remembering how it felt to let her own home go after Evelyn, Shasta understood why Róisín held onto the house. It hurt, but the good memories remained.

She pulled back onto the road and drove a little way until she located the parking lot of a hiking trail. Grateful to find it empty, she parked the car and focused on stilling her body and re-grounding herself before she gave into the urges and used her phone to search for the nearest store that sold alcohol.

It took longer than it had in Jackson's driveway. Her body shook harder, her heart skipped and danced around in her chest.

"There we go," she whispered after taking her first full, steady breath.

Then, knowing she still had time before Matthew and Jackson returned to his home, she let that tugging pull her just a little further. She closed her eyes and shifted.

When she opened them, her world went deadly quiet and her body stilled as she found herself looking into a pair of familiar hazel eyes.

"Hey, mom," Caid said, tucking two small children behind him.

THIRTY-FOUR

Tura shifted restlessly on the bench in front of Róisín's tea shop. She and Hecate had been quietly arguing about Hecate's planned next steps.

"It hurts when I use my magic," Tura began quietly. "Not the loom, no." She shook her head, then tugged on her bottom lip. "The rest of it. I still feel the echoes of what I had to do to Aoife in that room."

Hecate lowered next to her. "I know." She reached over and took one of Tura's hands between hers. "I also know how it makes you feel inside. You can't let it rule you. There isn't anything to be ashamed of. The stars guided that magic to you for a reason."

Tura lifted her head, her eyes damp. "And what reason was that? To be a monster?"

"No." She covered her hand with her own. "You're not a monster, Tura. You're a guide, and sometimes, when we need to guide the cruelest, or the most stubborn, we have to become the darkest form of ourselves."

Tura pressed her lips together, feeling her chin quiver. What Hecate was saying made sense, but it still didn't strip away that shame that gnawed on her weary soul.

"Aoife finally made good on the deal she made with you, didn't she?"

Aoife had, finally. But what good had it done? For six years, everything had been left behind in tatters. Now, Tura faced going back. Facing her mother after the centuries of plotting behind her back. The lies she had to spin. Her deceit against her own sisters. Would there be forgiveness for her and her actions when it was for the good of their people?

"If we get through this, yes," Hecate said. When Tura startled and looked up at her, Hecate continued, "We have been together long enough that I know her." She brushed a thumb over Tura's forehead. "What she has done to them, they'll see her truth. They'll understand why you did what you did."

"You sound so sure."

"Without hope, Tura, we have nothing."

They were startled out of their solitude by Elizabeth's approach. "Things are in place."

"And your mother?" Hecate asked.

"The wards have been stripped on the checkpoints," Ana replied. "However, the witch Anthony used to put them in place..."

Hecate's face fell and Tura felt her stomach drop.

"The family of the witch?" Hecate asked in a rough whisper.

"They were already able to get off-realm," Ana said. "The witch that created the ward was taken en route to their shift point in the northern province. Promised freedom, or the safety of their family, most likely."

Silence settled heavily over them.

Hecate broke the silence. "Runa and Aja are with the others?"

"They were leaving the north province just behind me. I overheard bits of what they said as I was working. Their plan is to go to Molennius to meet Ione and Lily. Shasta is on Earth to find and bring Matthew back," Ana said.

Elizabeth's eyes lit with mischief. "Well, isn't that delightful of Fate to treat us so good today?"

"It certainly makes this easier to have Matthew and Shasta here." Hecate rose from the bench.

Tura tipped her head to the side. She almost didn't want to ask, but she had to. "What happens now?"

Hecate rose, nodding to Elizabeth.

"Shasta should arrive there now," Elizabeth said, confirming whatever quiet question had been conveyed in the nod.

Hecate turned to Tura. "Now, time stands still."

THIRTY-FIVE

Róisín couldn't put to words how seeing Matthew standing before her felt. Her palms had become sweaty, and something akin to butterflies with teeth had taken flight inside her stomach and chest. Their wings beat and teeth gnashed furiously in their attempt to break free.

She caught Lina's eyes dart toward the kitchen door and knew she was looking for Caid.

"He's with the kids," Róisín said in a low voice.

They had come immediately when Abigail's frantic shout for help echoed through them.

Their squabble over who went where lasted five seconds before Abigail and Sloane came bursting through the back door. Caid swooped them into his arms and moved toward the edge of the property with Thomas in tow. Caid's magic was a fire in his eyes as he gave Róisín a look that showed her he was not okay with them being split up. She had nodded and moved to find Lina.

Matthew's eyes blinked quickly as he stared at her. His body remained still where he stood in the doorway next to a man with a similar build, copper-colored hair and eyes nearly the same color. The man caught Róisín's perusal of him and stepped forward, hand extended.

"Jackson Burke," he said.

His hand was warm, electric, and was that campfire smoke she smelled? Her head became foggy as she drew in the scent that had always been Matthew's and only his. "You're a witch."

He nodded. "My father, Declan, was Clarissa's brother."

Róisín couldn't stop the gasp that exploded from her.

"Surprise?" Matthew finally spoke. He blinked rapidly and lifted a hand to rub at one of his eyes furiously.

"I..." She shook her head, her words failing her.

"I'm not here to bring you back, Róisín." Matthew's voice was soft, sad, and just a little broken. "I just... I woke up this morning and something wasn't right here." He pat his chest. "The last time I felt this way was when Madigan was in Roidon with the Seer." He looked over his shoulder, then to Jackson, before facing her and Lina again. "Could we come in?"

Lina's hand found hers and gripped it tight.

Caid. Róisín knew exactly what Lina was thinking because it was screaming at her, too. He would still be able to feel their presence, know that they were there. However, both women knew he could *also* feel everything they were feeling in that moment, standing before Matthew and Jackson.

Róisín's anxiety, swimming alongside dread toward the distant mixed emotions of sadness and happiness that seeing Matthew brought on. Lina's defensiveness pulsing like a strobe light in a nightclub while her own anxiety danced.

Caid would come. Even if she asked him to stay put. He would feel it all and come. Because that was who he was.

No matter how many times she tried to convince herself she could do something before Caid ever found out, he was always there. His hand over her mouth to quiet any argument she had, nostrils flaring, angry that she had tried to sneak away from him.

Lina cleared her throat and motioned toward the living room. "Drinks anyone?"

Róisín blew out a breath and it lifted the strands of hair that had fallen over her face in her dash to the front of the house.

Lina's eye tracked Matthew and Jackson as they moved into the house, toward the living room. She put her hands on Róisín's shoulders. "You've got this. When he comes in, we will handle it. The three of us have a pretty good system going. And now"—Her eyes lifted, moving toward the men. She wiggled her jaw, her top teeth running over her lower lip. "What a mess."

Róisín snorted and rolled her eyes. "You have no idea." She rubbed her eyes with the heel of her palms. "We met someone last night."

Lina's eyes grew round. "Did you find her?"

"No. I wish, but nothing on Gea, yet. But..." Róisín shifted her weight from one foot to the next. "It's all finally coming together, Lina. I was right," she added in a whisper. "But there's more. So much fucking more."

Lina squeezed her shoulders. "Breathe. One thing at a time. Starting with this right here. My brother was right the other day. You need them." She lifted her index finger, eyes narrowed. "And if you tell him I said that you're dead to me. This is your chance. Tell him everything. Bring them into the fold. The more, the better." She pulled the refrigerator open. "I'm getting the water. You're confessing everything. We'll deal with the whole *my brother's alive* thing last."

"Not everything," Róisín said curtly.

"No, you don't have to go in there and tell them how you blew up a dress shop with a magical..." She waved her hands around, her mouth moving like she was searching for the words. "*Bomb* with all of your magic at once. Tell them about Gea. What Madigan said. What we've uncovered."

Róisín pressed her lips together.

Dammit.

Squaring her shoulders, she turned and entered the living room. "So..." Her attention shifted from Jackson to Matthew. "You have a cousin."

Matthew rubbed the back of his neck. "I have more than a cousin. I have a whole family, and that's not all of it. Róisín. My mother was Aunellion."

Her breath lodged in her throat, sending her into a coughing fit. "What? No. We would have known. My mother, she'd have..."

"You'd think, right?" A look of hurt flashed across his face, pinching his brow and turning the corners of his mouth down. "I can't explain the why. Shasta didn't even have any answers. But... but, shit, Róisín, there's so much. I don't even know where to—" His face paled and his mouth was left hanging open, the rest of his words not coming.

She knew what he saw behind her. She had felt him moving toward the house. Had felt the moment he entered. His magic radiated off him, wrapping around her like a cocoon as he came to a stop at her back.

"How?" Matthew croaked out. "I haven't seen my mother in years and Lucius, he's never..." His breath caught, and he shook his head.

"Something has happened in the afterworld and our dead can no longer cross the veil," a familiar voice said behind her. "He's alive, Matthew."

Róisín's heart stopped. Slowly, she shifted so that she faced Shasta.

"Hi, sweetheart," Shasta smiled, her eyes damp.

THIRTY-SIX

Marcelo's fingers flexed around the device clenched in his hands. Nolani had handed it to him nearly an hour ago, when she sensed him spiraling as the conversation shifted faster and faster around him.

"Write it out. It helps," she whispered to him when she handed him the stylus for the device.

He had been trying to keep up with the new knowledge of... everything.

Jessamyn had been working with Hecate, trying to free the witches of all the realms from Gea's hold. That was the part he kept circling back to.

How much of what held his realm hostage would be erased if they could rid themselves of Gea? Could Hecate, should her power be restored across the realms, be able to save them?

Save Anthony?

Or was he still going to lose his brother, and then spend the rest of his own days fighting off the monster inside?

That same monster that, at that very moment, stroked a nail along one of his lungs making him suck in a breath.

Nolani leaned forward, brows furrowed.

"I'm alright," he said quietly. With his free hand, he took one of hers and gave it a light squeeze. "I'm alright."

The monster had stirred when the arguing began between Ione and Lily. When Aja had tried to step in, Runa intervened.

"This has been a long time coming," he said. "Let them have this."

Aja folded his arms across his broad chest and stared down Runa. "Fine."

Ione and Lily were still arguing behind Runa, completely unaware.

"Just *think* about it, Lily, damnit!" Ione's hands waved in the air. "Alright, look. Let me try to appeal to your book nerd. Okay?"

Lily pressed her lips into a thin line. "Ione—"

"No. Earth's witches." Ione made a fist and lifted it. "Not one left. Not even to leave a record of anything behind for our *archives* to have on hand. The only thing left were the stories passed around, century after century."

"Well, that's how histories are told," Lily said.

"Yes. Then they're written. Right?"

Lily nodded.

"Where is she going with this?" Marcelo asked, trying to keep his mind off the sudden gnawing sensation in his stomach.

"I think we're going to find out," Nolani said.

"Not only was it never written, Lily, but we had Caid as living, breathing proof that there are witches on Earth. That alone should be enough to suspend whatever beliefs you have, and see that this is all so fucked," Ione said.

"I know it is, Ione. You forget, I was there. I was with them in the beginning. With Róisín in Shianshani. I didn't expect something like this." She cast a look around the room. Her cheeks turned red when she noticed all their eyes were on her. "But I knew something wasn't right."

"Then what the hell is going on?" Ione asked, exasperation clear in her tone.

Marcelo's monster rattled its invisible cage.

The reaction in Shasta's living room in Molennius had been new. It had been the first time in a moment of dread, of suspicion, that it even breathed. Normally, it was hunger that drove it.

Nolani's other hand closed over their joined hands. "Marcelo."

"I can't..." He ground his molars together. "I don't know what's wrong."

"I can *feel* it this time." She shuddered next to him. "Is it always like this?"

He pulled their hands up to his chest and then lay over his thighs. He wanted to speak, but it felt like his monster had its grip around his throat. Its claws digging.

"Marcelo?"

"I can't lose anyone else, alright?" Lily's words split through the air on a sob. "Is that what you want to hear? First mom, then Caid and Róisín. I got Matthew back, but..."

"Let them have this, huh?" Aja grumbled to Runa.

"I thought it was something else going on," Runa said.

"So did I," Ione admitted.

Marcelo struggled to sit up and take in the room. His vision blurred in and out of focus. His throat was like sandpaper when he swallowed. He squinted toward Ione and Lily.

"Lily, you can't hide from the hurt forever," Ione said softly.

Something about the lyrical note of her words soothed the monster and Marcelo found he could take in a slow breath. The pressure that had been assaulting his body began to ease and he felt Nolani shift closer to him. Her shoulder pressed against his arm, and the warmth of her magic washed over him, edging the rest of the darkness the monster had brought, away.

Ten rose and went to Lily's side, placing a hand at her shoulder. "We're right here with you. Just like always."

Lily stared at her for a moment, unblinking. "I need to talk to Matthew."

"He'll be here. Shasta said she was going to drag his ass back here so we can do what we all do best," Ione said.

"And if some of us die, it's okay to cry over us," Runa said.

Aja's head fell back, and he groaned. "You fucking idiot."

"What?" Runa blinked. "My sister fell from the top of the castle with a knife in her chest. *We both cried*. It's healthy. It's normal."

Marcelo turned his head slowly to face Nolani. She was watching the scene before them with rapt attention.

"That's not the point, you idiot," Aja said. "Now is *not* the time."

"I think it is," Cicile chimed in from where they sat on the sofa with their legs curled beneath them. "Air everything out now. So we go in with clear heads and hearts."

"Like group therapy," Runa said.

Aja drew a hand down his face. "What the fuck, Runa?"

Ione's smile was blinding. "I like it."

"Of course you would. That's why you and him are so damned perfect for one another," Aja said. He turned and stalked over to the love seat that Anelle was perched on.

"Go get your own seat," she said. She let out a grunt when he ignored her and dropped into the space next to her.

"This is better than television," Nolani said.

Marcelo wasn't sure he could agree. Although, he appreciated the distraction that the shift in conversation caused. Slowly he was coming more into himself, the monster edging away into the spaces he held it.

As he listened to Ione explain to everyone what an '*I Message*' was, he lay back in the seat, tugging Nolani against his side. In the night's dark, when they had gone to bed and everything was quiet, he would try to work out what had just happened. Was his monster changing? Or worse, was he losing control?

THIRTY-SEVEN

CAID AND RÓISÍN'S bodies tensed the moment the impact of Abigail's cry for help hit them.

He had just backed Róisín against the wall in their apartment and driven one of his hands into her hair, giving it a gentle tug, tipping her head back to expose her neck. His lips skimmed along the delicious sweetness of her skin, and he released a hum of delight.

"Caid," she said breathlessly.

He nipped her collarbone and rocked his hips against hers. Her fingers along his scalp sent his senses into overdrive and his eyes shuttered closed.

But their exploration of one another's bodies ended, without hesitation the moment Abigail called out. Not waiting for another one, and not wasting the time reaching for Lina, they immediately began grabbing their discarded pieces of clothing and shifted to Maine.

When they got there, the air was heavy with the smell of magic. There was a faint familiarity to it.

"I'll take the front, you take the back?" Róisín asked.

"What? No. You're not going alone."

"*Caid.* We don't have time for this."

"Dammit, Róisín—"

The back door burst open and Abigail and Sloane came rushing out.

"Uncle Caid! Aunt Ro!" Sloane called to them.

Róisín's magic rose around the quartet as she asked, "Where's Thomas?"

"Right here," Thomas said from where he was jogging toward them from the far side of the yard near the pool. "What's going on?"

Caid looked down at Róisín. "Five minutes," he said tightly. "You've got five minutes solo. It'll give me enough time to get the kids and Thomas somewhere safe."

When she turned to him, her eyes swam with every single color of her magic. So many that her irises had bled into the white.

Her voice was throaty and thick, dark, when she replied to him. "I won't need five minutes."

Then she was gone.

"Are you okay?" Thomas asked the twins, his hands shaking as he took each one by the face, peering into their eyes.

"Someone's here," Abigail said.

"Two people," Sloane added. "Men."

Caid's head snapped up, and he looked toward the house. Róisín's magic still filled the air, but it felt and smelled different from when she walked into the house.

"We need to go," his magic said to him.

He grit his teeth and clenched his hands at his side.

"What is it?" Thomas asked beside him.

Caid let his magic rise and reach forward for Róisín and Lina's magic. Beneath the heat and quiet rage of Róisín's, he could feel Lina's. It was jittery. It reminded him of the bouncy way Lina would act when she tried to hide something from him when they were younger.

"I don't know," Caid said quietly so that the twins wouldn't hear. "Which way did you come?"

Thomas nodded his head toward the small potting shed. "The only part of the neighborhood I can see from that corner is the Beckett's house and part of the McMann yard."

"Shit." Caid frowned.

The air in the yard warmed and a slight gust danced through the trees. *That* scent he remembered well. When he spun around, he moved so that he was fluidly tucking the twins behind him and stepping in front of Thomas at the same time. "Hey, mom."

Shasta's honey-colored eyes widened, and a soft gasp slipped past her lips. "H-How? The veil—" She lifted a shaking hand. "It's not…"

With a swallow, Caid reached out and took her hand, placing it over his heart.

"Oh, my—" Her fingers flexed in the fabric of his shirt. "You're really here. You're really *you*."

"*Uncle Caid?*" Abigail probed with her mind. "*Is that really grandma?*"

He gave her hand a light squeeze. "*It's… complicated. I'll explain later. With ice cream.*"

Abigail's tiny body vibrated with excitement behind him.

"They've gotten big," Shasta said, her head tipped to one side and her eyes dancing as she took in Sloane's face peering around Caid. "And" —She straightened—"Magic. When? Why didn't you reach out to me?"

Caid's mind scattered with all the things he wanted to say.

The apology. The explanation. The guilt that seeded inside wanting to make excuses. Instead, he shifted his weight so that his posture loosened and he was no longer squaring off against her. "Not in front of the kids."

Shasta chewed on her lip for a moment, then nodded. "Is Matthew inside with the others?" Despite the steadiness of her eyes shining with unshed tears, her voice trembled.

Matthew. The familiar scent of magic he hadn't quite been able to place.

Lina appeared in the doorway, her eyes flaring wide and her hand slapping over her mouth when she saw Shasta in the yard with them.

Róisín's five minutes were up. And everything was going to change. Again.

"Shasta, hi," Lina said when Caid slid the door open and they all entered the kitchen. "H-how are you—Oh!" Lina's last words became muffled as Shasta embraced her tightly. "You're not mad at me?"

Shasta stepped back and looked from her to Caid. "No. Even when the three of you do finally feel comfortable telling me what happened, I could never be mad." She shook her head, then cupped Lina's face. "I love you like you were my own." She nodded her head toward Caid. "Him, too."

Caid's heart danced up his chest to his throat. This certainly hadn't been how he'd expected this to go. He expected anger. Shouting. Then for everyone to turn their backs and go.

Lina blinked a few times before lifting her hands and pressing her palms against her eyes. "I thought you'd be so angry with me."

"For what, sweetheart?"

"Well, there's me, for starters," Caid said.

Shasta turned to him and opened her mouth to speak, but her eyes fell to Abigail, who stood like a statue watching and waiting. Caid knew that there were parts of the adults lives around Abigail that her curious mind would do anything to know about. Shasta gave her a soft smile before facing Caid again.

"I was there, Kincaid." Her hand was warm at his shoulder. "Having lost Ev, I understand that pain and rage she felt in that moment. And it was righteous. So much was taken from you two. That's not to say that I don't hate that she felt she *had* to do that. I could have helped her, hid her. Hid you both."

"She wouldn't have taken that risk with any of you," Caid said.

"She threatened to ward me," Lina said and snorted.

Shasta's smile was wide. "I have no doubt that she would have, too."

"Oh, don't I know it." Lina lifted her eyes over Caid's shoulder to where Thomas stood. "And he'd have gladly helped her. *Both* of them."

Shasta sniffed and waved a hand before her. "I came here to tell Matthew about the veil, but this..." She sniffed again. "This is a little sunny patch in the shit that's going on."

"The veil?" Lina asked at the same time Caid's chin fell to his chest and he said, "Shit."

She cleared her throat. "I don't want to ruin this moment with you two, and knowing"—She tipped her head toward where Caid could now hear Róisín's voice in the living room—"She's here too. But, Hells. It's a mess. No one can cross the veils. We have a mass exodus of witches from Shianshani because the curse is still *very* real. Marcelo did everything he promised his people and the witches that he would do. The general election came, and to absolutely no one's surprise, they elected

Anthony. Except, the problem is, while he was leading office, *his* curse awoke and he attacked Cassius. Now he hates witches and wants them all dead. He's executed nearly a quarter of the population." Shasta's chest heaved as she tried to catch her breath once the words stopped tumbling from her lips.

"What's *execution*?" Sloane's voice broke the silence that had fallen over them.

"I'm gonna"—Thomas motioned toward the back door. "Take them for a walk into town for ice cream."

"Wait," Abigail said. "Uncle Caid said he'd take us for ice cream once he explained who she was." She pointed to Shasta.

Caid knelt in front of her and held a hand out. "I promise I'll still take you for ice cream. Even if it's right after you finish the one your dad's taking you for."

She kept her eyes locked on his as she took his hand. "Promise-promise?"

"Cross my heart." He ran one of his index fingers crisscross over his chest.

"Okay!" She bounced on her toes, then leaned forward to brush a kiss over his cheek.

"Sorry," Shasta said when it was just the three of them remaining in the kitchen. "It's been a while since I've been around kids, and they were so damned quiet."

"For once," Lina mumbled. "Come on. Róisín, Matthew, and Jackson are in the living room."

"Jackson?" Caid and Shasta asked in unison.

THIRTY-EIGHT

MATTHEW'S DAY had quickly gone to shit. He still wasn't sure if it was good shit, or bad shit as he dragged his eyes away from Caid to where Shasta stood.

Jackson had filled the room in on what he had told Matthew, and Matthew did his best to answer the questions that had come his way. Not that he was any help. His head was swimming and at one point, he was sure he was seeing triple.

How he hadn't passed out yet, he didn't know.

He had only hoped to either get a tip on where Róisín was, or pass word onto her through Lina. Instead, he had found not only Róisín, but Caid as well.

Caid was *alive*. They hadn't gotten to that part yet. Shasta came into the living room, her words coming out in a rush about the veil, and the Goddess being in the afterworld looking for a missing Sister Future. Then, she had zeroed in on Jackson and began rapid firing questions at him.

This had been a mistake. One chaotic, colossal mistake.

He leaned forward and rested his elbows on his thighs. The pounding at his temples grew more and more furious with each passing second.

He had done this all out of order. If there even was an order for him to follow.

Then again, his mother and father had shifted everything around on him to begin with. So, who was he to say that he was doing this wrong?

Matthew tried to sort out his thoughts and emotions, but the onslaught of new information Shasta came with made the task feel impossible.

Róisín was okay. Or at least she seemed mostly okay. There was something there just beneath the surface that she was holding close. What had the past few years been like for her? For Caid?

He swallowed the thickness building in his throat and lifted his head. Lina had disappeared back into the kitchen to refresh drinks. Shasta stood next to Róisín, their arms linked like both women were afraid to let go. Caid was behind Róisín, arms folded across his chest and his eyes trained on Róisín.

The jagged line at the base of Caid's throat drew Matthew's attention.

Matthew hadn't been there in the moment everything had happened. He had been battling his way across the massive courtyard with Marcelo and Lily, had gotten there just as Róisín was leaving with Caid's body.

But he had seen it after. When Shasta couldn't tell him what had happened, she had shown him.

The scar moved with Caid's swallow and Matthew squeezed his eyes shut, trying to pinch away the red wash of blood.

"Hold on, let's take a few steps back here," Shasta's voice snapped him back to the room around him. "You don't know why you couldn't leave Earth, just that you couldn't?"

"Correct," Jackson said with a nod. "Our only connection to realms beyond had been Clarissa, Lucius, and,"—He tipped his head in Matthew's direction. "Matthew."

Shasta chewed on her lip for a moment, her eyes dancing between them. "You two could be brothers. Couldn't they?" She asked Róisín who stood next to her.

Róisín squinted. "Jackson's more of an Earth and Matthew's more fire."

This conversation was not happening. Was it? Here he was, sitting on the sofa in Róisín's, no *Lina's* living room, nearing an emotional break down, and they were comparing *color pallets* of him and his cousin?

"It just makes little sense," Shasta said. "You're forbidden to leave Earth." She pointed at Matthew. "You don't find out you have family until, well, that's not the point. The point is, you spent time with them and didn't know who they were. Clarissa, shit, how in the Hells did I never know in the three hundred years I knew her, that she was Aunellion?"

"Because she was trying to keep her family safe," Róisín said softly.

Caid stepped closer so that her back was against his chest, a shield.

Every pair of eyes in the room turned to her expectantly.

"That night, in the ballroom when he was dancing with me, Madigan tried to convince me it wasn't power he wanted. When I questioned him, he revealed it was more justice, maybe even vengeance, he wanted. We can't forget the Seer is, *was*, his parent," Róisín said.

Two hours later, Lina was curled at one end of the sofa, her eyes blinking slowly as she clearly struggled to keep herself awake. Jackson had shifted around in his spot two cushions over and was now completely sprawled out. His own eyes looking to be heavy with sleep as well.

Caid hadn't moved from his spot in the doorway, but at least Róisín and Shasta had finally stopped pacing and sat.

Matthew picked at the edge of one of his nails, one thought hammering at his brain over and over.

Everything they had known had been a lie.

And for what? What had been the cost?

Brenna and Lucius's lives.

Jessamyn.

His time trapped in Aunellion and the demons that hung around his shadows in the days since.

The broken bits and pieces that Róisín had clearly left behind in

Talista that day. He saw it in the way she held herself tighter, more rigid than before. The clipped and concise way she relayed information to them of what she had learned over the years.

It was most noticeable in the way her magic felt in the room with them. Hotter and louder, darker than what it had been before.

"Ah, shit." Lina groaned from her spot. "Abby feels so awful about that. It was the first thing she said when I came to the door after feeling her panic."

"It's okay," Róisín said. "Given we've been in here for at least two hours already and that," she motioned to the wall clock, "hasn't moved at all..."

"Batteries died," Lina mumbled.

"Sun hasn't moved either," Caid said.

Matthew blinked the swarm of thoughts away and swiveled to the window. No, the sun was still high in the sky, just as it had been when he arrived. He let his chin fall to his chest. Closing his eyes, he took a few slow breaths. The spinning in his head intensified.

"What could it be? *Who* could it be?" Shasta asked.

"I think why is a more appropriate question," Jackson said.

Matthew felt the burn of eyes on him and lifted his head to find Róisín's turquoise eyes unblinking on him. Her mouth was turned down into a frown.

"What is it?" He asked.

"I think..." Her eyes stayed on him, the pupils dilating until they swallowed the irises. "I think we're out of time." Her lids fluttered close and her jaw tightened.

Did she mean them? She and him? All of them?

"Róisín?" He leaned forward. He cast a nervous glance up at Caid, who was already moving across the room to kneel in front of her.

"Caid." Her hands reached out to him, grasping blindly.

"Breathe, Róisín." He took her hands in his. He stacked them, then placed them against his chest. "Breathe."

"It's happening," she said in a low whisper. "I can't... I can't stop it."

Next to Matthew, Jackson straightened.

"It's just us," Caid said. "We're at Lina's with Matthew, Shasta, and Jackson."

"I'm right here, sweetie," Lina called across the room to her.

Róisín's eyes fell closed. "I've got it. It's okay. I've..." She pressed her lips together and her nostrils flared.

"I'll go get you some water." Shasta pushed quickly to her feet and disappeared into the kitchen.

"You good?" Caid reached up and smoothed a lock of Róisín's hair from her face.

With her lips still in a tight line, she drew in a breath and nodded.

"Here, hon." Shasta handed Caid a glass of water.

"Thank you," Róisín said. "Um, what were we talking about?"

"How it's time to bring everyone in and get us all on the same page," Shasta said.

Matthew tipped his head to one side, wrinkling his nose. That had *not* been what they were talking about. Shasta shook her head at him.

"Ione and the others are in Molennius right now," she said.

"No," Róisín said firmly. "Everything we say and do needs to be done here. Hecate has retained her power and strength here. She can protect us if we're here. Nothing, and I mean nothing, going forward happens in any other realm."

"Alright then." Shasta stood. "We get some rest, and then we'll all..." She glanced around the living room. "I don't want the kids to be involved. And if they're anything like you two." She gave Caid and Lina a pointed look. "They can't be trusted to not try something."

"I still have the cottage," Róisín said. "We can all meet there. Tomorrow?"

"That should be enough time. Right?" Shasta asked Matthew.

He rose on shaking legs and nodded. "We'll head back down to the coast."

"You may as well stay for dinner," Lina said. "All of you. We've still got plenty of day left."

"I'll help you get something made," Shasta said.

Matthew leaned closer to Róisín. "Are you okay?"

"Hm? Oh, yeah. I'm fine." She waved his concern away. "It was just a bit of a panic attack. That's all."

Matthew knew better. The way her skin flushed first, then her body seeming to light from within. That hadn't been a panic attack. That had been her magic.

He needed to talk to her, but he didn't know how or what to say.

Thankfully, she must have sensed it, because she spared him when she rose to her feet and held out her hand to him. "Walk around the circle with me?"

THIRTY-NINE

Tura let out the breath she had been holding just as the edges of her vision hazed, feeling Hecate approach her side.

"You are safe here, Tura," Hecate said softly. A moment later, Hecate's warm hand was at the small of her back. "You need to use your magic, but only here, with me, where I can still protect you."

Tura reached out, her pale fingers stroking the pattern of the projected loom before her. Her words a whisper breaking free. "What if she's found a way?"

"There are too many *humans* here who hold religions that believe." She pressed a kiss to the side of Tura's head. "I am the mother of magic and witches, my little love. To all who walk this beautiful blue and green sphere."

"Which is probably why that bitch wants it so bad," Elizabeth said, breezing into the living room of Caid and Róisín's apartment carrying a tray of coffees. "Who doesn't love a two-for-one special? Witches *and* humans? I know I'd be down."

Tura could only stare at her. Elizabeth and Ana differed from the witches that she knew. Then again, her window to the realms around her had been tiny. Who was she to judge?

"How much longer can we hold it?" Hecate asked.

Elizabeth turned her wrist to look at her watch. "Our magic should hold for another hour before it fades. Time will not move normally, but trickle. Which," she shrugged, "gives us a bit more time."

"Why did you do that? Stop time, I mean," Tura asked.

Hecate walked over to a cupboard and pulled down a glass, then turned on the faucet. "The more time they have to convene, to talk, without the pressure of a ticking clock, the more the mind will absorb and think. To be prepared." She took a long drink of water. "When time does begin to move, they are clearheaded and ready to act. If we cannot do this, end this, Fate itself will step in, and we'll *all* find our endings."

"Is it only here?"

"Ana secured Molennius," Hecate said.

"And I secured Shianshani," Elizabeth added. "With help, of course. Anelle is quite brilliant," she said to Hecate. "Jessamyn would be proud."

Hecate frowned down at her drink. Then, with a shake of her head, she set the glass next to the sink and returned to Tura's side. Her voice soothing in Tura's ear, she asked, "What do you see?"

On an exhale, Tura faced her loom. She trailed her fingers along the hundreds of threads along the top, then moved her way down, down, down, until she reached the bottom. Nearly one hundred thousand threads in all. Less than there were only a few years before.

"We need to heal Shianshani," Tura said. "But how?"

"One step at a time." Hecate leaned closer to her. "Now use it, Tura. If it comforts you, Elizabeth is now here with us, offering more protection."

"Me too," Ana said, almost breathlessly, after shifting into the room with them.

"And Ana," Hecate said. "Breathe, Tura. We will watch over you while you go."

Tura let her eyes fall closed as her magic sang through her. It warmed her veins and danced to every corner of her body. She wasn't sure what this type of magic was called. Everything had a name, a classification, except for the true magic that she and her sisters held. She knew it was only because their mother didn't want others to know. To everyone, the Sisters only read the looms, acted on fate, and sealed those actions away for eternity once they came to light.

The sweet and tangy smells of the herbs from Róisín's collection faded, replaced by the smell of soot and something rancid that burned her nose.

When Tura opened her eyes, it was as though she were standing amid a battlefield, and not at the gates of the afterworld.

No, she realized as she took in the desolate surroundings, this wasn't a battlefield. This was something else. A keening noise sounded in the distance. With a swallow, Tura moved toward it.

FORTY

Róisín walked next to Matthew down the sidewalk. Their bodies were stiff and neither of them had yet to speak.

What did she say to him? Was an apology enough?

She had left. Torn apart every connection she had and then ran away.

Róisín had been hurt. But so had Matthew. He had endured the Fog Fields in Aunellion. Lost Lucius.

And then she had run away.

Sorry would never be enough. Regardless of why she had done what she had.

"How?" Matthew's question was rough.

"Yesterday, I'd have told you my magic was slow. It took a little longer to work," she said quietly.

Matthew stopped walking and waited for her to face him. His green eyes were steady on her. "And now?"

"Now I know that my magic of life has limits. Not everyone can be saved. No matter what I do or how hard I try." The tightness growing in her throat at the thought became painful. "What if it *had* been his time, Matthew? What if Gea's actions at the loom had been a part of it all?"

He moved toward her quickly, wrapping his arms around her. "Don't," he bit out. "Don't go there. Okay?"

"I can't shake it." Her breaths came faster now. That heat and pressure building inside her again, just as it had in the house. She clamped her teeth together, trying to hold it in. She would *not* become a bomb right there on the sidewalk over something that hadn't happened.

Matthew stroked a hand over her back. "He's here with you now. That's what you need to focus on. You're both here, right now. I don't know what you two have been through since Talista, but in the end—" His arms tightened around her. "You're still here. Together."

The smell of woodsmoke surrounded them. Then the warmth of his magic of fire tickled along her skin. Slowly, her shoulders sagged, and her magic receded. The pressure easing.

"Are you okay?" Matthew asked, stepping back.

Unable to lie, she gave him honesty. "No. I'm not. I don't know if I ever will be. And you?"

He shrugged. "Same." He turned his head and glanced back toward the house. "Everything is so fucked up, isn't it?"

"I'm sorry. For leaving."

He looked down at her. "I'd have done the same. Shit, Róisín, you forget, *I did the same thing.*"

"That situation was different."

He crossed his arms over his chest. "Was it, though? At least you said goodbye. I didn't even give you that. I took off in the middle of the night, then disappeared for an entire decade."

"Is that why you're not mad at me?"

His mouth opened, then closed. "I'm hurt. Not mad." He pursed his lips, then nodded. "Yeah."

"Want to punch me in the face?"

"What? No." Then the laughter bubbled out of him. It shook his shoulders first, then his entire body. He bent and rested his hands on his thighs. "I deserved to be decked."

"You did," she said with a nod.

"Look, Róisín." He sighed heavily. "We were all in it, but you were in the middle of it. Madigan wanted *you*. Gea wanted, Hells, *still* wants you. I am not going to stand here and pretend to know how it felt before or at that moment. I do know how I'd feel if Lily died. What I'd want to do." He held his hand out to her. "I'd want to burn it all down and leave nothing behind."

"I'm sorry I hurt you," she said quietly. "I won't stop apologizing."

"No. I know you won't. And I can see my insistence that we're fine isn't going to stop you." He lifted an eyebrow as he stared her down. "So, what will?"

"Go home. To Lily." Hecate had said they all had a part in this. That Fate had placed their stars in the same sky for a reason. But everyone had already given and lost so much. If there was a way she could spare them...

"Excuse me?"

"Things are..." She dropped her gaze down to his still outstretched hand and bit her lip. "Things are different here, Matthew. Earth's witches, they haven't lived with Gea's imposed limitations. They've been free. *Always*. It's not safe. Gea has no interest in any of you. Go home."

His face turned to stone, and he pulled back his hand. "Róisín."

"Please, Matthew. I can't tell you what's happened." She shook her head. No, she wouldn't. The parts of her that had become bent and lost their light. He could never see those. Not her best friend, her brother. "But I'm not the person you knew six years ago. She's—" She swallowed and drew in a deep breath. "She's gone."

"I wouldn't expect her to still be kicking around, Róisín. I saw what happened."

She took a step back.

"Shasta, she kept trying to tell me, but could never get through it. I don't know why..." He drove his hands into his hair. "I wasn't in a good place myself. I'd inherited just before we got to Talista that day. Everything in here was a fucking mess." He slapped a hand against his chest. "And then it all happened. I got there too late. I couldn't do anything. Caid was already gone."

"W-what did you see?"

"Everything that Shasta saw in that moment." When she moved to take another step back, he reached out for her. "Stop. I'm not saying this to push you away, Róisín. I just got you back. I'm not going anywhere. Yeah, I've found out my mother had an entire family hiding here in Montana and Jackson's in the house right now. But you and I? We're family. You're the only thing that feels like family I have left."

"Matthew—" She blinked back the building tears. Tearing at her was the urge to fall against him, hold him tightly and never let go; and the urge to force him back to Ely because she didn't want to lose him.

"I don't care who you think you are, or what you think you've become. I'll always love you, Róisín. I'll always be at your side." His fingers tightened when she tried to pull away. "Please don't make me fight to be there. Because I will."

The first tear splashed onto her cheek and she exhaled a shaking breath.

"My jokes aren't as good as they used to be, but I promise I can still make you laugh once in a while."

She studied him carefully under the sun that had finally started its descent from the sky. His red hair was sticking up and out all over from running his hands through it. The green of his eyes had taken on a sheen from his own tears. His mouth was curved into a slight but pinched frown.

"You don't have to tell me anything. Just let me be there," he said softly.

"Okay," she said finally.

"Okay?"

Not trusting her voice, she nodded.

He grabbed her and yanked her against him, causing her to let out a squeak of surprise when she crashed against his chest. "Thank you," his words rumbled from his chest, against her ear.

She brought her arms around his waist and squeezed. "I missed you."

"I missed you, too." He kissed the top of her head. "So fucking much."

Róisín squeezed her eyes closed and tried not to think of how much his feelings for her would change when he found out that her magic had become a literal bomb inside of her. Or when he found out the rest of what she had done in their years apart.

"Now that we've got that settled," Matthew sniffed. "Can I ask you a question?"

Here it comes...

"I need some, uh, relationship advice."

She pulled her head back and looked up at him. "Excuse me?"

"Yeah." He scratched the side of his head. "Lily. I would've thought I had this all worked out this far in, but I'm still a fish out of water, apparently. She's not so hot on letting me be supportive of her when she's going through shit. I don't know what to do or how to handle it. And I don't want to be a jackass about it."

When Róisín realized he was being serious, she tipped her head to one side. "Have you tried talking to her about it?"

"She keeps telling me she's fine. Nothing's wrong." He linked their hands together and walked back to the house. "That we have an entire pantry of muffins, bread, and other baked goods, says otherwise."

"She's like Shasta, then. Except instead of trying to cook it away, Lily's trying to bake it away."

"Exactly. It makes me feel like shit because she's done so much since we got home. She was there helping me search for the Burkes. She and Ione got Nanette to agree to take some of the Shianshani refugees. She's helped settle the refugees at home. The gardens she's cultivated have helped feed thousands in Ely." He dropped his voice. "She helps me get through the flashbacks when they knock me down."

What was left of her heart cracked a little at his words. At what he had lost. What would Lucius have to say about her actions? She cleared her throat, pushing down that rising flood of emotion, and said, "And you want to be for her what she is for you."

"Even just a little. But she won't let me in to *be* that for her. I don't want to force it, but I have to do something."

Róisín moved closer and lay her head against his shoulder. "To be honest? You've just got to talk to her, Matthew. You may have to be firm. Don't give her an out to tell you that everything is fine. It'll be uncomfortable, but you're going to have to push."

"Goddammit Kincaid James McGrath! I told you to take your boots off!" Lina's shout from inside the house carried down to where they had stopped in front of the house.

"She hasn't changed at all, has she?" Matthew asked.

"She was a lioness from the start," Róisín said with a smile. "Nothing can be mightier than that."

FORTY-ONE

SHASTA STOOD at the back door of the house, watching the activity in the backyard. It had changed so much since the last time she was there. The pool, the treehouse, the spattering of toys throughout the yard. It was clear that this was where Lina and Thomas had settled with the kids. Her attempt at watching from a distance had been for naught. They had all still slipped around her in secret.

They owed her nothing. Their lives were theirs to live, and she was just a bystander.

Still, the ache that throbbed at the center of her chest grew hands and dug in deeper as she watched the twins weave their hands together and hang like monkeys from Caid's outstretched arms.

Thomas and Jackson stood just beyond the patio, drinks in hand. She could hear them chatting about Maine's coastline and the fishing industry Jackson's girlfriend's family was a part of. A family of mermaids working the ocean, Shasta mused with a smile.

Caid's burst of laughter drew her attention back to him. He spun in circles, the twins' bodies now swaying outward with the movement. Abigail squealed for him to slow down, while Sloane urged him on, begging him to use the wind to speed them up.

"He's so good with them." Lina stood next to her. "They adore him."

"Don't we all?" Shasta asked with honesty.

"I'm sorry, Shasta," Lina's voice was soft.

"For what?" Shasta turned to her. "This?" She motioned with her hand toward the yard.

"I lied to you."

"Oh, sweetheart." Shasta wrapped her arms around her. Neither she nor Caid had said anything about their parents, but Shasta had quickly understood that the siblings had very little semblance of a relationship with them.

"I knew, already, when you and Matthew came to tell me," she confessed against Shasta's shoulder.

Shasta stroked her hair, then ran a soothing hand in circles over her back. "You don't have to tell me anything, Lina. Just as I don't expect Róisín or Caid to. If you want to, any of you, I'm here to listen. But," she pressed a quick kiss to the top of Lina's head, "I'm not owed any of that. I'm just happy that you're alright. All of you."

They parted and turned back to the yard.

"Me too," Lina whispered and leaned into Shasta.

Grief was crawling up from her belly, and Shasta cleared her throat. "Oh." She blinked when Sloane disappeared. "I see Caid taught them how to shift. No, what did he call it? Do the blinky thing," she said with a chuckle.

"I wish I could blame my brother for that one." Lina shook her head. "That was Róisín."

"Really?" Shasta lifted a brow in disbelief.

"Oh, yes. The shifting, the best way to throw a water balloon for maximum damage. Ah, and the best places to hide with a Nerf gun to scare the bejeezus out of me. We can't forget the wheelies on the bicycles." Lina sighed heavily and Shasta bit the inside of her cheek to stop herself from smiling. "She's also helped Sloane learn ways to read around his learning disability, taught Abby how to draw and paint. She's sat with the both of them more times than I can count after a fight to mediate apologies."

Shasta's worries for Róisín ebbed the more Lina spoke. Róisín hadn't fallen into a dark space after Talista. She had dug her feet into life and bloomed. She had been *living*. Shasta found herself wondering if Róisín had realized that.

"Don't get me wrong. Caid's done his fair share. Slingshots, dirt bikes, hidden doors in the tree house he and Wyatt built for them..."

The smile Shasta had been holding back broke free.

"*Abbyyyyyyyy!*" Sloane shouted.

"Well, you kind of *did* ask for it," came Caid's rough voice in response.

"Ha!" Abigail bounced on her toes.

Thomas glanced over his shoulder toward the house. When he saw them at the door, he stared at Lina with his brows raised.

"See what I mean?" Lina mumbled.

Shasta gave her shoulder a squeeze. "I guess that answers my question about how magic is going."

Lina snorted. "I wish there'd been a bit more time before it came. Having the three of us all at once? It was a little chaotic at first. They've picked it up so much faster than I have."

"They're young, their brains like sponges. Because—" Shasta winced when Caid became suddenly drenched. Sloane shrieked from the tree house and darted inside of it.

"Oh, dammit." Lina closed her eyes and rubbed at her temples.

Caid knelt next to Abigail. His sandy haired head bent lower so that they were nose to nose, and his mouth began quickly moving. They were plotting, planning.

"Should we step in?" Thomas asked, his head appearing through the door.

"Nope. Sloane knew what he was getting into, starting something with his uncle. It's on him." Lina lifted her eyes to the tree house. "Sorry, little dude. It was nice knowing you." She sighed again and faced Shasta. "Caid picked it up quickly. He was so natural with it and now? Now it's easy to forget it's only been seven years that he's had magic. He's just as skilled and quick as Róisín."

Of course he was. She had seen his determination in the months after Róisín's death. He had blamed himself for that day and not being good enough, fast enough. Knowing that, she didn't need to imagine how hard he pushed himself after Talista.

"I'm sure you're just being hard on yourself."

Lina frowned. "Róisín says it's just because I try to control it instead of working with it."

"Our magic is a marriage, a partnership," Shasta said.

"That's exactly what Róisín said."

"And she's right." Shasta studied Lina's profile for a moment. The determined set of her jaw, the way her nose flared with each breath. "I can help you."

Lina blinked and looked away from the yard. "But, with everything—"

"If there is anything I've learned over these last many years, is that even when it's all going to shit? Life still goes on."

She pressed her lips together and nodded. "I'd like that."

Shasta brought an arm around her and kissed her cheek. "Me too."

Forty-Two

CAID RUBBED his towel over his head then wrapped it around his waist. Reaching for his shirt, he realized it wasn't on the hook by the shower where he'd left it.

"Róisín? Have you seen my—" He paused in the bathroom's doorway.

Róisín sat cross-legged on the bed in the shirt he had been searching for, and nothing else. He tipped a brow up, waiting. Instead, Róisín's eyes remained unblinking on the wooden chest at the foot of the bed that he had built for them to store blankets in. Her bottom lip had been tugged between her index finger and thumb. She was rolling it back and forth between the digits.

"Róisín?" He crossed the room to her.

"Do you..." She cleared her throat. "Do you still love me?"

His body stilled. "What?" He flinched at the harsh, shocked way the word cut through the air. When she lifted her head and looked at him, he saw her cheeks were damp. She had been crying.

"The way that you did at first, do you still love me?"

His breath caught in his lungs and at first he could only blink. Which was a mistake. She took his silence to mean that whatever worry it was that was simmering inside of her was founded. Fresh tears splashed onto her cheeks. It was all that it took to have him moving again. He pulled her from the bed and into his arms. The honey and lavender smell of her wrapped around him, and he breathed it in deeply as he cupped her face in his hands.

"Why?" He asked roughly. "Why are you asking this?"

Her brows knit together, a swirling knot of skin appearing where they almost touched.

"What did you and Matthew talk about? What did he say to you?" His mind went into overdrive with thoughts. What did he do? How could he fix this? How did he soothe her worries and show her he loved her? What had he said or done to make her feel otherwise?

She shook her head. "He didn't say anything. At least about how I've changed."

"Then why?" His heart thundered in his chest. The vibration of it making the organ dance up to his throat.

"It's just..." She stepped back and wove her fingers together. "It's quiet again, and in here—" She pulled her fingers apart and tapped her temple. "It gets noisy. Everything I've said and done. And when you... When you said earlier that I'm not who you met that night in the meeting." Her eyes shuttered, and she sniffed quietly. "I know I'm not. I think she's gone for good. I can't get her back. I don't even know if I *want* to get her back." The knuckles of her hands grew white from the tension of her clenched fists.

"Róisín." Desperation clawed at his lungs as he struggled for air. "*I'm* not the same person you met, either. Do you still love me the same?"

Her eyes grew round. "Of course I do. It's different, Caid, you haven't—"

"Haven't what, Róisín? You have done nothing that I haven't."

She shivered.

"I'd do it again, Róisín. For you. For us. So, tell me, how is it any different?"

"I... I don't know." She squeezed her eyes shut. "I don't know."

He thumbed away her tears, then kissed each cheek softly. "If anything, I love you more. So much more now than I ever believed I could ever love someone. Every day." He brushed his lips over each of her closed eyes. "I fall deeper and deeper into that love for you."

The tension slowly seeped from her body, making her slump slightly. He moved his hands to her hips to hold her up.

"Even if what's in here"—She pat her chest—"Is so dark and angry most days?"

Caid pulled back. "You've met the voice of my magic, Róisín. You've *felt* what it's like inside me." He lifted her into his arms. "It doesn't make you a bad person." He laid her on the bed. "Everyone gets angry. We all rage and fight. Darkness accompanies it. It doesn't make us bad people." He kissed her softly. "Even good people can do bad things sometimes."

"I've done a lot of bad things, though," she whispered.

Things that kept her alive is what she meant. Whereas the things he had done hadn't just been to keep himself, or her, alive.

We keep the things in the dark," his magic whispered to him. The words skittered along his spine.

He sat next to her and brushed a strand of hair from her face. "You're still a good person."

"You sound so sure."

"If anyone would know who you are inside, it's me."

Her eyes swam with bright blues, greens, and purples and he realized his magic had reached for her to soothe her, and hers had responded, welcoming it. Róisín's cheeks flushed, and heat coiled at his core.

Slowly, he lifted his hand, then trailed his fingers lightly from her throat to where his shirt had fallen open on her. "I love the way you whisper that little pep talk to yourself, every morning, over your cup of tea or coffee." He brushed his knuckles along the softness of her skin, down her chest, pausing just below her navel. His eyes trailed the movement, watching in fascination as the goosebumps rose in the wake of his fingers.

She let out a small gasp. "You hear that?"

"I hear everything, baby." His fingers stroked along her thigh. "Every noise of happiness you make. That hum when you step into the shower under the warm water. The off-key songs you sing when you're organizing your stock room. I hear it all because—" He lowered his head to one of her nipples, slowly circling it with his tongue. "I've never been able to take my eyes off of you."

"Caid," his name was a whisper.

"I love you, Róisín. Everything you are and everything about you." Caid nipped her shoulder. "From the way you knead your toes against my thigh when we're on the couch at night." He shifted his hand from her thigh, moving it closer to where he could feel the heat beckoning to him. "To the way you feel in my arms, every night and every morning."

"Caid." Her hips lifted in search of his touch.

"You never tried to change me." He pulled his gaze away from his wandering hand to her face.

Her body stilled and she frowned. "Of course not. Why would I?"

"You've always loved me for exactly who I am, without conditions. I need you to know that my love for you is the same. Every single part of you is who you are. To change any of that is to change you. I love *you*. As you are now. As you will grow to be."

Her eyes filled. She lifted a hand, resting it against his cheek. He closed his eyes and leaned into her touch.

"I'll burn the realms for you, Kincaid McGrath," she said.

Caid would too, for her. He brought his mouth to hers, kissing her hard. When he shifted his hand, stroking along her folds first, then slipping two of his fingers into her warmth, he took advantage of the way she opened her mouth to moan. He dove his tongue in and plundered. Feasted.

Her hips rocked against his hand, and he thrust his fingers in deeper. She arched off the bed, whimpering into his mouth. Caid hummed and worked his way along her chin, pressing soft kisses, stroking his tongue down her neck.

She swore softly and dug a hand into his hair when his mouth closed over one of her breasts. He sucked and laved the skin there in time with the thrusts of his fingers, reveling in the taste of her, the feel of her warmth and her body rolling against him.

Róisín's fingers flexed in his hair as she held him against her. Her breaths came faster, her body trembling beneath his touch. When he felt her walls gripping his fingers, he withdrew them.

"Shh," he said when she protested. He shifted lower, slipping his fingers into his mouth, tasting her.

"But—"

He stared down into her heavy-lidded eyes. Holding her gaze, he moved down her body. He lowered his mouth to the inside of her thigh, pressing a soft kiss there. With his tongue, he trailed up, up, up. She lifted onto her elbows, watching as he closed his mouth over her clit. He gently nipped first, before closing his mouth over her swollen nub and sucking hard.

Her head fell back, a low, deep moan escaping. Settling himself between her legs, he lifted them so that they rested over his shoulders.

"Always so wet for me." He stroked his tongue along her core a few times.

"Please, I can't..."

Caid's magic rose inside him, cool instead of warm. Instead of dousing the heat that had built to an inferno low in his belly, he burned hotter. Their eyes held as he brought his tongue back to her at the same time he hooked his arms around her legs, holding her in place. Then he dove into her sweet heat.

When his magic reached his tongue, turning it ice cold against her heat, her hips bucked and she rocked against his face with a throaty moan. Caid curled the tip of his tongue, tracing a circle around her entrance.

Róisín's back bowed. A sob exploded from her, then her hips rocked frantically against him. As her orgasm coated his tongue, he hummed in delight.

Her hand still fisted in his hair as her body rolled beneath him then snapped bow tight, before it trembled and she let out a small gasp, followed by a quiet moan.

Caid could feel the way the muscles in her lower stomach fluttered in the wake of the second orgasm. He dragged himself away, shifting her legs off him before he rose over her. Her hands moved to splay over his chest where his heart had beat a violent dance against his chest and rib cage.

When one of her hands moved from his chest, reaching to take his swollen cock, he gripped her wrist and dropped his forehead to hers.

"Don't." He clenched his teeth, pushing down the inferno that was raging in his core. "Don't." He would explode the moment she did more than touch him there. As it was, he was barely containing himself.

Róisín shifted beneath him, then guided him back to her. He lowered against her, slowly. He feared if he thrust into her the way he wanted to, he would come before he was fully seated.

Her touch was soft as she stroked her hands along his back. She traced a finger along his bottom lip. On a breath, he slipped his tongue over the tip. Her eyes stayed on them, watching in fascination as he pulled her finger into his mouth, sucking lightly.

"She could take it all from us, but she can never take this," Róisín said thickly. "I love you, Caid. So fucking much there'll never be enough time to show or tell you."

He smiled down at her. "Fates be damned," he said. Then he rocked against her.

Her legs came around him, and she lifted her hips to meet his thrusts. They moved together, slowly, so deliciously slow. Their magic danced together, making the air thick and heavy around them as he whispered his love for her against her face, her neck, shoulders. Her own odes came around her pants as her fingers dug into his back, arms, scalp as though she were trying to anchor herself here.

The base of his spine lit up, electricity buzzing along the length of it to the base of his skull and back before reaching around his hips and tightening. When she clenched harder around his cock, he moved deeper, harder, faster.

Róisín's head fell back onto the pillow, her body pressing against his. Her legs squeezed him, her fingers bruised his forearms where she gripped. Her warmth slicked over him as she fluttered around him and he couldn't hold on any longer. The release that came made his body ignite in a wave, and he felt the hairs along his skin rise in its wake.

He tried to not collapse on top of her, bracing himself on his forearms, but she pulled him down, wrapping herself around him.

"Let me hold you," she begged.

"I've got an easy hundred pounds on you, Róisín." He tried to push off her, but she doubled down and he felt the help that her magic was giving her.

"I don't care. I just... I need this, Caid."

His heart tumbled free of his chest, falling to his feet as under-standing weighed it down. The uncertainty of what was next crashing down around them both. He knew she would protest, but he used his magic to free himself. Before she could say anything, he scooped her into his arms and walked toward the bathroom.

"We clean up first." He set her in the shower and turned the water on before going to the closet to grab fresh towels. Stepping under the spray with her, he smoothed the hair from her face and kissed her nose. "Then we go to bed, and you can hold me until we need to go tomor-row. But only if I can hold you back."

She nodded, then said the words that shot an arrow through his falling heart. "Promise to not let go."

FORTY-THREE

Róisín burrowed deeper into the blankets, letting the warmth her body had created beneath them wrap around her for another moment before she forced herself to surface from sleep.

Time wouldn't wait any longer for them. The shelter they had built, insulating themselves against the realms beyond Earth, would be torn down that day, and they'd be thrust back into the chaos.

Fear tickled the base of her skull.

Slowly, she stretched, then rolled to her side. Not wanting the day to begin, but knowing they needed to take the next steps, she forced her eyes open. The marked flesh of Caid's neck greeted her. Raw and angry. The scream bubbled up her throat from her chest. She jerked back and saw his face in profile, his golden, tanned skin from the Greek sun now a pale gray. His lifeless eyes on the ceiling overhead.

The scream ripped free from her throat, and for a moment, she was unable to move. Before the sound of it died out, she was vaulting herself off the bed and slamming against the wall as her flailing body became tangled in the sheet that had come with her.

When she screamed again the sound was choked off as her heart jumped into her throat, making it harder for her to breathe.

"Róisín!"

She ground her teeth together and shoved her hands into her hair, fisting it. The tug sent a ripple of pain over her scalp, down her neck. The next scream that exploded from her came out as a sob.

"Róisín!"

Warm hands cupped her face.

"Róisín," the familiar voice was softer now.

Fingers pushed her hair carefully from her face and shifted the sheet.

"Róisín," Caid whispered her name. "Look at me."

Blinking through the tears that burned her eyes, his face slowly came into focus. His brows were drawn together, and his hazel eyes blazed as they danced over her face. The blue-gray of his skin was gone, but it was still paler than normal.

He was there with her. He was alive. Her nightmare had not only startled her awake, but him as well.

"I can't go back," she stammered and shook her head. "I can't... I can't go back. Caid, I—"

He pulled her against him, his arms strong around her. His heart thundering in his chest against her ear.

Her body shook harder and harder until it was as though she were being violently rocked. "I can't go back."

The words began spilling out of her mouth over and over like a defiant chant, louder until they rang off the walls of the room.

Caid held her tighter, stroking a hand over her hair, pressing his lips to the top of her head.

Róisín's voice grew hoarse, her throat turning to sandpaper the more she repeated the words. Tears rolled down her cheeks, splashing onto his shirt. The dam had broken. Everything she had tucked inside behind that anger, behind that rage, pushed free and she couldn't stop it. Grief was drowning her. It wrapped around her ankles, tugging her deeper. The surface growing further from reach.

"Come with me," Caid said quietly. "Please."

She tried to speak, but the only noise she could make was a gasp before the sobs took her over again. Instead, she nodded and clung to him.

A moment later, the warmth of Ely's two suns washed over them and she could draw in a full breath. The air was earth and wheat. He had taken them to the Rose Valley.

"Caid." Panic began clawing at her chest, her throat.

"I've got it," he said. "Don't worry."

The air shifted quickly around them and then stilled. Digging into her well, she found the strength to straighten her bowed body, pulling back enough to look up at him.

"A little trick I've been working on." His cheeks colored pink, and he smiled softly at her. "Wyatt may be human, but he makes a pretty solid training partner."

"It's a..." She turned her head, studying how the rose-colored wheat stalks in a circle roughly four meters around them stood still, while beyond, they waved in the gentle breeze. She crawled away, a hand outstretched, until it was met by something cold, hard. Suddenly, that hardness moved toward her, nudging her back. With a yelp, she scrambled back to Caid's side.

"I can change its size." He nodded toward the invisible wall. "It will move, too."

She looked up at him, blinking.

"It will also stay in place should anything"—He pointed to the sky —"Fall on us."

"Caid—"

"It won't melt, burn, whatever. It's—" He scratched the back of his neck. "It's bullet proof. *And* it can withstand the impact of a 2029 Ford F-250 crew cab moving at one hundred miles per hour." He gave whatever surrounded them a satisfied nod.

This is what he and Wyatt had been doing all those times they disappeared for hours on end. Why Wyatt had sometimes returned with Caid looking weary. Or worse, the times he had come back to the cabin bruised and Róisín healed him before he went home to Leslie and her two boys.

"It took some time to figure out what elements to use to make it as solid as it is now," he continued, rubbing his jaw. "Once we got that down, it was getting myself connected to it enough that it matched my reaction time. *Then* it was getting it dialed into my magic enough that it would sort of be... a step ahead of me." He said his last words in a whisper.

"Why didn't you tell me?" She asked.

Quiet blanketed them and she took in the tightness of his jaw, the way the joint flared out on each side as he clenched it. The lines around his eyes and lips. He had been so steady, moving forward, never looking back, but at that moment, she realized he had done just as she had. Buried Talista deep inside in a corner. She knew he had been training the best he could with Wyatt, but she hadn't realized that he had been doing something like *this*. Something to protect himself.

"It's not just for me." His voice tugged her from her spiraling thoughts.

"I can't go back." The silence in the shield became deafening. Her heart picked up its pace until it was like a jackhammer trying to crack her chest to free itself. The edge of her vision grew hazy. "*We* can't go back."

"It ends with us, Róisín."

"I can't—" A rough sob burst from her. "No," she said more firmly, slapping her palms against his chest.

His eyes shuttered and his chest heaved with his breaths. He pressed his lips into a tight line. His eyes shone, filled with tears when he opened them. "Let it out. Use me. Anything you need." He reached out and thumbed a tear away from her cheek. "You're safe here, Róisín."

The resignation in his tone had her anger rising to dance alongside her grief. She hit his chest again and shook her head.

"For Sloane and Abby," he said.

She fisted her hands, wanting to shout at him, but her words became trapped. Emotion taking over her mind and body.

He stepped closer, his eyes steady on hers. "For our kids. For theirs."

Róisín pounded her fists against his chest, her lungs screaming for air around her sobs. She would go back to it all, she knew she would. As much as she wanted to stay on Earth with her family, she knew she couldn't. They would risk it all, again. She hit Caid again before fisting his shirt in her hands and pulling him closer, burying her face in his chest.

Caid lowered them to the ground. "We'll make it right. Even if not for us, for our family."

Róisín had no doubt that they would. If they had to forfeit everything for Lina or the twins, for Shasta, Matthew and Lily, they would. She remembered how at peace Lucius had been the day he knew he was leaving them all. The day he knew he was going to bring Matthew home, even if it meant that he wasn't coming with him. Even if it meant his end.

So, they would. If not for themselves, for their loved ones. For family.

Tipping her head back, she looked up to the sky over the valley. Her mind was a race of thoughts, round and round. She caught one and her heart calmed. "Caid?"

His thumb was gentle as it stroked over her chin. "Hm?"

"Can you," she blinked, shifting her attention away from the sky, she looked at him. "Can you teach me?"

He nodded, his throat bobbing with his swallow. Wrapping her in his arms, he told her, "Come on. We've got a few hours before we have to go to the cottage."

FORTY-FOUR

"THIS IS an awful idea," Anelle said from where she stood next to Marcelo. "Do you know how dangerous this is?"

Marcelo shifted his weight from one foot to the other, then turned to face her. "I need to try, Anelle."

She frowned at him. "I can give you fifteen minutes. Drop and go, then come back for you." With hasty, jerking movements, she wrapped her deep red braids around one of her hands. Then, her eyes like fire on his, she slapped them atop her head and tied a piece of leather string around them, securing them. "I don't care if you're not ready. I'm not facing my brother and Runa if something happens to you while you're there."

Marcelo gave her a slight nod and swallowed hard. Lifting his hand, he reached for hers. Together, they blew out a defeated breath, and then Anelle whisked them away to the castle.

"Fifteen. Minutes." Her breath was hot at his ear before she shifted away, leaving him alone inside his brother's suite.

"Go away," Anthony's voice was gravelly when he spoke.

"I can't, Ant."

"So." He rose from his chair. "You've come to kill me. Finally."

The gravity of his brother's situation slammed into him with the force of an entire realm falling on him. The skin around his bloodshot eyes had become thin, the veins webbing dark beneath them. His cheeks were gaunt, making his sharp cheekbones appear more severe. The years, or the monster within, had caused his light, wheat-colored hair to darken. It fell to his shoulders in a dark mass of curls.

Anthony pushed that hair from his face, spearing him with a wicked grin much like the one Marcelo had seen upon his father's face the more the monster took hold.

"I'm not here to kill you, Ant." Marcelo fought to keep his voice soft.

Anelle was right...

"Well, you certainly didn't come to share a meal with me, *brother*." Anthony stalked closer, into the light from the window. Blood streaked the front of his shirt. "Then why?" He asked when the tips of his toes met Marcelo's.

Marcelo clenched his jaw, his own monster beginning to claw at him from the inside. Slashing at him, demanding its release. It wanted to battle Anthony, and it burned his guts, his lungs, his heart as it raced to rise.

"How do you do it?" Anthony asked.

"Do what?"

"Live?"

Marcelo drew his brows together.

"Every day." Anthony lifted a hand to Marcelo's chest. It took every ounce of control to keep from flinching. "Right here." He tapped a finger over Marcelo's heart. "It rages against me. Then it crawls into my throat, to my head, where it beats against my mind like a hammer. Until I feed it."

"The more you give in, the more it wants. The louder it gets," Marcelo said.

Anthony slid his hands up Marcelo's chest, brushing along his neck. His pupils dilated as he stroked his index finger along Marcelo's steady pulse. It was when Anthony licked his lips and the skin beneath his eyes rippled that Marcelo reached a hand up. Anthony hissed when Marcelo's fingers wrapped around his wrist, squeezing.

"Kill me, Celo."

Marcelo released his hand and stepped back. "No."

"Why not? The witches will build a statue of you in the capital square." Anthony sneered at him. "They'll worship you like their pitiful Goddess."

"That's not what I want, and you know it."

"Were you not with *her* before you came here? I know you two are hiding in the Northern Provinces. I know that Aja and Runa are the ones that are running the transports out of the realm." Anthony scrunched his nose, then spun around, giving Marcelo his back.

Beneath it all, he was still Marcelo's younger brother. Somewhere buried beneath the monster, he was still just a man, afraid. That was what Marcelo needed to remind himself as he stared at his brother's back. The once broad expanse of it now slender, hunched.

"The great Prince Marcelo. Always were the apple of everyone's eye," Anthony said bitterly.

"It wasn't like that before, and it isn't now. You know that. You can fight this, Ant." Marcelo took a caution step toward him. "We can fight this."

Anthony's chin fell to his chest. "You can, but as you can see, I can not."

Marcelo laid a hand on his shoulder. "He forgives you." The shoulder beneath his hand heaved, then shook. "He wants to help you get through this."

"He—" Anthony's breath hitched and he shook his head. "He can't come back here. I can't let him."

"You know Cass as well as I do. You can tell him no, and he'll just do what he wants, anyway."

The remark made Anthony chuckle lightly, and the pressure that had been building in Marcelo's chest eased slightly.

"I didn't want to," Anthony whispered. "I panicked. I needed to give them something, or they were going to come for me. So I, I gave them the witches. I've let it consume me since."

"You need to fight it, Ant."

When Anthony faced him, he saw the red lines of tears staining his cheeks.

"What if there's a way?"

"There *is* no way, Celo. Or have you forgotten? You've gotten to live with your soul's heartbeat every single fucking day since the day father died. You get to wake next to her, kiss her, *love* her."

"You could have all of that with Cass."

Anthony's bark of laughter cut through him. "I remember when *you* were the pessimist, and I was the foolishly hopeful one."

Marcelo felt the sudden urge to take him by the shoulders and shake him. This wasn't his brother. Anthony was always full of hope, love. He was funny and kind. The man that stood before him wasn't even a husk of his brother. This man was someone else entirely.

"Do you trust me?" Marcelo asked.

"Despite it all?" Anthony swept his arms out wide. "I do."

"Then trust me on this, Ant. Please. There's been developments. We've—"

"It's time," Anelle said, wrapping her arms around him.

"No! Wait!" Marcelo struggled against her hold, but it was too late. They were already shifting away.

Except they didn't go back to Nolani in Northern Prindell. They went to Molennius where everyone was once again gathered, Shasta having returned.

"How nice of you both to finally join us." Aja's words were low, vibrating Marcelo's chest where his heart was still racing. He needed just a few more minutes with his brother. Just a few more. Aja's eyes moved from Marcelo to Anelle and narrowed. "You and I will talk about that stunt later."

"Shove it," Anelle said. "We're both fine."

"That's not the point," Aja said. "It's a risk that neither of you needed to take. And there will be repercussions. He's a loose cannon and it will *not* take much to provoke him."

"No." Marcelo stepped so that he was between the fighting siblings. "No, he won't. He's defeated. Locked inside his room, hiding from everyone."

"That means nothing," Aja said. "And you know it."

"Excuse me, but if you three are done bickering, I'd really love to hear why it's a group excursion, *immediately*, to Earth," Ione's voice lifted over theirs.

"What?" Aja snapped upright, eyes landing on Shasta.

"We're going to Earth. Preferably immediately," Runa said.

Shasta put her hands on her hips and sighed. She looked at Aja and said, "What he said. I will tell you everything when we get there. Grab whatever you'll need for at least a week because if we can avoid returning to the realms before then, it's best. I need to check in with Helen, make sure we're good here on our end with the refugees."

Marcelo frowned. What had happened when she found Matthew?

"Anelle?" He glanced at Anelle, whose knitted brows showed she was just as confused as he was. It was Aja's wide eyes, unblinking, as he stared down Shasta that had Marcelo's heart picking up its pace so quickly it began thrashing against his ribs.

Shasta dipped her head slightly at Aja before she walked over to Ione.

"What's happening?" Marcelo asked.

"It's no longer safe for us to be here," Aja said.

Marcelo was unable to ask more questions as Aja grabbed Anelle by the hand and the pair quickly shifted away.

"Celo?" Nolani's voice was small at his side. "Are you okay?"

Wordlessly, he took her in his arms and crushed her to his chest.

"We can still save him," Nolani whispered against his chest. "There's still time."

Marcelo could only hope she was right.

FORTY-FIVE

LINA DROPPED heavily onto the sofa next to Thomas. She had expected Abigail to hit her with questions when she had gone up to tuck her in, but she had been eerily quiet. When Thomas said Sloane had reacted similarly, Lina found herself in the laundry room folding their clothes. Then, scrubbing down the machines. Anything to keep her hands and mind busy.

Exhausted, she nestled against Thomas and yawned.

"What do I have to say to get you to stay?" His voice rumbled against her ear.

"Nothing."

He stiffened beneath her.

Had she wanted to go? Yes. She wanted to be there and do whatever she could to help. To feel that satisfaction of making Gea pay for all the ways she had damaged her family. Arguing with Caid and Róisín earlier had felt right. *Going* had felt right.

Then reality smacked her in the head. No, the laundry detergent bottle *fell* on her head when she slammed the dryer door closed so hard, it rattled the wall it sat against, and the shelf overhead.

Who was she kidding? Helping Róisín had been easy because she was more of a secretary. A bookkeeper. What was next? Lina didn't know the first thing about *fighting*. Caid had always handled everything for her. Protected her. Until Thomas came into her life.

"Lina—"

"I'm not going, Thomas."

His hands were gentle as he took her by the shoulders to move her so that he could look at her.

"I have absolutely nothing to offer them, except being in their way. I'm only tough in here." She tapped the side of her head. "The first time I see something out of the ordinary, I'm going to run screaming."

Thomas frowned at her. "You sell yourself short, baby. You're the toughest person I know."

She chuckled and shifted so that she was sitting. "I don't know how to use my magic all that well yet, either. Going against a super old, powerful witch is a bit out of my wheelhouse."

"You'd figure it out quick enough," he said.

She squinted at him, scrunching her nose. "Are you *trying* to get rid of me?"

"No. I just don't like you thinking you're not capable, when you are."

"Oh, Thomas." She lifted a hand and rested it on his cheek. "You already have me." She wiggled her other hand, her wedding and engagement rings twinkling in the light of the living room lamp. "You don't need to schmooze me."

He reached out and took her hips, then pulled her onto his lap. "Just because I have you"—He kissed her nose— "Doesn't mean I'm done schmoozing you. Schmoozing is my way of loving you."

The bridge of her nose burned and her heart galloped in her chest.

"I also don't like seeing you so down on yourself. No, I'm not talking you into going. To be honest, I'm fucking relieved as hell you're staying." He shrugged. "But I also don't want to see you beat yourself up as less than. Because you're not."

"I couldn't bear to leave you." Her breath hitched. "Leave Sloane and Abby."

He brushed her hair over her shoulders, his soft brown eyes steady on hers.

"I've seen what Caid and Róisín have been through. I can't." She shook her head and bit her lip. "I can't lose them. But even more, I can't lose *you*. No, that's not right. I don't want to leave, because we don't have much time left. I can't give a moment of that up. It's selfish, I know—"

He pressed his index finger against her lip. "Shh."

"I don't want magic anymore." The tears that rolled down her cheeks were hot. "I don't want to live for hundreds of years after you're gone." Her sob stole the rest of her words.

Thomas pulled her against him and wrapped his arms around her. He stroked a hand over her hair, then pressed a kiss to the side of her head.

"This isn't how it was supposed to be," she whispered against his neck.

"I know, baby, I know."

How quickly everything had unraveled and become a mess. It had been easy to be heartbroken that Caid would be the only one to have magic. To miss something that she didn't wholly understand. Just as it had been easy to not have her reality placed in front of her when hers, Sloane's, and Abigail's magic woke inside of them.

Having their house filled with witches, listening to them talk and theorize on what Gea was doing, how to attempt to set things back to right, it uncovered something inside of her. They were going to live on, without Thomas.

Lina had grabbed Róisín before she and Caid left, asked her if she was okay, if going back to it all was going to be okay.

"She took him from me once, and as long as she's out there, she can do it again," Róisín said, her tone filled with anger and defiance. "I can't let her take him, Lina. Even those minutes, those hours without him..."

She knew. Her best friend, her sister, didn't need to finish. The shadows had clung to them since their return, but it wasn't until she had watched Róisín slip out of the church during Wyatt and Leslie's wedding and later found she and Caid clinging to one another in the building's shadow, that she had truly understood.

Lina had stepped out of the hall next to the church to retrieve Abigail's leggings and ballet flats, knowing her daughter well, and knowing that it wouldn't be long before Abigail was scaling something, or taking on a dare from one of the boys. When she closed her car door and turned back to the buildings, Wyatt had been approaching, his head on a swivel.

"Caid and Ro?" He asked.

Lina frowned and nodded to where her brother and sister-in-law stood. She had felt Róisín's emotions rise despite their distance in the church during the ceremony. Had felt that panic settle its claws in her. She had also caught the fringes of Caid's magic when it had risen and reached out to Róisín in the effort to soothe her. To assure her he was there. He was okay. They were okay. Lina had been grateful for it, because even just that little had helped soothe her own rising emotions.

"They'll be okay, right?" Wyatt said.

"Honestly?" Lina frowned. She watched Caid lift his big hands to cup Róisín's tear-streaked face. He lay his forehead against hers. Lina could hear the gruff, rumbling tone of his voice as he gave his assurances to Róisín over and over. "I don't know. I want to say time, but... This scar is deep, and I don't know if those parts will heal for them. I know what they looked like after. I can't imagine what it was like for them—during." She swallowed and blinked back tears. "I hope they just need more time. They deserve to be free. To be happy."

Wyatt nodded. He brought his arm around her shoulders and gave her a half-hug before kissing the side of her head. "Time is something we always want more of, but never get enough of," he said.

Now as Lina curled against Thomas, burrowing her face against his neck, she felt the weight of Wyatt's words.

FORTY-SIX

MATTHEW SPENT the entire trip back to Jackson's house trying to convince him to go back to his family. If not to Montana where his mother, Matthew's *aunt* lived with their cousins, then remain on the coast with Nadia.

Jackson argument against that was that what was happening impacted him and his life, his future with Nadia, just as much as it impacted Matthew.

"I can fight," Jackson said. "My father, my uncles, they all made sure I knew how to use my magic and my own strength. I'm not a pampered Earth pet."

By the time they had pulled into Jackson's driveway and Matthew parked next to what he assumed was Nadia's car, Matthew had relented.

"You go in there and talk to her about it first," Matthew said, pointing to the house. "She needs to know the risk. What it can mean."

Jackson turned to him and slowly lifted a brow. "Haven't had too many serious relationships, have you?"

"What's that supposed to mean?" Matthew wanted to wince at the bite in his tone.

"If I take off on her to go do something that could mean the end of my life without saying anything, I know she'd probably hunt my dead ass down, bring me back, only to beat the hell out of me all over again. Of *course* I'm going to talk to her. This is her life, too."

"And if she doesn't want you to go?" Matthew asked.

"She knows what this means for us. Nadia will be scared, yes. But she won't stop me."

There was a surety in Jackson's eyes that Matthew wished he had when it came to Lily and his relationship. She would tell him it was okay. She would even come with him to help as much as she could. But deep down, would she want to stop him? Lucius and Clarissa had been, perhaps, the best role models a child could ask for when it came to love and relationships. How was he failing so tremendously with his own? How was he still trying to figure it all out this many years in?

How did dad juggle it all and still love mom the way he did?

Maybe that was where the fault lay. He was trying too hard to emulate his father. As a leader to their people, as the backbone to this iteration of what he called family now. As Lily's bonded. And he wasn't Lucius.

"I need to go home," Matthew said abruptly.

Jackson only stared back at him.

"I'll be back by mid-morning, Earth time. Then we can go meet everyone at the cottage."

Jackson blinked.

"What?" Matthew huffed out the word.

"I'm only fifty-seven, and the last we were together before this, I was a kid that rolled in the muddy riverbanks and barked like a dog." He ran a hand through his hair and sighed. "But we're family, Matthew."

Matthew's heart gave a heavy thump against his chest. *Family.*

"Maybe not today," Jackson continued. "Someday. If you need an ear, I'd like to think you trust me enough to lend you mine."

Matthew nodded and swallowed around the lump that grew in his throat. "Thank you."

"Now, go talk to your girl. Smooth out whatever's making those edges frayed. I'll see you in the morning."

Before Matthew could respond, Jackson was pushing open the door to the car and striding up the walkway to his front door, whistling.

MATTHEW STEPPED INTO THE HALLWAY AND LISTENED TO the sounds of the manor in Cascadia. He knew from what Shasta had said that everyone had gathered in Molennius after her and Ione's discovery in the afterworld. Shasta had been heading there from Maine to bring everyone back to Róisín's cottage in Ireland. However, something had tugged Matthew toward Ely. Home.

Had she gone to Molennius, learned about the afterworld, and then returned to Ely to wait for him? Or had it been something else that had driven her back to the manor?

"Lily?" He called out and gave her line a gentle tug. He had been trying more and more lately to use their tether to pinpoint where she was. More of a comfort than a need. She had been who he instinctively reached for when the memories crept up, trying to smother him.

Moving toward the kitchen, he kept his ears open and magic reaching.

"Lily?" He paused in the doorway to the kitchen.

Something akin to nervousness trickled down along their tether and he spun around, facing Lily, who stood at the other end of the hall.

"We need to talk," she said.

"What did Nanette say?"

Her brows came together, her forehead wrinkling. "What?"

"When you and Ione went to Roidon." He stalked toward her. "What did she say to you?"

"She said," she began, almost breathless, and took a step back. "She said they had room for some of the Shianshani refugees. We talked about—"

"What else did she say?"

Lily took another step back and bumped against the wall. She pulled her bottom lip between her teeth and lifted a hand to rub along the base of her neck. "Matthew—"

He lifted a hand and placed it against the wall next to her head. The smell of her flooded his senses. He wanted her. But not yet. "You've been quieter than normal, Lily. And I'm not accepting that you're just... fine. Not anymore. Talk to me. Let me be here for you."

"I am fine, though. It was only our trip to Roidon. To talk to grandmother."

"That's not all." He leaned closer. Let his nose brush against hers. "Stop hiding from me. Please."

"I'm not—"

"Lily."

Her shoulders sagged and her eyes fell closed. "You're going to hate me."

Matthew frowned. His other hand lifted, and he stroked his knuckles over her cheek. "Lily, you could tell me that you've decided to leave me and go back to Roidon. And still I could never hate you."

When her eyes opened, they were a bright, blazing amber, damp with tears. "I could never go back. I could never leave you."

"Then what is it?" He hated how desperate the words sounded.

"I... I have. I don't know how to—" She pressed her lips together. "This was so much easier when Ione was yelling at me in front of everyone," she said in a rush.

Matthew's magic prickled along his spine. "Ione yelled at you? When?"

She placed a hand on his chest. "It's okay."

"No, it's not."

"Matthew..." She sighed. "I deserved it. For the way I've been behaving."

He begged to differ. Instead of arguing with her about it, he waited.

"When my mother died, it felt like I had been torn into pieces. The pain was unbearable. I made a promise to myself that I would never, ever hurt like that again." She chewed on her bottom lip. "I think that's why I turned to books so often. Why I let myself become that quiet, nerdy book girl. It made it so much easier to..."

"Hide."

"Exactly. I kept my head down and did everything grandmother asked of me. It was easy, and it was safe." Wrapping her arms around herself, she shifted her weight from one foot to the other. Her eyes remained downcast. "I ran from you that first time you kissed me because I was scared. I was feeling so many things for you, and you were right in the middle of everything with the others. If you had gotten hurt, *I* would hurt. I couldn't—" She hiccupped. "I couldn't bear it. So I ran. I tried to hide."

Matthew reached out and hooked a finger under her chin, lifting her face to his. "And then I went and disappeared on you. I'm so sorry, Lily. I will be until the day I die."

"You did what you had to do. I can't fault you for that." She blinked, spilling the built-up tears down her cheeks. "I ran again, after. That's why I went with Róisín. It made it easier to shove my feelings down, and not deal with them. I stayed distracted."

And then Caid had died. Róisín had left. Shianshani fell apart, and the realms were plunged into chaos.

"Lily…"

"After Talista, there wasn't anything to use as a distraction. So… I baked. And baked. It was helping. Just as helping Brent with the records to find your family helped. But it, it creeps up on me. And it *hurts*. So much. Right here." She rubbed at the base of her throat. "Like hands, squeezing. I can't—" Her fingers fluttered against her skin and she gasped in a breath of air. "I can't make it stop. Even now after all these years."

"Lily—"

"I have these nightmares that we never got you back. That you're still trapped in Aunellion in the fields. Or *worse*, that you get pulled back there because Fate didn't want you to come back home. I know they're just nightmares." Her voice dropped to a whisper, and she said, "But sometimes when I wake, you've already gotten up for the day and it's easy to let that nightmare grow roots."

Matthew drew in a steadying breath. His heart was beating in heavy thumps inside his throat. Each beat sending a shockwave through his body and his muscles tightened in response. He stepped forward and brought his arms around her. Gently, he pulled her close. "Don't shut me out, Lily. I can't bear the thought of you hurt, and it kills me a little right now, knowing that you've been holding this inside for so long. Let me in. Let me help take the pain away when it rises."

She pressed her face into his chest in response.

"Please."

The tips of her fingers pressed deeper into the skin at his back as she clung to him.

"We can go slow. Small steps, but please, don't shut me out." He tightened his hold on her.

"I-I'll try."

At that moment, that was enough for him. The door had been cracked open and all he could do was remain patient. Show her he was there, still. Forever. Eventually, she would open the door all the way.

He bent slightly and swept her into his arms. With his foot, he nudged their bedroom door open and walked with her to their bed.

"I could never hate you, Lily." He lay next to her. "I love you." He brushed his nose along her neck, then pressed a light kiss to her cheek. "You could rip my heart out and smash it to pieces beneath your foot, and I'd still love you."

Lily's touch was soft against his scalp when she pushed her hands through his hair. She stroked down to his neck, then banded her arms around him. He let her pull him against her and burrowed his face in the crux of her neck.

"I could never do that." She pressed a kiss to the side of his head.

Matthew brushed his lips to her shoulder and shifted so that he settled between her legs.

"I love you, Matthew." She stroked her hands up and down his back and drew her knees up to make more room for him between her legs.

"Lily."

"Hm?"

"You've just been crying," he said against her throat before kissing it.

"So?"

"We've just talked about ripping hearts out and stomping on them." He nipped lightly at her jaw. Heat coiled at his core. Shifting upright enough to look down into her golden eyes. "You've been open with me," he whispered the words. "Vulnerable. I can't..."

One of her hands moved down his back to his ass. She gave one of his cheeks a light slap before squeezing it.

"I thought you wanted to try for babies," she said, an eyebrow lifting.

"I also thought, until not even five minutes ago, that you wanted to leave me to take your heiress' place back in Roidon."

She rolled her hips upward.

"Lily." He said her name deeply.

"Shasta found you?"

He stilled. Not that he had forgotten what the last several days of his life had been like, what doors had opened that would never close again. Or maybe, just for this moment, he had.

"If what Aja and Runa have said is true, and what Shasta and Ione have learned..."

Matthew didn't know what Aja and Runa had said, but he knew what Róisín had said. Shit, Caid. He was alive. Róisín was in Maine. The things they had said about the Goddess. A witch. A pretender. *Traitor*.

"This could be our last moment alone," Lily continued. "Make love to me, Matthew. Please."

His body began a war against itself. He had wanted to tell her everything at that moment. It could soothe her hurts, her worries. Caid was alive and Róisín was coming back to them.

"Matthew."

What he wanted, and what she wanted, warred inside him. She was telling him what she needed from him after he had just asked for just that. He hesitated a moment before bending his head and taking her mouth with his. She tried to maneuver them so that he rolled and he chuckled against her mouth.

"I thought the request was for *me* to make love to *you*." He let a hand travel down her chest, cupping her breast. As he kneaded the soft flesh, her eyes fluttered closed and her body rolled under his.

With a grin, he tugged her shirt and the cup of her bra down. Her skin was warm against his mouth as he sucked deeply.

Lily's hands stroked into his hair again, and she arched to press her chest against him.

Matthew hummed against her and slipped down her body, using his magic to strip away their clothes as he went. The smell of late spring rain and blooms surrounded him as he drew closer to her core. It filled him, warmed him. His cock stretched and throbbed in response.

Everything changed again once the day was over. This moment with Lily was his solace, his reprieve from worry, from fear.

He lowered his mouth, hovering just over her clit.

"Matthew." She reached for him, her hips lifting in invitation. "Now. I can't wait."

When he stroked his thumb over her clit, down through her folds, he agreed. "So wet and ready."

"Then don't play."

His head shot up to find her watching him across her body.

"What do you want, Lily?"

"You. Now. *Please*." She put emphasis on the last word.

He took a moment, stroking along her center, teasing his fingers over her entrance. When he circled his thumb over her clit, her hips rocked. She cursed and tried to bat his hand out of the way to replace it with her own. Instead, he linked their hands together and closed his mouth over her clit.

Lily's other hand dove into his hair, gripping, holding him against her. Her body rolled and rocked, igniting an inferno within him.

"Matthew," she grit out.

He released her and lifted back over her. "You're sure?"

She nodded and widened her legs for him.

"I'll always be there for you. No matter what, okay?" He remained still, his cock just at her entrance, waiting for her response.

"Always?"

"I know everything with Nanette was conditional, Lily." And it made him rage like nothing ever had to know that fact. "But with me? Never. It'll never be like that."

Her fingers flexed briefly at his shoulders.

"Okay?"

"Okay."

Matthew rocked himself into her, and they became lost in the dance of ecstasy and love.

FORTY-SEVEN

Róisín watched the tops of the trees sway in the light breeze from where she sat on the porch swing of their cabin. They had returned to Maine and spent hours working with her magic to create even a semblance of a shield. While Caid had been satisfied with her quick progress, she was not.

What if he got hurt and couldn't shield himself?

What if Gea got too close and siphoned his magic away and he couldn't create his own?

Would hers be enough?

Would she be fast enough?

That had been what haunted her the most about that day. She hadn't been fast enough.

The sound of Caid's flesh tearing carried on the wind and whispered in her ear. Shivering, she tucked her chin into her sweater.

He was alive. Caid was with her.

Her eyes fell closed as her mind chanted the words over and over.

Warm lips against her forehead had her eyes opening. The concerned hazel gaze that was on her had her lifting the hand not holding her coffee mug and brushing her fingers over the stubble on Caid's jaw.

"I love you," she said softly.

He brushed his lips over hers. "I love you."

Róisín tipped her head back when he stayed positioned over her. "You good?"

She wanted to lie to him, tell him she was fine. But she was so damned tired of being strong. Of holding it together and burying it deep. "I don't know."

Caid lifted her legs, sat on the swing, then laid them over his thighs. He stroked his hands along her calves, every few strokes giving them a light squeeze.

"What do we tell them?" She asked.

He shrugged. "The truth."

"Is it that simple?"

He looked up from where he had been watching his hands on her legs. "Yes. We've been here, digging for and getting answers. Trying to find her and stop her. What else is there to tell?"

"What if it isn't enough? Matthew and Shasta are the exception. A part of my family. The others..."

"Well." He drummed his fingers against her leg. "We can't stop them from feeling what they feel or doing what they may end up doing. What matters is what *we* do. And we won't stop."

She burrowed her face back into her sweater so her next words were muffled. "You sound so sure."

"I'm not sure about any of this, Róisín." He reached toward her and took her coffee cup. After he placed it on the railing, he slid an arm behind her back and tugged her to his lap. "There are two things I am sure of in life. That's it."

She shifted so that she was straddling him. "What are those two things?"

"No way in fucking hell is Lina getting involved in this."

Róisín nodded. On that, they could agree. They had both argued against it, and she was shocked Shasta had sided with Lina. Although Róisín had been helping Lina learn how to harness her magic since it had awoken, it had been little, basic things. Nothing to prepare her for the risk that waited for them.

"I've been trying to find the words to convince her to stay. Helping me before, it was... different. She wasn't truly at risk of anything. This..." Róisín frowned. "She'll be so angry with us, but I think she'll understand. I *hope* she'll understand."

She had to. Róisín could never live with herself if something happened to Lina. If she took the twins' mother from them. Róisín knew what it was like to navigate life without a parent, and they were already at a disadvantage with Thomas being human.

"What's the second thing?" She asked in a whisper.

His eyes were bright on her. "You."

She pursed her lips and drew her brows together.

"Remember when you said that you had been an unmoored ship, drifting?"

Róisín nodded.

"You're *my* anchor, too."

She drew in a breath, pressing her lips together to keep her chin from quivering.

"No matter how this goes, you need to know that, Róisín. I didn't even realize it at first. How I was just drifting through life, not really living it. Until you. Even in our darkest moments, I can say that I've *lived*. With you, because of you, for you."

"Caid..."

"The only thing I would change in my life would be asking you to dinner sooner."

"I'd have said no," she immediately replied.

His body shook with his laugh.

"I don't like the way some things have happened for us." Her body quaked as the shiver at the memory of their deaths rolled through her. Caid drew her closer, wrapping her in his warmth. "But I wouldn't change any of it."

Caid pressed a kiss to the top of her head. "We should probably go make Lina mad at us."

"We could just go to Ireland without her."

"No. She'll track us down, which is worse."

Róisín sighed heavily and buried her face in the crux of his neck. "Good cop, bad cop?"

"You be the best friend," he said, squeezing her thigh lightly. "I'll be the big evil brother."

FORTY-EIGHT

THE WOODEN screen door slammed against the side of the house and Sloane came racing out like a rock off a slingshot toward Caid's truck.

"She's got *iiiiiiiiice*," he screamed as he ran toward them.

Róisín's eyes were wide on his when Caid glanced at her.

"I didn't teach her that," he said and lifted his hands. "I swear."

Slowly, one of her brows rose.

"Don't look at me like that. I seem to recall a certain aunt teaching the hellions how to shift."

She snorted softly. "I still miss you calling it the blinky thing."

Caid shifted the truck into park and pulled the keys from the ignition. "I could still do that." He twisted and leaned closer. "You ready?"

"Nope." She shook her head.

Before she could say more, Abigail ran by Caid's window, cackling maniacally. "Maybe we should let Leen come. Just forbid her from leaving the cottage. Give her a break from the madness here."

They watched Abigail chase after Sloane. She was circling him, pushing him toward the back of the house, both kids knowing they were not allowed to show anyone outside of the family their magic. The backyard, though, was fair game.

241

Sloane edged around Lina's SUV, just enough out of sight of the neighbors, and he froze, realizing his mistake. Abigail, seeing her opportunity before her, immediately trapped him in an ice block.

"She's good," Caid said. The awe in his voice clear.

"She's very methodical in everything she does. Even her school-work," Róisín said. "And he's a, what's the expression? A bull in a China shop."

"Sounds exactly like Lina and I." Caid laughed and pushed open his door. "Just the other way around. We should probably break this up, shouldn't we?"

Róisín nodded. "Definitely."

"It wouldn't be stalling."

"No. Never. It's helping."

He looked down at her. She had pulled one cheek between her teeth and he could see her molars chewing the skin. "Want me to go talk to Lina and you wrangle the heathens?"

Releasing her cheek, she tipped her head up.

"I'll break the"—His eyes darted toward Sloane—"ice in there with her, and you do it out here with Sloane. Then come in and do your good cop thing."

The echoes of her nightmare still cast shadows in her eyes, beneath them, and bracketed her mouth with tight lines. He could feel it humming between them in their connection. It was like a swarm of bees looking for a way out of his body.

He paused and took her hand in his. This was it. There wasn't any more talking about going back. It was a real thing happening at that moment. He swallowed down his own fear, his own anxiousness, and tugged her closer. There was so much he wanted to say, promises he wanted to make that he wasn't sure he could keep.

Instead, he brushed his lips over hers and said, "Don't scare them too much."

A corner of her mouth lifted. "I won't. I've gotta keep top spot over their uncle."

Caid stroked his thumb over her hand before releasing it and making his way to the house.

"God dammit, Abigail, *where is my baking pan?!*" Lina shouted from the kitchen.

"What on Earth would a six-year-old want with a baking pan?" Caid leaned against the doorway and folded his arms over his chest.

"You'd be surprised," Lina muttered, slamming another cupboard door closed. "I just want to get the bread in before it gets hot out. It's still two weeks until summer officially starts and they're saying it's going to be almost eighty all week long." She stomped over to the pantry. "Which means there's going to be a heat day at school for sure. Probably an early dismissal one day and canceled the next."

"Leen—"

"It'll push the school year, again. We didn't have many snow days, and we were all looking forward to an early summer vacation," she continued, as though she didn't hear him. Something crashed to the floor in the panty and she let out a string of curses. "Thomas wasn't supposed to need to go to work for another week. But they called this morning, and he has to go Tuesday for *three* days." Her voice was muffled inside the pantry. "I made the mistake of checking my email when I got up today and school—"

Caid stepped in front of her and placed his hands on her shoulders. "Leen."

"What?" She blinked up at him.

"What's wrong? You only ramble like this when something's up."

She swatted his hands away and returned to the oven. "I do not do that."

His chin dropped to his chest. This was one scenario he had *not* been prepared for.

"A-Ha! Ouch. Shit." She pulled away from the lower cabinet, rubbing at the back of her head. "Found it."

"Huh. A pan in a cupboard, how strange."

She side-eyed him. "It was in the fancy dinnerware cabinet."

"You have fancy dinnerware?"

"If you two jackasses hadn't eloped, you'd have gotten wedding gifts, too."

"We didn't elope," Róisín said, coming into the kitchen.

Lina set the pan on the counter and turned to them. "Did we go dress shopping?"

"No," Róisín answered hesitantly.

"Did you two get to eat dozens of cupcakes to pick which flavor you wanted your wedding cake to be?"

Róisín inched closer to him and it made him want to chuckle. He placed his hand on the small of her back in support.

Lina put her hands on her hips. "You got married in the *woods*. You called us all a week before and said just to meet at this dummy's spot." She waved a hand toward him. "Wyatt would know where. Follow him. So yeah, it was an *elopement*."

"You won't convince her otherwise," Caid said to Róisín from the corner of his mouth. "Let her have this one."

"You two don't have to give me anything." She turned her back to them and set to work preparing her bread loaves. "I'm not going."

Caid's body stilled. He wasn't even sure his heart was beating. Róisín let out a long, quiet breath next to him.

"I don't know why you two have to be weird about it," Lina said.

"We're not. We just thought..." Caid shifted his weight and rubbed the back of his neck. "Shit. But, yesterday?"

"Was yesterday." She tucked the pan into the oven, then gave them her attention again. "Last night I realized not only am I *not* equipped to handle this shit beyond looking at maps and reading books." Her shoulders sagged. "My babies, and Thomas. I don't have forever with him, and who will take care of them if we're all dead?"

Caid flinched.

"And you're sure about this decision?" Róisín asked, making Caid jerk his head around to look at her wide-eyed. "What? I want to make sure once we leave she doesn't change her mind and try to find us."

"The thing about Lina is, once her mind is made up, it's made up," Caid said, casting a glance to his sister.

"And yesterday when I argued about going, I wasn't totally positive," Lina added. "It just felt right to go. Then everyone left, and the reality sank in like a fucking rock."

The three of them let out a breath, sending Lina and Róisín into a fit of giggles. The tension of the moment broken, the women stepped toward each other and embraced.

"Kick her ass," Lina said. "And please try not to die." Her hazel eyes lifted to Caid's. "Either of you."

"We can promise to try not to," he said. The thickness building in his throat making his words gruff as he spoke.

"Come here, asshole." She waved him closer. "Oh, Jesus." She yelped and let out a squeak when he bear hugged her, lifting her off her feet. Her lips were warm as she kissed each of his cheeks. "I love you."

He held her tighter and buried his face in her hair. "I love you."

When he released her, she wiped at her face and gave them a small smile. "Now, get out of here. Go do that magic thing and make the world a better place for our kids."

Once they had made their rounds saying goodbye to the twins and Thomas, Caid drove them to Wyatt and Leslie's house. It had taken Caid years to open up to Wyatt about what had happened to Róisín, then to himself. Some days he wished he hadn't. That he had spared his best friend from knowing. Other days, he was grateful for Wyatt. And he would not leave again, knowing that he may not come back, without telling his best friend that he loved him.

"If you make it back, does that mean we're done beating the shit out of ourselves?" Wyatt had asked. "I know you're going to stay young forever and whatnot, but I need to remind you I am almost fifty and very much feel almost fifty."

"I dunno, man. Shit." Caid shook his head, "Lucius once told me it wasn't always like this, but…"

"It's always been like this to you," Wyatt finished.

"I want to believe it's better on the other side. I don't know, though. Hecate, she's the real Goddess or creator, whatever." He waved a hand. "She's a wild card. I can guarantee I'll see her again, given she's my great-great-grandmother—"

Wyatt spit his drink out and began coughing. "Say what now?"

"Wild, huh?" He scratched his jaw. "Her daughter decided she was done being a witch. By her not practicing anymore, the magic went quiet in her, my grandmother, then my dad."

"But you, Lina, the kids?"

Caid shrugged. "We didn't really get around to that part. She said there was more. Told us to take the night, live our lives. She'd be back. Then Matthew showed up at Lina's and everything went to shit."

"That had something to do with how damned long yesterday felt, didn't it? I swear that sun didn't move an inch for *hours*. Leslie said I had sunstroke and dragged me to bed."

"I don't know for sure, but I think it was." Caid ran a hand through his hair and stood. "If I don't come back..."

Wyatt pushed to his feet and wrapped his arms around him, giving him a firm slap on his back. "I love you, man."

Caid fought to keep his tears at bay. "I love you, too."

Wyatt sniffed and stepped back. "We'll find a way to each other on the other side. I know we will. If you... this won't be the last time we see each other."

Caid could only nod, his emotions thrashing inside like a storming sea.

The ride back to the cabin was quiet. Caid's eyes focused on the road ahead, while Róisín stared out her window, the wind making her hair dance around her face.

When they pulled to a stop in front of the cabin, he pat the steering wheel twice before climbing out and stepping around the back of the truck to where Róisín waited. Caid had expected her to take his hand as they had done so many times before when shifting. Instead, she moved so that they stood chest to chest.

She tipped her head back. "Kiss me."

"What?"

"You heard me, Mr. McGrath. Kiss your wife."

Something inside of him, next to his heart, settled into place and he could breathe again. She did that to him. Centered him. Calmed all the racing thoughts and the thunder of his heart. He bent his head and took her mouth with his. The sensation of the shift overtook him, just like a blink. He wanted to laugh against her lips at the thought as it came to him, but the smell hit him first, grasping right onto his gag reflex and yanking. His body tried to heave up the contents of his stomach.

They jerked apart. Caid backed up a step, his eyes burning and his stomach twisting tighter. He bumped against the Jeep parked in the cottage's driveway. Beneath their feet, the ground shook.

"What's that smell?" He asked. His stomach rocked and rolled harder, trying to heave up its contents.

Róisín studied the glen. "I don't know. Do you see anything? I can't."

He squinted. "I see—"

It appeared before them suddenly. It was as tall as the skyscrapers he had seen in New York and just as broad. Skin the color of night wrapped around it tightly. Its mass of muscles bunched and flexed as it moved. The sunlight caught it, revealing the texture of what looked like billions of small, finely pointed needles.

As it neared, not only did the smell of rotting skin grow stronger, but he could see the wisps of smoke dancing around it. Feel the heat radiating from it.

"What is that?" Róisín's voice was barely a whisper. "What is that?" Her voice grew louder. "What is that?" She tried to scramble back. "WHAT. IS. *THAT?*"

He brought an arm around her waist and pulled her against him. His voice a whisper in her ear. "You don't know?"

"I-I've never seen anything like it."

"We need to get out of here, now."

The thing, the beast, the *whatever* it was, snapped its jaw together. The sound sent a shockwave through the air, pressing them back against the side of the Jeep.

"Wait." Róisín gripped his arm tightly, nails digging into his skin. "What did it just say?"

"What?!" He whisper shouted. "It didn't say anything. It gnashed its fucking teeth at us."

"No, no, no." She pressed her fingers harder. "It did. It said something. Listen."

Caid's magic screamed at him in protest, but he didn't shift them away. Grinding his teeth together, he bent his body over Róisín's when it snapped its jaw again, sending another wave out.

"*Sssssstephennnnnn—*" it snapped again, smoke curling into the air from its mouth. "*MccccccccKennnnnaaaaaaaaa.*"

"Daddy?" Róisín's body tensed against his. Then she gasped. Her entire body tightening like a string on a bow. "I know what it is."

"Care to share?"

"It's one of the darkness's demon hounds. It broke through the veil."

"Hound?" He bent them lower to the ground as a tree sailed over their heads. "That doesn't look like a god damn dog to me."

"I don't think they're really dogs. They're trackers. Caid, it's looking for my father."

"Well, he's not here, and we shouldn't be either."

He adjusted his grip on her and readied to shift. Yet, it was too late. The demon had spotted them. It let out a bellow and smashed one of its feet against the ground. Caid braced against the riot beneath their feet and kept them both upright.

"You're going to do something stupid, aren't you?" He asked her.

"Yup," she said. Then she broke free of his hold.

"At least you admitted it this time," he grumbled before breaking into a sprint to follow her as she ran toward the demon.

FORTY-NINE

"HEY, PARKER, stop hitting on my lady," Matthew said from where he sat across the table from the blond-haired boy.

Parker's cheeks flamed red.

Matthew had yet to tell Lily about Róisín, or Caid. Before they had left Ely, he had gathered that Ione had told her about the veil, and that somehow Aja, Runa, and the others had already known most of what Matthew had learned about Gea.

Which left him filled with questions. And suspicion.

Jackson reached over to ruffle Parker's blond hair, giving him a wink. "When do we hit the road for Ireland?"

"Ireland?" Lily's attention shot to Matthew.

Now it was Matthew's cheeks that burned.

"Ah." Jackson winced and rose. "We'll get this cleaned up."

In a blink, it was just Matthew and Lily left in the room.

"Matthew."

"What?" He croaked out.

"Why are we going to Ireland? Is that where Shasta is? Are the others coming too?"

Matthew turned his hands palm up and sighed. Could he tell her everything here? Or would it be best to wait until they made it to

Ireland? He drained the water from his glass and decided on meeting in the middle.

"When Shasta found me, after she, Jackson and I talked, it just made sense. Jackson said they were all forbidden to leave Earth's realm. My parents worked triple time to keep mine and my mother's connection to the Aunellion Coven secret."

"Why?"

"Why what?" He leaned back in the chair and crossed his arms over his chest.

"Why weren't they allowed to leave Earth?"

"Jackson doesn't know. He just knows the punishment was incredibly strict if they tried. Now with what's been said about the Goddess... Steering clear of the other realms seems to be the safer bet until we get it sorted."

Lily stared at him for a moment. Finally, she rose from the table and set her napkin down. "I hope you don't expect me to ride there in a car."

Relief lightened the weight of his shoulders. "We've got to cross the Atlantic Ocean to get there."

"A boat? Oh, Hells no, Matthew."

"No. We'll shift. Once Jackson's ready, we can go." He came around the table. His fingers brushed along her arms, down to her hands. He wove their fingers together and lifted her hands, then pressed soft kisses to the backs of them. "I promise, when we get there, I'll tell you everything. Shasta will help it all make sense, because it still doesn't to me."

She gave him a small smile. "You better. I'd hate to turn you into a tree."

"We good?" Jackson ducked his head in and looked from her to Matthew.

"Let's get this show on the road," Matthew said. He leaned close to her ear. "I'll be right there, at your side. I promise."

She pulled back, her brows knotted.

"Onward ho!" Jackson hooked his arm through one of Matthew's.

Instead of the peaceful, serene glen that Róisín's cottage sat in, they arrived to a thunderous noise, and the reek of decay and sulfur.

A large creature let out a roar that had the trio flinching backward. Lily released Matthew's hand and clasped hers over her ears.

Róisín ran into their line of sight, full speed, toward the creature. She released a warrior's battle cry as flames engulfed her arms and she leapt into the air. Vines burst from the ground beneath her, rising quickly to create a stairway toward the beast.

"Róisín!" Caid's voice barked out from one side of the yard. "Here!"

Lily released her ears. One hand reaching for him, her fingers digging into his forearm.

"Matthew, the veil, Caid—"

"Jackson," Matthew snapped out. "Get Lily out of here. *Now!*"

"No, I can help!" She reached for him as Jackson looped an arm around her waist.

"Go, Lily. Please," Matthew said. "I need you to be safe."

She opened her mouth to argue, but Jackson was quicker.

WHAT FELT LIKE AN ETERNITY LATER, MATTHEW'S FEET SKID across the gravel of the drive, diving out of the way of an incoming stone spear. When Jackson returned, they had battled side by side. It hadn't been what Matthew had meant when he'd said to take Lily and go. Jackson had insisted he could hold his own, reminded him *again* that he too was a part of this.

And Jackson had indeed held his own. Getting back up every time he was knocked down. Wielding his magic with ease. Latching onto the demon like a dog hungry for bone. Matthew could only wonder what life for Jackson had been like for him to fight as he had.

It had been the roughly fifty-foot trip through the air into a tree, then landing on a rock, that had knocked him out.

Now, the demon had Caid trapped beneath the upturned Jeep. Another long stone spear holding it in place.

"Go!" Caid shouted at Róisín. "Get out of here!"

"You can just fuck right off, Kincaid McGrath," Róisín shouted back. She gripped the spear staff in her hand and it burned bright red.

Matthew paused long enough to let his brows fly upward in shock. Never had he heard Róisín speak like that. Not even when they were sparring in the training hall. And he had prodded, poked, and teased her.

"I can't do that if you're *dead*!"

Caid's retort had Matthew moving again. He dug deep, grasping hold of the other elemental magic he had. The fire shifted clear, making room for it to rise. Using the wind, he catapulted himself into the air, landing with a thud against the demon's massive chest. The heat at his hands burning the mottled, pricking skin with a hiss.

Matthew clawed his hands, in part to hold on as the demon swayed back a step, and partly to drive his fire deeper.

"Dammit, Caid, you're going to get yourself killed!"

He gripped tighter and tossed a look over his shoulder. Freed, Caid was now scaling a leg. His fingers were icepicks, gashing the leg. Black spurted from each puncture as he went. Róisín's body was glowing, brighter with each moment that passed.

"You heard what Hecate said," Caid's voice was growing closer to where Matthew was.

"She didn't... invincible. It... one moment... could be it. Be your fate," bits of Róisín's response drifted up to him.

The desperation in her tone was clear as the blue sky overhead.

Something shifted around them at that moment. The demon stilled. Everything quieted.

A blast slammed against Matthew's chest and he was sailing through the air. The sound in his ears was awful; high pitched and grating against his eardrums. It grew louder until his ears rung.

He braced for an impact that never came. Instead, as though a hand caught him, and righted him slowly, his feet settled on the gravel like he had just taken a small hop. He looked around him, searching for what could have been the cause of his soft landing when groaning near the front steps drew his attention.

"What the hell was that?" Jackson grumbled, rubbing at his temples.

Relieved to see him conscious, Matthew stumbled toward him. "Some type of demon I believe."

Jackson squinted up at him. "How much did I miss? Probably all of it, right?" Jackson tried to get his feet under him to stand.

"Five minutes? I don't really have an—" Matthew began.

"You stupid, *stupid* man," Róisín's half-shriek, half-sob cut him off.

Instead of helping Jackson up, Matthew dropped next to him. Together, they watched the battered pair before them.

"Ah, shit, that hurts." Caid hissed and winced when Róisín took his face in her hands. "Easy."

"What were you thinking?" She asked, her hands jerking slightly, making Caid's head shake. He winced again and squeezed his eyes closed.

"How long have they been together again?" Jackson asked.

"Seven years? Almost eight?" Matthew said.

"What was I thinking?" Caid's voice rose quickly before dropping again. "I was thinking I didn't want to watch you die," Caid said. "Again."

"That's it?" Jackson asked.

Matthew hummed and nodded.

"Did you think I wanted to watch *you* die? Again?!" Róisín shook Caid.

"They've been through a lot," Matthew said, rubbing at a tender spot on his jaw.

Jackson snorted. "I'd say so if they've both seen each other *die*."

Matthew had been there when Róisín had died. Had seen her lifeless body fall from the sky. Felt that frantic dance in his chest as his heart raced up his throat before it ceased all movement. He would never forget that fear that she was gone forever. How it made a thick, black rage bloom inside him as he raced off with Lucius to find Madigan. Nor would he forget the relief that flooding him, sent tears streaming down his face when he learned she was okay.

He shifted next to Jackson and watched Caid yank Róisín against him, his thick arms wrapping around her.

When Shasta had let Matthew see what had happened in Talista, he had seen the pain twist Róisín's face. The way it had changed her, had broken her, and the magic that spilled from her in the courtyard the moments after Caid had grabbed Madigan had reflected that.

The change to her face had been the most startling. Her eyes had shifted to complete black. Like an abyss. And the skin around her eyes became webbed with black veins. Her tears were bright red rivers flowing down her cheeks.

The power of her magic had felt different, felt new around Shasta and Caid's lifeless body. It felt unchained and wild, just as Caid's had when it had woken inside of him.

The magic Matthew felt still filling the air around them now was *far* more than that.

If he asked, would there be an answer?

"Ah, shit." Jackson hissed next to him. "I think my leg is broken."

"Pretty sure my entire body is broken," Matthew said.

Róisín had walked over to them and now stood at their feet. "Come inside, I can patch you all up."

Matthew blinked and looked up from the gash he was prodding with a finger on his arm. Caid was limping toward them, wincing with each step he took.

"You two kiss and make up?" Matthew nodded his head toward Caid.

Róisín glanced over her shoulder. "I guess it never really leaves us, does it?"

Matthew gripped the baluster of the bottom step and pulled himself to standing. He groaned when he straightened himself. Looking down at her bruised face, he frowned. "No. It doesn't. The only thing we can do is not let it take us down when it pays us a visit."

She let out a shaking breath and nodded.

He and Jackson leaned on one another, taking the steps to the door one at a time.

"Come on, you oaf. I need to get you healed up," he heard Róisín say behind him.

"You gonna kiss it better?" Came Caid's retort.

Jackson chuckled. "Fuck, that hurts. I miss Nadia. Damn, do I miss Nadia right now."

"You know the Trifoan mers have more life magic than we do," Matthew said offhandedly.

"What?" Jackson's step faltered, and they almost fell against the door.

"We've all got that drop that helps us heal a little faster and live a little longer." Matthew leaned his shoulder against the door to nudge it open. "It's not the same as Róisín's full life magic, but they have enough to heal others when they're hurt or sick."

Jackson's brows rose. "No shit?"

"I shit not," Matthew said before waving him into the cottage.

"I wonder if she even knows that. From what I gather, her folks don't talk about it much. Only enough to help them learn to control the change when they're in or near water."

"Parker?"

Jackson paused near the sofa. "Yeah. His dad is human, but I guess it doesn't matter. It isn't like when humans and witches have kids. Hit or miss. The mermaid magic is always dominant."

Matthew couldn't imagine how hard it was to be a parent of a mermaid child, surrounded by humans.

"Sit, all of you," Róisín instructed.

All three men hissed in pain as they fell to the sofa and chairs.

"How's your head?" She lowered in front of Jackson.

"Well, I had a Jeep thrown at me," he replied and shrugged. "Then I was chucked into the trees. So, it hurts. A lot."

"Here." She waved her hands for him to lean forward.

It was then that Matthew saw it. The glint of a small silver band on her left ring finger. How had he missed that yesterday? He let his gaze linger on it a moment longer before he shifted to look at Caid's left hand.

And saw a thicker silver band wrapped around his ring finger.

FIFTY

TWO YEARS AGO

THE BLADE cut through Róisín's side just below her ribcage from behind. She ground her teeth together, swallowing down the scream that wanted to break free as the searing pain burst through her body.

"We only need a bit of the magic, sweetheart," the deep male voice said behind her. "We won't leave you completely dead."

Her magic pressed at her. The heat from it making the sweat that had formed along her hairline drip down her neck, trailing along her spine. It wanted to break free. Create that explosion, just as it had in that house two years before.

But she couldn't. Caid was inside the building with her.

Moments earlier, she had heard his rage-filled shout, followed by the sound of gunshots. She tried to reach for him, but through the waves of pain thrashing her body, she couldn't locate just where he was. But she knew he was alive, he was okay. The steady beat of his magic at the center of her chest gave her that comfort.

Quietly, she let whispered words slip past her lips as fire engulfed her hand. The words from the worn, black, leather-bound book she had unearthed in one of the witches' black markets just weeks before. The book that pushed her a little further toward the edge. The book that revealed that even more of her life, the lives of the witches in the other realms, was nothing but lies.

Spell work was not only to create wards, or power exhausting glamours. Spell work helped gardens grow to feed more hungry mouths. It was for protection. For good.

Very few spell works existed for darkness. Cronan's book had been rare.

To only the realms beyond Earth it seemed.

On Earth, the falsehoods had been stripped bare, revealing the truth beneath. Piece by eye opening painful piece.

Spell works were good and bad, but only based on the intent of their user. And the well of spell works was bottomless. There was one for anything a witch could imagine.

Róisín had been drawn into the store front, by some unseen force. Drawn to the shelves, and one little black book in particular. She had flipped page after page, her magic growing warm and full within her body.

Now, as she turned to the witch that had driven the blade through her, she would put one of those spell works to use.

To send a message.

Because before had done nothing to stop their quest for her death magic. Not even when she decimated them.

"What—" The man's gray eyes widened.

Róisín tipped her head to one side. "You look cold," she said in a low, otherworldly voice.

He stepped back and lifted his hands. "No. No, no, no," he chanted.

There was no escaping. She let her magic glide her across the floor, lifting her hand of flame. Her palm lay flat against his chest.

"No. Please, no."

What was he seeing when he looked at her now that he hadn't seen before? What was it that had made him change from believing he could kill her and take her magic, to becoming a man filled with so much fear, he had soaked the front of his pants? His chin quivered as he repeated his plea once more.

"Please—"

"Burn."

The flame was pulled from her hand and into his body. The smell of burning flesh hitting her nostrils, making her eyes water. As the flame consumed him from the inside out, and his screams bounced from the stone walls, she turned her back to him.

She needed to find Caid. They needed to get out of there. She had made a mistake. *Again.*

After two years, this was proof that she still didn't know what she was doing. How was she ever going to stop Gea if she was still walking blindly into traps like she had in this run-down church?

No. She hadn't made a mistake.

Just as with the first Oathkeeper, they had just been trying to protect their families. Themselves. It was a dance that Róisín could understand.

Which was how this time, walking away from the burning witch was easier. That heavy stone that sank in her stomach when she saw the broken bodies littered around her the other times was absent as she neared a door at the back of the church.

Instead, a cold resolve settled over her.

Whatever she needed to do to keep her family safe. To keep herself alive.

Because she wasn't done yet.

Gea was still out there.

Róisín gripped the knob. It groaned as she turned it and the hinges protested loudly when she yanked the door open. Right as Caid drove a broken chair leg through the eye of a witch.

FIFTY-ONE
NOW

Róisín dropped her exhausted, weary body onto the top step of the porch. Resting her elbows on her thighs, she buried her face in her hands and blew out a breath.

Sleep. She had wanted sleep so badly, but she needed to hold on. The others would be there at any moment.

After what had just happened, she wasn't even sure that her sleep, when she got it, would be restful. She was sure that her mind would be ripe for a nightmare to bloom. After the one she'd just had...

The door closed quietly behind her.

"I'm sorry," she said, her face still in her hands. "I'm so sorry. You have every right to be angry with me." She had seen the way his lips curved down after spotting her ring. The way he had zeroed in on Caid's hand and noticed his.

I should have told him yesterday. I should have told him everything.

"I... I don't know how I feel." Matthew sat next to her. "I'm not mad that you did it. I think I'm just mad that I missed it." He scratched his jaw and nodded. "Yeah. I fucking missed my best friend's wedding."

"I'm sorry," she said again.

"Don't be. You two have..." He stretched his long legs out, then tipped his head from one side to the other. "You grab those little spots of happy, and peace whenever you can, how you can. Getting married? That was one of them. And"—He glanced sidelong at her—"Whatever you've needed to do to survive, you did it. *Both* things make me happy. I have just one question, though."

Her muscles tensed and her heart slowed to a crawl. She struggled to keep her voice even. "What's that?"

"Did he wear flannel at the wedding?"

The snort that escaped her sent her into a coughing fit and made her eyes water.

"It's an honest question." Matthew grinned at her.

"He wore a linen button up, actually." She looked out over the ruined yard.

"Wanna tell me what that was all about?"

"I—" She rubbed a hand down her face. "Things were different already when the power of my magic was restored at the well source." She released a heavy breath. "But after Caid–after... it was a lot. A *lot*. I couldn't control it. Do you know how embarrassing that is? After one hundred eighteen years, to not be able to control my magic anymore?"

"What happened?" He asked softly.

"I blew up. Literally."

"What?" He straightened. "Obviously you're alright. At least physically, but, shit, *how*?"

How much did she tell him? Could she ever find the courage to confide in him? Would he ever tell her about his days on his own after? What had happened in Aunellion with Lucius? They were all so broken, she couldn't help but wonder if they'd ever be whole again.

Róisín cleared her throat and crossed her arms over her chest. "I was in the wrong place, at the wrong time. It sort of"—She used one hand and gestured it in a circle around her upper body—"Just kept building inside of me. Getting really hot. Pressing against my skin. The more I tried to hold it in, the more it wanted out. And then I couldn't stop it." She made a fist, then spread her fingers. "Boom."

He motioned toward the driveway and the dark spot where the demon had been. "And that's what that was?"

She nodded. "It took forever, but I've finally learned how to control it. I think..."

Silence fell over them, and she found there were so many more things she wanted to say, wanted to tell him.

"Is it because you're not tied to us anymore? Because you severed that connection?"

She lifted a shoulder. "Honestly, I don't know. Maybe? Caid's magic has always been this wild energy in our connection. So noisy, and... thrashy."

Matthew nodded. "Sort of how yours feels when we're in the same room or near each other."

She turned to him. "Seed magic. It has got to be the seed magic."

"What?" His brows lowered over his eyes. "What in the Hells is that?"

"It's—"

"Well, this is a surprise," Ione's voice came from where she stood with a slack-jawed Runa in the garden.

Róisín straightened and tipped an eyebrow up. "What? That Ione Wallingsford didn't barge right in for a change?"

"Oh, that?" Ione waved a dismissive hand and started toward them. "I'm a changed witch. Runa's tamed my wild ways."

Runa's soft snort told Róisín otherwise.

"I'm referring to you." Ione pointed. "That's something both Shasta and Lily forgot to mention."

"Probably because Lily only just found out herself," Matthew said. He pushed to his feet and let out a small, pain-filled groan. "Where is she?"

"On her way with Shasta." Ione rolled her eyes. "She dropped in on us, said we needed to get here pretty much yesterday, because you needed help with—" She turned in a slow circle. "Something."

"We have it taken care of," Matthew said.

"I can see that," she said. "So." She looked Róisín over, then tipped her head to one side. "Now it makes sense why Shasta said we were to gather *here*."

"How much did she tell you?" Róisín asked. Her pulse hammered against the corner of her left eye. The sensation vibrated along her temple and covered her scalp.

"Not a lot. She knew where Sister Future was. We had to come here.

She and Aja blinked some type of code at one another." She shrugged. "Then we all were sent to get whatever we thought we'd need and told to be here."

"Except Lily caught us before we could get that far," Runa finally spoke.

"All of you?" Matthew asked.

"No, just Runa and I. Shasta had already gone to Helen. Aja and Anelle were gone before Shasta had finished saying the last word. Ten and Cicile went with Marcelo and Nolani," Ione said.

Róisín swallowed hard. Everyone that was left of their group would be descending on the cottage, in mere moments, most likely.

Runa's maroon eyes were on her. There were words he wanted to have with her. She could feel the tension coiled in his body from where she sat.

"And you're sure Lily's coming back here?" Matthew asked.

"I'm right here," Lily said. She stood next to Shasta, who was eyeing the turned over Jeep. "Are..." Her eyes darted from Matthew to Róisín. "Are you all okay?"

Matthew started down the steps toward her. He jabbed a thumb in Róisín's direction. "Perk of knowing a witch with the magic of life."

"What was it, do you know?" Shasta asked after she pulled her attention away from the ruined car, and back to them.

"It was a demon hound," Róisín said. Slowly, she rose. Her magic tickled beneath her skin. She knew it was trying to distract her. To lighten the heaviness that had settled inside. She wanted to tell it to take her away again. To flee.

Ione gasped and began cursing. Shasta's eyes grew round.

"That's not all." Róisín struggled to keep her voice even. To breathe. Everything inside of her was growing tight, and her magic fought to fight it, to soothe her. "It was looking for my father."

"Stephen? But he's in the afterworld still." Shasta's forehead wrinkled, and she frowned.

"Shasta and I saw him with our own eyes when we crossed," Ione added with an emphatic nod.

The screen door slammed shut and Róisín heard two pairs of feet cross the deck.

"*Hot damn*," Ione squeaked. "You made it through too?!"

"I never crossed," Caid said.

"Wha—how?" Ione moved past Róisín, up the steps. "You're warm."

"What's warm got to do with anything?" Jackson asked.

"Who are you?" Runa and Ione asked at the same time.

"Jackson. His cousin," Jackson said.

"You're warm," Ione repeated.

Róisín turned in time to see Ione poke Caid and for him to scowl down at her. "When the dead cross the veil, they're more cool to the touch."

"So you"—Ione tipped her head back and squinted at Caid—"Are very much alive." Her smile was blinding. Róisín could practically hear the woman's brain kicking into overdrive. "Which begs the question, how?"

Caid opened his mouth, but then closed it, pressing it into a thin line. Róisín saw his discomfort in the tense way he held his body, unmoving. They still hadn't spoken to anyone else about the hours after. The days after. The years. They had only given parts of it. Who Gea was. Tura. His thread...

"Let's go inside, give the others a minute to get here," Shasta said, pushing past everyone, moving toward the house. "Then we can go over it all, *one* time," she called over her shoulder.

Róisín felt her shoulders drop at the same time Caid's had.

"What you tell them about what happened is up to you," Matthew said next to her. "You know that, right? You don't need to tell them anything more than what relates to the Sisters, Hecate, and Gea."

She used the back of her hand to swipe at the fresh tears and nodded. He gave her shoulder a light squeeze, then went to Lily. After a moment, it was just her and Caid still outside.

He lifted his eyes from her and settled them on the Jeep. "I should probably find some time to get it fixed."

"Why? It's been sitting there, rotting for years."

Caid walked down the steps and cupped the back of her neck. "Maybe since seeing it, I haven't stopped thinking about a certain day..."

Despite everything, her core grew hot and tight.

"See?" He flashed her a quick grin. "I'll even get a top for it, so we can make it a four-season thing."

She laughed softly. "Damn you, Caid."

"Anything to not have to see you cry. It wrecks me when you do." He brushed his nose against hers. "I can't stand it when you hurt."

Róisín leaned into him. Bergamot, wood, and musk scents surrounding her, anchoring her. "I'm sorry I yelled at you."

His fingers threaded through her hair. With a gentle tug, she was looking up at him again. "I'm sorry I yelled back."

"Stay close? When the others get here?"

"Always."

Part Three

"The candle flame gutters. Its little pool of light trembles. Darkness gathers. The demons begin to stir."
——Carl Sagan, The Demon-Haunted World: Science as a Candle in the Dark

FIFTY-TWO

THE SOUND that crawled from Tura's throat, into her mouth to fall from her lips was unfamiliar and rough. She stumbled and sunk to her knees, her chest igniting with a searing pain.

What had she done?

She had abandoned them. Had left her people to her mother's hand. And this...

Blinking away the tears that crowded her vision, she saw the emptiness again.

Gone was the sprawling world of the afterlife for witches. No longer was the landscape dotted with the homes that sheltered each witches' afterworld, the roads and pathways that meandered, connecting them all.

Had it been her mother that had done this? Or was this just the natural action of things without Tura's magic present?

The keening picked up again in the distance and drove Tura to her feet. On shaking legs, she shuffled toward the sound. Her magic pressed at her, wanting release. The strain of repressing it exhausted her here more than it did on the other side of the veil. If she were going to contain it, she hadn't long.

For if she didn't release her magic so that the afterworld recognized her as its Queen, she would face the same fate that any living witch faced when they broke the veil.

Death.

The afterworld would claim her as a new soul and she would be forever lost.

The magic within stroked her spine, up, up, up, until it tickled her mind.

Her sisters needed her.

If she released her magic, their mother would feel the connection flare to life again. Then, all hope would be lost.

They would never win against her.

Tura's mind became thunderous and her temples throbbed.

"You shouldn't be here," a voice said to her left.

She came to an abrupt halt, her head spinning around, searching.

"It's not safe. Not with her wandering around with her monsters, screaming."

"Who are you?" Tura asked. She squinted through the dust that had kicked up from the wind that whipped across the deserted space. Faintly, she could make out the outline of a lean-to. "How are you here?"

"I think I should ask *you* those questions as you're the one that is new."

She took a cautious step forward. Would have taken more, but the keening was now pitched higher.

"They can smell you," the voice said.

If that's what I think it is, it's one of my children, of course they can smell me.

If it was what Tura thought it to be, she would have no choice but to use her magic. It would be the only way to drive it back to where it belonged.

Tura shook herself free of her thoughts. "Wait. You said someone was here?"

"The eery white-haired woman. She's been here for..." The voice trailed off. "I do not really know. I still do not understand how time works here. She's been here for a long time, though. Shouting for a lass named Tura."

Everything in Tura went still.

How? How had her mother still crossed without Tura's magic?

That had been the moment everything for Tura had changed.

The day she had come to the afterworld to welcome the new witches and send their magic to their inheritors, but no one had come.

Curiosity had struck her and she had wandered her Hells. The witches in the in-between that did not belong. There had been no traumas for them to heal from before they moved on. Their deaths having been natural.

In the belly of the darkness, she found witches locked away that had lived good, lawful lives and had pure hearts and souls. Yet there they were, being tortured by the demons.

Tura began watching her mother. Noticing how their mother touched her, just a simple brush of the hand over her shoulder, more often than her sisters. The only way a siphon could pull away another's magic or life force.

After weeks of quietly following her mother, she learned the truth.

Gea de Oro was not the Goddess of all witches as she had even convinced her daughters she was. She was stealing the magic of other witches at the gates to the underworld. Powers that she had craved for herself. Ones that could lift her status among them even higher.

When she couldn't meddle because fate ran far deeper, her mother was condemning them to the darkness once they crossed the veil.

Everything that Tura had known, had been a lie.

If it hadn't have been for her discovery, she would have never learned the truth. She would have never learned of Hecate.

Her sisters wouldn't be in danger.

"You're her, aren't you?" The voice dragged her back to the present.

Slowly, Tura nodded.

A figure moved from the lean-to. As it neared her, Tura automatically stepped back. "I'm not here to hurt you. It's not safe for you here. Now that I know it is *you* that is Tura, it's most certainly not safe for you."

Tura looked up and studied the man. Features of his face familiar, yet not. "Stephen McKenna."

His pupils flared briefly.

"The woman..."

"If I'm to read lips correctly, Shasta Fiero called her the Goddess," Stephen said.

Tura couldn't breathe. Everything inside of her squeezed tightly for one brief second, then stilled. "No," she croaked. "It can't be. She can't exist here like that. Not without..."

Stephen's hands were at her waist, holding her up.

"Shasta... you said Shasta was here?"

"She and another."

The ground at their feet trembled and the air around them grew hot.

"You must go," Stephen said. "I've been able to shelter from them. I do not believe you will have the same luck."

The laughter bubbled out of her, filling the silence that fell between them.

Stephen cleared his throat. "Are you alright?"

"Fate." She grit her teeth together so hard, her jaw creaked with the tension. She should have known better. She was Fate's forward hand. Despite her best efforts to keep half of herself locked away, she should have known better.

Fate always won.

In the end, no one was a match for it, and the destiny it wove. Not even Gea de Oro.

At that moment, seeing the large, looming figure wrapped in black smoke coming nearer, Fate was here to collect.

She had unknowingly set her own table, then sat down to dine at it. Was Sister Present watching this unfold on her loom? Would Sister Past tidy the lines these threads wove once the moment had gone to make it forever so?

Swallowing, Tura turned to face Stephen. If she was going to release her magic, even just a little, he needed to be prepared.

Especially should her real face be exposed.

"It is a pleasure to finally meet you, Stephen McKenna. I am Sister Future, known to many as Tura, Daughter of the Goddess." She glanced over her shoulder at the creature now recognizable as Crev, a demon in her guard of the darkness.

Stephen dipped his head and extended his hand. "Hello, Tura."

"I should also tell you, my mother is not a goddess. She's merely another witch. One that happened upon a stroke of luck and continues to try to grip it in her hands. And"—She pointed—"That is one of my children."

Stephen blinked at Crev. "Children?"

"One of my creations. They should also not be here." She faced Crev now. Her skin was burning and tight from the press of her magic. "I'll need to use some of my magic to send him back to the darkness. I apolo—"

The clicking noise from Crev's throat made her stop.

"Wait." She lifted a hand to her throat as if trying to slow her breathing.

Crev was nearly upon them now. The clicking he was emitting was clear.

"He..." Tura shook her head. Her mother had taken *her* children and set them out like hounds. Anger boiled inside of her.

"What is it?" Stephen was at her side now. His stance showed her he was ready to fight. Even if what they faced was over thirty feet tall, and pure demon. He hadn't been on her loom when he lived, but she had seen. Hecate had been her eyes in Earth's realm. In the great wars of Earth, Stephen had been a fierce warrior.

Of course he would fight and not back down.

Tura would have softened at the recognition of his kindness, his pureness, if not for what she had just discovered.

"My mother. She's still somehow able to use my magic. And she's using my children to search," Tura trailed off. Could she do it? Use just enough of her magic to force Crev back to the darkness, but not enough to send echoes of it through her connection with her mother?

She had to try. There wasn't a choice.

"Stephen, where is Brenna?"

"I-I don't know. She was in Evelyn's afterworld when they all disappeared. She couldn't leave. They were both trapped inside."

Tura pursed her lips and wrinkled her nose. No, whatever was happening in the Hells had nothing to do with her magic. It had *everything* to do with her mother. The question was, why? Turning back to

Crev, she interpreted his clicks for Stephen, settling the missing piece to the puzzle.

"Brenna McKenna," Tura said. "Where is Brenna McKenna."

Stephen's eyes grew round. His nostrils flared with his anger, his protective urge for his wife. "It's looking for Bren?"

It was. Because they had set to rights Brenna's misplacement in the hells. She was never meant to go to the in-between. She was always to go to the afterworld to be with her father. With her friends. To cross and help Róisín and the others when it came time to face Madigan, to face Gea.

To reset the balance.

Like a combination lock, the last number rolled into place and clicked.

And forced Tura's hand.

Fighting to keep the full power of her magic at bay, she stepped toward Crev.

FIFTY-THREE

SHASTA PINCHED the bridge of her nose with her thumb and forefinger, then squeezed her eyes closed. Tension, uncertainty, and fear had filled the room as what everyone knew to that point had been woven together. The puzzle pieces fitting tidily.

It wasn't a drink that she had wanted. It was Evelyn.

Oh, how she missed Evelyn.

Slamming into her all at once, her head was pounding a full concert at her temples.

Evelyn's soft skin beneath her hands. The hearty, full sound of her laugh. The sweet smell of berries and pine that was her scent. How her lips tipped up just a little more on the left than the right when she smiled.

Her heart was beating sharply against her ribcage.

Would she ever have the chance to tell Evelyn that she loved her again? Even if it was just one more time?

The room around her had fallen silent. Aja had given them all that he had known, what Jessamyn had known and done. Then Shasta and Ione covered what they knew of the afterworld, what Brenna, Stephen, and Evelyn had told Shasta.

Then Róisín spoke.

Uncertainty had radiated from Cicile and Ten, who sat on the far side of the room, preferring to observe and take notes instead of interacting. Anelle had tucked herself behind a chair, leaning against a windowsill. Her eyes remained steady on her brother's, even when he was not talking, leaving Shasta sure that they were having a quiet conversation in their minds.

Ione and Lily sat on a low sofa. Their energy pulsing through the room had worried Shasta. Something had happened with the sisters.

Shasta tipped her head to one side, studying the sisters now. Ione's jaw flared with how tightly she clenched it. She wanted to speak, but was holding whatever it was in. Lily's eyes were downcast, her hands clasped so tightly, her knuckles had bleached white.

Had it been Nanette?

Róisín's slow intake of breath drew Shasta's attention. From the way Aja's large hand drew down his face, she knew she had missed something. So lost in her thoughts and emotions, she hadn't been paying attention when she needed to be the most plugged in she had ever been in her life.

"You can go back to Shianshani," Róisín said, her voice low and deep. "I have spent the last six years here, with witches at my back, trying to take my head off, piecing all of this together and searching for her without *you*. I can keep going without you."

Runa's jaw flexed and his nostrils flared. On the sofa beside where he stood, Ione rose. Her brows were pinched as she looked from Runa, to Róisín, and back. She gave Runa a slight shake of her head.

"You all can," Róisín said, louder. Her eyes moved around the room, settling on Shasta for a moment, before she looked at Caid. She held his gaze as she spoke to the rest of the room. "Shianshani. The afterworld. You're not bound to the need to be here. *I* am. And I have enough shit to deal with from the witches here in this realm." She turned back to Runa. "I will not have another seething in a corner over every breath I take. Now, if you'll excuse me, I'm going to go outside, scream obscenities at the trees, then go back to what I was doing."

The room remained still and silent as she walked out. After the front door clicked closed, Aja smacked the back of Runa's head.

"The fuck?" Runa rubbed at the spot.

"You're an idiot," Aja said.

Ione hummed her agreement, which shocked Shasta.

Marcelo cleared his throat from where he stood behind Shasta. She shifted to face him and Nolani. Nolani had her bottom lip captured between her teeth. Her eyes darted around the room before they settled on Marcelo and she dipped her head.

The couple had been the only ones in the room that Shasta had felt hope radiating from.

"What if..." Marcelo shifted his weight from one foot to another. "What if this is all tied together?"

"And if with Gea's death, everything, even what has happened with Celo and Anthony, are—" Nolani shifted her hands back and forth in front of her, "put back to rights?"

A jumble of noises bouncing between Ten and Cicile had everyone looking away from the couple.

"They could be on to something," Ten said. She snapped her fingers at Ione and pointed to the tablet she held in her hands. Despite having access to technology far easier than before, the cousins still opted for pen and paper most times out of habit.

Ione rose and handed Ten her tablet, then crouched on the other side of the coffee table to skim over the loose papers of the notes the cousins had taken by hand.

A tense, heavy quiet settled over the room as the trio combed over every word spoken in the last few hours.

Shasta rubbed at her chin and turned back to the others just as Caid and Aja were giving one another a nod. As Aja passed Caid, he pat his shoulder. When Caid saw Shasta watching the interaction, he tipped his head toward the front door.

"I think Celo and Nolani are onto something," Ione half-mumbled the words as she spoke. "But we're missing something." With papers in hand, she stood.

"What possibly could we be missing?" Lily asked. She uprooted herself from her spot on the sofa and joined her sister.

Ione scratched her nose, then blinked down at her papers. "That's what we need to figure out."

"Why don't we call it for the day? It's late, and we're probably all hungry." Shasta attempted her best menacing squint in Runa's direction. By the way his shoulders dropped and his chin hit his chest, she could only guess it worked. She hadn't known what prompted Róisín's words, but the way he had held his body tight and tracked her every movement, something was there. Something was wrong.

Runa had promptly buried himself in Coven affairs so that he could take the steps needed to relinquish his role as leader to Aja. Then everything had fallen apart shortly after. Never had he taken the time to grieve the loss of his sister.

Shasta caught Anelle by the wrist as she made to slip by her. "Go to Trifoa and check-in with Beatrice on the refugees."

Anelle's red eyes brightened.

"Be careful and return by morning."

"Are you sure?" She asked.

Shasta kept her voice low when she replied. She didn't know who else had observed the pair together to see what had been so crystal clear to her. "Am I sure that I want you to have what could be one last moment of peace with the woman you love, Anelle? Yes, I am."

In a rare display, Anelle threw her arms around Shasta. She pressed a warm kiss to her cheek. "Thank you." When she pulled back, she frowned. "What about Aja?"

"He knows you're our best at stealth. Lying by omission is something that I'm not above, sweetheart." She smoothed the backs of her knuckles over Anelle's cheek. "I've sent you off to slip into the realms to check on our refugees. Yours and Beatrice's story is not mine to tell. He'll know only what I tell him."

Anelle placed her hands on Shasta's shoulders. "Thank you."

And then, she shifted away.

The only ones remaining with her were Jackson, who had stood in the background, silent and taking everything in, and Matthew and Caid, who were staring at one another, unblinking.

"You two." She looked first to Matthew and Caid, then to the back door. "Take it outside. Talk first. Then hit each other. But only if need be. Have whatever it is settled by seven. We're all going to sit down and have dinner like one big, happy family."

Before any of them could respond, Shasta stalked from the room, toward the kitchen.

FIFTY-FOUR

THE SCREEN door creaked open behind Róisín. By the heaviness of the footfalls down the stairs, she knew it was Aja. She drew in a breath, holding it as he lowered onto the bottom step beside her. Waiting.

She had felt it in the collective way everyone had straightened when she had spoken to Runa. The shock. They had never seen that side of her. Hells, Róisín hadn't even known that she could *be* that person she had been in her living room moments before.

There had been glimpses of her. That night in Roidon with Madigan and Aoife. Each interaction with Madigan in Talista. It hadn't been until she lost it all, and something inside of her had snapped, never stitching itself back together.

For six years, she had also been the one with the higher knowledge of magic, their people. She had been the only one who could read multiple languages. The reins were at her feet, and she'd had to grasp them to move them forward.

Everyone was together again, but that hadn't changed that for Róisín. She could recognize the importance of repairing and restoring Shianshani for their people. Of what was happening with their after-world. However, she knew above all else, the most important piece that needed to be removed from the board was Gea. She didn't know how to fix the curse that the brothers still bore, or how to make Shianshani safe again. Her gut told her that cutting the head off of the snake would not only be their best path to freedom, but possibly the only way to set *everything* back to rights.

"Jes had gone to the Northern Prindell Province with her mother and Runa when he—" Aja cleared his throat, "when they needed our well source to strengthen the magic needed with the spell work to remake him as he had been meant from the beginning."

Slowly, as quietly as possible, Róisín released her breath through her nose.

"When Jes came home, something was different. We had never truly followed the Goddess." He rested his hands on his thighs. "Our Coven always walked the line necessary to retain her support. But Jes... she always felt something was off about her. None of us had ever spoken with her. She was just as mystical to us as the humans' Gods or Goddesses." He lifted a hand and pointed to the cloudless sky. "Someone living there, watching us, never interacting."

"I guess you could say I'm questioning my religion..." Her conversation with Lina all those years ago filtered back to her.

"That trip sparked something in her. For a while, it was scary how much it consumed her. Diana tried to bring her back to us, to pull her back together and refocus her." He shook his head. "She was lost to it."

Róisín shifted slightly so she could see him fully.

"It was by chance that she stumbled on some type of summoning spell." He rubbed his jaw where the joint fluttered briefly. His eyes fell closed and his shoulders drooped. "I was with her when she tried it the first time. I didn't trust the words. We didn't know where they had come from and by then, she had shut Diana out because of Diana's insistence that she stop."

Róisín's voice cracked as she spoke. "What happened when she tried the summons?"

"Hecate came."

She couldn't stop her hand from shooting out and grasping his wrist. "Aja."

"That first time was so messy. Jes and Hecate were both talking at once. I couldn't keep up. Jes was asking question after question, while Hecate was trying to explain who she was, *what* she was. Jes got weaker and weaker, and the magic that was holding Hecate there just... couldn't anymore."

"Aja."

"It was the second time she told us about you."

She squeezed his wrist tighter. "Second?"

He nodded. "Jes wanted to do it again almost immediately. It took so much out of her, she was in bed for days. I didn't leave her side because I feared the moment I left, she'd do it again, and to be honest, I didn't trust Hecate. I didn't trust that she was who she claimed to be, or what her motives were. While Jes recovered, Diana and I tried to find some mention of her in our texts. When Diana wanted to see if anyone had an oral history about Hecate, something inside of me panicked."

"You didn't ask anyone."

"Not a soul." He shook his head again. "I made Diana swear to secrecy, and when Anelle came looking for me after a few days, I said nothing to even her."

"What I know of this whole situation, it's good that you trusted your gut," she said.

"I don't know. Some days I wish I had told someone else. Then maybe Jes would still be here. Maybe we would have been able to change her fate."

Róisín thought of Caid. What Hecate had said about Gea ripping his thread from the loom. A direct interference with fate, which was how he had come back.

Only because fate isn't done with him yet. A small voice niggled at the back of her mind.

Her magic grasped for it, chased the voice down, trying to catch it and shove it deep down inside of her. To protect her.

"There wasn't anything you could do, Aja," she said. "If fate marked it, it would have happened regardless."

He glanced at her sidelong. "Just one more day would have been enough. Just one more day so that her last seconds wouldn't have been with a knife in her heart as she plummeted to the ground."

It was a feeling Róisín knew too well. "Tell me about the second time, please. Something tells me that's why you're out here, right now, letting me know all of this. That you're not out here to smooth things over, or make excuses for whatever is up Runa's ass."

His chuckle was a low rumble as it rolled from his chest. "He'll come around. His behavior is out of character at the moment, and I think that's because by seeing you, he's forced to actually face Jes's death. He can't run from it anymore like he's been doing." He pulled her hand free of his wrist, then clasped it between his. "The second time, both of them were far more rational. Jes asked questions, Hecate answered. Then Hecate told us everything about Gea, the Sisters, and you. At first, admittedly, we thought it was something like a prophecy. When you came to save our jungle, Jes had wanted to go to you, to meet you."

She studied his profile. The firm line of his jaw. The way his joint flexed, flaring near his ear when he clenched his molars together. "Why didn't she?"

"In Hecate's words, the stars had yet to be cast by fate."

"What in the hells does *that* mean?"

Aja shrugged.

"Wait." Róisín blinked. "When I was in Shianshani..." She began mentally ticking off the years.

"What is it?"

"Caid hadn't been born yet."

His brows knotted.

"That's what Hecate meant by fate not having cast the stars yet." As another piece of the puzzle clicked into place, her body hummed. The vibration of her excitement caused the hair to rise along her arms and up her neck. "Caid was a part of whatever it is that I am. Our fates have been woven together since before we were even born. Hecate had been waiting for *him* because it was he who would re-awaken *their* magic."

"Shit."

"What was the prophecy, or,"—She shook her head—"I mean, what did she tell you about me?"

"That it all lay with the last witch of Legianne. The witch that could bring the realms together and would end Gea's rule over us. That a witch of earth and water would free the children of fate."

284

Róisín's heart stalled, and she struggled to take in her next breath. *"Unite the Covens..."*

Surely that had *not* been what Gea had meant when she said those words to Róisín in the Dead Forest. It didn't make sense.

Did Gea know Róisín's fate? Could she read Tura's loom?

"By freeing the realms of Gea's rule, it would free Hecate from the walls that lock her out," Aja said. "The balance of power would be restored above and below."

"The veil." Róisín's words were a soft whisper.

"That's the only thing I can think of, yes. Except we knew nothing was wrong in our Hells. Jes, she—" His chin fell to his chest.

"Did Jessamyn know?" She moved closer, but hesitated to reach for him. To what, comfort him? Could she? Should she? Admittedly, she barely knew him.

"She knew she would be a part of it. She would help you do what you needed to do." His voice grew thicker as he spoke. "She also knew that she wouldn't get to see our freedom, or Hecate's."

Róisín's breath caught. Jessamyn had fallen from the castle parapet, believing it was that pivotal moment. Yet, it hadn't been. It had, however, been the catalyst. So much had gone wrong. So many pieces were still missing.

"I failed, Aja. I failed Jessamyn."

He lightly squeezed her hand. "No, you didn't. You're here now. We knew nothing about Caid's part in this. Hecate always said 'the last witch of Legianne,' so we could only deduce that it was all tied to one. You." His eyes moved across the glen, shifting slowly as he took it all in. "But... a witch of earth and water..."

"Would be Caid." She scratched her chin. Her thoughts were bouncing around inside, smashing against her skull. She tried to piece them together, feeling that something was still missing.

Aja nodded. "It would appear that all of us are pivotal to this."

"Well, that won't work because we're not all on board."

He glanced over his shoulder at the door. "I'll handle Runa."

"I don't want you to have to do that, Aja."

He rose and tipped his head from one side to the other. "He refused to step into the role of Coven leader after Jes's death and named me in his place." He extended his hand to her. Without hesitation, she took it and let him lead her toward the door. "I've yet to need to do more than get our people to safety, so we can consider this my first true act as Coven leader." He stopped at the screen door. "Besides, Jes isn't here anymore to tell me to stop punching him." He gave Róisín a wink before opening the door.

She hesitated at the threshold, turning back to him. "Thank you, Aja."

"You did what you had to do. We've done what we've had to do. In the end, we're here, right now. That's what matters. We take what we all know and go from there, working together."

A throat clearing in the front hall had her turning. Runa's brows kissed and his mouth was turned into a deep frown. "Could I... Do you have a minute?"

Róisín looked over her shoulder at Aja. He was watching Runa. After a moment, he gently cupped Róisín's elbow and gave a shallow dip of his head before squeezing by them and disappearing into the cottage.

"Walk my mother's path with me?" She lifted one of her arms and motioned toward a small path that wove around the gardens closest to the house and out into the glen.

Runa's face relaxed. "I'd like that."

FIFTY-FIVE

"DON'T YOU dare say you're sorry," Matthew said. "Don't you dare. I still don't understand what happened, how you're here. I'm not going to question it. I'm just really fucking glad you are. Not just for Róisín, she really deserves to be happy, to be loved like you love her, but..." He gave himself a second to swallow the thickness that had filled his throat. He ran a hand through his hair and shrugged, trying to feign casualness. "For me, too. Call me selfish, but I kind of like having you around."

Caid straightened. His arms still crossed over his chest. The fingers on his biceps flexed. "Why? So you can throw me under the bus the next time you take me to fight a Krogor?"

Matthew's heart stopped and the silence that fell over them was heavy. Then Caid snorted, quickly covering his mouth to stifle the chuckle that followed.

"You fucker." Matthew punched him lightly in the shoulder and grinned at him.

"You gave me the perfect opening. I'd have been an idiot not to take it."

Matthew swatted at him. Laughter bubbled up inside him and he had to press his lips together tightly.

Shasta had scolded them like schoolchildren, misreading their stances as though they were readying to fight one another.

"So," Jackson drew out the word. "You two aren't going to punch each other?"

Caid shook his head, and Matthew said, "Nah. You and Shasta have it wrong. I'll grab us something to drink. Let's go out to the patio and talk?"

"I'm gonna go check in with Nadia." Jackson jerked a thumb toward the stairs. "I'll come out after."

"He seems pretty unfazed by all of this," Caid said.

"Given he was kept more up to speed on our Aunellion roots and whatnot, it doesn't surprise me. This is probably just another day for him." Matthew shrugged.

Caid was silent for a moment. Then he turned toward the back door that led to the patio.

"Hey, Caid?"

He stopped and turned.

"I'd have done the same damned thing. You two have made the choices you've had to in order to stay alive. No one can fault you for that. Even the others."

Matthew's heart hammered through his chest, crashing against his lungs as Caid's hazel eyes took him in.

Finally, Caid spoke. "Even if they did, it wouldn't change any choice I've made. I'd make them all again." He ran a hand through his hair. "And if any of them can't get over it enough to be a part of this, to help us? I won't stop them."

With that, he turned on his heel and disappeared through the door.

Matthew hadn't been sure what the deal had been with Runa in the living room. Judging by Aja and Ione's reactions, they did. And neither agreed. The others? Matthew had to admit he didn't know.

He had been so steeped in finding his family, learning more about Lucius, fighting the reality that no, Lucius would not walk back in the front door of the manor hardy and whole, and juggling the Shianshani refugee situation, that he had paid little attention to any of the others.

Even Lily.

"Are you okay?" Lily asked, almost as though he had summoned her with that heart crushing thought.

He wrapped his arms around her and pulled her against his chest. "I'm so shit at this relationship thing, Lily. I'm sorry."

"What's this all about?" She asked, her voice muffled by the fabric of his shirt.

"If I'd been better at it, I would have pushed you to tell me what was wrong sooner. You wouldn't have had to shoulder all of that on your own. I could have been there for you. Supported you. Held you." He squeezed her tighter.

"I wasn't exactly doing a bang-up job myself, Matthew. Between fighting with Ione about it, and finally talking to you about it," Her breath hitched. "I realize I should have been more forthcoming. We're a unit, but we can't be when one of us is hiding from the other."

Matthew stroked a hand over her hair. "I knew something was off, but instead of coming to you, I just waited. That's on me. No matter how you spin it."

He wasn't sure what drove him to that new desperation he felt. That push to hold Lily so tightly, she became a part of him. His heart was still thrashing in his chest and his lungs ached with how tightly they squeezed.

"I want everything between us in the open, always." He pressed a kiss to the top of her head.

She let out a small squeak when his arms tightened again. "Matthew, you're squeezing too hard."

"I'm sorry. I just..." He forced himself to loosen his grip and step back. Cupping her face in his hands, he tipped it up to his. "I don't know. I'll apologize until the day I die, then I'll cross the veil every day after to keep apologizing."

Lily brought a hand up to cover his on her cheek. "I'm sorry, too, Matthew. I should have been honest. I know I can't take that back, but can you be patient with me while I learn?"

"We'll be patient with each other. As I work to be a better partner, and you work to not bottle everything inside." He brushed her hair over her shoulders. Stepping closer, he pressed a kiss first to her cheek, then against the side of her neck. When he kissed her bare shoulder, she laughed softly. "You're a very petite person, Lily, and I'm awful at puzzles. If you keep trying to hold it all in"—He swept his lips over her collar bone—"you'll explode. I'll try my best to put you back together, but you can't blame me when your nose is where your knee is supposed to be."

Her head fell back as her laughter exploded out of her. The sound of it and the feel of her skin beneath his lips, loosened and calmed his chest.

Lily gave him a slight nudge. "I love and adore you, Matthew McArthur. Now, if you'll excuse me, I was actually down here to grab some water for everyone. I should probably do that before Ione calls some cavalry somewhere."

"Has she said anything about what she thinks is missing in all of this?"

Lily shook her head and frowned. "Her instinct has never been wrong, though. Which means there's something we've either over-looked, or haven't found yet."

Matthew blew out a harsh breath and ran his hand down his face with a groan. "Fuck."

FIFTY-SIX

TWO YEARS AGO

CAID HAD fucked up. But he couldn't think about that now. The broken chair back swung toward his head and he ducked low, spinning and kicking his leg out. Right into the side of the blond-haired witch. Four others lay dead on the floor around him in the small back room of the abandoned church in Prague.

A groan to his left drew his attention, almost costing him his head when the blond witch swung the chair toward him again.

Make that three witches dead. The one he had just shot, close range in the chest with the last three bullets of the gun he had wrestled away from the first witch he'd killed, kicked his legs against the ground, trying to gain purchase and roll over.

Caid clenched his teeth and moved quickly. He dodged another incoming blow as he raced across the space, dropping low to swipe a stray blade from the floor. His lungs burned with the exertion of the fight that his body had been in for the last several minutes, or hours. He no longer knew.

He only knew that he had to get out of that room. He had to get to Róisín.

That he still felt her presence inside of himself, her heart beating next to his as it had been doing every day since he had come back, had been the only thing that kept him from letting his magic completely take over and rage.

He knew what the result of that would be. The bodies ripped apart and blood painting the walls of a warehouse office had shown him just what he was capable of when he let his magic lead. Róisín's heart had been a slowing thump next to his. Fading. And he'd snapped.

Caid drove the blade into the neck of the squirming witch, then pushed to his feet just as the blond was advancing on him again. The chair back slammed against his forearm, sending it splintering more. He caught one piece, spinning it in his hand for a better grip. Drawing his arm back, he used all of his remaining strength to swing forward. The chair piece made a squelching noise as Caid made contact with the witch's eye socket. Just as he was driving it deeper, the door to the room swung open.

The witch crumpled to the floor and Caid spun to Róisín.

"Are you okay?" They asked one another at the same time.

"Your face," Róisín said. Her frown was so deep, it looked as though her lips were going to touch her jawline. "We need to get you home so I can heal you."

"I'm fine. Where's the Oathkeeper?" He looked around the room for something to wipe his hands on before he went to her. Never would he touch her with someone's blood on his hands. That had been a promise he had made himself that first night they had found themselves two against many.

"She..." Róisín swayed. She reached out and gripped the door handle. "She left after she gave me the information on the necklace."

When she swayed again, Caid was at her side, arms wrapping around her. Pulling her up, against his chest, he shifted them to the cabin.

Róisín had passed out, her eyes closed and face pale. Her magic poured from her body, leaving a hot metallic scent in the bedroom around them. Gingerly, he tugged her t-shirt up, revealing two large gashes at her side.

"Lina..." his magic hissed at him.

"No. She doesn't need to see this. I can take care of her."

"The Oathkeeper."

Caid's head snapped up.

"You made... promisssssssssse."

The Oathkeeper had broken her promise. Just as Caid had known she would. However, unlike her, Caid had never broken a promise in his life. He had no plans to start now.

"Oh, that's so fucking cool. It really *is* a blink," Lina whispered as she shoved into the bedroom, the door slapping against the wall from the force of her movements. Harsher, she demanded, "Where is she?"

Caid turned to face her, but before he could move to block her view of Róisín, Lina's eyes grew wide.

"What hap—" One of her hands slapped over her mouth, her eyes growing wide. "Holy Jesus, *fuck*." The words sounded jumbled behind her hand. "Did she get stabbed with a giant steak knife?!"

"How?"

"I've felt you both all morning. I don't know what happened, and I don't really care to. The kids are at daycare for the next four hours, so move out of my way." She shoved around him and gingerly lowered herself onto the edge of the bed to look at the wounds closer. "Why isn't her magic... you know... doing the thing?" She tugged on her own shirt. "Shit, it's hot in here."

"*That's* why it's hot in here. Her magic is trying to heal her."

"Alright." Lina rose and tugged her long-sleeved shirt off. "Boo-boo stuff in the bathroom?"

Caid nodded.

"I'll get her cleaned up and sit with her while she heals. You"—She quickly looked him over—"Go get whoever the hell did this to her."

"Thank you, Leen." He leaned forward and pressed a quick kiss to the side of her head before shifting away.

IT TOOK HIM TWO HOURS TO GET A TRAIL ON THE PRAGUE Oathkeeper. Another thirty minutes to bribe his way into the den in which she spent her time.

"I didn't break my promise," she said, not looking up from her cards when he walked through the velvet curtains of the room. "I gave her everything she needed to know about the necklace."

Caid stood silently across the table from her. Her skin was a creamy white, almost like it had never seen the light of day in however many years she was old. Her mahogany-colored hair was piled atop her head in thick dreadlocks, secured by a length of red leather strapping. Brightly colored feathers hung from her ears.

Flipping a card over, she lifted her gaze to him. Her orange eyes alight with curiosity. "Would you like me to read your cards?"

Still silent, he moved across the room. His magic rose inside of him, wrapping around him. It urged him to let it lead this dance.

No, Caid said to it. *We do this together. I want her neck in my hands.*

"Sit." She gestured to the chair across from him. "Unlike my human clientele, I promise to read my cards true."

He lowered into the chair. Placing his elbows atop the table, he leaned his upper body over the cards. They were nearly face to face. "You've already broken one promise to me." His voice was low, rumbling. "Why should I trust you won't do it again?"

"I gave her the photo of the necklace. It's last known whereabouts." The Oathkeeper swallowed loudly. "I was not lying when I said I did not know where it is now. Probably for the best. You two are crazy to look for that bitch, Gea. She'll eat you up like she has with the witches in the other realms."

"It's no different from what you all have tried to do to us here."

The Oathkeeper blinked.

"I told you what would happen if you broke your word. If you let the wolves in. All you had to do was give us the information we sought. But instead, you whistled."

The Oathkeeper tried to stand, but Caid reached out quickly with both hands and snagged their wrists.

"Sit." He watched her tongue dart out over their bottom lip. "Unlike you, I *promise* to keep my word."

"I—" The rest of her words died off as ice moved from her fingertips, swallowing them instantly.

Caid released his hold on her wrists and stood. The sound of the den outside the door had risen in the few minutes he had been in there. The patrons already drunk and rowdy. He started for the door, but stopped and turned back to the Oathkeeper.

Her crystalline form was frozen with eyes wide, earrings flared out from the movement of her head in mid-shake. Mouth still open with the words left unspoken.

To his right sat a small table with trinkets atop. He picked up a small rose carved from cherry wood. Stroking his thumb along one of the petal edges, he knew he would be a fool to ignore fate. As he moved back to the door, he tossed the rose toward the Oathkeeper. The sound of shattering ice followed him through the curtain.

When he got back to the cabin, he found Lina sprawled out on their bed, next to a still sleeping Róisín. Her words were low and whispered as she stroked Róisín's hair.

"The wounds have healed," Lina said to him, but kept her attention on Róisín. "She hasn't woken yet. I remember when she was in the hospital after you both fell. The way her magic burned her."

It was a glaring reminder to him that Lina had known of Róisín magic much longer than he had. The fear and uncertainty that had filled him in the hospital room after their fall tickled along the edge of his senses now. She had been in pain that day, brutally so, and he had yelled at her. Had walked out on her. Because he was scared. Scared to lose her.

"She was burning up, so I kept patting her down with a cloth. Like I did then." She shifted so that she was sitting up now. "I think she was badly hurt inside, and it's still healing her. She isn't as hot, but you'll need to keep an eye on her. Help her stay cool."

"Leen." He held open his arms and motioned her over.

"I filled a pitcher with water and put it in the fridge. She'll need that when she wakes."

"Leen."

Finally, she swung her legs over the edge of the bed and rose. He expected her to slowly lean against him, instead, she crashed against him. Her arms wrapping tightly around his waist.

"I don't know what happened. I don't care what happened. I only care that you two are okay, and whatever it was has been taken care of," she said.

"We will be and it has."

She stepped back.

"You really don't have to be a part of this, Leen. The closer we get, the messier it'll get. It always does. This won't be any different."

Pressing her lips together, she nodded. "I want to be with you two for as much of it as I can. I don't know about until the end." She looked over her shoulder. "But this stuff? Please don't push me out. Let me be here. For you both. Okay?"

"Okay." He brought his arms around her and pulled her in for another hug.

She was old enough to make her own choices, and he knew he couldn't keep her away from the dark side of this new life of theirs. But it would not stop him from trying.

FIFTY-SEVEN
Now

CAID'S THUMB swiped at the condensation on the sides of his glass, his mind lost to the memories of Prague just two years before. He knew Róisín had tried to absolve him of the guilt he had felt. Had tried to take it for herself. He had been the one to track down that Oathkeeper. Something about her had caught his attention. She had known too much about Gea. More than any of the other witches they had met.

A flock of birds flew overhead, crying out as they soared.

Róisín hadn't known that he had gone back. What he had done. Lina had only known he had handled it. She didn't know how. It was his secret to keep.

His fingers tapped the glass. He had never let the thoughts creep in that he had made a mistake in not telling Róisín. Not even when she'd struggled with her own actions.

Caid squeezed his eyes closed. He was a piece of shit. He needed to go to her. To tell her.

"We keep the things in the dark," his magic repeated to him.

Except this time, he ignored it. Shut it out. Slowly, the dark, smokey feel of it disintegrated.

"You two make a good team," Matthew said from where he sat across from him.

Caid blinked, clearing his thoughts, and lifted his attention to him.

"I mean, you two have always made a good team." He shrugged. "That"—He gestured toward the front yard—"was a different type of teamwork, though. You two have been through some shit."

Caid noted it was clearly a statement, not a question. "The witches here are... different."

"How so?"

"Well, they're noisier than you and the others for starters," Jackson said, joining them. "Do you all have something against alcohol in this group? This was shoved all the way in the back of the fridge."

"Aja stocked the fridge, which means he probably did so with Shasta in mind," Matthew said. "Odds are, it's a holdover from the last time we were all here."

Jackson took a long drink from the bottle and immediately spit it out. "What the hell is this garbage?"

Matthew chuckled. "Almost seven-year-old beer is what that is."

"That's awful." Jackson used the back of his hand to wipe his mouth.

Caid looked away from him and found Matthew staring back at him. "She didn't start again, did she?"

Matthew shook his head. "No. She's been sober since dad..." His voice grew thick, choking off his words. He cleared his throat. "It's a precaution. Aja's been like her big brother since Talista happened. Well" —He let out a soft snort—"Bigger only in the sense that the dude is massive. I think he's a good two centuries younger than her. Give or take."

Caid mentally noted that he needed to really talk to Shasta. To check in with her. She was the one who had been there to help him when his magic woke. While Róisín recovered, Shasta worked with him on learning how to work with his magic. Then, she had been the one to unlock the door to lead him to his Coven's roots. She had looked out for him. And, when he noticed the changes in her, he had been drawn to help her, too.

Her heart was big, and she openly gave him a piece. He had a feeling that she would have, even if he hadn't been with Róisín.

"Anyway. Explain noisier." Matthew was looking at Jackson. His brows pulled down and together so tightly they were knotted.

Jackson pointed at Matthew. "Your magic. It's like a... whisper. It's soft and gentle. Almost relaxing to be around."

Caid couldn't hold in his snicker. Matthew shot him a glare.

"Whereas with him." Jackson gestured to Caid. "It's like a fucking cannon coming at you. Followed by a missile."

Matthew lifted his left brow. His green eyes scanning Caid's figure. "Why *is* that? I've always noticed that about him. Róisín's, now, too." He shifted in his chair. "She started to say something about seed magic, but Ione, being her usual self, well..."

Caid scratched at the side of his neck. "It was something Tura said." He shrugged. "How Gea has, but no." He straightened and set his elbows on his knees. "It doesn't really explain it. Hecate's loss of power is because the witches in the realms stopped believing her to be their creator. In turn, they just forgot about her all together."

Jackson and Matthew sat quietly, watching him work through his thoughts.

"Tura said that seed magic was pretty straight forward. Take a seed, do that spell thing on it, then plant it. Someone consumes it and whatever the spell is, it becomes a part of that person."

"So, Gea used something like a forgetting spell?" Matthew asked.

"Shit," came Jackson's whispered response.

"Maybe." Caid set his glass on the table between them. "What if it was more? When we came back from Wurbray, Róisín had mentioned her magic felt different. Like it was freer. I don't think that had anything to do with what happened that day."

Matthew leaned forward. "What exactly *did* happen? No one ever told me."

Caid pulled his bottom lip between his teeth, rubbing them over the skin. "Something was there. *In* the well source. Everything the well source was trying to give Róisín, whatever was there, it was trying to take it away from her."

Matthew jumped to his feet so quickly, he almost upended the table.

"What?" Caid leaned back to keep his eyes on him.

"Aoife. When she came to me in Aunellion. She said something then that didn't make sense." He paced away toward the edge of the patio, then back. "Fuck." He rubbed the back of his neck, then scratched the top of his head. "Give me a sec."

Jackson turned to Caid, brows high on his forehead.

"Ah!" Matthew spun back to them quickly. "She was trying to convince me she wasn't as bad as the Milsenetts. Rambling on and on. She said something about their well source. How she would never have made her people suffer the way the Milsenetts had." He swept his arm out wide. Caid could see the rapid-fire beat of Matthew's pulse at the side of his neck. "Then, *'Our well source had a sedative to help with that.'*"

Caid doubted there was any sedative involved. Róisín's screams of pain from that day still haunted him.

"And if she could fuck with the well source to do that, now we know how she was taking their magic." Matthew dropped into his chair with an audible *oomph*.

Caid's magic rose with a speed that had his muscles tensing. As it coiled around his veins, he struggled to stay rooted in his chair. There wasn't anything he could do now. Nothing he could have ever done. Aoife was gone before Róisín had ever come into his life.

"Okay, so that explains it," Jackson said.

"Not really," Matthew said. "I noticed it was a little different when I came home, but nothing like it is now."

"Maybe Gea used the seeds to dull the magic? Chain it?" Caid said. "Everything the other day when Hecate and Tura showed up at the tea shop was a jumbled mess of trying to say as much as possible. We were supposed to talk to them again, but Hecate still hasn't—"

"Still hasn't, what, great-great-grandson?" Hecate asked, making the trio jump.

FIFTY-EIGHT

LINA SCRAMBLED through her morning routine. She had woke with curiosity's flames licking at her heels, urging her to move faster, faster. Weighed down with two armloads of grocery bags, she finally stumbled in through the front door of the house at almost noon.

She paused, listening to see if Thomas had left yet for his business trip to Boston. Before she had left to bring the twins to school and run her errands, she had asked him to wait for her. Then again, her plan had been to be in and out of all the stores she needed to go to quickly.

Of course it had to be a day when everyone had also been out, and had complaints to file with her for the next town meeting.

While Lina was no longer the select board's chair, she had remained on the board. Even when she hadn't run, the town had written her in with far more than enough votes to secure a seat.

With Thomas's flight set to leave Bangor just after one that afternoon, she knew he could only wait so long for her. On a sigh, she trudged into the kitchen and set the bags on the table, then pulled out her cell phone.

One text from Thomas, time-stamped just fifteen minutes earlier, read, *We need a helicopter and a helicopter pad so I can stay longer when you need me. I'll call when I land. Love you.*

Her heart danced in her chest. She would never understand how she had gotten so lucky to be loved by someone like Thomas.

Thinking of his love for her had her snapping out of her love induced haze and righting herself back onto the tracks of her morning's mission. Her brother. Their Coven. Hecate and what their connection with her would mean for them should the others succeed in destroying Gea.

And there was only one, small, fluffy rabbit that would have the answers.

Lina was going to do whatever she needed to put a stop to the secrets.

She thought it childish and only caused more harm than being forthright.

If David didn't fess up, she'd turn him into a stew that she and Caid would share in a celebration of Gea's end.

WITH HER EYES ON THE TREE LINE AT THE EDGE OF THE YARD, Lina drummed her fingers on the top of the plastic container of raspberries. Not that she was nervous. No. She was a plotter, diplomatic. Every conversation she approached with reason and the aim of discussion.

This was going to be a confrontation. A confrontation she had zero preparation for. Her subconscious had tackled her in her sleep, taking advantage of the millions of thoughts about the twins, the end of the school year, Thomas's trip, dinners, upcoming summer camp, and the endless worries for Caid and Róisín.

A flash of white hopped from the woods and she straightened.

"I don't know why you hesitate," she called out to him. "They know you're here. And I know *you* know that they're gone."

That rankled her. David had to have known what Hecate was doing. He may not have been there when the day essentially stood still, but there was nothing that could convince her he didn't know.

"The children must be excited about their summer break from school," David said.

Lina looked down her nose at him. "This isn't a social call, rabbit."

His ears fell back and laid against his fur.

"I can't credit my parents for anything growing up, except for knowing who and what I didn't want to be as a parent, a friend, and a wife. I learned everything I know from my brother." She leaned forward. "Do you know what the most valuable lesson he ever taught me was?"

"No?" David said.

"I was thirteen, almost fourteen. As a woodland creature, you are probably unfamiliar with the ways of the human teenage mind, especially a social teenager. However, I'm *more* than happy to tell you. We. Know. Everything. Or, at least we think we do. No one can tell us otherwise. Even if it's for our own good. We're gonna do what we wanna do. Full stop."

He tracked the movement of her hand as she sat the raspberry container on the table next to her.

"My friends were having a sleepover one weekend. Caid had said I couldn't go. I'd just failed nearly every single one of my freshman midterms." She clasped her hands together. "I was pretty much living with him at the time. He'd moved out right after he turned eighteen. Didn't matter anyway, our parents were, once again, off at some fancy weekend event thing down in Portland." She unlaced her fingers and waved one hand dismissively. "Even if they *had* cared about us kids, I still would have had to crash at his place that weekend. He'd still have been in charge of me." She snapped open the lid and took a raspberry out. "Looking back, I get why he said no. I'd failed the tests, it was enough to drop my grade point average below where I needed to stay at to keep myself on the swim team. Failed the tests and got booted from the team until my grades came up." Lina popped the raspberry in her mouth. "Teenage me didn't get it. I thought he was an asshole. I hated him for ruining my life. He wasn't going to stop me, either. Once the big lug fell asleep, out I went. My plan was to go to the sleepover, but make up an excuse why I had to leave early so I could get back home into bed before he woke up. You probably know how the rest of this goes."

"You made it home late," David said. Not a question or statement, but it sounded more like a suggestion.

"Oh, no, no." She grinned, taking another raspberry. "Everything went off perfectly. Sure, I only had a few minutes lead on Caid waking up. I'd literally just shoved my overnight bag under my bed and buried myself under the covers when I heard his bed creak down the hall."

"I'm afraid I do not understand this lesson that he taught you."

"Because the story isn't over yet." Lina could only hope that she and Caid were far from done making more stories together. This couldn't be it for her brother. She refused to accept it.

Look at how quick it happened before, the little voice in her head reminded her, making the next breath she drew in shake.

"That weekend, Caid sat like a good big brother and helped me study for the retakes the teachers so graciously allowed. He even picked me up on the days I had to stay late to take the tests after school. I passed, of course. The swim coach told me once my week suspension for grades was up, I could come back to practices. I see it now, but I didn't then. Just how *too* perfectly everything went that week." She nudged the raspberry container further back onto the table, out of sight from David. Was it mean to taunt him? Lina could admit that, yes, it was. However, her give a damn meter was broken at the moment. "A full week later, that Saturday morning, I came into the kitchen to a full breakfast. *That* is when I knew something was up."

"Your parents?"

"Nope. Caid. He can make a hell of a breakfast spread. Had to learn how to cook, or else he and I would've starved." She smiled at the memories of all the mornings they had shared in the little breakfast nook of their house and later his apartment. Her heart pushed against her chest. Would she survive if he didn't come back this time? Yes. She would. For Thomas and the time they had left. For the twins.

Lina swiped the container from the table and set it in front of David. He hopped back at the abruptness of the act and looked up at her.

"'*You can hate me, Leen. Scream at me, hit me, curse me to hell.*' That's how he opened the conversation that morning. I knew. Right in the pit of my gut, it sank like a rock. That knowing sensation. He knew I'd snuck out, that I'd lied, kept secrets from him. I'd *hurt* him in a way that cut *me* far deeper than it hurt having him tell me I couldn't go that day."

David inched forward.

"*Lies and secrets are the worst kind of betrayal. They show someone that you deem them unworthy, while making yourself untrustworthy.*" She crossed her arms over her chest. "You've been a part of this whole thing, David. From the start. You've been welcomed into my family. You've *become* family. To take a page out of my brother's book, you can hate me, scream at me. Please don't curse me to hell. I'd like to be able to come visit my kids once this veil mess gets straightened out. But the secrets and lies? They end *now*."

"I have—"

"Enough. You certainly have lied and still keep secrets. You told Róisín you were a charge of Future, *not* the Goddess. You have been privy to all of this." She swept her arms out. "That day Shasta and Caid came to take me to that island, you *knew*. Enough with the bullshit, David. You may be a magic rabbit, but I can guarantee if I skin you and cook you, you'll taste just as good as a regular one."

David's front paws landed on a patio stone, and he dropped his head.

"You knew who Caid was, right from the start, didn't you?"

"Yes."

"And me?"

"Both of you, yes. Not of your magic, but who you were to Hecate."

Lina squeezed her eyes shut. "That day at my old house. You knew everything about the Jordbrand Coven."

"About that—"

She squealed and stomped a foot. "David!"

"There isn't a Coven under the name of Jordbrand," he squeaked out the words.

The air fled her lungs. "What do you mean?"

"The realms, they never had what we now consider assigned Covens. There once were many, many of them spread around the realms. All of them cohabitating like the witches in this realm do. No leaders or rulers. That was something that fell into place as Gea rose to power and her magic took hold of the people."

"The others don't have a clue about this, do they?"

"N-no. Unless Future and Hecate tell them."

Lina covered her mouth with a hand and took a moment to gather her racing thoughts, trying to pluck out her next question. "Jordbrand isn't even a thing? But it was in those books Shasta and Caid found that led them to that island."

"To be completely honest, I'm not sure how or when the name of Jordbrand was assigned to this realm. Or by who."

"Could it be a plant?"

"No, it's a name," David said.

"That's not what I freaking mean. Could someone have planted the name as a... distraction of sorts for Gea and it just happened to take root over the centuries?"

"Oh. Well, I suppose it could be."

She reached down to the container and grabbed a handful of raspberries. Tossing them into her mouth, she chewed thoughtfully. "Hecate, she can't get to the other realms?"

"Correct. Mostly."

"David."

"She has been blocked from the other realms. However, she can still feel and see what is happening there," he said.

"Is it possible that she caught on to what was happening with this new witchy order of things, and to maybe, say, distract or keep attention off of the *one* place she could remain, created a fictional Coven to lead the realm? Then, maybe kill them all off, fictionally, to keep Gea's interest in the realm to a minimum?" Lina's thoughts were racing so fast, a headache was thrumming at the base of her skull.

"It is possible. Only she would know that answer, I'm afraid." When Lina only stared back at him, unblinking, he quickly added, "Sorry. I truly am. As a hand for the fate of future, I've always been limited in how much I can say or do. Even what I know. I'm just to watch and help guide the involved parties toward what fate has ruled for them."

Lina pursed her lips. "Dammit."

"What?"

"I want to stay mad at you for being a little, fluffy, white liar. But I get it."

"So you're not going to eat me?"

She burst into laughter. "The twins would never forgive me."

FIFTY-NINE

MARCELO TIPPED his head to one side. His eyes remained on Nolani's frame through the door to their en suite bathroom, while his hands were deft across the sketchpad. The charcoal scratched over the paper as he drew wave after wave of her hair, tumbling down her back.

"You're staring," she said over her shoulder before bending to turn the water off.

"How can I not?" He moved his hand to smooth the sketched lines of her waist.

"Put that pencil down and come join me."

His hand froze.

"I know you heard me."

He followed the movement of her hands as she worked a braid into her hair and pinned it atop her head. Then, as she stepped into the bathtub.

"Celo." She nearly whined his name. "My shoulders are tight."

Marcelo's core grew hot. His cock tightening almost painfully. He dropped the pencil and book onto the bed. Then, with every ounce of control he could grasp hold of, sauntered into the bathroom. Leaning against the sink, he crossed his arms over his chest.

Nolani's eyes did a slow, almost lazy, perusal of him from head to toe, and almost all the way back to his toes, but her gaze lingered at where he knew his length was pressing against his pants. After a moment, she laid her arms on the tub edge and rested a cheek against her stacked hands.

"I can't make you stay, can I?"

Unable to find his voice, he shook his head.

"Celo—"

"You can't, Nolani. And you have to stay here with the others. It's safer."

The water sloshed over the sides, spilling onto the tile, as she shifted her weight and pushed to her feet. "And it's safer for you? Are you that blind? He may be your brother, but you've said it yourself. The monster is in control."

"It isn't like he's the only one that has one inside," Marcelo said.

"You may have yours, and you may be brothers, but he is not like you. I just—" She threw her arms out. Her brows came down over her eyes as they drew together. "I don't know how to get you to *see* that."

He drove his hands into his hair, the urge to scream and shout tearing away at his inside. "It's because he's my brother that I have to try."

"You've *tried* to help him before." She wrapped her arms around herself. "You shielded him from your father, from the court, from all of it. It built a strength inside of you to deal with the curse. He doesn't have that. Why can't you see?"

Marcelo had seen. Just as he had seen his brother's frail form and smelled the faint smell of death all over him. It was Anthony's decay, not that of a feast. Bile rose in his throat, making his eyes water as he recalled the way the smell had hit him the moment he had entered the room.

He had made his mind up in that moment, even before he knew of Róisín's return to them. Before the lines had started to finally connect.

Before there was a chance of their freedom from the monster within.

And even if that freedom came, Anthony *would* die. Marcelo knew that. He didn't see any way, once his monster was gone, that Anthony could survive long enough for the healing process of what had happened to his body to begin.

No, he would not, could not, leave his brother in his darkest hour.

"I can't leave him to die alone, Nolani." His voice was thick, the words cracking like logs in a fire.

Her chin trembled. "What if you die, too?"

Slowly, he approached the tub where she stood. He cupped her face in his hands and brushed a kiss over her lips. "We were never promised forever. Our time always had a limit."

"No." Her breath caught, and she shook her head. "No, don't say that."

He thumbed away a tear from her cheek, then pressed his lips against where the dampness still lingered. "It's our truth. I love you, Nolani. And I'll be grateful to my last breath for all the moments we've had together." He kissed her jaw. "How much my heart has always been full with you, and for you." His lips grazed along the column of her neck. "Every waking moment since that day you crashed into me." He pressed his lips to the skin of her shoulder. "Even when it was all going to shit, I've never felt more complete than I have with you in my life."

Nolani threw her arms around his neck and pulled him into the tub with her. The water slapped against the wall behind it, and more spilled over the sides and the front. She brought her legs around his waist, rolling her hips against him.

Her voice breathy, she asked, "Will you at least let me be the one who brings you?"

Marcelo pulled back to look down at her. Her eyes glittered with the lingering tears that clung to them. "Only if you promise to be quick and immediately return. I can't..." His throat tightened, stealing the rest of his words.

"I promise." She brought him closer and crushed her lips to his.

SIXTY

Róisín walked into the kitchen and found Shasta with her head inside the oven. "It's gas, remember?"

"Why is everyone fighting? Ouch. Shit." She rubbed the side of her head once she straightened. Her head tipped to one side for a moment before she said, "Ah-ha!" And turned a knob at the front.

Róisín dropped heavily onto a stool at the island. She had forgotten how much extra noise so many people in one space made. Her life could be easily split into thirds. For each part, she had only ever been one half of a duo. She and Brenna after Stephen passed. She and her grandmother after. Now, she and Caid. Shasta, Matthew, Lina, Lucius, and Clarissa had been there or were there, but nothing constant.

A door slamming upstairs made her flinch. Her senses were in overdrive, even more than they would have been after a few hours with the twins.

She and Runa had wandered Brenna's pathway for nearly an hour. Róisín had let him lead the conversation, asking her questions. As she gave him answers, she studied him. She learned his quiet tells. The nervous tick at the corner of his left eye. Or, when he had been asking questions about Talista, when she had been with Anelle and Jessamyn on the castle roof, how he pulled the right corner of his bottom lip in, pressed it between his teeth twice, then tapped his fingers against his thighs.

Everyone handled grief differently. It didn't take her long to deduce that Runa hadn't tried to handle his at all.

That became much clearer when she had asked him questions. He hadn't wanted to lead his Coven because he felt the role had never been meant for him. By giving it to Aja, someone so close to Jessamyn, he could keep pushing forward, and hold the grief at his back.

"Seeing you," he had begun before snapping his jaw shut. It had been too late. She had already seen the way it quivered. "I have to face it. She's gone. And she'll be really gone if we don't fix all of it."

"We will." She reached out and rested one of her hands on his forearm. "Gea, the curse, the afterworld. All of it."

"Celo and Nolani think it's all tied together."

That thought had awoken something within her. Something that had driven her to seek Lily when she and Runa parted ways. After both women had shed enough tears to flood the valley just south of the cottage, Lily had revealed that yes, it was likely that something connected everything together. They just needed to figure out what that something was.

Lily had assured her she, Ione, Ten, and Cicile had been on it, but then the heavy thump, followed by Ione's giggle, sounded overhead.

"She's just doing a little extra research," Róisín said, casting her eyes toward the ceiling.

Lily snorted and slapped a hand over her mouth. "Oh, gosh, that was so rude of me. I shouldn't laugh like that."

Róisín reached forward and tugged her hand from her mouth. Holding it in hers, she gave it a light squeeze. "I missed you. A lot. And I'm so sorry I didn't say goodbye."

Lily gave her a sad smile. "Don't be sorry. I know how it felt not knowing if I'd get Matthew back, and feeling that way before our bond even was tied in place... If it had been after? Especially with everything he and I shared with one another—" Her cheeks flared red. She shifted their joined hands, then stroked her thumb over Róisín's. "We move forward from here. No looking back."

Róisín ducked her head to catch Lily's eyes. "We move forward. Together."

"Hm?" Shasta turned and gave Róisín a confused look. "Forward together? What's forward?"

Róisín blinked at her, then glanced around the kitchen, coming back to the present moment.

"You said something about moving forward," Shasta said.

"I..."

Shasta leaned over the island. "Sweetheart, go lay down and rest. You're exhausted."

"I'm alright. It's just a lot being around everyone again."

Her honey-colored eyes danced back and forth. After a moment, she rested her chin on her palm. "Mm, no. I'm not buying it. That may just be a part of it, but unfortunately for you, you have your father's pasty complexion. You've got two black eyes and not the kind you get from getting punched. It's okay to take a minute."

"I've taken plenty of minutes." She extended her index finger and bopped the end of Shasta's nose. "Unfortunately, judging by the sun's standoff yesterday and the demon hound in my front yard this morning, there are no more minutes to take."

Shasta sighed and pushed away from the island. "Shit. I could really use a drink right now."

Róisín stood. Once she was in front of her, she wrapped her arms around Shasta's waist.

"I want most to see Ev again. But oh—" Shasta's chuckle was watery. "I can't wait to get my hands on Lucius's pretty face. What a muck up of it all I've done. And it's his fault he left *me* to be the grownup around here."

Róisín sniffed, blinking away the burn building in her eyes. "Do you think he made it to Clarissa? Before..."

"I hope so. After everything those two had been through, I hope they're rolling around in some flower patch I know she has in her afterworld."

Róisín smiled at the thought. She thought back to a time when she and Matthew were in their twenties. They had just returned to the manor after a night out with friends, expecting it to be dark and quiet.

Instead, they had found Clarissa wrapped in Lucius's arms as they swayed to a soft, slow song coming from a record player in the corner.

Matthew had rolled his eyes and made a gagging motion. But Róisín had stood quietly, watching their love for one another for just a moment before joining Matthew in the kitchen.

Pulling away from her embrace with Shasta, she used the backs of her hands to wipe the wetness from her cheeks.

"I can make us mocktails," Róisín said.

"Aja stocked the fridge when he got here and there's nothing in there except water and milk. He's been my witchy sponsor over these past few years."

Róisín glanced around the kitchen, taking in the sounds of the house. She quickly located Caid in the back and guessed that was where Jackson and Matthew were as well. "Given everyone's fighting, or hiding, I'm pretty sure I can slip out and be back before anyone notices. I'll get the stuff for a clean sangria."

Shasta's eyes darted toward the backdoor that lead to the patio. "He'll kill me."

"No, he won't. He loves and adores you far too much, *mom*." Róisín winked at her.

She rolled her eyes and looked up at the ceiling. "Go. Quickly. Under five minutes. If he comes in and you're not back, I'm playing stupid. It's all on you, sweetheart."

Róisín didn't have the heart in that moment to mention that Caid would know the moment she left. For all the times Róisín tried to convince herself she could be off and back before he even noticed, she had always known better. Their tether may no longer exist, but somehow, their connection was stronger than before.

She leaned forward to give her a quick kiss on the cheek. "I'll be right back."

SIXTY-ONE

MATTHEW'S SPINE had snapped so straight when Hecate appeared, he felt like he had gained a few inches in height. Before he knew what was happening, questions were pouring from his lips.

"Did my father know about you? What the Hells is this seed magic stuff?" He kept his eyes on Hecate, but pointed at Caid. "Is Fate going to take him back once this is over? That's kind of a shitty thing to do, you know. Can Gea mess with bonds? Like make her own as she sees fit? Because if I find out she messed with Lily and I for some personal interest of hers, I'm going to—"

Hecate lifted a hand to silence him.

To her right, Jackson dropped his chin to his chest. His shoulders shook slightly with the laughter he was failing to hold in.

When Matthew turned his head toward Caid, he found him staring back. One brow high on his forehead. A slight smirk tipping his mouth up. He gave Matthew a shallow nod before grinning at him. Then Matthew sucked in a sharp breath and whirled.

"*Great-great-grandson?!*" He shrieked out. He glared at Caid. "You and Róisín failed to mention *that*."

Hecate smoothed down the front of her shirt before leaning back in her seat. Silver-gold eyes were bright on him when she lifted her head and tipped it to one side. "Kincaid and Lina are my great-great-grand-children."

That one sentence deflated Matthew. His shoulders sagged, and he practically melted into his chair. What the fuck was going on? Neither Caid, nor Róisín had mentioned that at all in the past two days.

"That explains why your magic is the noisiest I've ever been around," Jackson said. He lifted one of his legs, resting his ankle on his opposite knee. "If you've got *that* kind of power thrumming through your body... Shit. I've gotta admit I'm pretty jealous. The things I could do." He nodded. "I could end world hunger."

Matthew groaned and covered his face with his hands. The more time he spent with Jackson, the more there was absolutely no denying they were related. It was exactly the kind of remark he would have made to break the tension.

"Why'd you mess around with time yesterday?" Caid asked.

"You all needed it. Time. Something that you've always had in short supply when you needed it most, and has always damned you in the end." She nodded first to Matthew, then to Caid.

"Why didn't you do it before? Aja said the day lasted forever in Molennius, so you can't use the excuse that your power is weak beyond Earth," Matthew said.

"Ana and Elizabeth," Caid said, earning a nod from Hecate.

"And their families. It was far from easy work, and unfortunately for us, they will be out for several days because of it. The power it took from their magic to not only travel to the realms and remain shielded from Gea, but to perform the magic needed to bring the days to a stop in each realm." She shifted in her seat, crossing her legs. "We tried once before, when you were all in Greens Glen with Madigan."

Caid shot upright. "You knew."

Slowly, Jackson lowered his leg and sat up.

"You knew what was going to happen to Róisín." Caid stood. "You knew she was going to *die.*"

Jackson let out a quiet gasp.

Matthew ground his molars together. His fingers dug into the armrest of his chair, holding him there.

Hecate remained seated, but lifted her chin, sending her white hair tumbling behind her as her head fell back so that she could look at Caid. "I did," she said quietly. "I also knew that Fate wouldn't allow it, but I still tried. I still tried to do something before it even happened. But we... *I* failed. It was a new magic, even to me."

Caid turned his back to them. His shoulders high, almost to his ears.

Matthew sat, frozen. The chaos of that day in the ravine haunted him. It *all* haunted him. The ravine, Alleyette with Mildred and Henry, his time in Aunellion... They had molded together to become like a second skin on him.

He cleared his throat and pulled his attention from Caid. "What made it work this time? Isn't Earth the realm where you still have all your power?"

"Yes, my full strength remains here." She was still watching Caid as she spoke. "It took a lot of practice. A lot of restructuring the way I worked the magic. I also needed to be careful to not draw unwanted attention." She swung her gaze at him. "Fate would not take kindly to me wiping out an entire species in order to save myself and mine."

"I thought you were, like, above fate, though," Jackson said.

"No one is above fate," Hecate said. "Not even I. I'm beholden to it and its whims, just as the rest are. It helps keep the balance between all. Keeps the order of everything and everyone, preventing one singular person from obtaining ultimate power."

"Explain Gea, then," Caid said.

"And seed magic," Matthew added.

"When you all return, I'll explain Gea's use of seed magic in all of this. As it's something you all need to be aware of," Hecate said. "Fate, on the other hand." Shadows passed over her eyes and her mouth tightened into a thin line. "Well, it appears that it is suffering the consequences of its own actions."

Jackson lifted his head, eyes on her.

Caid's body stiffened.

Matthew felt a heat wash over him from his magic. The urge to explode strong. Had Lucius been a consequence of those actions? If that was how Caid was there, next to him, alive and breathing, why not Lucius?

316

"I do not know why it allowed her to push the limit so far. Only that it did. We all have our place, our purpose, out—" She rose quickly. The color quickly drained from her face. "I... I need to..."

And then she was gone.

"What. The. Fuck." Jackson's throat bobbed.

Matthew scrubbed a hand over his face and slumped back into his chair. "Did she just admit what I think she did?"

Caid tipped his head from one side to the other. The crack his neck made loud enough for Matthew to hear. "Yup."

"What, fate just said, 'Hey, let's see where this goes' when Gea started going off the rails?" Jackson reached across the table and swiped Matthew's water. He brought it to his lips, tipped his head back, and downed its contents in three swallows.

"Yup," Caid said.

"And we were all just left to the mercy of it," Matthew added.

Jackson set the glass on the table with a heavy thud and stood. "Now *we* have to fix fate's fuck up."

"Yup."

Jackson shook his head. "Is that all you've got to say?"

Caid's brows came down over his eyes casting a shadow. "If I say what's really in here"—He tapped the side of his head—"lightning will probably strike me down. Now, if you'll excuse me, I need to go find my wife because it's her life that hangs in the balance all because fate decided it was going to fuck off and play a game of fifty-two pickup."

Matthew and Jackson watched him turn and stalk toward the house.

"Shit," Matthew frowned.

"We're fucked, aren't we?"

Matthew sighed, then pushed to his feet. His eyes were on where Caid had slipped back into the house. That feeling he had just shaken since finding Róisín and Caid reseeded itself. Only this time, what grew there had claws. As it grew, those claws dug themselves deep into his insides.

They were all truly fucked, just as Jackson had said. However, that pit in his stomach, taking root and growing with such force and speed that it made his magic flare inside, told him that his best friend, his sister, and the man stalking into the cottage like a storm cloud, his brother, were going to suffer far more than any of them.

Matthew's eyes burned with the angry tears that built in them. For Róisín. For Caid. For Lucius. Clarissa. Brenna. *Himself.* How many more would suffer because of this?

"What do we do now?" Jackson asked, coming to stand next to him.

"We find a way to fuck fate up. And save them."

SIXTY-TWO

SHASTA SNORTED, causing the mouthful of sangria to spurt past her lips. She slapped a hand up to hold the rest in, snorting again. Only this time, the act sent her into a coughing fit.

"I couldn't help it! It's not like I had ever been around babies before that," Róisín said. Then she threw her head back and cackled. "There was poop everywhere. That awful kind because he had just started eating like... *real* food."

Shasta wrapped a hand around her waist. "Oh, goodness." She gasped, her tongue shifting in her mouth magnifying the noise, sending them into a fresh fit of laughter.

Róisín slapped her thigh, her eyes glittering with tears from her laughter. Suddenly, she stopped and straightened, looking over Shasta's shoulder.

"What?" Shasta turned. Aja stood in the kitchen's doorway, arms crossed over his chest, eyes on the two glasses on the island. Shasta picked her glass up and offered it to him. His eyes narrowed on the glass. "It's virgin."

"Excuse me?" He blinked, looking from the glass to her.

"This." She slightly tipped the glass back and forth, making the liquid slosh around inside. "It's a virgin."

"She means nonalcoholic," Róisín chimed in. "She's not drinking."

Shasta stretched her arm out further. "Try it."

Aja took the stem of the glass between his thumb and forefinger. He lifted the glass to his nose to smell the contents. "It smells incredibly sweet."

"I may have gone a little heavy on the sugar this time around," Róisín said.

He brought the glass to his lips. "It has a surprisingly nice taste." A soft hum sounded from his throat. He licked his lips, and asked, "Where is everyone?"

"Ten and Cicile are in the room they picked, probably doing what they do best." Shasta took the glass back and set it on the island. "Organizing everything into one so we can see where the holes are that we need to fill."

Aja nodded before walking over to the counter where a pan sat on a cooling rack. "Oh, Shasta." His voice had dropped, the deeper timber of it making Shasta want to giggle. He bent over the dish and inhaled loudly before humming in delight. "You know I'm not going to share this, right?"

Shasta gave a half-shrug, then gestured to the other cooling racks and pans. "I made more than enough. Salad in the fridge. A pasta, one with some greens. That beet and carrot one Ten likes."

"Auntie Shass, taking care of us all," Róisín whispered behind her.

"Cooking helps me think," Shasta said. Scooting around the island, she opened the oven door and peeked in at the last batch of dinner muffins.

"And?" Aja sat next to Róisín at the island. "What have you come up with?"

"Not much. Only more anger than I started with." The confession heated her cheeks. "Everything has been a lie."

"Not everything," Róisín said. She rested her elbow atop the island. Cradling her chin in her palm, she added, "Everything here with all of us, that's been real. The truth."

"And what we've done to get the witches from Shianshani to safety," Aja said. "Your leadership. With your people, with us, after..."

"I know." She pressed her lips together and willed away the ache building in her heart. "All the rest of it. The silly rules. The way we all blindly followed them. They dictated so much of our lives through choices rooted in fear of the consequences. When in reality, they were in place to keep us under *her* foot."

The timer on the oven buzzed. Sliding mitts on, Shasta removed the golden muffins.

"Then we just need to fix it, so we can have the same freedom the witches here have," Róisín said.

"It was what Jessamyn was working for. Not just our freedom in Shianshani, but everywhere." He shifted on his stool. "She was ready to lead the change from our home, no matter the risk."

Shasta didn't miss the way he said the last part directly to Róisín. Or the way Róisín's nostrils flared with her exhale. The way her shoulders dropped slightly.

"Ten and Cicile are accounted for. The others?" Aja pulled Shasta's glass toward him, earning a curious glance from Róisín. Her lips pursed, an eyebrow tipped up when he sipped the drink again.

"Ione and Runa were fighting," Shasta said.

"Ah, no, they were not. At least not when I left the living room." Róisín downed the rest of her drink.

Aja's eyes followed her movements as she rose and went over to the sink. "Are you making more?"

"Absolutely. Especially if those are done." She waved a hand at the muffins.

Aja's mouth formed an *O* and his eyes lit. After he collected himself, he asked, "Marcelo and Nolani?"

Shasta frowned up at the ceiling. Marcelo and Nolani's choice of room had been just overhead. "They were fighting too."

The remark seemed to take Aja just as off-guard as it had Shasta hearing the muffled angry words earlier. "About?"

"Anthony," Shasta said. Her throat tightened, and an ache grew in her chest. Anthony had been so sweet and caring, funny, and full of sunshine and hope when she had met him. She hadn't seen him since the monster within had awoken, but to think of him in such a way broke her heart.

Róisín handed her a fresh glass. "The curse... it really controls him?"

"Marcelo said that the monster within has completely taken over," Aja said. "Anthony appears to be a bystander in his own body."

Róisín picked at her muffin. "Would it break the curse if we can succeed in destroying Gea? Lily said Ione thinks Celo and Nolani were right about it all being tied together. Gea has to be at the core of all of this. Right?"

Aja scratched his jaw but said nothing. The tight line in which he held his mouth, the flex of his jaw were indicators he was biting back what he really wanted to say. Knowing that the words were not what any of them needed to hear in that moment.

"That's what we hope," Shasta said. "Many birds, one stone."

Aja's face relaxed. The appreciative smile he gave Shasta was grim. He reached out and took another muffing from the rack. After scrutinizing it for a moment, he tossed the entire thing into his mouth.

"Where do you *put* it all?" Róisín was staring him.

"Right here." Aja pat his stomach.

"I had one muffin. One. You've had—" Róisín's index finger pointed to each of the empty spots of the pan. "*Ten.*"

He finished his drink and shrugged. "I've never really had home cooking like this."

"Ever?" The shock was clear in Róisín's question.

"Never. My family dynamic was... tricky growing up. Often it was just Anelle and I. We ate whatever, whenever. To have this now?" He swung his arm out and gestured to the spread of food around them. "I'm not going to pass up the deliciousness of it all."

Shasta's chest grew warm as her lungs expanded and her heart danced. She could have easily lost all of this. She nearly had. Every time she had reached for a drink and filled herself with alcohol, it had slipped a little further away. A renewed strength to stay sober surged through her. There was nothing that could entice her to bury herself in a bottle again. Not even with the make-up of reality's face washed away now.

"If you want a muffin, I suggest you snatch it now before—What? What is it?" The harsh scrape of Róisín's stool vibrating along the floor snapped Shasta back to the kitchen.

Caid stood in the doorway like a thunderstorm rolling in off the water, eyes darting around the room, taking in everything.

"It's not alcohol," Shasta said.

"What? No." He shook his head and ran a hand over his face. "It's not. No." He shook his head again. "Sorry. It's... Hecate came."

Aja lurched to his feet. The stool banged against the floor. "Is she?"

"No. Not anymore. She ducked out with next to no warning. The same as she came."

Róisín was standing at his side. Her voice low when she asked, "What did she say?"

"Not much. She didn't stay long." He slipped his arm around her waist, then pulled her to his side. "The only thing she said was that fate was paying for its actions, letting Gea have too much room to roam."

Shasta frowned. No, Hecate had said more. She saw it in the way Caid's fingers flexed their grip at Róisín's side. How his other hand fisted and unfisted. "We're left holding the bag?"

"Bingo," he said.

"It's safe to assume yesterday's standstill was her, yes?" Aja asked.

"It was. She found a way to stretch time or something and knew it was important for us to have it." He lifted his free hand and ran it through his hair. "She said she's coming back. I don't know when, or why she left. I just know that she kind of tapped out for a second, then got really pale before she did."

"What now?" Róisín asked.

Shasta surveyed the kitchen and sighed. "I guess now, we eat."

SIXTY-THREE

CAID FOUND Róisín in the bathroom of their room later that night. It hadn't taken long for the smells of everything Shasta had cooked to fill the cottage, luring everyone into the kitchen with hungry stomachs. No one spoke of Gea, Hecate, or Tura. Instead, they shared stories from their lives that filled their evening with chuckles and full-bellied laughter, replacing for a few hours the fear and uncertainty that sat heavy inside of them all.

As the noise of the room grew, Róisín had drawn more and more inward. He saw it happen more than felt it. When she had moved close enough to him that he could snag her by the waist, he excused them both and carried her upstairs to their room.

She had immediately gone to shower, filling the room and bedroom with steam that smelled of her fresh lavender soap. When he had stepped into the room, she stood at the vanity, finger combing her damp hair, wearing one of his old Boston Bruins hoodies that fell to just above her knees.

He came up behind her. Wrapping his arms around her middle, nuzzling her neck.

"Don't let it take you away from me," he said against her skin before pressing a soft kiss where his lips had grazed. "I can't reach you when you go there. And one of these times—" His throat tightened, sealing off the rest of his words.

Her body melted into his. "I don't want it to. I'm trying. It just... it sneaks up on me so fast and grabs me before I can take a breath."

"Talk to me. Not this half-assed shit you've been giving me, either."

She turned in his arms. "How do I tell them what I've become? What my magic is now? I can't even explain what it is, or how it happens. Hells, I'm still fighting to control it fully. You saw what happened at Lina and Thomas's. Caid, I almost blew the fucking house up."

He lifted a hand and nudged her hair back from her face. Then he moved his hand to tip her chin up. "But you didn't. Almost doesn't count."

She snorted and closed her eyes.

"Look at me, Róisín."

Her eyes squeezed tighter, sending a tear leaking from the corner of her eye.

"Róisín," he said her name softer this time.

Finally, she opened her eyes. The turquoise color of them shone brightly.

"It'll be alright."

"Will it? You heard Hecate, fate has checks and balances. It's seen what happens when it lets just one witch take too much power for themselves. What about me? I have my entire Coven's worth of magic pulsing inside of my body, Caid." She drew in a shaky breath. "And I was born with the true magic of life, something our people have not had in any Coven for at least a thousand years. What if—" She pressed her lips together, her chin quivering. "What if fate wants me next?"

Everything inside of him stilled at that moment. It hadn't been a new revelation. Not to him, and now he realized it was something she had been thinking about, still.

"I haven't been a good person here," she said. "It's the same damned story as before. Just this time, it's not Gea pulling the reins."

"I still tried to do something before it even happened. But we... I failed."

Hecate had known Róisín was going to be okay, yet she had still tried to stop her from dying. She had tried to interfere with fate. If fate turned its sights on Róisín next, could he trust Hecate to step in again? To try again?

He liked it better when the information was fresh. He had discovered he always did. Because once they got the chance to think more on the information, to talk it out, that was when the comfort of sense and the pieces coming together, fled. The doubt crept in, fear racing in right behind it.

And that's where they all were now. The commotion of it all had settled, and they'd all had quiet moments for everything to sink it. Moments to dwell on certain things that stuck out and caught their attention.

This, Róisín's magic, was Caid's and hers to share.

"If you go, I go." He cupped her face in his hands. "I'm not doing this veil shit, living over here without you, waiting for you to come to me for blinks and breaths at a time."

Her hands settled at his waist. "I can't." She shook her head. "I can't either. Shasta's been doing it with Evelyn, and Lucius and Clarissa did it, but, no." She stepped closer to him. "If you go, I go."

Caid bent his head and took her mouth with his. The kiss was slow. Delicious. He pulled back and stroked his knuckles over her cheek. "Not tonight. Right now is just another night for us. A night where I get to do this—" He kissed her again. A little deeper than before. Their tongues twisting and stroking. "And this." He kissed her forehead softly. "And"—He moved his hands to her ass and lifted her—"This." He set her on the towel stand and was just moving to nestle himself between her legs when she let out a yelp as the stand collapsed. He had been quick enough to grab her, to pull her back before she had fallen with it.

Together, they looked down at the splintered piece of furniture.

"I guess that one wasn't built by a great-great-grandfather for his wife that had thirteen kids?" Caid asked, sending them both into a fit of laughter.

Her laughter died off abruptly. "Caid?"

"As many as you want, Róisín. One, or twenty." He swept her into his arms, bringing her to the bed. "Can we just, uh, not do the twins thing? Visits are good. Trying to parent them?"

The corners of her eyes crinkled with her smile. "Silly man, we don't get to pick that part."

"I know." He lowered next to her. "It's on Thomas's side, anyway. So, I think our chances are slim."

She released a soft sigh when he tugged the collar of her shirt down, kissing, then nipping her shoulder. He moved lower, nudging the hem of the shirt up. Her fingers threaded through his hair as he kissed and licked his way up toward her breasts.

"Caid?" His name a breathless whisper.

"Hm?" He closed his mouth over one of her nipples and sucked deeply, making her back arch.

"Get on your back."

His head snapped up. "Excuse me?"

Her hand was warm against his cheek. "You heard me. On your back. Or..." Her eyes shifted away to the edge of the bed. "You could sit at the edge of the bed. I know you like to watch me take you."

The way his core turned into an inferno at her statement, there was no denying just how much he enjoyed watching her.

"How about this?" He flipped their positions so that he sat against the headboard. "Makes it easier to tuck you beneath me after." He winked at her, making her chuckle.

She dragged his shorts down. Slowly, she lowered her mouth to his cock and circled her tongue around the tip. Pausing, her eyes lifted to his. "That's if you're not too tired. *After.*"

SIXTY-FOUR

Róisín felt Caid's warm breath at her ear the moment she squeezed her eyes shut, finger pinched on the bridge of her nose. "You good?" He asked.

Her words were mumbled when she replied. "No. I need a break. Air, or something."

It had been Lily's startled yelp when she entered the kitchen that morning that brought everyone sleep mussed and rushing. Hecate and Tura sat perched at the island. Tura looking tired and worn; Hecate wore an amused grin.

Over two hours later, a buzzing had grown in Róisín's ear. It was now near deafening. The kitchen was unbearably hot, slicking her back with sweat. A bead of it rolled down her back. Wetting her lips with her tongue, she forced herself to focus.

It wasn't all of them gathered in the kitchen that had spiked the panic attack to take root and thrive, as it had been the night before. That morning, it was the repetitiveness. Hecate had started all the way at the beginning. Details Róisín and Caid had already relayed when they'd initially gathered.

And Tura was hiding something. It was in the way she shifted her weight from one foot to the other, often. How after Róisín had detailed the appearance of the demon that had come, that it had been saying her father's name, Tura had kept her eyes downcast.

Nolani stood in the back corner with Marcelo, clinging to him as though she would never see him again. She had heard their argument. Had known Marcelo was planning to leave them to be with Anthony. Feeling the weight of Róisín's eyes on her, Nolani looked away from Hecate.

At that moment, Róisín wished she could tell Nolani that it would all be okay. That she and Marcelo would have their happy ending. That they could have peace for whatever time he had left.

Róisín wished she could tell them *all* that. Especially herself. Caid.

"We can go outside for a second," Caid said.

"I need. Just... one second." She cleared her throat so her voice would be louder, stronger. Steadier.

Caid squeezed her hand in his.

"Breathe..." his magic's words brushed along her sweat-soaked spine.

"I have a question," Róisín said.

Hecate immediately stopped talking about Elspeth and faced her.

"You said that Gea pulled a thread from future's loom." Róisín stepped forward. "Nothing has happened yet on that loom. How, if it was never pulled from the loom of the present, did it happen?"

Hecate shifted to Tura. "This is where you come in, my dear."

Tura's shoulders rose and fell sharply with the breath she took. "The thread was only ever present on my loom. It was a mercy fate had given us. Perhaps if my sisters had awoken to what our mother was doing, it may have been different. I'm sorry I cannot give you a better explanation, but that is the only one I have."

Everyone's heads swiveled to Caid, recognizing what Róisín and Tura had meant.

"Your loom held his past, present, and future?"

"Given what happened when Gea pulled the thread, it would seem to be that way," Tura said.

Róisín felt Caid's magic, like a cool hand, settle over her racing heart. "When did she pull it?"

Tura shook her head. She wove her fingers together, then pulled them apart. "I'm not sure. She pulled it in such a manner that the end was still woven in along the lines of the others around it. It wasn't until —" Her breath hitched. "After that I went over the loom trying to find out what I had missed. Everything had been perfect. It had been *ready*. That day was our turning point to freedom."

Which meant everything, the chaos in Shianshani, the refugees, all of it, would not have happened if the thread had remained.

"So that was the tipping point for fate to say enough is enough with her?" Her magic began to push and expand inside her. Her lungs began working double time, and the edges of her vision faded out into black.

The threat isn't here, she tried to tell her magic. *Just like the other day. These people are* safe.

Her magic nudged her to look at Hecate.

Hopefully.

After a moment, her magic retreated. Her lungs and heart slowed. As her body calmed, she felt Caid's chest pressed against her back. He had moved closer when her magic flared. He knew the signs.

Across the kitchen from where she stood, Matthew caught her attention.

"You okay?" He mouthed to her.

She nodded back.

"It was the first time she tried to truly change fate," Hecate said.

Shasta's brows shot up and her mouth fell open. "And all the other times?"

Ten waved a piece of paper from where she stood between Lily and Cicile near the doorway. "We've got quite a list of offenses here."

"You can rewrite how fate falls, but you can never change it completely." Tura lifted one hand. "Aoife had always been cast to die around eight years ago. There were a multitude of ways fate cast it to happen. The tension between her and Mildred had come to a head. One end had been at Mildred's hand through poisoning. It was an opportunity mother seized and took control of herself."

Ione waved her stylus in the air as she frowned down at her tablet. "So, what you're saying is, as long as it keeps our fate on the path set, Gea can step in and meddle?"

"Anyone can," Tura said with a slight nod.

Ione tapped on her screen, moving to stand back next to Runa as she did.

"I have a question." Shasta crossed her arms over her chest. "For you, Hecate."

"I shall do—"

"No." Shasta sliced a hand through the air between them. "You will not *do your best*. I want straight forward. I had a part in all of this from the moment she"—She pointed at Tura—"came to Bren. I'm owed the truth. As is she." Her finger moved to point at Róisín.

"Shasta's pissed," Matthew whispered behind Róisín making her jump and spin around. "I've never seen her so mad."

She could only blink up at him. Only seconds before, he had been on the other side of the room. He was right, though. Shasta had always been the calm, rational one. The soother. At that moment, anger was burning so brightly in the woman that was her mother's best friend, the room had begun to seethe with it.

"Why Róisín? You said it yourself. The only thing that can kill you is death magic. Bren was a wielder. Why not one before Bren?" As Shasta had spoken, she had moved closer to Hecate. Now the two women were almost toe to toe.

Hecate held Shasta's stare. "Gea's quest began barely six centuries ago. Which would make Brenna, then later Róisín, the only death wielders alive."

"I repeat"—Shasta's hands fisted at her sides—"Why Róisín?"

"You would sacrifice your friend?" Hecate tipped her head to one side.

Róisín felt Caid's fingers gripping her forearm. As Shasta and Hecate spoke, Róisín had been moving closer to Shasta. Aja had, too. He stood just a step behind her now.

"Either way, I lose Bren, right? Answer my question." Shasta had squeezed her knuckles so tightly, her hands had gone from chestnut colored to white. Her veins rose dark blue against the skin.

Róisín gasped as Hecate's words hit her. "Aoife was over six hundred years old. That's how she knew who Gea was. That's why she... Fucking *hells*." She brought her hand to her chest. It suddenly spasmed, then squeezed so tightly she couldn't breathe. Her magic rose in a panicked fury, trying to free her lungs. The room grew too bright, too hot.

"Róisín?" Someone's worried voice came from her left.

"You've gotta breathe, baby," Caid's tone was soothing in her ear.

"I can't..." Her chest heaved as she gasped.

"Lay her down," came another voice. Shasta.

"I've got her." Caid's strong arms swept her up and held her close. The steady beat of his heart against her ear paired with the coolness of his magic wrapping around her had the calming effect he intended. When he began to leave the room, she said, "No. Wait. I'm okay. I just... I need a second."

"Are you sure?" He looked down at her with knitted brows. The hazel in his eyes now danced with explosions of golds, greens, and browns.

She licked her lips and nodded.

"Here," Ione appeared before them with a glass of water. "Drink this. Preferably all of it. That's what usually helps me when I'm two seconds away from passing out."

Róisín took the glass and drank half of it before trying to get Caid to release her. His grip only tightened. Ione watched her expectantly. Sighing, she brought the glass to her lips and finished the rest.

"Will you put me down now?" Róisín asked. At first, she was sure he was going to argue because his arms didn't budge. Then, he loosened his grip, allowing her to slide down him until her feet hit the ground. However, he didn't fully release her. He kept one arm at her waist to hold her close.

Ten approached and looked over Ione's shoulder at the tablet. "May I?"

"Of course." Ione handed it to her. "What are you thinking?"

"Me thinks the plot just thickened," Ten said theatrically. "If Aoife was alive before Gea took power..." Still holding Ione's tablet, she turned to Hecate. "Madigan, too?"

"Madigan was just a child when the Seer was taken, right?" Róisín wasn't sure who to look to for confirmation, Hecate or Tura.

"He was nine," Tura said.

"So..." Ione's hand rose to her throat.

"He knew who she was this whole time, too," Ten said.

"What are we looking at for time here?" Ione looked down at her wrist, tapping the non-existent watch with her stylus.

A shadow passed over Hecate's face and her features hardened. Lines forming around her mouth, near her eyes, and between her brows. "That, I do not know. With fate making itself felt as much as it has in the past several days, it tells me we do not have much." She lifted a hand and waved her index finger back and forth. The sound of Ione's mouth snapping closed was audible. "I am unable to stop time again, even here. It would take much longer for me to attain that ability again than what we have time for."

Shasta shook her head and chuckled. "What do we do now, oh mighty one?"

Runa, who had somehow stayed completely quiet during everything, barked out a sharp laugh and quickly covered his mouth with his hand.

"Now, unfortunately, we wait," Hecate said. She held out her hand for Tura's.

"Wait?" Róisín asked. "You just told us we don't have time to *wait*."

"I cannot help with the games that fate chooses to play," she said, shifting away with Tura before any more questions could be sent her way.

"She's kind of a snotty bitch," Ione said.

"Dammit, they still didn't say what the Hells this seed magic stuff was." Matthew dropped his head back and groaned up at the ceiling.

"Seed magic?" Lily asked.

"It's something Gea's done to, I don't know." He shrugged.

"Tura said it was how Gea could gain her power over us," Róisín said. "It obviously didn't work on all of the older witches. Madigan and Aoife are prime examples of that. What are the odds Mildred knew?"

Lily tapped her chin and pursed her lips. "Let me see what I can find out about it. Maybe it'll give us more insight into what she actually has done to us through it."

"It'd sure be nice to find a way to break it." Matthew motioned around the room. "Something tells me if we could at least break ours, it'll give us a better chance against her."

Cicile pushed away from the counter near the sink. "I'll start with cross-referencing the two conversations, ridding ourselves of doubles."

"We need to establish a timeline." Ione scribbled something on the tablet before looking at Lily. "We'll tackle this first, then the seed magic?"

"What about me?" Runa asked.

"You can come if you want. But you're not just going to sit there, belching, and flipping through magazines noisily. You're going to *help*."

He placed a hand on his chest and gasped. "I do *not* flip pages noisily."

"At least you're admitting the other half of it. Come on, you big lug." Ione shook her head and grabbed a handful of his shirt, tugging him into the living room.

Once the room cleared out so that it was just Róisín, Caid, and Shasta remaining, Róisín crossed to Shasta. Without a word, she wrapped her arms around her waist. They each let out a heavy breath, then tightened their arms, holding one another tighter.

"I love you, Shasta."

"I love you, too, sweetheart." She stepped back and gave Róisín's shoulders a light squeeze. "And you, too, kiddo," she said to Caid.

"What, I don't get to be called sweetheart, too?" Caid asked.

One of Shasta's brows lifted. "If that's your thing..."

Caid chuckled before taking her in his arms and bending to kiss the top of her head. "I'll take whatever you want to call me, mom."

Róisín watched Shasta sink into his embrace and for a moment could feel that seed inside, the one that would bloom into a spray of hope, take root.

"Alright, shoo you two." Shasta blinked rapidly and waved them toward the door. "Don't eat though. I'll make us a late lunch."

Caid took Róisín's hand and shifted them away to the cabin.

"Caid, we don't really have that much time," Róisín said.

"And"—He tugged her against him—"I only need thirty minutes."

The weight of her panic fell to her feet, and she burst into laughter. "Ambitious." She pressed her face against his chest.

"I've been told that before," he said.

Pulling back quickly, she tipped her head back to look at him.

"For work."

"Sure." She made to move away, but he slipped an arm around her waist before she could. "Caid—"

"Are you okay?" He brushed his nose against hers, then moved to nuzzle her neck.

Leaning against him, she brought her arms around his neck. "No. I'm not."

He lifted her, bringing her into their bedroom. "Talk to me."

"It just..." She shoved her hands into her hair. "It's a *lot*. After so long, it's like the answers are all finally coming together, but it's all at the same time. I can't stop feeling..." She lifted her hands and waved frantically. "Gah! Like it's all still unraveling. Like *I'm* unraveling. Right at the seams."

"I won't let you." His whispered words tickled her shoulder before his lips met the skin there. "I'll follow you around with a needle and thread. Every time you start to fray, I'll mend you."

Her chest grew heavy and her heart thudded.

"I won't let you," he repeated.

She stroked her fingers through his hair. He leaned into her touch and closed his eyes.

"Caid."

"Hm?"

"Make love to me."

His eyes flew open, their hazel color bright and dancing. The intensity with which he stared at her had her lips parting slightly. A tremor rolled through her body, causing her to release a ragged breath.

For just a moment longer, they lay like that on the bed, staring at one another, bodies growing warmer. Then, Caid took her mouth with his like a man starved.

SIXTY-FIVE

SHASTA SET the casserole dish on the cooling rack, then yanked the oven mitts from her hands to rub at her temples. The kitchen island was covered with all the food she had cooked and baked in the last hour. Now she eyed the spread. It was enough for a horde. Far more than any of them could eat in a week, let alone one sitting.

"Sha, this is enough food for an army. More than the two of us could eat in a month. What's wrong?" Evelyn's voice echoed softly in her mind.

"Nothing is wrong. I just... I need to think. Organize. My brain, it's..." Shasta began aloud. She frowned before adding, "Great, now I'm talking to a memory."

Evelyn's scoff echoed through her head. *"You only cook like* this *when you're trying to work something out in your head. So again, what's wrong?"*

Shasta sighed and turned away from the food. "It's better than turning to the bottle to run from it all," she said.

Turning the faucet on, she scrubbed at the pots and pans. Her mind was indeed churning. There had already been a lot happening, and the new information was overwhelming. Everything she knew, a lie. Everything she and Brenna had done had been for something... else. That had been what stung the most. The lies that had cost her best friend's life.

She closed her eyes as though the act alone would be enough to keep everything in. Keep it all from spilling out. She wanted to scream, to cry. Something primal inside her wanted to slam the pot she held in her hands against the countertop, over and over until something broke. Either her or the pot.

The quiet of the cottage around her grew louder until it was like static vibrating against her eardrum. When she opened her eyes, her vision was blurred, spots dancing along the edges. Blowing out a steadying breath, she gripped the front of the farmhouse-style sink basin.

"Are you alright?" Aja's deep timber came from behind her.

"I'm..." Her shoulders rounded.

His hand on her shoulder was warm, comforting. "Breathe, Shasta."

The urge to curl inward warred with the urge to lean into him.

"Please tell me you haven't come with more revelations that just dig our hole even deeper." She cringed at how clear her desperation was in her voice. When he said nothing, she straightened and turned her head to look at him over her shoulder. "Aja."

"Marcelo has gone back to Talista."

She turned her body away from the sink and crossed her arms over her chest. "Why has he gone back?"

Aja ran a hand over the top of his head. "It's..." His hand fell away, slapping lightly against his thigh as it swung down to his side. "Marcelo is convinced Anthony is at death's door. Waiting for the curse to release its grip on him so that he can die. Anelle said he looked starved. Mostly skin and bones now. Marcelo, he—" He pressed his lips together and fell silent.

"It has gotten that bad?"

Aja only nodded.

"Cassius?"

"What would be the point? He's defenseless even against a dying monster. We can't put either of them in that situation."

Shasta's hand came to her mouth. The sting of tears burned at her eyes. "But they love each other, Aja. We can't do that to either of them. Cassius has to know, and the choice has to be his."

Aja stalked around the island and dropped onto a stool. He scrubbed a hand over his face and let out a deep growl. "I want to give him that. Trust me. I just..." He dropped his head to the island top. "Fuck!"

She put her hands on her hips, her chin falling to her chest. She took a moment to collect herself, pull in her emotions. Moving around to stand next to him, she put an arm across his back and brought her face to his. "Being a leader isn't easy," she said softly. "The choices we're faced with making."

He turned his face to hers. His red eyes had shifted to black with the rise of his magic. "I never wanted this. I shouldn't *be* in this position. Marsenna and Cassius shouldn't need to be stowed away in different realms for their safety. They should be home." He sat up quickly and Shasta followed suit. "Marcelo shouldn't have to be counting down the hours to his brother's death. If fate—" His breath caught on a shaky exhale. "If it hadn't gone on holiday, where would we be?"

Shasta cupped his face in her hands. Warm tears splashed onto her cheeks. "I learned a long time ago to stop thinking about the *'What ifs'* because they only sent me to the bottom of the glass in search of a way to ease my pain. I don't have the answers, and I wish I did. What has happened? We need to move past that."

His words that came next did so in a cracking whisper. "I miss them. So much that sometimes I don't know if I can keep going."

The burning in her chest from her heart cracking didn't come slowly. It was fast, and it was angry. The rage that bubbled inside her grew hotter, tearing at her heart more.

Everything, everyone they all had lost because of *fate*.

"I don't think we have a choice, Aja. We have to keep going. To see everything put to rights; for them. For all they worked for."

His eyes danced as he studied her. The tremble of his chin nearly finished breaking her. He had always been stoic in the years that she had known him. Soft-spoken, yet sturdy and sure. To see him before her, beginning to crumble into pieces—

"—can't just, damn you, Matthew!" Ione's shout interrupted him.

Shasta and Aja quickly moved to the hall to find a wild-eyed, panting Ione standing next to Runa.

"What is it?" Shasta asked, looking down the hall, searching for Matthew and Lily.

"Matthew." Ione spun around, her hair flying upward with the movement. She stomped into the living room without another word.

Aja brought his attention to Runa. "Care to divulge a little more information?"

"Matthew popped in, said something to Lily that made her go"— He flared his eyes wide—"And then..." He pressed his hands to his cheeks and gasped. "Róisín and Caid showed up. Matthew didn't even have to say *anything* to Róisín, and she did this." He made his eyes grow large again. "Then said, 'We're coming with you.' And, well, that's that. They're gone."

"Gone where?" Shasta asked.

Runa shrugged and Aja groaned.

"That's why Ione's pissed," Runa said.

Shasta turned to Aja. "Go to Marsenna, then Cassius. It has to be their choice." She motioned to Runa. "I'll try to figure this out."

Aja gave her a nod before shifting away.

"Why's he going to talk to Marsenna and Cass?" Runa's attention remained on where Aja had been standing.

"If Anthony really is dying, they need to know." Shasta drew a hand over her face. "I could make some chicken piccata. Leftovers can't hurt anyone," she said.

Runa's brows knitted together. "What?"

Her head fell back, and she stared up at the ceiling, a small chuckle escaping her. "Oh, Ev. You were always right."

SIXTY-SIX

MATTHEW TAPPED a finger against his chin as he studied the destroyed Jeep in the yard. Jackson had slipped off to call Nadia. Lily was with Ione, Ten, and Cicile. Runa lurked in the background, doing just as Ione said he would do: thumb through the pages of a beat-up magazine, noisily. Marcelo and Nolani had ducked somewhere. He hadn't seen Anelle since the day before, so he could only assume she had been sent to check on the refugee statuses across the realms, as stealthy as she was.

Bored, he had slunk back into the kitchen to help Shasta, to feel useful. To keep his mind occupied. She waved her hands at him like she was sweeping up dust, shooing him away.

Which left him in search of something else to occupy his racing mind and silence the thoughts.

Everything had fallen apart, and now that it was coming together, at a blinding pace, everything was too... *everything*. It made his body vibrate from the onslaught.

Reaching inside, he poked at his earth magic which often lay curled, sleeping, within. He took a step back and nudged the ground up beneath the Jeep. Roots escaped the packed earth. They wrapped around the twisted, dented heap of metal.

He led the roots along the driveway, back toward where the Jeep had been parked before. It settled with a groan back on its four tires. Matthew didn't know what he planned to do with the vehicle. He passed by the front window on the way out of the kitchen and saw it sitting there in its sad state and felt the pull to go out to it.

Now, with his hands on his hips, he realized he didn't know all that much about vehicles of any type. He loved to drive them. Especially fast ones.

No, he wasn't completely helpless. He knew some of the basics. However, he knew absolutely nothing about how to get what sat before him in operable shape again.

"Can't hurt any to take the smashed shit off," he said.

Without tools on hand, it was going to come down to his magic and his strength.

Cracking his knuckles, he stepped closer and set to work.

"How does mom know the Burkes?" His question spun into his mind so quickly, he almost dropped a door on himself.

He remembered his mother's smile, so full of love and life as she said, *"They're family..."*

The Burkes *were* his family. One half of him.

That she had hidden her Aunellion lineage, now that he knew of what Gea had done, made sense. Although her magic of sight had come and gone, making any vision she had muddy, faint, she still had it. By default, being Aunellion made her a target for Gea.

Clarissa had done what she could to keep herself safe.

In hopes of buying her family time to break Cronan's curse.

In the end, Matthew didn't inherit her sight. It was her elemental magic that came to him and helped amplify his own. He was sure he could walk up to Gea, shake her hand, and she wouldn't bat a lash because she wouldn't feel what she was searching for.

The puzzle sat before him half finished. It was the rest that he couldn't find the pieces for.

He still had yet to figure out why they had kept it hidden that Lucius was truly his father.

Matthew yanked the hood open and scowled down at the motor. "What am I missing?"

It couldn't be *who* Lucius was. It had to be...

"Oh, shit." He rapped his head on the twisted end of the hood that hung low. "Oh. Oh, *shit.*"

He spun on a heel and raced toward the house, shouting for Lily as he went.

"What?" Her eyes were wide when she met him in the doorway to the living room. "What is it? What happened?"

"We need to go," he said. "Now." Relief flooded him when she took his outstretched hand without hesitation.

"Can't it wait?" Ione asked from where she sat on the armrest of a loveseat.

"Don't have time," he said. "Someone tell Jackson I'll be—" The front door swung open, bringing with it Róisín trailed by Caid.

Her eyes locked on his. With a small nod, she said, "We're coming with you."

"Good." He looked beyond her to Caid, who mirrored Róisín's nod.

"Matthew!" Ione was on her feet, advancing toward where the quartet stood in the hallway. "You—"

He never heard the rest of it because they had shifted away to Ely before she could finish.

"YOU WANT TO DO WHAT NOW?" CAID'S TONE WAS PITCHED high with shock. The sleepy rasp of it had now made him almost sound like a teenager entering puberty.

Matthew turned away from the wall they stood before in Lucius's study. No, it was Matthew's study now. This was his home. With Lily.

Caid scratched the side of his head, squinting at the enormous built-in bookshelf that spanned the wall, floor to ceiling.

"Take it down," Matthew said.

Caid clucked his tongue. One eyebrow lifted. "Seems like a perfectly good unit, though." He walked over to it and tapped his knuckles on a shelf. "Sturdy, too."

"I'm pretty sure we're going to find there's something behind it," Matthew said.

Lily's hand was warm on his forearm. "Did you remember something Lucius said?" She asked softly.

"Kind of? It's a little fuzzy because I was only fifteen when he told me." He motioned to the wall. "It'd track with how he had my mother's papers hidden."

"Let me get this straight. You think there's what, a room? A bunch of hidden safes?" Róisín joined Caid at the bookshelf and began tipping out the books that lined the shelves. "Are we looking for a lever of some sort?"

Matthew shook his head. "No."

She paused in mid-reach and turned to him, nose scrunched and lips pursed. "No hidden room?"

"No. Dammit." He dropped onto the low sofa that faced the shelves. "I don't know."

Lily sat next to him. "How about you just tell us what made you think to come here?"

He sat back and sighed. "I was taking apart the Jeep." He winced and looked at Caid. "Sorry, man, I know it's yours, but—"

"Don't worry about it. It can be a project vehicle to keep us busy after all this shit is done," Caid said.

Matthew smiled at him. "I'd like that." He wiped his hands on his thighs, then blew out a breath. "Okay. Anyway, I just wanted to keep my hands busy and slow my head down. Know what I mean?" They all nodded. "I got to thinking about Montana and mom. The things she said when we were there that were just flat out... weird. Lucius, too. Which made me think about him and trying to figure out why they kept it a secret." His gaze shifted to the shelves. His voice had dropped to almost a whisper when he added, "Kept *him* a secret." Tipping his head to one side, he let his eyes trail along a visible seam of one section of shelving.

Caid followed his line of sight and shuffled down to the seam. He ran his fingers along it, nodding and humming.

"You think?" Matthew pushed back to his feet and went to him.

"Could be. I need—" He pat his back pockets. "Wait." He lifted his hand and a clawed end tool that looked to be made of stone formed.

"The ice swords made sense. We were outside. That," Matthew's attention remained transfixed on the tool. "After seeing that..." He looked up at Caid. "She really *is* your great-great-grandmother, and fuck do you have a *lot* of power." When Caid only shrugged a shoulder, Matthew had to fight to keep down the bark of laughter that wanted to explode free. Of course, to Caid, it would all seem normal. He'd always had that wild and free power to his magic.

"Step back." Caid motioned him away.

"Lucius said something back when I was a kid about his father. I guess it'd be my *grandfather.*" Matthew blinked. Even almost a decade after learning the truth, it still startled him. "He was the one to put an end to testing and recording of magic in Ely."

"Wait." Róisín stepped forward, her face pale. "Testing? Like, what kind of testing?"

"Ely wasn't always like this. Peaceful. That was something that came with Lucius's father. Before... it was bad." His voice dipped low with his last words. "I thankfully got the summarized version, " He wet his lips. His muscles tightened, trying to hold him still as shudders from the memories of what Lucius had said threatened, "but I could tell that Lucius, dad... his father couldn't protect him from them. Dad thinks, *thought*, that was what confirmed his father's stance on the testing. He was already planning on ending it when he became Coven leader, and seeing his own kids be put through it made him snap."

"The fight between Lucius and Demitri, that was about the testing, wasn't it?" Róisín asked. "He wanted to start the testing again, but Lucius didn't. The only way Demitri could accomplish it would be to take the leadership from Lucius." She shuddered. "I only met him twice, but it was enough to—" she shuddered again.

"I don't know for sure, but I think so. It wouldn't surprise me. He's twisted enough to want to do it."

"Got it!" Caid called out. "There's nothing—" A thump sounded. "Hold on." Another thump, this one sounding higher pitched. "Right here. Matt, I need a hand."

"Why did they keep records of the testing? What was the testing *for*?" Lily asked.

"Instead of taking the magic at face value like every other realm did," He ground his teeth together, growling as he and Caid pushed against the tool. The wood cracked, then splintered. "Ely extracted cells from each witch once their magic woke and analyzed it."

"Fuck, can I just..." Caid waved a hand at the shelves.

Matthew frowned at them. He hadn't wanted to totally destroy the structure. Anything he could hold on to that kept the memories of Lucius close to him. But... "We have no choice. We don't have much time."

Caid hesitated, eyes steady on Matthew's.

"There's a room back there." He pointed. "With all the files of all the witches from Ely, before my grandfather became the leader of the Coven. One of them *has* to be dad's," Matthew said.

Caid pressed his lips into a thin line. His throat bobbed with a deep swallow. Then he turned back to the shelves. Seconds later, wood and books were scattered in heaps. The wall behind the shelves revealed a wide door that looked to be made of steel.

"A secret weapon," Matthew whispered. "Should there ever be a war among the realms, the Ely Coven leader could access the files of our witches and know exactly who to force into conscription. Stack the deck to win."

Lily let out a small gasp, and Róisín released a stream of curses.

"How do we get in?" Caid flipped the tool around in his palm, then gripped it, readying to strike.

"We break it down," Matthew said.

Sixty-Seven

Róisín stepped into a small, unfamiliar room. There was a warmth to the room that settled deep into her marrow. It made her want to sink onto the sofa near the fireplace and nap. The scent of honey and dough lingered in the air. She turned in a slow circle, confusion settling deep, seeping through her skin.

Gone was Lucius's study and the books she had been in front of only moments before. No longer did she hear the muffled conversation between Caid and Matthew on the other side of the broken bookcase.

Where was she?

Her magic crept higher, ready. She called out, "Hello?"

The soft creak of a floorboard replied and made her whirl around.

That was when she saw them. Three looms, each held by a deep maroon toned wood frame, the wood so dark, the knots appeared black.

Everything inside of her stilled except her magic, which thrummed louder, hotter. Ready.

Before she could step toward them, a figure entered the room from her right. The flash of pale blond hair and a gold hued cloak made her magic thrash inside her even more. It wanted vengeance. Justice.

Gea leaned closer to the middle loom. Her fingers moved up and down, never touching, only tracing from a distance the lines of the millions of threads that moved frantically along the loom. With a nod, she shifted her attention to the one on the right.

Róisín wondered if Gea could sense her presence. Sense that anger that had overtaken her despite her best efforts to tamp it down and keep herself rational and calm.

Could she feel the way Róisín's magic burned and pressed against her skin, trying to break free, to explode and take their surroundings with it?

"Never go into a fight angry. Unless you wish to face your end," Brent had told her and Matthew over and over during their trainings. *"Your enemy will use it against you. Make you trip over it and onto their blade. Magical and literal."*

Gea's lips moved, her mumbled words impossible for Róisín to hear from where she stood across the room.

"There," Gea said clearly. Her finger touched the loom, a wicked grin growing across her face, twisting her features into something dark and ugly. She pinched the green and gold thread between her fingers. Quickly, the grin morphed into something of disgust. Almost like touching the thread made her ill.

Róisín's head buzzed. A dizziness settled in and made her vision blur. Her legs suddenly felt weak. She reached behind her for anything to grab hold of to keep herself steady.

"I have had it with your meddling," Gea said before she pulled the thread further from the loom. "Since the day"—*tug*—"The Byrne family came into existence"—*tug, tug*—"You've all been a thorn in my side." *Tug.* The thread finally released its hold on the loom where it had wrapped around a burgundy-colored thread.

Róisín's throat squeezed. An invisible hand wrapping its fingers tightly around it. She tried to breathe, tried to gasp in even the slightest of breaths. Her magic changed track. Pulling back, it danced in panic; clawing at the hand.

Unable to move, unable to breathe, Róisín realized at that moment what she was seeing.

"My mother, she pulled a thread from the loom that day," Tura had said, her eyes on Caid. *"A beautiful green and gold thread."*

She was watching the very moment her entire world had gone dark.

The moment that haunted her every second since. Could she change it? Could she stop it?

Even at the thought of moving toward Gea, Róisín found herself met with a wall. She and her magic reached out, pounding against it to no avail.

"I told you once, Aoife, you cannot stop me." Gea twisted the thread. It grew taught. "I will find out how you keep coming back. I will stop you. Then that stubborn granddaughter of yours." With a sharp tug, the thread snapped. "So Hecate can see me take her precious Earth before she draws her last breath."

The air in the room grew heavy. Róisín's heart hammered faster, harder. Her lungs clutched, desperate for air.

Aoife. Gea had thought the thread was Aoife's.

Aoife had not only known the truth of Gea, but *knew* Gea.

Just as the beautiful pattern the green and gold thread had made on the loom had unraveled with Gea's pulls, the tangled mess of the truth unraveled before Róisín.

Gea had pushed and pushed Róisín, trying to exhaust her, to wear her down with menial tasks. *Dangerous* tasks like going to realms of witches that had just attempted to end her life under the guise of peace before a war. When the reality was, a war wasn't coming to them.

Róisín had been right. From the moment the thought had hammered at her skull, she had been right.

Gea wanted her gone. No, not because of who her family was. Not as punishment. Because her death magic was the key to Gea's complete rule.

Uniting the realms instead had backfired on Gea. Made Róisín stronger. Made *all* of them stronger. And united. It wouldn't be just Róisín that Gea had to face. It would be all of them.

Just as fate had intended.

As Róisín's vision swam, a chuckle escaped.

Róisín tried to take in a breath. Her head had grown light and unconsciousness slipped up and along her body. She struggled against it, trying to focus on her thoughts, and Gea.

Gea balled up the thread and walked over to a door. She knelt and lifted a floorboard and tossed the thread in the space beneath. Voices sounded to her right. Feminine voices, laughter. The Sisters. Gea lightly stomped on the floorboard to resettle it, then with hasty movements, she brushed her hands over the loom, smoothing the frayed edges of Caid's torn thread.

The moment the Sisters came into the room, darkness swallowed Róisín.

SIXTY-EIGHT

WITH SHAKING hands, Alina, Fate's hand of the present, lifted her sister from where she had collapsed onto the floor only moments before.

Senna, the hand of the past, had been in mid-sentence when her body seized. Her eyes rolled back into her head, and she crumpled to the floor.

"Sister, please." Alina gently pat Senna's cheek. "Please wake up. I cannot lose another sister."

Behind her closed eyelids, Senna's eyes flitted back and forth. A second later, her nostrils squeezed inward on a sharp breath.

Her umber eyes flared opened. "Something's wrong. Something's happened."

"Wh-what do you mean?" Alina moved back slightly to give Senna room.

"Fate, it has," she glanced around the room, "it has shifted my magic away from me. I can no longer feel it."

Alina's pulse flitted next to her left eye.

"Is this what fate had in store for us? Is this our time ending? First Tura, now me?" Senna's eyes were wide, her chest heaved as her breaths quickened.

"Tura is still with us. We would have felt it otherwise," Alina said.

"Would we?" Senna struggled to bring herself more upright to sitting. "*Nothing* since she disappeared, Sister. I feel it all less and less with each passing day. How long has it been? Days? Years? And Hells," she frowned, "I can no longer feel the Hells, nor the fates cemented in eternity. Are they still held true?"

"Our looms would let us know if they were not."

Senna glanced at their looms. "Not if fate was moving on without us."

Alina looked over her shoulder to the door of their small cottage. Together, they tried every day to open it. To leave. To find Tura, the hand of the future.

Every day, they remained trapped. The door remaining impossible to open. Impenetrable to their magic.

"Sister?" Alina asked in a whisper.

"Yes?"

"I've just realized I've never been able to leave this home."

Senna's eyes settled on the door. "No. You've left. I know you have. We all have."

"Not I. I've been here every day since mother built this home for us." She turned to Senna, her eyes damp with tears.

"I—" Senna stiffened. "I've only ever been able to go to the Hells. To make sure..."

"Sister."

"I can't remember."

"Do you think?"

"Not Tura, no."

The sisters faced one another.

"Mother," they said in unison.

Their mother had them bound to their home, to their duty.

Somehow, Tura had broken free.

"Mother has taken our magic."

Sixty-Nine

A COLD, snaking sensation slithered along Caid's spine. It coiled around his neck, then stroked down his chest to his heart. His magic slapped at it like it was an errant child. It only made the sensation wrap tighter.

Next to him, Matthew mumbled as he read over the file Caid had found that contained Lucius's birth certificate and testing when his magic had awoke.

The mumbling stopped and Matthew went stock still.

Something erupted inside of Caid. "Róisín."

"Something's here," Matthew said. "Lily!" He dropped the file and darted back into the study. "Róisín!"

Caid already knew that Róisín wasn't in the manor. That coldness, much like his magic, had a voice. He closed his eyes and willed his heart to slow so he could focus.

There. In the valley.

On an exhale, he shifted away.

He arrived in the Rose Valley, finding himself greeted by the rose-colored wheat stalks he had seen just days before. Only as he faced them now, they towered over him, waving at him as they bent in the wind.

"Róisín!"

The wind leaned the stalks in unison toward the center of the valley.

"Róisín!" He called out louder.

"I feel her..." His magic pushed him forward a step.

"Get me to her. Now."

He let his magic take over his body. It moved him deeper and deeper into the stalks, the smell of damp earth surrounding him.

What felt like an eternity of lefts, rights later, leaving him sure that he was only making circles, he came upon Róisín. She sat on the ground, face cast up to the sky. The wind had tossed her hair over her face.

He said her name softly, "Róisín."

She remained still. A strand of hair catching and rising on a gust.

Caid walked around and knelt in front of her. He gently brushed the hair from her face. The hair at the nape of his neck rose on end. Róisín's eyes, once a brilliant blue that always reminded him of the warm waters of the Caribbean on a sunny, cloudless day, were now milk white.

"What has her?" He asked his magic through clenched teeth.

His question was met with silence.

"Dammit!" He had meant to be gentle with her, but the tension in his muscles had him gripping her by the shoulders, hauling her to her feet with him as he stood. "Róisín!"

Her head dropped back.

He banded an arm around her back and placed his other hand behind the crown of her head to tip her face back to his. "What. Has. Her?"

"I seek but do not find... No. It's there. It's..." his magic finally replied. *"It is from beyond us. Beyond us all."*

The rustling sound of wheat just ahead of him had him tearing his gaze from Róisín's pale face. His body tensed, muscles ready to move.

Matthew burst through the stalks with Lily's hand clutched tightly in his.

"Is she?" Matthew asked around heaving breaths.

"I don't know. She's..." He looked down at Róisín's face. Her pulse danced along the side of her throat, and he could still feel her inside of him, along with something else. But what?

Lily cleared her throat. "The white eyes. It means someone has thralled her."

Caid didn't need to demand an answer from his magic again. The growl that escaped his throat was enough. It flared inside, then surged outward, almost like it had that day in the Nianti Fields in Legianne. As it wrapped around them, Caid sank to his knees, clutching her against him.

"Come back to me, baby." He whispered and stroked a hand through her hair. "Please." His thumb trailed along her jaw. "It's not our time. Not yet."

Sweat beaded and trickled along his spine at the heat from his magic as it pulsed around them. He leaned closer to her mouth and tried to listen for her breaths. The blood rushing through his veins was all he could hear. A heaviness settled against his chest. It pressed and pressed until his vision blotted, his lungs protesting.

No. Not again.

"Róisín!" He took her face between his thumb and index finger and shook it lightly. "Don't you dare. Róisín!" His limbs shook as he moved them so he could lay her on the ground, her skin clammy beneath his touch. He could feel Matthew and Lily move closer to them. Feel the way their magic pressed inward, reaching for his and Róisín's, responding to the panic they all felt in that moment. His magic gently nudged them back, keeping the space between the two couples.

Caid's fingers brushed along the smoothness of Róisín's cheek as he moved his hand to cup her jaw and tip her mouth open. He had just bent down over her when her eyes sprung open, and a rasping gasp clawed its way from her chest, exploding from her open mouth.

"C-Caid?" The bridge of her nose wrinkled as she squinted at him. The whiteness that had overtaken her eyes slowly faded.

Unable to speak, he sat back on his heels and buried his face in his hands.

"How did I get down here?" She asked.

His hands fell away from his face, and he looked up at her, unable to find words. He was an asshole, he knew it. But he was frozen. His entire system was trying to climb its way back up to functioning after crashing down, down, down until it was in that pit where his fear of losing her had resided since that day in the ravine.

"What is the last thing you remember?" Matthew asked. He and Lily had inched close enough to be within arm's reach.

Róisín had moved so she was now sitting. She rubbed at her temple and frowned. "We were in the study. I was skimming through books. Lily was at the desk combing through Lucius's papers you had out. You both"—She looked at him, then to Caid—"were in that room you found behind the shelves."

"Did anything happen? Did you see anything?" Lily asked.

"I..." Róisín blinked. She pressed the heels of her hands against her eyes and shook her head. Her shoulders shook, and that was enough to break Caid free of whatever hold he was under.

Leaning forward, he took her in his arms and brought her against him. He buried his face in her hair and drew in the scent of her. Tightened his arms around her and let her warmth, her *life*, seep into his skin, to his marrow. She was there. She was okay.

He brushed his lips over her forehead. "Where were you?"

"What do you mean?" Róisín's voice was muffled by his shirt where she had pressed her face. She gripped him tightly, her fingertips pressing deep against his skin as she clung.

"I felt something. Something new, different that I haven't felt before. It wasn't here, but it was—" His arms tightened again in reflex. "It's hard to explain. Something had you. Some*one*. My magic said it was from beyond us all."

"What does that mean?" Matthew asked. He had, at some point, lowered into a squat, one knee resting on the ground.

"That's—" Caid hissed out a breath when Róisín's nails bit into his back through his shirt.

355

"We need to go." She released her grip on him and tried to stand. "We need to find Hecate, Tura."

Not wanting to hurt her, Caid released her. Rising to his feet, he helped her up and slipped an arm around her waist. "Slow down," he said when she swayed against him. "Breathe, Róisín."

"We don't have time," she said.

"Róisín, you were just flat out on the ground. You didn't even blink," Matthew said. "It was like you were..." His throat bobbed. "Just —" He let out a shaking breath. "Take a second."

Caid spun her slowly to face him. He took her face between his hands. "What happened?"

"I saw, Caid." Her eyes filled with tears. "I saw it all."

He stroked a thumb over her cheek, swiping away a tear. "Saw?"

"I-I don't know where I was, but there were looms. Three of them." Her hands came up to cover his. The next words she spoke were so low, he almost didn't hear them. "I saw Gea take your thread."

Everything that was struggling back online inside of him, in one breath, slammed back into full operation with such force, he flinched.

"Caid, she didn't know. She *doesn't* know," Róisín said.

He fought to keep his voice even. "Doesn't know I'm still alive?"

"No. She doesn't know it was *you*. I don't think she knows about you at all. Especially if what Tura said is true." Her teeth chattered. He pulled his sweatshirt over his head and tugged it over her. "When she was at the loom, she was saying Aoife. 'I told you once, Aoife, you cannot stop me.'" Tears splashed onto her cheeks as she spoke. "Just before she ripped it out, she said she'd find out how she kept coming back and stop her from doing it again, then she was coming after me. She was going to make Hecate watch as she took Earth's realm before she killed her. With my magic."

His jaw snapped shut. Matthew's magic flared hot next to them as he stood.

"She's going to have to live through me first," Caid said.

"And me," Matthew said.

"I can't fight worth anything, but I'll be damned if I stand by," Lily said. "I just got you back. Both of you. I'm not saying goodbye again."

"Don't you get it, though?" Róisín looked at each of them. "Gea didn't know that Caid was on the loom. She doesn't know he exists. What are the odds she doesn't know the connection with Hecate?"

Matthew tipped his head to one side. "Given Hecate only had Elspeth, then Elspeth only had one..." He shrugged. "I don't think anyone outside of Hecate's circle would know about him."

"Or any of us," Lily said.

Caid's hands fell away from Róisín's face. "That gives us the upper hand, right?"

"It just may." Róisín nodded.

"We need to be careful." Lily wrapped her arms around her middle and shifted closer to Matthew. "She's still powerful, and she's still dangerous."

He wrapped his arms around her, bringing her against him. "Unhinged if what Ione and Shasta saw in the afterworld means anything."

Caid scratched his jaw. "Basically a ticking bomb. What do we do though? We have all of this"—He shifted his hands in circles before him—"information, but what do we do with it?"

Róisín turned to Lily. "Have you all been able to find any thread that we can grab and follow? Or has Ione figured out what she thinks we're missing?"

"Not yet. It's all just information right now, like Caid said. A time-line of everything. Which, now that we have it, why Aoife, Mildred, and the rest were on the mission to power that they were, it all makes sense."

"They knew who she was and wanted it for themselves," Róisín said quietly. "Even Madigan. After he brought his parent home, he wanted the power and rule."

"We need to get back to everyone," Matthew said, looking at Róisín. "Maybe with what you've seen, we can come up with something. *Anything.*"

With all the talking they had done, Caid wasn't sure what help it would be. Even with what Róisín had seen. The wheat stalks rustled in the wind, the breeze feeling like a phantom hand along his spine.

"Then let's head back," he said.

"I'll get that file and meet you back at the cottage." Matthew reached for Lily's hand.

"Wait!" Róisín lifted a hand to stop him. "You found something?"

"Caid found dad's file with his birth certificate and shit." Matthew scratched at his jaw. "Dad, uh, well..." He blew out a sharp breath. "Turns out dad had a bit of sight in him too, it would seem. Not much. It doesn't look like it ever really manifested into something useable for him."

"It would have been just enough for Gea had she known. She didn't want to take any chances. Not just to hunt him down." Róisín covered her mouth with her hand.

"Yeah." Matthew rocked back onto his heels. "Makes everything mom and dad did, and said, so much more understandable."

The only sound around them for a long moment was the rustle of the wheat blowing in the breeze.

"She won't ruin any more families," Róisín said. "Not as long as we still live."

SEVENTY

"YOU DIDN'T tell them about Crev." Tura stood near the door just inside Róisín and Caid's apartment in Greece. She had been staying there with Elizabeth and Ana before they had returned to their families to rest after exerting so much of their energy holding time.

Hecate paused at the threshold of the kitchen. She glanced over her shoulder, a brow raised high on her forehead. "And neither did you."

Tura pulled the sleeves of her sweater over her hands.

"Fate only allows even me so much leeway to step in. I'm to create, intervene occasionally when our people go a little *too* wild. And that's it. It is also worth mentioning, they were not completely open with us," Hecate said. She opened the refrigerator and pulled out a block of cheese.

"Can you blame them? Look at what's happened. All the lies and deception. The loss." Tura could place herself in their shoes, and with no doubt, know that she wouldn't trust herself or Hecate either.

"If there's no trust, then what is the point?" She sliced the cheese. "Grab a plate."

Hanging her head, she walked into the kitchen and took down a plate. She watched Hecate arrange the squares of cheese around the edge. "We've done nothing to earn their trust."

Hecate plucked a grape cluster from the basket on the counter. "Have you not done what was needed to guide them all together? To shake the tree a bit when they got stuck and needed a,"—She popped a grape into her mouth—"nut of information to fall into their lap?"

"None of it was free from deception."

"Look, Tura, we are all far from perfect. Sometimes our hands get dirty doing good work. You tried, you really did." Hecate set the cluster on the counter and moved closer. "Sometimes, despite trying, we are too late. Other times, we have to do the hard things. Aoife knew better than to do what she did in Roidon. She pushed back against you, and she paid the price." She put her hands on Tura's shoulders. "I know you don't like when you need to show those parts of you. What it means when they see your true face. You can't come back from it, so you never make that choice lightly." She pressed a kiss to Tura's forehead. "Aoife didn't give you the choice. Her actions forced you that day in the darkness. You have to release that blame you lay upon yourself."

Tura's chin dropped. "Easy for someone to say that isn't a monster."

"Tura," Hecate's voice was soft as she hooked a finger beneath her chin. "You are not a monster. You are a Goddess."

"Of the Hells. Which makes me a monster."

"You are a beautiful creation, my child. *My* beautiful creation. Not only to see the future, but to foster and care for our people when they've moved on through the veil. To bring justice for those others have wronged."

Tura squeezed her eyes shut. The Goddess of the Afterlife. A blessing and a curse because not all witches were good and just. Witches like Aoife, Frederick, Cronan, Madigan, they faced a much darker afterlife in which pain and brutality for eternity were their sentences for the lives they lived before death. Tura hadn't been able to endure it despite it being a part of her creation. The punishments took pieces of her soul each time. So, she created the demons.

Tura sucked in a sharp breath. Her lungs were burning, and her heart had slowed to near stopping.

"What? What is it?" Hecate's hands gripped her biceps. Tura swayed, and she moved her hands, banding her arms around her.

"Tura?" Hecate's voice shook. "Talk to me. What's happening?"

Tura forced her lips to move, but her voice would not come.

A warmth washed over her, seeped into her. Hecate's magic, probing.

"Something's wrong," Tura stammered the words.

"What?" Hecate's arms tightened around her.

"I can't—" Tura vision blurred. At the edges of her sight she saw... No, that couldn't be. Could it?

Her sisters gathered in the front room of their cottage. Two looms to one side. But her sisters were on the floor. Alina held Senna in her arms. Just as she was weak, she could *feel* the same weakness in her sisters.

What was happening to them?

She couldn't feel any of her gift of future. It was as though that magic had fled to an unreachable place.

"Fate." Her voice was hoarse. "It's changing."

Hecate closed her eyes and stilled. "No. It's intervening."

Tura jerked forward, her body curling. She ground her teeth together as a wall of pain, hot and furious, slammed into her.

"Breathe." Hecate lowered her to the ground. She smoothed a hand over Tura's hair. "Breathe."

Tura panted and curled tighter.

After what felt like an eternity, her body calmed. Blinking to clear the fog away, she reached with her mind to her loom. A wave of relief washed over her when she saw it. The threads of the future dancing, creating endless patterns. Slowly, she sat upright.

"What do we do now?" Hecate asked.

She pressed the heels of her hands against her eyes. "I don't know what it means."

"Fate has stepped in and acted itself. That means something. We don't know with who or about what, but something has happened. You felt your sisters, didn't you?"

Tura nodded.

"Then we need to figure out who fate reached for, and what that person needed to see or know." Hecate rose to her feet and helped Tura stand.

"Wait." Tura gripped the edge of the counter. A silver thread had woven its way nearly all the way down the loom, brushing alongside the deep burgundy one Tura always had an eye on. "Róisín."

"And?" Hecate prodded when Tura went silent again.

Tura swallowed hard. Her stomach burned as the acid churned in it like a storming sea. She was going back to the afterlife, and this time, she would have no choice but to use her magic.

"The Seer."

A smile bloomed on Hecate's face. "The final piece of the puzzle."

Tura frowned.

"Unfortunately, this is where you and I have to part ways for a bit, child." Hecate approached her.

"No. I cannot—"

Hecate cupped her face in her hands. She smiled down at her before pressing a kiss to her forehead. "You can do it, Tura. Finish this."

SEVENTY-ONE

"THAT'S ALL fine and dandy, but how do we find and *kill* her?"
Everyone in the room turned away from Róisín to look at Runa.

"I think that's what we're trying to figure out from all of this, babe." Ione gave his arm a squeeze.

He glanced at Róisín, mouth turned down in a deep frown. "What do you think?"

The question, his delegation to her, at first caught her off guard. She squared her shoulders. "We need to focus on finding her first. That's what we were doing before."

"She has her stuff strewn around the realms," Ione said. "We could always use the spell work from your mother's book."

Róisín thought of the necklace. The Oathkeeper. Her body tightened and her magic stretched, ready.

"I took care of her," Caid said in a low voice from behind her.

She glanced over her shoulder at him. His face was tight lines and shadows, almost like it had been something he hadn't wanted to tell her. "When?"

"While you healed at the cabin. Lina sat with you in case you woke up and needed something. I went..." His throat worked with his swallow. His jaw flexed.

"Thank you," she said.

Surprise lit his eyes.

She reached behind her and laced their fingers together before turning back to everyone else. "It's worth a shot to try again. But we need to know for sure it is hers, or else we're just wasting our time."

"What are our other options?" Anelle asked. She had rejoined them late that evening once dinner had been cleaned up and everyone was dispersing to their rooms. Despite what they faced, she seemed a little lighter in her step.

"We could ask Tura," Lily said.

"I think if she knew where her mother was, she would have happily told us at this point. That woman is terrified of her, and I think only Gea's death will ease any of that fear," Ten said. She shuffled the stack of papers her notes were scrawled on. "There has to be a way we can narrow it down to at least a realm. Go from there."

Cicile chewed on their bottom lip, blinking rapidly. "We don't have enough information to do that."

"Dammit." Ten let the papers fall back onto the table in front of her.

"We could draw her out," Caid said. He still held her hand but had moved to stand beside her. He was growing impatient. Róisín could feel it in their connection. The way his energy had shifted after they learned Gea didn't know whose thread she had pulled.

Something in his tone made her skin prickle. When she looked at him this time, his attention wasn't on her. She glanced across the room, following his line of sight. Matthew's green eyes were staring, unblinking, back at Caid.

Pulling her attention away from him, she said, "She wants me. I'd be the easiest sell to get her where we know we can overpower her."

It had been enough to shake Caid free from whatever thoughts he had of going into it alone, or for he and Matthew to go after Gea without the rest of them. Just as she had intended. She didn't need to reach into his mind to know. It was in the way he held his body, primed for action.

Shasta quickly stepped between them. She placed a hand on Caid's chest to stop him, then looked to Róisín. And winked at her. "It's too risky. Too much can go wrong," she said.

Róisín knew she was playing with fire when she said, "Not if we plan it right."

The sound that rumbled from Caid's chest was a near growl.

"She's not wrong," Aja said, earning a smack in the arm from Anelle. "What?"

"It's like—" Anelle waved a hand toward Caid. "Come on, help me out, Earth Boy. The thing about the cows."

"Leading a cow to slaughter," Caid said through his clenched teeth.

Anelle snapped her fingers. "That. No, she isn't wrong. But yes, to what Shasta said. Too risky. We're all dead if Gea gets her hands on Róisín's magic. Not just Hecate and Róisín."

The room fell silent.

"Have you lost your fucking mind?" Caid's voice echoed in her head.

"Have you?!" Her words came barreling through their connection so hard, she nearly spoke them aloud.

"It's late. We're all running on very little sleep." Shasta nudged Caid back a step. "Go to bed. We're short on time, and even shorter on room for error. We have to get this right. The first time. Because we won't get a second chance at this."

"Sounds like an excellent plan." Ione took Runa's hands and pulled him from the room. "We'll see everyone in the morning!"

Ten and Cicile slipped out behind them.

Shasta's eyes darted between Róisín and Caid. "Don't kill each other." She motioned for Anelle and Aja to follow her as she passed them.

Matthew and Lily were next. Not before Matthew said to Caid, "You don't have to ask."

Once they were alone, Caid's hands were at Róisín's shoulders, and in a blink, they were standing in their bedroom of the cabin.

"What was *that* all about?" She shouted at him at the same time he repeated, "Have you lost your fucking *mind*?"

Placing her palms against his chest, she shoved him back. "Fuck you."

"Dammit, Róisín. You can't just walk around waving a white flag in the air for her."

"Why not? You know I'm right. It would be the easiest way to get her where we want her."

He slapped his hands on his hips. His brows came down over his eyes, transforming his face into something dark and angry. "Nothing's changed, has it? You're still ready to walk into the fire, alone if it means saving everyone else."

"Isn't that what *you're* planning to do, you asshole? Or is it different because it's you? Hm?" She came toward him. "It's different that you get to go get yourself killed, right? Easier to leave me behind."

"That's not what I mean and you know it."

"And it's not what *I* mean, Caid. Just because I said I would draw her out doesn't mean that I'm stupid enough to face her alone."

His face went slack. "You're not stupid. Headstrong and stubborn, yes. But not stupid."

"Then admit it. It's a start. If we plan it right, this can be the end. For all of us. But we need to be *all* in. Every single one of us."

He drew a hand down his face, then held it out, reaching for her. She took a small step forward, but it was enough for him to link their fingers together and tug her against him. His words were thick when he spoke. "It's too much like before. Too much can go wrong. One second, you're dancing at some fancy gala, the next, Madigan is on top of you, taking your magic. And I... I can't, Róisín."

She pressed her face against his chest. His heart thundered against it. Her own heart was pinched in her chest. Just as her lungs were. She was afraid to move, afraid to breathe. If time could just hold on for a second, again.

"It's only one option. Just one." She wasn't sure who she was trying to assure, herself or him. He was remembering Talista as the moment he had nearly lost her, while she was remembering it as when she *had* lost *him*.

Exhaustion tugged her down. She tried to stifle her yawn but failed.

"Come on." He pulled her toward the bed. "We need to get some sleep."

"I should probably shower. After being in the valley like that, I'm gross."

Caid laid next to her, then leaned over her to press a soft kiss to her lips. "And I smell like I just rolled out of hell. It can wait until morning."

She wanted to argue, to get up from the bed, go into the bathroom and scrub it all away. Instead, she burrowed against him, her head on his chest. A breath later, sleep had claimed her.

* * *

As she slept, Róisín found herself back in Roidon. The Seer turning to ash and floating away on a gust of wind.

Gea dressed in pale blue, flowing linen. With each step she took toward Róisín, it swirled around her legs. *"Without the house, the Seer drifts..."*

Róisín kicked her legs free of the blankets and rolled onto her back. The memory shaping her dream; tugging her deeper.

"Do not fret... without the house, they are nothing..."

Somewhere outside of the dream, Caid reached for her. His hand smoothed over her bare stomach, thumb stroking for a second before he hooked his arm around her and brought her against him.

"I've got you." His whispered words filtered through the leaning, twisting trees of the Dead Forest to her.

The dream flickered around Róisín. Gea shifting into Madigan. Dark trees melting away, revealing other couples dancing, whirling around them.

"One day, she just swept in and took them from us..." Madigan spun Róisín around, then brought her back against his chest. In her ear, his voice low, he said, *"Bound them to that house for eternity..."*

Róisín sat up with a gasp.

SEVENTY-TWO

MARCELO STOOD facing the dark wood of the door to his brother's suite in the castle. The coldness on the other side waited for him. Its frigid fingers reached beneath the door for his ankles.

"I don't like this, Celo." Nolani had her lips pressed together so tightly they had become colorless. "You should come back with me."

He stepped closer to her, selfishly wanting to steal her warmth. "I have to be here with him." He brought his arms around her. "I can't leave him alone, Nolani. He has no one."

"For good reason."

"Are you to say if it were Tizan or Bastian, *both*, you'd leave them on their own?"

The sigh she released made her body sink deeper into his embrace. "What if you don't come back?"

Marcelo's arms tightened. He may have been the stronger brother, in all ways before the monsters had woke inside of them, and after, but he would be foolish to believe that in his brother's state, Anthony couldn't be more ruthless and brutal. Desperation could drive a man well beyond his limits. The chance Marcelo's days would end before his brother became very real the moment he stepped into that room.

"What if he—"

368

His lips crashed against hers, quieting the rest of her questions. He didn't want to spend what could be his last moments with her, with his heart, his soul, his everything, arguing.

Marcelo wasn't going to let his brother die alone.

Even if their monsters faced one another in those last days.

"Marcelo." Nolani's breath was hot against his lips.

He took her face between his hands and kissed her again. Softer this time.

"You move on, Nolani." His forehead rested against hers. With his thumbs stroking over her cheeks, he whispered, "If I don't come back, if he..." He swallowed hard. "There will be another that will find you. Love you. Let them. You deserve a world filled with happiness."

Nolani closed her eyes, sending tears down her cheeks to his thumbs. "Celo."

"Please. Nolani, promise me. Promise me you'll move on."

Her body quaked in his arms. Her golden tiger's eye-colored eyes shone as she looked up at him.

"Please."

Her chin dipped slightly. "I may move on, but you'll always have my heart."

He threaded his fingers in her hair. His chin trembled as he struggled to keep his emotions in. She didn't need to see him break. Squeezing his eyes closed, he had just pressed his lips against her forehead when the door opened.

"Nolani, you can't—Gah!" Anthony's nails dug into the wood of the door. "You can't be here," he gasped the words out.

Marcelo quickly pushed her behind him. "Close the door, Ant. Give us a moment."

"Celo, she needs to—" He clutched his stomach. The skin around his eyes rippled.

"Close. The. Door. Ant."

Anthony slammed the door shut. The howl of pain he released once it latched had Marcelo's muscles bracing.

Nolani's fingers dug into his forearms, pulling him, turning away from the door and moving them further down the hall.

"Celo, he's... I..." She covered her mouth with a hand, her eyes wide with horror.

"Now you see why I need to be here."

She looked past him to the door.

"He's right." Marcelo tucked a strand of her hair behind one of her ears. "You can't be here any longer."

She brought her hands to her face. "If he can't control it, please." Her voice shook. "Do everything you can to come back to me."

He covered her hands. "If I can't—"

"I promised. I don't like it, but I will keep that promise." Nolani rose to her toes and kissed him. "I love you."

"I love you. Stay with the others. Whether or not they succeed, stay with them. They'll keep you safe." He released her hands and stepped back.

Her hands fell to her sides, fisting. She stood silent for a moment. Her eyes darting over his face, like she was committing it one last time to memory. Finally, she shifted away.

"Is she gone?" Anthony's voice was thin and muffled through the door.

Staring at where Nolani had been standing, an emptiness quickly filled where Marcelo's heart once beat. Yes, she was gone. He could only hope she would stay away. Leave him to this choice. On his own. He straightened and faced the door. "Let me in, Ant."

Part Four

"Meet me at the end before I turn into sand."
—— **Kush**

SEVENTY-THREE

R ÓISÍN FROWNED at the overflowing basket of fruit on the counter in the apartment. There had been one banana left when the bottom completely dropped out of her life, again, with the arrival of Hecate and Tura. Someone had been there. Her magic immediately flared, reaching out around the small space.

"This is cute as fuck." Ione dropped onto the loveseat. "Oh, it's like a cloud." She nestled deeper into the cushions. "I need one."

Lily came to stand next to Róisín. "What's wrong?"

"Someone's been—"

"Oh. Róisín, hello." Tura shifted before them.

"You've been staying here," Róisín said.

Tura's cheeks turned dark pink.

"Whatever. It doesn't matter." Róisín pushed the books she had swiped from the dining room table in the cabin against her chest. "It's perfect actually that you're here. You can help."

"I can?" Tura pursed her lips. She looked down at the books she now held. "What are we doing?"

"That's an excellent question. This blanket is fabulous," Ione said. "I need you to decorate mine and Runa's place when we get one."

When Róisín looked over to the loveseat, she saw Ione had wrapped

376

herself in Róisín's favorite sherpa lined blanket. "The credit for the blanket actually goes to Lina. It was a Christmas present."

"It's just so..." She wiggled and tightened the blanket, then yawned. "Comfy."

Lily walked into the living room. She set a tablet and two books on the coffee table. "Why just us? And why the urgency?"

"No, the real question is, why so sneaky about it?" Ione said.

"I had a dream. Not really a dream, actually." Róisín sat in a chair across from Ione. She reached for the tablet. Tapping the screen on, she sorted through the notes they had. "Something Gea said to me in Roidon has been following me since. I've never been able to pinpoint why I can't shake it."

Tura's face paled. "What did she say?"

"A lot of weird, cryptic stuff. It was when she told me to unite the Covens. Once everything settled—" She found the pages she was looking for and paused to read over them. "I got this feeling it was a, well, a scam for the lack of a better explanation. Like she wanted something else from me." Róisín popped the stylus from the case and highlighted the details Lily had noted about the night in Roidon. Then tapped forward to find the notes about the day in Talista. "*That* suspicion was confirmed when I saw her rip Caid's thread from your loom."

The books Tura held fell to the floor with a thud. "How? How did you?"

Róisín shrugged and highlighted the next set of notes. She pulled the highlighted parts into a separate document, then handed the tablet to Lily. "Fate? I don't know. I just know I was there, *somewhere*. It was a small room with a stone fireplace. Looms, three of them."

"Our home. My sisters and I..." Tura stooped to pick up the books. "Why didn't you tell us?"

"It only happened this afternoon. After you and Hecate had left." Time was not on their side that morning. She had slipped out of the cabin while Caid was still sleeping. Then, she had dragged Lily and Ione from the cottage while *their* significant others slept.

"It'd be easier if she knew," Lily said.

Releasing a heavy sigh, Róisín brought Tura up to speed.

"Hecate's family remains. *All* witches, and here maybe as well?" The relief in Tura's voice was palpable.

"Why is that important?" Ione asked from her blanket cocoon.

"For starters, about the time that Gea finds out that Caid, Lina, and the twins are Hecate's direct descendants..." Róisín had to stop herself. She could feel the way her magic was stirring inside at the threat of just the possibility. Closing her eyes, she took in a deep breath. She reached for her magic and stroked it gently with her senses. She was safe. They were safe.

Her eyes flew open. She scrunched her nose, brows drawn, as she stared Tura down. "The Jordbrand Coven. That's not real, is it?"

Tura's lips pressed into a thin line and she shook her head. "That came as she was losing her reach in the realms. Elspeth was living here, and Hecate was able to convince her to *stay* here. Together they created the false history of an Earth Coven under the name Jordbrand."

"That also happened to have died off," Ione said, tone flat.

"If there was no Coven to covet in this realm, Gea would keep her focus elsewhere."

Ione snorted. "Gea didn't think to, oh, I dunno, take a visit to Earth to see if there were witches here?"

"Think about it though." Lily set the tablet down. She shuffled through the book stack and lifted one. After thumbing through a few pages. "Everything back then was recorded by hand. You could easily create a record of a birth, death, even a *war* that would be taken as fact whether it was true or not."

"Which, dammit, I'm stuck." Ione wrestled with her blanket until her arms were free and she was sitting upright. "Doesn't make sense. Because if I wanted to usurp someone like Hecate, you can bet your damned ass that I would be personally going to each realm."

"It will be the mistake my mother made that she will come to regret."

The coldness of Tura's tone had them slowly turning their heads toward her.

"I hope," she added off-hand.

"Hope?" Róisín arched a brow.

Tura's eyes locked onto Róisín's. "I've... I've seen the threads change between two futures."

"What does that mean?" She asked.

"It's never happened before. Not like this. Any time a thread changes paths, it always will settle on one. This, however, it's different. All of your threads move between two paths. Consistently. Yours more than the others." Tura sat next to her.

Róisín put a hand on Tura's thigh. "Tura, where is the Seer?"

"The Seer?" Lily and Ione asked in unison.

"That's why we're here. Everything you highlighted were things mentioned about them in both of those incidents," Lily said.

Róisín nodded. "The Seer drifts. That's what Gea had said in the Dead Forest. I couldn't figure out why my brain kept chanting it over and over all of these years. Then in my dream tonight, it, and something Madigan said too, brought it all together."

Lily shifted her weight, tucking her legs beneath her. Resting the tablet on her knees, she held the stylus in her hand, poised to take notes. "What are you thinking?"

"Gea bound the Seer to the house in the Dead Forest. She said that without the house they drift." She watched Lily tap out what she had said on the screen. "However, Madigan said that the Seer was bound to the house for eternity."

"Didn't the house get destroyed that night, though?" Ione asked.

"Yes and no," Róisín said. "It collapsed. Which means that it's still there."

Lily tapped the stylus on her thigh. "Róisín, the Seer isn't."

"We know that. They're *somewhere* though. They turned to ash and floated away—"

"Which means the bind on the house and Seer had grown weak over the centuries," Tura interrupted. "If it still held strong, they would be trapped with the rubble."

Róisín lifted a finger. "This is why we're here."

One of Ione's brows lowered over an eye while the other lifted high on her forehead.

"I think if we can find the Seer, get them back to Aunellion, it will be the catalyst to the end of this all," Róisín said.

Ione clucked her tongue. Lily gasped. Tura, however, burst into laughter.

Róisín moved so that she was sitting sideways. "Are you withholding something, Tura?"

"No. I'm just…" She pat her chest. "There's something tickling me here. I've never felt it before. It's like… bubbles? Yes."

"She's going mad," Ione muttered from the loveseat.

"Nerves?" Lily suggested.

"Oh, I know nerves. I've felt them since the moment that I discovered who my mother really was and what she was doing. This is,"—A smile bloomed on her face—"Lighter."

Róisín reached over and took one of her hands. "That, Tura, is hope."

"I like it. It's a pleasant feeling."

"It is," Róisín said.

"We're going to Roidon?" Ione untucked the rest of herself from the blanket.

"We are." Róisín nodded. "I've got some notes in these"—She tapped the books she had brought. "That can probably help us."

Ione leaned forward and grabbed one of the books. "How are we doing this?"

"That's why I brought everything from the cabin," Róisín said.

"Wait. You weren't even at the cottage?" Ione's eyes flared wide.

"Once you all went to your rooms, Caid brought me home. I've grown so used to it just being us. All the extra noise has been…" She wiped her palms on the legs of her jeans. "Last night, we weren't exactly in the mood to be quiet and Shasta was right. We all needed sleep."

Ione cackled. "Oh, sweetie, Runa and I weren't quiet either."

"No, they really weren't." Lily narrowed her eyes at her sister. "It's weird, like we don't have this sound blocking spell."

"Pfft." Ione rolled her eyes. "Not like you and Matthew don't knock the headboard when you have company."

Lily's cheeks reddened.

"We weren't '*knocking the headboard*,'" Róisín said. "It was more us yelling at one another."

"Oh." Ione's eyes fell to her book.

"Are you two okay?" Lily asked.

"We're good, now. Or we stay that way as long as we get this all figured out before he realizes I'm not anywhere near him anymore."

"Hence the urgency," Ione said.

"Hence the urgency. Not just that we clearly don't have much time with this, but that too." Róisín tugged at a lock of her hair.

"Let's dive in then." Ione flipped open her book.

Twenty minutes later, the rest of the puzzle they were trying to build came together.

"Removing the Seer from Aunellion was my mother's first act to all of this," Tura said.

Róisín rose from the sofa and stretched her arms overhead. "It appears that way."

"It stands to reason that you're right about your theory then." Ione nudged the blanket off and stood. "Which means we need to test Lily's theory."

"What?" Lily blinked up from the tablet.

"I think you're onto something with getting a piece of the house and using Brenna's spell work." Ione tugged the band from her hair, then used her fingers to comb it.

"If they're drifting, what are the odds that means they're just scattered ash floating around the realms, though?" Róisín asked.

"If they're bound to something, it will reform them," Tura said.

"Re-bind them to something from the house?" Róisín asked.

"Anything would work, but that would be easiest, yes." Tura rose. "I could help. If you'd like me to, that is."

"You're one of us now," Ione said, standing.

Lily looked at her watch. "We have about forty minutes, tops, Earth time, before we're all noticed to be missing, and it gets ugly. Matthew won't notice I'm gone until he wakes."

Róisín knew it would be the same for her and Caid. Unlike the tether bonded witches share in which a witch had to intentionally reach for their bonded to know they were still there, Caid and Róisín's hearts seemed to beat in one another's chests now. A constant presence, near or far. For Caid, as long as he felt Róisín's heart, he wouldn't stir from sleep. Once he woke?

Róisín looked around the room at each of them. "Then we better get a move on. Even Roidon time, that doesn't leave us much room."

Seventy-Four

S HASTA CUPPED her mug between her hands. Lifting it to her mouth, she blew across the top of it to cool it. The cottage had finally fallen quiet, yet she found even the idea of sleep impossible. She had lain in her bed until the pre-dawn light had lit her room.

"Is it okay if I join you?" Nolani's voice came from the doorway, pulling Shasta's attention from her tea.

Shasta smiled at her. "Of course."

Nolani quietly padded across the room, her own mug clutched in her hands. She and Marcelo had been noticeably absent at the last gathering. Judging by Nolani's swollen red eyes, Shasta knew why. It didn't surprise her that Marcelo stuck to his intent to be with his brother. He was loyal, honorable. And Shasta had been witness to how close the brothers had been... before.

"It isn't easy," Shasta began. "My late wife, Evelyn, she was a helper. Something inside of her was just drawn to it. However she could help, she never hesitated."

Nolani slowly lowered her mug to her lap.

"During this realm's second Great War, she signed on to be a spy for British Intelligence. I hated it because it put her right in the path of danger."

"W-what did you do?" Nolani asked.

"I told her how much I loved her. Then I told her to come back to me."

Nolani placed the mug on the table in front of them. She clasped her hands tightly together, her knuckles turning white. "It's what I told Celo."

Shasta reached over and laid a hand over Nolani's. "It's all we can do, sweetheart. We need to let them be free to make their own decisions."

"It-it's so hard. What if—" She sniffed. "What if he doesn't come back? He's not like us. I won't get to see him again. Ever."

Shasta's eyes filled with warm tears. "I'm so sorry, Nolani."

"If he dies, Shasta, how do I let him go?" Nolani lifted her tear-stained face. "How do I keep my promise to move on?"

"I wish I had an answer," she said, her voice thick. "I'm still working on my promises to Ev. Day by day. One foot in front of the other."

Nolani's breath hitched, and a sob broke free. Shasta moved closer and took her in her arms.

Around her sobs, Nolani asked, "Will the curse break if Gea dies? Were we right?"

Shasta's chin quivered as the emotions rose inside of her to near spilling. There were false assurances she could give, but she remembered Brenna's words the day Shasta found herself on Brenna's sofa in this same situation that Nolani faced.

"There's a chance it may not. You have to be prepared for that." She stroked a hand over Nolani's hair, rocking with her. "You need to be ready to face the chance your future may not involve Marcelo."

When Nolani's sobs grew louder, shaking her body, Shasta ground her molars together and held her tighter.

"If that happens, I will be there for you." She pressed a kiss to the top of Nolani's head. "I will help you, every day, survive. That's my promise to you."

"Ione!" Runa's shout from overhead startled them both, breaking them apart.

Shasta tipped her head back.

"Ione!"

No, she hadn't imagined it, the pure panic that filled his tone. Something was wrong.

SEVENTY-FIVE

I T WAS the hollowness in his chest that drove Caid from sleep. His
eyes flew open, arm immediately reaching for Róisín only to be met
with a cool pillow and empty space.

"Róisín?" He called out.

Sitting up, he focused on the bathroom, expecting to hear her soft
humming as she showered away the dirt and grime from the valley. Only
silence met his ears.

"Róisín?"

Pushing back the blankets, he got out of the bed and moved into the
main part of the cabin. His heart gave him what could only be consid-
ered a half beat. The place next to it where he always felt Róisín was
empty.

"*We cannot find...*" His magic hissed in an angry, impatient voice.

He swallowed down the fear that was trying to choke him. Gripping
the doorframe of the bedroom, he pressed his magic out. He pushed it
deeper into the woods around them.

"*She's not—*"

"I know," he snapped. "I fucking *know.*"

There was nothing. No trace of her, or her magic. The connection
inside of him was gone. He could no longer feel any part of her.

She was gone.
He shifted away with a roar.

SEVENTY-SIX

Róisín used her foot to nudge a rock aside. "This was an awful idea. Who let me talk us into doing this?"

"More like why did any of us agree to it?" Ione huffed from where she was digging in the dirt with a stick.

"For what it's worth, I didn't expect it to just be..." Róisín threw her arms out wide. "Gone."

Lily, who was crawling around to Ione's left, on her hands and knees, paused. "I mean, it shouldn't *be* gone, though. It hasn't been nearly close to long enough for the forest to have taken it back."

"About that." Tura's voice carried a tremor to it. "Why does it feel like they're watching us?"

"Because they are," Róisín said.

"What?!" Tura yelped. A second later, she was sprinting back toward them from where she had been at the edge of the forest searching for any remains of the house.

Róisín called over to Lily, "How much longer do we have before we can expect company?"

"Seven minutes." Lily stood and brushed the dirt from her knees.

"Fuck—shit! I've got something, I think!" Ione's digging grew more frantic.

Róisín climbed over the log in front of her and knelt next to Ione.

"Here. You were here more recently. I was maybe seventy the one and only time I trekked out here." Ione shuddered. "The Seer gave me the heebie-jeebies."

"Is it?" Lily dropped next to them.

Tura followed shortly behind.

Róisín pressed her thumb against the object Ione had handed her, pushing a chunk of dirt free. "What is it?" She pulled the bottom of her shirt out. After rubbing the fabric against the object a few times, the debris was cleared. "A door hinge pin?"

"If it's a part of the house, it will work," Ione said.

Róisín handed it back to her.

Lily leaned in to get a closer look. "I say we give it a shot and see what happens. We've got five minutes before two angry men show up, shouting at us for taking off without them."

"Three," Ione said. "Runa will know if you're missing along with me, that Matthew can use the tether to find you, and he'll tag along."

"What happens if they show up?" Tura's eyes darted between them.

Róisín scrunched her nose. "A fight. Not just because I snuck off, but because this is probably pretty valuable information." She motioned to the pin.

"Why didn't you want to tell them?"

Ione looked at Róisín, expectant.

"Time primarily. Bringing everyone up to speed, and the time it would take for everyone to hash out their theories. I know Lily's academic mind very well from our time together." She sent Lily a small smile. Lily returned it with one of her own, her cheeks turning a faint hint of pink. "And Ione was the only one who was able to figure out Cronan's book and the curse."

"A lot of good *that* did," Ione mumbled, thumbing the door hinge pin.

"It may not have been able to save Marcelo and Anthony, but something tells me we still need it," Róisín said.

"Three minutes before angry men," Lily said.

"Spell, Ione." Róisín said. "We can hash out the rest later."

Ione's eyes fell closed. Her lips moved with her whispered words.

The hair on Róisín's arms rose as the smell of Ione's magic's energy filled the air. "What?" She asked when Ione's brows pinched.

"It's the Seer's," she said. At her confirmation, the trees around them began to creak and sway.

"And?" Lily asked when Ione said nothing more.

"I guess it's a good thing I know how to cross the veil," she said.

Lily and Tura began talking at once. Róisín lifted a hand, waving it to silence them. "What do you mean, Ione? Are they dead?"

"No. They're still alive. Somehow, though, they've crossed the veil into the afterworld."

Róisín looked at Tura. "How is that possible?"

"I-I don't know. It shouldn't be possible to cross and remain among the living. The longer you stay, the more life you lose until there's nothing left."

Tura's rapid blinking told Róisín there was more. She took the pin from Ione and held it up in front of Tura. "You better talk. Now."

"Sixty seconds," Lily said nervously.

Tura looked from Ione, to Róisín. "I can take you."

"Take me where?" Róisín asked.

"To the afterworld."

The quartet rose to their feet in unison.

"How?" Ione stood next to Lily.

Her shoulders sagged with her exhalation. "I'm the Goddess of the Hells. Aside from my magic of future sight, a gift from fate, I am also who our people call Mother Death. I created the Hells. The afterworld where we rest for eternity. In-between while we seek redemption into the afterworld. And... the darkness. The demons are my children."

Róisín's brain took a half-second to catch up to what Tura was saying. She was speaking so rapidly, Róisín had been sure she had heard wrong.

Opting to act first, question later, Róisín lifted her shoulders and held her hand out to Ione. "Take us. Ione and I. Lily, go back and tell the others everything. *Do not* let them come for us. The fewer, the better."

"But—"

Lily's complaint was cut off as Tura gripped Róisín's other hand and whipped them away to the afterworld.

Seventy-Seven

Róisín felt as though she were being pushed through one of Sloane's buckets of slime. Her body trying to propel her forward, but the stickiness of the veil wall grabbed hold of her. Gritting her teeth, she let her magic flare, pushing her forward and through, landing face first on pale gray dirt.

Groaning, she pushed herself to her knees. "Ione?" She whispered.

"Over here."

Róisín rocked back onto her heels, then stood. Her eyes took in the desolate space around them, the air heavy, oppressive on her lungs. The silence, so abrupt after the windstorm on the other side of the veil, felt deafening.

Spinning in a circle, she searched for Ione.

"Hells, these are Runa's favorite pants on me," she heard Ione mutter at her left. Róisín had managed two steps toward her when she was halted by a voice.

"Róisín?" That was her father's voice.

When she turned to him, he stood in a torn shirt, dirt covered pants, with his mouth hanging open. His eyes shone with tears.

"Oh, daddy, no." She shook her head and ran toward him. "I'm okay. I'm not—" Her words died in her throat when she collided with him, throwing her arms around his shoulders. "Daddy."

His arms came around her tightly, lifting her off of her feet as he hugged her to him. "If you're not, then how?"

"I'm just looking for someone." She squeezed him tighter before letting go, and he released her. When her feet touched the ground, she looked over her shoulder to where Ione was trudging toward them. She was still cursing, fingers playing with a rip at the thigh of her jeans.

"I know you," Stephen said, his eyes on Ione.

Ione stopped and looked up. "Brenna's husband. Stephen? You came to Ely with her." Ione shifted her weight, turning her head to Róisín. "He's human, so I'm guessing that's why he's not stuck in any of the afterworlds."

"What?" Stephen's brow wrinkled.

Ione jabbed a thumb in Róisín's direction. "I've been hanging out with her enough lately to know the questions before she even asks them."

Stephen looked between them. "We can't be out here in the open long. We should find shelter."

"Dad—"

The ground rumbled beneath her feet and an ear-piercing shriek split the air.

"That's why," he said. "Come on. Follow me."

They slid and ducked their way across the barren space of the afterword for what felt like an eternity before Stephen tugged the women behind a lean-to made from what appeared to be charred wood.

"If you go deep enough, there are trees," he said.

"Where are all the afterworlds?" Ione asked.

Stephen dropped heavily onto a log. "They began to disappear not long after Brenna and I got here. A few weeks ago, after we returned from seeing everyone in Ely."

"That was... that was over six years ago," Ione said quietly.

"Six—" Stephen covered his mouth with a hand.

Róisín reached out and took his other in hers. "Before they disappeared, what did it look like?"

His gaze shifted, looking beyond her. "It was *alive*. It was quite an experience going from sleep to waking here. For a moment, it was as though it was before the war and I was still alive. My brain"—He rubbed his temple furiously—"I was fooled at first. Even more when Brenna, my beautiful Brenna, was before my eyes." His mouth curved into a lopsided smile. "There were streets, before," he continued, motioning with a hand to beyond the dusty lean-to. "The afterworlds were more like homes. Folks could come and go, visit, cross the veil." He scratched his jaw. "Well, most could. The troubles with the veil had already begun to happen. Everything seemed to move rapidly after our arrival, however."

Ione clucked her tongue. "Róisín."

"Where's mom?" Róisín asked.

Stephen nodded to the sparse landscape. "Wherever Evelyn is."

Róisín covered her face with her hands and bit back the urge to scream. How were they going to find the Seer if they couldn't even find the afterworlds?

"Ione, you need to go back. You need to get Tura to cross," Róisín said.

Ione snorted and shook her head. "That's like telling Caid to stop wearing flannel."

Róisín sighed heavily, hoping it would suppress the chuckle that fought its way up her throat. "At this point, I think we need to risk anything crossing through. We can just add it to our list of shit we need to take care of."

Ione stood and thumbed the tear of her jeans again. "We don't have much time left, Róisín."

"I know. Which is why we need her, Ione. If she's the Goddess of our Hells, she has to have the magic we need to fix this." She looked at her father, who was watching them closely. "Hecate's been too protective of her and her magic."

"We get to be the bad guys," Ione said.

"I don't *want* to be, but at this point"—Róisín lifted her hands and shrugged—"You and I are the best ones for the job."

Ione flashed her a quick grin. "Give me five minutes. Be ready, because she may be kicking and screaming when we get here," she said and shifted away.

SEVENTY-EIGHT

CAID HAD gone to Lina first. By the time he had gotten to Greens Glen, he had calmed himself enough to come to her door casually.

"Did you save the world?" Lina asked, slipping snacks into lunchboxes on the counter.

"What? No, not yet. Have you seen Róisín?"

She spun around to face him. "Excuse me? Did you just... Kincaid, tell me what is going on right now, and no." She pointed a finger and wagged it at him. "Shut up, I'm not done. Because I know that one of you can tell when the other one *blinks*. For you to not know where she is, something's wrong."

That was all it took to deflate what he had left of control. He covered his face with his hands and would have growled, shouted anything, but he knew the twins were still sleeping. They didn't need to be a part of this.

"I can't feel her anymore, Leen." His words were a broken whisper. "It's just hollow in here. Completely empty." He thumped a hand against his chest.

Lina's hands came to her neck first, then covered her mouth. "Is she?"

395

"I don't know." His voice grew thicker, his emotions threatening to drown him. "I can't feel if she is or not. Leen—"

She nearly leapt across the kitchen at him, her arms coming around him. "Don't. Don't go there, okay? It's probably some stupid witchy thing for us here in this realm. You've heard her say many times over the years how different her magic feels now. How it's always changing inside of her and whatever. That's probably what it is."

He knew Lina didn't even believe her own words. She was speaking too quickly, and her body shook as she embraced him.

"Go to Ireland. I'm sure she's there. Okay?" She stepped back and took his face in her hands. "She's fine. It's Róisín."

He licked his bottom lip. That was the problem. He knew Róisín too well. Knew the risk she would take for them all. Something new bubbled up inside of him; hot, acidic. Eating away at him.

Lina shook his head lightly. "She's okay, Caid. Go. And let me know."

He pulled her in for a quick hug. Not trusting his voice, he nodded to her, then shifted to Ireland.

"Where is she?" Caid shouted, pushing into the cottage, nearly colliding with Runa.

Shasta burst into the hallway from the living room, a wide-eyed Nolani in tow. "Why are you two *shouting*?"

"Where's Róisín?" Caid asked.

Runa glanced from him to Shasta. "And Ione."

"What the Hells is all the shouting about?" Anelle trudged down the stairs, rubbing her eyes. Aja thudded down behind her. He squinted at Caid and said, "You look like you want to kill someone."

"Right now, I do," Caid said between his clenched teeth. Somewhere between Greens Glen and Ireland, that feeling had flared to life inside him. He didn't know what he was raging against, whose neck he wanted wrapped in his hands, but the dark rage burning inside of him wanted death.

Shasta slowly lifted her hands, then pressed them to his shoulders to turn him around. She nudged him toward the living room. "Come sit down so we can figure this out. Anelle, go grab Ten and Cicile and—"

The front door flew open, banging against the wall of the front entrance. Matthew stepped inside, tugging Lily behind him. "It seems the ladies have been"—Matthew's eyes dropped to Lily briefly—"Working a theory."

"A theory?" Shasta asked.

Matthew nodded towards them and Lily blinked at him.

"I'll butcher it," he said to her. "That will only make it sound worse than it is." He waved a hand toward Caid, then Runa. "Which will make those two snap. I know I would if I heard someone tell me what you're about to say and it was you involved."

Lily pressed her lips together, her nostrils flaring. "They crossed the veil."

"What?" Everyone shouted at once.

"Why?" Shasta asked. "How?"

"Tura took them," Lily said.

Caid started toward the door, but Shasta's hand gripped his biceps. "Caid."

He let Shasta's touch anchor him as he fought against the need to track Tura down, demand answers, demand entry to the afterworld.

In a shaking voice, Lily kept her eyes on her hands folded in front of her as she relayed Róisín's quest to find the Seer and a way to return them to Aunellion. Believing that if they did so, it would be the pivotal shift in returning Hecate to power, and drawing Gea out.

"But how?" Shasta asked.

They all turned to where Ten and Cicile stood at the back of the group clustered in the hallway. It was Cicile that stepped forward and spoke. "I think they're on to something. Cronan's curse on the Aunellion Coven was powerful. Are we sure that it's tied to the return of the Seer to the realm, though?"

Everyone turned back to Lily. "I don't know," she stammered. "Madigan told Róisín that he wanted to bring them back to Aunellion."

"Which means it's a stretch," Shasta said. Her grip on Caid's arm loosened.

"Not necessarily." Aja moved the rest of the way down the stairs. "We still have the original curse, and they"—He nodded toward Ten and Cicile—"have Ione's translation. Exactly how Cronan wrote it."

"And?" Anelle elbowed Ten in the side.

Ten exhaled loudly. "If they can find the Seer, it will work. *Until the restoration of my beloved amongst our realm*," she said.

"Will it break the curse as Frederick placed it?" Nolani asked from where she hovered just inside the doorway to the living room. "Even with his warded words?"

"It *should* completely break down any trace of it," Ten confirmed. "Because the core of Frederick's is Cronan's. If that no longer stands…"

"What happens when the curse breaks? How does it tie to Gea?" Runa cracked his knuckles. Caid could feel he was itching for a fight, just as Caid was.

"It would be a two-fold thing if it's successful." Ten extended one hand. "Releasing a curse that is on the scale Cronan's is will be a massive push of energy out into the realms because the Aunellions still living are so spread around." She extended her other hand. "Paired with the blow breaking what Gea has done with the Seer will cause…"

"It throws the realms into chaos and zaps some of Gea's power?" Matthew asked.

Ten grinned at him. "Oh, it's gonna cause a massive mess."

Shasta's fingers flexed against Caid's arm. "It will not only draw Gea out, but it'll do it when she's not at her full strength?"

"It's pretty genius if you ask me," Ten said.

Caid felt Lily approach his other side and looked down at her.

"We were in Greece," she spoke low from the side of her mouth.

He was getting ready to shift to the apartment to wait for Róisín, but Shasta's next question halted him.

"Wait. What do you mean Tura took them to the afterworld?"

Lily's eyes darted away from Caid to the floor. "Tura is Mother Death."

From the collective gasp they all made, Caid's guts plummeted to his feet.

SEVENTY-NINE

LINA STOOD in front of the shop, a smile tipping up her lips. Would Róisín come back and reopen it once things were settled? How many times had their talks centered around tea and coffee? More than Lina could count in their seven years of friendship.

The blinds were drawn, the Closed sign hanging in the door, but Lina knew. She felt him there, a big, moody black cloud.

Caid.

Sloane and Abby had been out of the car for school before she had even come to a complete stop that morning with their excitement for the last days of school energy filling them. When she returned home, Thomas had known what she was going to do. He kissed her softly and told her to be gentle with Caid, then sent her on her way.

She gripped the knob. Her magic worked through the mechanism, twisting, turning, pushing. With a click, the door unlocked and she stepped into the shop. She came to a halt at the sight of her brother, hunched over, elbows on the counter with his hair gripped in his hands.

"You found her."

His head moved with what she could only assume was a nod.

Lina cautiously stepped closer. The energy pulsing off him differed from how it had been when he came to the house that morning. "And? Why are you here?"

"Because I can't go where she is." He finally straightened and Lina had to hold herself in place. The lines of his face deep, his eyes overly bright, and the tendons in his neck looked like they were trying to burst free of his skin. She wanted to run to him, throw her arms around him, tell him it would be okay.

Finally finding her feet again, she walked to the counter and peered down at the papers strewn across it. She recognized Róisín's scrawling words.

"What's all this?"

Caid cleared his throat and stacked the papers. "I found it all upstairs." He reached for a leather-bound book. "Her notes about the Seer and everything. I tried... I wanted to make heads or tails out of it all."

"To help." Lina's eyes tracked his hands as he finished shuffling the papers, then tapped them against the countertop to neaten the stack.

"To go to her if she can't make it back."

Lina felt the sweat prickling along her top lip. "Caid, where is Róisín exactly?"

"She, Ione, and Tura went to the afterworld. Lily said they tracked the Seer there earlier this morning." He was staring down at his hands, unblinking. His knuckles had turned white with the strain of how hard he gripped the papers.

"Shasta said—"

"I know what Shasta said. So does Róisín. And they went anyway." His words were short, curt, and snapped at Lina like a whip. His face crumpled when he looked up at her. "I'm sorry, Leen. I'm so fucking sorry."

She put her hands on his shoulders, turning him to face her. Then she wrapped her arms around his waist. "She'll be back. She hasn't left you behind." She rested her head against his chest. "Róisín never does anything without a plan. Even if she's the only one that knows the plan."

"That doesn't help at all." His voice rumbled against her ear.

"She won't go without you, Caid. Trust me."

He snorted and stepped back. Nodding toward the back door, he said, "Come on."

For just a moment, she could only watch him disappear through the door. Glancing down at the papers, she grabbed them, then followed.

Caid was opening another door at the top of a set of stairs by the time she had caught up to him.

"Something to drink?" He asked over his shoulder.

"Water is fine." She took in the front room of the apartment. The small touches of her brother and Róisín scattered around. Knick-knacks, shoes, stacks of books.

A glass of water broke her line of sight. She slipped it from his hands and studied him over the rim as she took a long drink. Everything from the defeated energy, his rounded shoulders. It was an unfamiliar sight to her. Never had she seen her brother in this way.

"Why can I still feel that anger pulsating off of you like you're ready to punch holes in the wall and rip someone's head off?"

He scrunched his nose. "I'm not angry." He fell back against the cushions. " I'm just... angry."

"See? Now, tell me *why*."

Caid tipped his head back and closed his eyes. "She wasn't there, Leen. When I woke up, she was gone. And I'm not talking about physically not there." He drew a hand over his face. Then, he rubbed his chest. "Here. I couldn't feel her anywhere. It was fucking terrifying thinking something had happened to her, and I'd *slept* through it. How much of a piece of shit would I be if I'd slept through her needing help?"

A dawning light rose over Lina, splitting her heart. "Is it because she crossed the veil that you can't feel her at all?"

"It's the only thing that makes sense."

"You didn't ask Shasta?"

His nose wrinkled. "I didn't stick around. I had to get out of there."

"Oh, Caid." She frowned.

"I fucking hate this. When do we get normal? When does all this stop?" His voice cracked on the last word and his body shook against hers.

Pressing her lips together to keep in the quiet sob that wanted to escape, she lay an arm across him, giving him a side hug.

"What if something happens to her and she can't get back, Leen? What then?"

Lifting her head, she willed her chin to remain still and her voice to be steady. "Then you cross over and get her. Bring her home."

Over her head, he sniffed.

"Now, do you want to know what our favorite bunny told me about our family?"

His body tensed against hers. "What do you mean?"

"Apparently, there isn't such a thing as the Jordbrand Coven. Not just that, but there aren't even supposed to be specific Covens. That's a Gea thing. Split everyone up and assign them to specific Covens with rules and whatever." She let out a squeak when she was tossed aside by the motion of him sitting up quickly.

"What?"

She righted herself and pushed the hair from her face. "Before Gea went on her crazy power trip, witches all intermingled in the realms. Just like they do here. There wasn't a Roidon Coven, Ely Coven, any of them. We all existed like one big, happy, witchy family. No specific leaders, nada."

"No." He waved a hand, shaking his head. "The Jordbrand thing. It's not real? Why's it in so many of the books Shasta and I found? Why did my magic go full throttle after we went to Sweden?"

She turned her hands palm up and shrugged. "David told me as much as he knew. He said Hecate would have the answers for us."

He scowled at her. "I guess that means Hecate's going to get her wish."

"What wish?"

"She wants to hang out with us. Get to know us."

"Is she at least nice? Nicer than mom and dad?"

He stared at her, wide-eyed. Then they burst into laughter.

EIGHTY

MARCELO'S EYES traced the charcoal line of his pencil. He knew the line well. His fingers had traced it thousands of times, if not more. The pencil faltered, and he had to pause. Flexing his fingers, he tried to push away the thought that he may never stroke a finger along Nolani's jaw again.

Shoving the pencil and notebook to the side he stared sidelong at Anthony.

Anthony's frail body stood, back hunched, facing the window that overlooked Talista. His bony hands were clasped behind him. Head cocked to one side as though he were studying a piece of art on a wall.

Marcelo knew it was the monster inside, watching, stalking. The people on the streets beyond the castle were prey, and Anthony's monster was hungry.

"Where are your guards?" Marcelo asked.

"My guards?" Anthony spoke to the glass before him. "They fear me. They rarely come to my wing. Afraid of catching my... disease."

Marcelo placed his elbows on the armrest of the chair. "Senate? When was the last time they saw you?"

"Four months ago." He turned slightly and pointed to the tablet on the bedside table. "We use that thing most times for meetings and updates."

"What are you telling them? When they don't see you on the camera?"

Anthony shrugged. "I suspect I have another month before they ask questions. By then, I'll be ready anyway, so what does it matter?"

"Ant..."

"Don't, Celo. I know that's why you're here. Not to be here if or when they can break this curse." He turned to him. His eyes and nose had changed into the monstrous form of the curse, but his mouth remained Anthony's. "I'm dying. You know it."

Marcelo rose and went to stand next to him. "Not if I have anything to say about it."

"The only way I live, Celo, is to eat. And I refuse to—Gah!" He bent over, gripping his stomach.

"Breathe." Marcelo put his arms around him. Anthony's molars creaked, his nostrils flaring with a harsh breath. "Come, sit."

Anthony leaned his weight on him, letting him lead him to the chair that Marcelo had been sitting in. Still curled forward, he hung his head, placing his hands at the sides of his head.

"Ant." Marcelo dropped into a crouch in front of him.

"It hurts. The gnawing inside gets worse each day." He rocked. "There isn't much left inside of me for it to consume."

The bridge of Marcelo's nose burned. He had to focus on keeping his breathing and his words steady. "You can fight it. I know you can."

"I can't. Can't you see? I'm not like *you*. I can't..." Anthony gasped, his body stiffening. "Father was right about me."

"Don't." Marcelo shook his head. "Don't. He was wrong. About us *both*. You need to push through this, Ant. We'll show him. We'll show him he was wrong about us. Then, we make this realm everything it was meant to be."

Anthony's hand shot out and grabbed Marcelo's forearm. His nails dug into Marcelo's skin making him hiss in pain.

"You... sound..." Anthony sucked in a ragged breath. "So sure."

"I am. I knew the moment mother said she was having another child that it would be you and I. Always."

Anthony's voice was raspy, faint, when he spoke next. "What if it wins?"

Marcelo shook his head, swallowing down his heart that had lodged itself in his throat. "I won't let it."

Anthony scoffed. The tension in his body released, and the fingers at Marcelo's arm loosened. His body shook. "It takes a little more from me every time I fight it."

Marcelo rose. He took the blanket from the end of Anthony's bed and wrapped it around his shoulders. An anger, hot and heavy, built inside of him as he watched his brother wrap the blanket around his trembling body. Anger at the Dionomis' before him. At Frederick. At fate.

At Gea.

If Róisín failed, could his monster face down Gea and end it for them all?

EIGHTY-ONE

T URA CHEWED on her lip and paced near the place she had slipped Róisín and Ione through the veil. The ticking in her head keeping time. Her heart hammering in her chest tried to drown out the sound and her thoughts.

The sandstorm had died down mere seconds after they had crossed. A sign from Fate that despite her task to guide Róisín, Ione, the others forward on this journey, *this* was pushing the fibers of the loom that held the threads to its limit.

A chill ran along her spine, squeezing the nape.

She had just wrapped her arms around herself when Ione's upper body came through the veil. Tura let out a small yelp and jumped back.

"We need you." Ione reached for her.

Before Tura could protest, Ione was yanking her through. "I can't—
"

"Shut it." Ione pointed toward the near barren landscape. "How in the fucking Hells are we supposed to do this, Tura? Look! Look at what has happened to your Hells."

Tura *had* looked. She had seen exactly what had happened to the once beautiful, lush and vibrant afterworld filled with the seemingly endless landscape of post-life worlds their people created after they passed through the veil. The dim grey, dirt filled scene before them shattered her.

"Wait!" Tura tried to pry Ione's hand from her wrist. "Where is Róisín? Where are we going?"

"I don't quite understand Hecate's methods. I get that she really holds no power outside of Earth. I saw that in Shianshani, where nearly an entire Coven had believed her to exist and even then, it wasn't enough. But—" Ione came to an abrupt halt and faced her. "I'm not Hecate. Even if you were my sister, I'd be dragging you across this shitscape, yelling at you."

"I—"

Ione lifted a hand and shook her head. "There's zero excuse. We're running out of time. We won't know if this will work if we can't even find the Seer. I don't know about you, but I'd like to find them. Quickly, so we can get back to Earth and get the axe to your mother's neck. I want a damned family with Runa, no matter how that looks. I can't *do* that if you keep being a big assed baby about using the magic Hecate gave you."

Tura blinked at her, unable to find words.

"Now. We're going to Róisín and Stephen. You're going to use that magic to fix this. We can't wait any longer for it to be your choice. You're going to get us all fucking killed if you don't. Then what?"

Tura lifted a hand to her chest. The weight of Ione's words settling heavily there.

"Come on." Ione tugged her forward again. "We need to grab the Seer and get the Hells out of here so I can go tell Runa that I'm sorry, and beg him to forgive me, before he decides I'm just a worthless piece of shit like everyone else in my life has, and leaves me."

"Oh, Ione, you're far from worthless."

Ione scoffed. "Shows how well you know me, *Fate*."

Silence fell over them as they made their way toward where Ione said that Stephen and Róisín were sheltered. In the distance, beyond the mountain lines, Tura could hear snaps and snarls. It didn't take long for those snaps and snarls to move closer.

Closer.

Sweat broke out across her upper lip.

Closer.

Her hounds had escaped the darkness.

Closer.

And they were coming for them.

She lifted a hand and rubbed her throat, her magic wanting to be freed. The skin along her face prickled, then itched. Who she was beneath trying to slip out.

No, no, no. I can't. I can't. Mother will know. She'll find me. The others will see me. And it'll be over. They'll never look at me the same again.

Closer.

Tura squeezed her eyes closed, her breaths coming quicker.

"What's that noise?" Ione asked.

My babies.

If Tura didn't use her magic, Róisín and Ione would be trapped in the afterworld. Forever.

And her mother would win.

Hecate would die.

They'd all be ruined.

EIGHTY-TWO

Róisín wanted to sit. However, the raised hairs on the back of her neck urged her to remain standing, ready to move. Stephen stood next to her, his posture tight, eyes steady on the direction in which Ione had left in.

"She'll be able to find her way back, right?" Róisín asked.

"We have to hope she can. It all looks the same out there."

"How long have you and mom been separated here?"

"To me, it feels like it's just been a few really long days." He tucked his hands into the pockets of his pants. "But if what Ione said is right..."

"It is, daddy. It's been six and a half years since you and mom came to the cottage."

Stephen rocked back on to his heels and ran his tongue across his teeth. "You and Kincaid?"

"We got married, finally." The smile she flashed her father hurt her cheeks. "I—" *Oh, no. Oh, shit.* Shit. *I left without...* The reality of what she had done slammed into her, trying to steal her breath away. He had to be awake and looking for her by now.

Róisín tried to reach for him, to let him know, but there was nothing.

Panic dug its claws into her chest, then her throat.

He'd understand. He'd *have* to. It was an honest mistake.

Róisín knew she was kidding herself. If she couldn't feel him, he couldn't feel her. Which meant he probably thought...

"Róisín?" Stephen's hand rested on her shoulder. He had moved to face her, studying her with brows drawn low. "Are you alright? You girls really shouldn't be here. This is dangerous."

"I'm..." She swallowed hard. "Daddy? I messed up."

With both hands on her shoulders, he shifted her so that they were eye to eye. "I doubt that, my Calon Bach."

"Caid died, daddy. Not long after you and mom came. There was a lot going on, and Shasta said it would be best for us to keep quiet until we knew what exactly was happening and how everyone was going to handle it. Only it got worse. It got *so much worse.*" Her eyes stung, but there were no tears there. "And in the end, Caid died."

His brows came together, and he frowned. "You said you two were married."

"Thankfully, it wasn't his time." Instinctively, she blinked, her mind telling her to push away the wetness in her eyes. Her vision was still clear, eyes dry. *Too long. I've been here too long.* What created life inside of her was fading. "We feel one another here." She put her hands on his chest. "Like an echo. Except, right now, there is no echo. Which means I can't let him know I'm okay. Everything happened so fast, and I left without telling him. Now if I can't, he can't and—"

"Shh." He pulled her into his arms and stroked a hand over her hair, then rocked back and forth with her. "It will be alright."

"Damn right it will. I brought our lucky ticket," Ione said.

"We don't have long," Tura said just as a long, high-pitched howl rang out.

"Hell hounds?" One of Stephen's brows shot up. "Those are new."

"New?" Róisín and Ione asked in unison.

Stephen's gaze was hard on Tura. "You didn't tell them?"

"No," Tura said in a clipped tone.

Ione's eyes widened and she glanced at Róisín.

"We don't have time for this." Róisín stepped between them. "Your magic, Tura. We need it. *Now.*"

Another howl rang out. From the way Stephen moved closer to her, she wasn't imagining that it sounded closer.

"Tura. We're nearly out of time. If you don't, then what? We let her win?" Róisín tried to keep her voice soft and light, but she couldn't. She could feel the way her body was changing. The way her magic was changing. *Too long.*

"For all that I do, I apologize," Tura said in a low voice.

"What does she mean?" Stephen asked.

Tura took a step back from them and straightened. The air around them grew warm, smelling of sulfur. Sounds of clicking and snapping sounded from Tura's body.

Then her hair fell to the dirt at her feet and Ione gasped.

"Tura—"

Róisín reached out, snatching Ione's hand before it could get any closer. "No. Don't touch her. Give her space."

A noise akin to a snarl emanated from Tura's throat, drawing Róisín's eyes there. It was then that she realized she was staring at bone. Tura's *spine.*

"Jesus, Mary, and Joseph," Stephen whispered next to her. "She didn't do that the last time."

Tura's skin had thinned to the point of translucence. It wrinkled and sagged off her skeleton. Stray wisps of hair that hadn't fallen to the ground hung around a gaunt face with hollowed eye sockets. Her nose was no longer. In its place were misshapen holes. Slowly, her near black lips curved upward, cracking and bleeding as she smiled.

"Welcome to the Hells." Her voice was deeper, gritty when she spoke. That soft, songlike whisper she always spoke with, gone. "Don't say you weren't warned."

The trio stood frozen, speechless, as Tura turned her back to them and whistled.

Hunched shapes with what appeared to be melting skin bounded toward them. Their legs were misshapen, gnarled, long and short. Bones jutted out from skulls and sides in the places their skin was missing. Black smoke trailed after each, like a flag of night.

Their size continued to grow and grow as they neared. They were still several feet away, and Róisín judged them to be larger than any animal she had ever seen before. In any realm. But these weren't animals. They may not look like dogs, but their growls and howls proved otherwise.

When they approached, the smell of decay flooded Róisín's senses. She covered her mouth and swallowed down the urge to gag. The small noise she made garnered the attention of the largest beast, its eyes of fire landing on her. Stretching its neck until it was almost in front of her, the nostrils at the front of its dark snout flared as it took in her scent.

Something about her smell registered with it, and the torn flesh over its mouth curled back. Its snarl was guttural, lava dripping from its teeth hissing when it hit the dirt at their feet.

"Enough," Tura snapped. "You are *mine*. You obey *me*."

The beast shifted its attention to Tura.

"You don't belong here." She lifted an arm, hand outstretched. "Go home! *Ite domum*."

The beast chuffed at Tura, but made no move to obey whatever command she had given.

Tura flexed her hand. Róisín could feel the heat in the hollowed, eyeless stare she leveled at the beast.

"*Ite domum*," she said again, harsher.

Yelps echoed through the pack.

"I will destroy you all and create anew," she said. "*Ite.*" She pointed again. *"Domum."*

With one last look at Róisín, then Tura, the beast turned its back and approached the pack. Moments later, they were gone.

It was Ione's quiet yelp of surprise that had Róisín looking away from the black smoke that remained in their wake. She jerked back a step, startled to see Tura returned to the form that Róisín was accustomed to.

"I feel more comfortable like this, but they only listen to me in my true form," Tura said.

"True form?" Róisín asked.

Tura nodded. "Goddess. Mother Death. Remember? I used to be... less. As time has passed..." She shrugged so casually that Róisín thought she was hallucinating.

"Will your magic work like this?" Róisín waved her hands up and down. "I mean, it's shocking, yes. Don't feel you need to do all of this for us, though."

"For what I do next, I can do it like this," Tura said. "If they return, or should Crev have been freed by mother again…" She pressed her lips together and her cheeks tinged pink. "I will have to become the monster again."

Ione looked down at her watch. "Whatever works. I'm down. We've got eight minutes left before we're stuck. I'm *not* getting stuck here. I plan to live a very long life up top with that bald-headed hunk of muscle."

"It will only take a few seconds. Be ready, please. For it is a lot of magic. It will be loud. She will know immediately. There may be just enough of my magic left in her that she can come here." Tura smoothed her hands over the front of her shirt. "You have the piece, Ione?"

Ione pulled the door hinge pin out of her pocket and wiggled it between her thumb and forefinger.

"Let it guide you to the Seer. We stick together," Tura said before closing her eyes.

The sky overhead cracked with such force, Róisín's bones vibrated. Slowly, the deep gray sky lightened. Beneath their feet, the ground rumbled and shook. Grass and stone creeping upward and outward, consuming the dirt. Before them, around them, the landscape quickly began to change.

"Ouch!" Ione dropped the door pin. "That just got blazing hot."

Stephen bent and retrieved the pin. "It feels fine to me?"

Because you're dead, daddy. If it was hot for Ione, that meant it wasn't too late. Yet.

"Let me see." Róisín held out her hand. When Stephen placed the hinge in her palm, she sucked in a breath and clenched her teeth together. It scalded her skin with its heat. She looked at Tura who still stood with her eyes closed. "She said to let it guide us."

"She also said to stay together," Ione said. "I'm sticking with all of you. I remember what happened in Talista when we all got separated."

Róisín did too.

"Let the piece lead you." Tura's eyes were open now, their amethyst color bright.

"How? It's not exactly telling me where to go," Róisín said.

"It'll stay hot as long as you're moving in the right direction."

Ione groaned. "It'd be nice it if were more like a damned compass."

Róisín couldn't agree more.

Six minutes. They had six minutes to find the Seer and get through the veil.

Six minutes to find the Seer, *convince* them to come with them, and get through the veil.

Worse than their time constraint, they were going to need to convince the Seer to come with them on a hunch Róisín had. They couldn't prove they were right with their plan on how to be freed from Gea's magic.

"It's cooling," Róisín mumbled when they moved left towards a new stone pathway. They changed directions, heading further right than where Stephen's lean-to had once stood. Now a fountain stood tall, its water trickling down a stone tower into the basin. "Hot again," she said.

"Five minutes," Ione said.

"Really, Ione?" Róisín scanned their surroundings. When her father had said the afterworlds were more like homes, she hadn't thought he meant actual houses. Homes of all shapes and sizes were coming into existence all around them at the return of Tura's magic to the afterworlds.

Their task quickly became daunting.

"Ah!" Róisín nearly dropped the hinge. She switched hands and squeezed her aching fist closed. When she opened it, an angry red line marred her palm. She stopped and looked up. "Here?"

"Four minutes," Ione said. "Worth a shot, I guess."

"Go, go." Stephen waved them forward toward the sunny yellow door of a small Cape Cod style home.

Ione and Róisín walked up the narrow walkway. "Do we knock?" Róisín asked.

"Nope." Ione turned the knob and walked in.

"Ione—" Róisín followed her in, then stopped. She had only ever seen the man before them in photographs, but she knew. She knew those eyes. Her *mother's* eyes.

"Brenna?" His voice was hoarse from disuse.

"N-no. Her daughter, Róisín."

"Daughter?" He blinked his eyes quickly. "I have a?"

Not knowing what else to do, she stepped forward and embraced the man. "Hi, grandfather."

"Oh, shit." Ione covered her mouth.

Róisín glanced over at her, and there, just beyond where Ione stood, was the Seer.

EIGHTY-THREE

MATTHEW SWUNG the hammer at the rear quarter of the Jeep with a satisfied grunt.

"You good?" Jackson called out.

"I'm," *thunk*, "fucking," *thunk,* "fine."

"Sure, sure."

Matthew let the hammer drop onto the gravel and faced his cousin. "What?" He snapped.

"Hey, now." Jackson lifted his hands in surrender. "All of that in there"—He jabbed a thumb toward the house. "Then you and Lily disappear. She's back inside looking like she's lost her best friend. You're out here." He leaned around Matthew to peer at the Jeep. "I was gonna say wrecking this hunk of junk more, but that quarter looks pretty good actually."

"Lily looks sad?"

Jackson chuckled. "*That* is what you just took from all of that?"

Matthew raked a hand through his hair and blew out a breath. "I panicked and snapped at her earlier. If she's..." He looked beyond Jackson to the cottage. All he had wanted was for Lily to come to him when she was hurting so he could help her through it. If she was hurt now, it had been *him* that had caused it. She probably just said she

416

understood only to get space between them after he had expressed his feelings over what she had done. Told her how terrified he had been that something had happened to her. Now she was inside and, fuck. "Fuck."

"For what it's worth, I don't think that's what is bothering her. Her sister and her best friend are on the other side of the veil. Without her." He scuffed a foot in a circle. "That'd chap my ass a bit, too, if it were me. Being included in the first half of the mission, but getting booted for the second? The best part? Pfft."

Was Lily mad she hadn't gone with Ione and Róisín? She had been at Róisín's side while they had been in Shianshani. Trifoa and Baijiola, too, before peace settled over the two realms after the new leadership had been established.

The hand squeezing his shoulder brought him back to the yard, and Jackson.

"Don't take it personally, man. She reminds me a bit of Nadia. Which, from what I've heard Ione say about their grandmother, is sort of on par with how Nadia's ex was. I get the impression that Lily is still trying to find her voice and ask for what she wants."

"What do you want, Lily?"

"You. Now. Please."

Heat flashed through Matthew. He dropped his chin and rubbed the back of his neck, hoping he hid his face quick enough from Jackson. Clearing his throat, he asked, "Nadia's ex?"

When Jackson didn't reply, Matthew lifted his head.

"He's in prison, again." Jackson's brows came down as his eyes narrowed.

"Again?"

"Broke parole. Found Nadia and Park." He straightened, rolling his head back and forth. "It'll be the one thing I miss when the curse is broken." Extending his arm, he turned his changed hand this way and that. "Magic is a helpful intimidation tactic with humans. But this?" He waved his claws. "This works on anyone."

Matthew studied his hand. The way the fingers had tripled in size. Long nails with jagged edges glinted under the sun. "Your whole body really does that?"

"Yup."

They both watched as the hand changed back to normal. "I shift, too."

Jackson spun on him. "What? Why didn't you say anything?"

"Because it's not like that." He motioned to the hand. "I can turn into a fucking bird. Woo." He wiggled his fingers and rolled his eyes. "It just a part of the magic. Shasta's got some shifting ability too."

A corner of his mouth tipped up, eyes glimmering with mischief. "I bet she's a big cat. Like a lion or a jaguar. Rip you to shreds if you go after her babies."

"Honestly? I wouldn't know. She's never done it around me. Shifting, if you have that magic, it takes a *lot* out of you. Even if it is something small."

"No one will confirm it, but I'm pretty sure it's what kill—"

Shouts erupted from inside the house, sending both men sprinting.

EIGHTY-FOUR

CAID'S BODY began its attempt to pull him into sleep. It felt like days since he had awoken without Róisín next to him. He rubbed at his eyes, his body deflating with the groan he released.

Lina walked out of the bathroom and frowned at him. "I need to go grab the twins from their practices. Are you going to be alright?"

He had no choice. He had to be alright. For Róisín. She *was* coming back.

The ticking clock on the bookshelf he had built her next to the window mocked him.

After Lily had explained Tura's position to the Hells, she said Tura would give them only two hours in the afterworld to locate the Seer. Once the two hours passed, Seer or no Seer, they were coming home.

The question remained, which realm's time? Was it two hours in Earth? Molennius? Elsewhere? Two hours had long come and gone in the small living room of the apartment. The sun hung low in the sky now. The room grew darker as neither Caid nor Lina had moved to turn on any lights in the space.

Groaning again, he rubbed at his temple. Thoughts of Róisín becoming trapped beyond the veil had poked through his mind hours

419

before. Now, they used thread, weaving themselves together, pulling taught.

"I can call Thomas. He's working from home this week, so he could grab them."

"No." Caid sat up. "No. I'm just being a fucking idiot. Go. I'll be alright."

She stepped around the coffee table to stand in front of him. "Up," she said and motioned with her hands. "I want a real hug. Not some half-assed thing."

Standing, he took her in his arms as he had done thousands of times before. He swayed with her a little and kissed the side of her head. "I love you, Leen."

Lina jerked back, her eyes wide.

"Calling you a shithead, assface, or something like that just doesn't fit right now," he said.

She pat his back and gave him a small smile. "I agree. I love you, too, Caid."

He kissed her forehead, then released her.

"I want an update. From the both of you. The twins are at a sleep-over after I get them cleaned up and fed dinner. You can come to the house. We won't have to"—She wiggled her fingers—"magic them to their rooms or something."

Caid wanted to laugh. He knew that was Lina's intent. He just couldn't find that lightness in his chest.

"Hey." Lina's hand was on his face. "She's a tough chick. Smart, too. She'll be back. If not, she'll find a way to let you know she needs you. You said she did it before. She'll do it again. Okay?"

He tried to swallow down the thickness filling his throat. "Okay."

After she shifted away, his body collapsed back into the cushions. It hadn't just been that he couldn't feel her. It was more that she felt she needed to do this without him. No, it wasn't facing Gea alone, but they had been an unbreakable unit. The hundred different questions of why rambled around in his mind, halting when a warmth bloomed across his chest.

Róisín.

A crash sounded downstairs, followed by a stream of curses.

He threw open the apartment door and sprinted down to the shop.

"Caid, I—" Róisín rushed toward him, but he was faster. He caught her and pulled her against him. His hands digging into her hair, he closed his mouth over hers in a desperate kiss. Her arms banded around him, fingers pressing deep into his back as she clung to him.

"You two *do* have an audience," Ione's voice broke through his relief.

Caid laid his forehead against Róisín's and closed his eyes.

"I didn't know that would happen. I'm so sorry." Róisín pressed kisses all over his face. "I'm so, so sorry."

"Excuse me," Ione said. "I really would like to go do the same thing with *my* man. But what do we do with them first?"

Caid looked over at Ione. She stood next to the Seer and Tura. They had succeeded. What it could mean for them all had the ground beneath his feet feeling unsteady.

"We need to keep them in this realm. Gea can't know that we have them. Tura using her magic may cause us enough issues," Róisín said.

"Do we trust them alone?" Ione slid her gaze toward the Seer. "Sorry. It's just that we don't need you slipping off to your son again."

Red flashed behind Caid's eyes. His magic churned thicker and darker than tar.

Róisín put a hand on his forearm and gave him a light squeeze. "Not Madigan. Ione means Bernard. My grandfather."

Her words were monumental. Róisín had met her grandfather, Brenna's father, in the afterworld. The man who died because he wouldn't let Aoife kill Brenna for her magic. The man who kept Aoife at bay long enough for Brenna to escape, be free. To have Róisín.

"Are you okay?" He asked her.

Róisín looked away from the Seer to him. "Yeah. I think so. It was nice to meet him, and I wish we had more time." She turned back to the Seer. "Maybe we'll get those chances after we do this."

Caid caught Tura's attention. "Thank you," he said.

Tura's head lifted. "Pardon?"

He motioned to Ione, then tucked Róisín against his side. "For getting them there and back. For keeping them safe while they were there."

421

"Oh." She clasped her hands in front of her. "You're welcome."

"Please don't make me ask again," Ione said.

Róisín walked over to the Seer and held out her hands. "You knew. That day I came to you."

The Seer settled their long, bony hands atop Róisín's. "You're a clever child. Of course I did. I saw when it changed. When you wouldn't defeat my son in the ravine, as you were to do."

Caid's jaw made a snapping noise when he slammed them together, catching Ione's attention.

"Did you know he was coming back?" Róisín asked.

"I knew he had done something, but I cannot see beyond our own people." They moved their hands from Róisín's to grip her forearms. "Everything changed that day in my home."

"When she took you from your family?" Ione asked.

"No. When Aoife returned, and you"—They pointed to Róisín—"killed them both."

Róisín licked her lips. "Wh-what do you see now?"

"I see home." Their chin quaked as their lips spread into a smile.

Caid stepped forward. "Does that mean this will work?"

They lifted a frail hand to his cheek. "I see you free the children."

"The twins?" His heart slammed itself against his chest.

"The others." They turned to Ione. "You and the Lunestran child will build bridges to the future of our people."

Ione lifted a hand to her mouth, sniffling.

"And you, my child. Once again, I see two futures for you. Fate appears to be letting you cast your own stone."

Caid drew in a sharp breath.

Fates be damned.

But what did it truly mean? Would Fate let her be with her mother in the afterworld if she died facing Gea? Would she even be able to make the choice to *live*? If Fate was revolting against letting Gea hold as much power as she did, what was to stop it from taking Róisín and Gea together?

"I fail or succeed." Róisín's voice was steady and firm. Her shoulders lifted and she faced the Seer. She gave them a quick nod before taking their hand. "Will you go with Ione and Tura? They will take you to Shasta, the others. You'll be safe there. Here. With us."

The Seer dipped their head in a shallow nod.

Róisín turned to Ione. "We'll be behind you."

Ione winked at her. "Take your time, sweetie. I know I certainly am once I get back to the cottage."

Laughing, Róisín gave her a quick hug. "We don't have that kind of time. Not anymore." She lowered her voice to a whisper. "You should probably make it a quickie."

"We don't know what those are," Ione cackled as she took the Seer's hand. She saluted Caid. "Sorry I stole your girl. Forgive—"

The rest of her sentence was cut off by her shift.

"It's not her fault," Róisín said quickly, lifting her hands. "It was all my idea."

He prowled toward her, backing her against a wall. "I want to ask why. I *want* to have this out with you right here and right now." He placed a forearm on the wall next to her head, then lifted his other hand to cup her cheek. "But I also don't want to waste what little time we have left fighting with you."

Her voice was breathless. "I really am sorry."

"Me too. For whatever I've done to make you think slipping away in the middle of the night was what you needed to do." He brushed his lips over hers. "I'm sorry."

Caid lowered his hand, brushing his knuckles over her hips before he hooked her leg, lifting it. She lifted her other, wrapping both of her legs around his waist. He felt the tremor begin at the center of his being before it rocked through his body and tried to stop it, but couldn't. He brought his arms tightly around her and buried his face in her neck.

"Caid."

"I thought knowing," he began, his voice rough. Squeezing his eyes closed, he brushed his nose along her neck. "I thought knowing it was coming would make it easier than having it thrown before us like the last time."

Her fingers dug into his hair. She tugged his head back. "Don't." Her eyes glittered with tears. "Okay? We have right here, right now. We can't give in to what's next, because it can change at any minute." She moved her thumbs over his damp cheeks. "We take right now, while it's still ours."

He swallowed hard. His mind battling with it all. How he should have hugged Lina a little harder, a little longer, before she left. The wish he could do the same with the twins. Clank beer bottles just one more time with Wyatt and thank him for everything.

"They know you love them." Róisín's whispered words were warm against his cheek. "They know we love them."

His chest heaved out a heavy breath.

"One more time." She kissed him softly. "One more night. Just us."

"You said a quickie," his voice broke on each word.

She giggled and winked at him. "You heard that, huh?"

"I told you, I hear everything." The kiss he gave her was gentle despite the riot his emotions were having within. "Because you're the center of my universe." Holding her against him, he turned them toward the bedroom.

EIGHTY-FIVE

THE COFFEEPOT Shasta had been holding in her hand lay shattered at her feet. The chain of events that lead up to the moment now caused a flurry of chaos around her in the cottage.

Mere seconds after Ione had appeared in the kitchen, the Seer and Tura in tow, Runa had exploded into the kitchen, Aja close behind. Ione had let out a yelp when Runa tackled her in what Shasta had been sure was meant to be an embrace, because Runa would never harm a hair on Ione's head. Instead, the pair crashed to the floor. In between his apologies, he showered her face in kisses. Ione in response giggled, while also groaning about her back.

Aja had stopped dead in his tracks, his eyes wide and unblinking on the Seer.

Anelle popped her head into the kitchen. "What's going–shit, they're here. Ione and Róisín did it. Lily! Ten! Cicile! All hands on deck!"

The front door slammed open, making Shasta flinch. Matthew pushed past Aja, his eyes searching the faces in the kitchen.

"Lily's coming," Shasta told him.

His shoulders dropped. "What in the Hells is going on?"

"Is that?" Jackson asked, having squeezed around the people in the kitchen.

Matthew's head turned, and when he saw the Seer, he let out a small gasp. Looking back to Shasta, he asked, "Where's Róisín? Caid?"

"They're coming," Ione said from where Runa still had her on the floor. "Gah, let me up. The quicker we get this over with, the quicker we can—" She wagged her eyebrows at him.

Runa immediately leapt to his feet, pulling her with him.

While everyone settled around the space, Shasta bent to pick up the shards of the coffeepot. Aja knelt next to her to help. With each piece she picked up, her body vibrated harder. Until her hand shook so badly, she dropped the broken pieces she held.

Aja's hand closed over hers. "It's almost over," he said to her quietly. "We'll get to see them again."

"What if we fail, Aja?"

"Look at me."

She kept her eyes on the mess on the floor.

"Shasta."

Pressing her lips together to keep her chin from trembling, she lifted her gaze from the floor.

"We keep going until we win." He squeezed her hand gently. "If we let go of hope, Gea will always win."

Shasta drew in an unsteady breath. "We *will* see them again."

He gave her a soft smile, his maroon eyes bright. "We will."

Together they finished cleaning up the mess, dumping the shards in the trashcan near the sink. Shasta was near asking if Róisín and Caid were coming on that particular day, when the couple appeared in the doorway.

"Perfect." Anelle gave them both a curt nod. "Let's get this show on the road."

Ione wrinkled her nose at her. "You're battle hungry, you know that, Anelle? I hear therapy is excellent for those with a penchant for violence."

Anelle hummed. "I'll look into it. Maybe it will help me tap deeper into my inner warrior."

Ione rolled her eyes.

Shasta caught Róisín smoothing down her hair and lifted a brow. She flashed a wide grin at Shasta. A blush bloomed on Caid's neck, reaching his cheeks. He looked away from Shasta, smoothing his hand over the door trim, busying himself with inspecting it.

"It's like having a houseful of teenagers," she mumbled, making Aja laugh next to her. Enough was enough, though. As much as she didn't want to pull the stars from the sky crashing down on them, she had to. "Alright, let's get the next steps in this. If I'm to understand correctly, Tura restoring the afterworld has set things in motion and our count-down clock has begun."

"We're in our own episode of 24," Caid said. When everyone looked at him, confused, he continued, "A television show. Each episode spanned a day, and they were always showing a clock..." He waved a hand and sighed. "Never mind."

"Keifer Sutherland, right?" Matthew asked from across the kitchen.

"That's the one," Caid said.

"Good show," Matthew said.

Lily groaned. "I feel a sense of déjà vu."

"As long as they don't try to hash out which comic book character they want to be," Róisín said. "We're good."

"Now that's—"

"Enough!" Aja barked out.

The room fell silent and everyone looked down at their feet like scolded children.

Shasta cleared her throat. "Now. Where do we go from here? That's the only question you should be concerned with." She turned so that she faced the Seer and Tura. "I'm guessing you two can lead us in the right direction."

Tura stepped up behind the Seer and placed her hands on their shoulders. "I release you from the binds that held you from speaking your sight wholly."

The Seer's eyes fell closed, and they stilled.

"Has it seriously always been that easy?" Róisín asked.

Tura shook her head. "My sisters and I were warded from them. We were never allowed to be near them."

Shasta lifted a hand to her chest. The sisters of fate were powerful.

Beyond their looms, they each had magic that shaped witch kind. That Gea had made them unable to be near the Seer meant Gea had felt the trust her children had in her was breakable. That one, or all of them, would seek a way to break her hold. Her thoughts were spiraling at the severity of what Tura was doing, risking, should things go wrong, when the Seer spoke.

"The threads that are woven here and now will fray as you all move through the realms to release the binds that have long held us in place," they said.

"What the Hells does *that* mean?" Runa asked in a low voice.

"I think it means that we're not doing this together," Anelle said. Her eyes were locked on her brother, her face drained of color.

EIGHTY-SIX

R óisín blindly reached for Caid's hand. Their knuckles bumped together, and his fingers curled around hers, gripping tightly.

Did the Seer truly mean they were all going to be separated?

What was the point, then? Róisín wanted to ask.

Instead, she let Caid pull her closer. Squeezed his hand tighter. Let everything they'd had in the last seven years anchor her while she listened to the Seer tell them what came next.

"Wait, why are we going to the other realms *now*? Why can't that be something we do after Gea is gone?" Ione asked.

"We know not what will happen once her power over the realms no longer has a source to feed it," the Seer said. Their voice was growing in strength as they spoke. It had been raspy and faint at first. Róisín noticed they stood taller, their skin coloring a little more with each minute that passed.

"My mother relied on her siphoning magic at the gates to the afterworld to obtain the magic she has, and her power. Through her seed spell work—"

"*Finally,*" Matthew exhaled the word loudly, cutting Tura off.

Her eyes wide on him, she continued. "She used a spell work that would alter the mind and open a door that would leave it susceptible to her influence. The more witches that consumed the spell work, the more believed her to be the goddess. Until there was no one left to know of or believe in Hecate."

"What about our magic?" Matthew asked.

"That was another spell work she placed in seeds." Tura nodded. "It stifled a witch's true power to their magic. No one in the realms has been able to access their true potential in centuries. It was too much of a threat to her own power."

Matthew let out a sharp breath, cursing.

"This is insane," Ione muttered. "All this by, what, casting spells on *seeds*?"

"It is literally as it sounds. But it isn't as easy as that. The magic it takes to imprint the seeds with the spell work to sustain, pass down from mother to child..." Tura shifted her weight from one foot to the other. "That was how I found out she was meeting our people at the gates before they passed. Greeting them as their Goddess. Taking their magic before they entered the afterworld so that their family wouldn't inherit first."

"What happens now? If we're all to be separated, how will this work? She's been taking magic for almost one thousand years," Róisín said.

"Ione and Runa will go to Baijiola and help them prepare. Aja, you will be needed in Shianshani. Anelle will go to Trifoa to work with Beatrice. You, Shasta, will go to Nanette. She will need an old friend to help her guide them forward." Tura walked to each of them as she gave them instructions. She approached Matthew and Jackson next, Lily standing between the men. "Matthew, Jackson, you will restore the Seer to Aunellion."

Róisín wanted to protest. She had lost Matthew to Aunellion once before. They weren't even sure that this would be enough to free the realm. Matthew could be trapped there. Again. What it took to get him home the last time...

Matthew's eyes cut to hers and she pulled her lips between her teeth, biting down hard until she felt the copper tang of her blood. Caid's warm body was behind her. His arms banding around her. When he brought her against his chest, she could feel the way his heart thundered against her back.

"Where do I go?" Lily asked quietly.

"You will have the choice." Tura cupped her cheeks. "You can go with Shasta to Roidon, or you can go with Matthew."

Lily and Ione looked at one another over the island. Ione gave her a tearful smile and a small nod.

"I'll go with Matthew and Jackson. Bring the Seer home," Lily said.

Róisín covered her mouth, her fingers digging into her cheek, before the sob could break free.

"Ten, you will work with Brent in Ely. Cicile will go to Helen in Molennius." The cousins accepted their tasks with dips of their chins. She lowered their voice and moved closer to Cicile.

The room somehow grew even quieter as they all strained to hear the words Tura said to Cicile. When Cicile's head snapped up, eyes wide, they motioned to Nolani.

"You're to come with me," they said, taking Nolani's hands in theirs and squeezing.

Tura rounded the island and came face to face with Róisín and Caid.

"I cannot tell you yours, Róisín, as the Seer said, you have two paths revealed to us. I can only tell you that the time is near. You will feel a pull to return to Legianne. The fields—"

"There's nothing there anymore. The well source, it doesn't work. I tried when Caid—" She swallowed hard and shook her head.

"It has been cleansed of what Aoife had done. Ana and Elizabeth have been there to take care of it. She can no longer cause harm with the well source."

"When?" Róisín fought to keep her voice steady.

"Soon." Tura stroked a hand over her cheek.

"And me?" Caid asked roughly.

"I need you to come with me. Please."

"Now?" He asked.

"Yes. You will return, though." She held her hand out to him. "Nothing begins until Róisín is called to Legianne."

Róisín's eyes closed when she felt Caid's lips press against her temple. She held them closed as he whispered, "I love you."

It was the silence around her a moment later that forced her eyes open. Everyone was staring at her, waiting. Tura and Caid the only two no longer in the room.

"This just got real, didn't it?" Ione asked.

"Pretty sure the fact that the Seer is sitting in the kitchen with us is a good indicator of that, Ione," Matthew said.

"What now?" Róisín asked.

Shasta came up to her side and put her arm around her shoulders. "We wait."

EIGHTY-SEVEN

"WHAT IS this place?" Caid asked, turning in a slow circle.

"Home." Tura's response was a soft whisper filled with sadness.

Home? There was nothing there. Around them was an expanse of cold, gray emptiness.

"My mother, she..." Tura stood next to him, her shoulders rounded. "We began our lives in Alleyette. It was a small home. A swing in the tree just outside the kitchen window. A low, white fence wrapping around it. She used to watch us play in the garden."

Caid glanced down when she fell silent. Her lashes fluttered and two shining trails of tears rolled down her cheeks.

"Witches began to talk when others started to fall ill." She cleared her throat and gave a slight shake of her head. "When others lost their magic." Her head tipped to the side, frowning. "They burned our tree. That was the first thing. Then, it was the bright red paint. Buckets of it tossed over the front of our house."

In the distance, something caught Caid's eye. Squinting, he could make out the rough shape of a cottage with a thatched roof.

"She insisted they were jealous of her." Her heels scuffed as she walked. "*Still* tries to convince herself of that. The reality is, she has always been jealous of others. Nothing will satisfy her." She stopped walking. "Even if she killed Hecate and gained control of Earth. It would never be enough." With a sigh, she began walking.

When she looked over her shoulder, he followed her.

"Will you have a relationship with Hecate after?" She asked.

"I mean, I guess?" He shoved his hands into his pockets. "If she wants to. Shit, I dunno. If I live through this, sure."

Tura stopped again. It took him three paces to realize she had. She didn't need to say a word. It was written in the way her mouth pinched and her brows kissed.

"You know." His throat grew tight, a squeezing around his windpipe. "You know I live, don't you?"

She pressed her lips together and shook her head.

"Tura."

"No." It was a whispered word, but it cut through the air between them like a blade. "I can't. I can't do this. I'm not supposed to know those whose fates I see." Her head bowed. "Not like this. Not like all of you. I'm not supposed to get close, to shed my tears for them. Yet I cried when Brenna left. For Lucius. For Róisín." She lifted her head. Her eyes were rimmed red. Tears stained her cheeks. "For you."

"Then don't cry for us."

She let out a quiet, dark chuckle. "To everyone, we are these otherworldly beings. Without feeling. But we *feel*, Kincaid." She brought her palm to her chest. "My sisters and I laugh. We feel that sunshine in our hearts, what you all call joy." Her hand fisted over her heart. "We hurt. Feel sorrow. Grief."

He rubbed the back of his neck, then shrugged. "You're normal. Just like the rest of us."

"We're not supposed to be," she whispered.

"Look, I've got—" He lifted his hands, ticked off seven fingers, then wiggled them in front of her. "Almost a decade of this life under my belt. I don't really know how all of this works, but when you break it all down, you and your sisters are witches, right?"

She nodded.

"You each have a different magic, right?"

Again, she nodded. Except now, her eyes were brighter. Curiosity shining there.

"Just because the magic you have is the kind no one else has, it doesn't make you any different from the rest." He took a small step toward her. "I had shitty parents, too. Telling Lina and I the worst things they could, trying to make us feel small. Less than. I didn't get it when I was growing up. All it did was make me angry. Once I got older, I realized that not only did they not want to raise us, they didn't want us to succeed. They thought they were happiest with all of their things, but that's all they had." He moved closer to her. "Things. Their jobs were mediocre. They failed at parenting. Their friends came and went like the wind. They wanted us miserable, too. So, they talked shit. Just like Gea has done with you."

Tura's lashes fluttered, resting on her cheeks when she closed her eyes.

"How much longer will you let her voice be the loudest you hear?"

"I..."

"You went to Hecate. Everything you've done since to get us here." He looked around the gray expanse. "It's getting quieter. Or else you wouldn't be able to keep going forward. Maybe it's time to finally shut her up."

Her shoulders rose and fell with her breaths.

"Tura." He hooked a finger under her chin and tipped her head up. "Do I live?"

Silence blanketed them. Smothered him. Then she said the one word that broke him.

"Yes."

His heart moved to his throat, pressing against the walls of his windpipe. He wanted to go back to the cottage, to Róisín. Tura stepped around him, moving again toward her destination. With his muscles tight from the battle to keep himself there, he followed her until the cottage was in clear view.

It stood quiet, with weathered siding, white trim and a thatched roof. It reminded him of a cottage from one of Abigail's beloved fairy tale books.

"Out of all, this was what bloomed." Tura gestured toward the cottage. "A space she somehow created between realms. Where only we existed." She faced him now. Her eyes were still red and wet. The tears that soaked her face were dark purple.

"Why are we here, Tura?" He asked.

She moved her hand down his arm to wrap their fingers together and lead him away from the cottage. "I remember the very moment your thread appeared on my loom. It had been so long. So painfully long that I had doubted. Hecate has so much knowledge as our creator that I wonder what mine and my sisters true purpose is."

He looked back toward the small cottage.

"It is you that will save my sisters."

He stopped walking. "What do you mean?"

"You've always been the one to free the Sisters of Fate from the prison we've been trapped in for centuries." Tura turned to him, her amethyst eyes bright. "A child of earth and water will be born to free the children of fate."

Caid tipped his head to the side. "I can't just bust in there now, can I?"

Tura shook her head. "She will know the moment you reach the threshold of that gate." She pointed to the low stone wall where a wooden gate sat. "She needs to be engaged elsewhere."

"With Róisín."

"Yes." She nodded. "While Róisín is with my mother, you will be here."

He let his magic reach beyond him and crawl along the ground toward the stone wall, prodding, feeling. The magic just inches from the wall singed him and he bit back a hiss.

"I don't like it..." His magic snarled inside of him. *"It creates a hunger in us that rages."*

"Why me?"

"Only you, Lina, and Hecate can pass through the barrier. Aside from the power you hold, it is an unknown magic to mother. *You* are unknown to her.

EIGHTY-EIGHT

Róisín was sitting at the kitchen island across from Matthew and Jackson. Lily sat next to her. A haphazard pile of playing cards was piled between them. It had been impossible for any of them to focus on anything other than what came next. Jackson found the deck of cards in a table drawer in the living room and it had started with a game of poker, but quickly devolved into several rounds of Go Fish.

"Any twos?" Matthew chewed on his bottom lip, his eyes hard on the cards in his hand.

"Which one of us are you asking?" Róisín asked.

"You."

She waved a hand at the stack. "Go Fish."

"Dammit," he muttered. He reached over, plucked a card, cursing under his breath.

Lily giggled next to her. "Jackson, do you have any Kings?"

"Yes, ma'am." He whipped a card from his spread.

Róisín surveyed what she had left for cards. "Lily, do you..." She lost the rest of her words. Her breath caught in her lungs, her chest almost stilling.

Matthew straightened. The hand holding his cards hit the island top with a thud. "What?"

437

"Róisín?" Lily placed a hand on her back.

Róisín squeezed her eyes closed. Tura had been *wrong*. It hadn't been a pull she felt; it was a yanking. Like a cord tied around her heart. It pulled *hard*, beckoning her to Legianne.

No. Caid had yet to return from wherever Tura had taken him. She couldn't go yet. She needed more time. Needed one last hug. One last kiss...

"Róisín." Matthew was next to her now. He turned her stool so she faced him, taking her face between his hands. "Róisín!"

"It-it's time."

Face paling, his throat bobbed with his swallow. "Shit."

"I'll go let the others know," Jackson said. "I need to call Nadia one last time, too."

Matthew's mouth opened and closed. The words didn't come. Instead, he pulled her to her feet and wrapped his arms around her. Lily's arms came around her from behind.

"I love you," Róisín said against Matthew's chest. "I love you both. So"—She gasped—"So damned much."

Matthew hugged her tighter. His body shook against hers. "I love you, too."

"This isn't goodbye," Lily said in a low whisper. "We'll see each other again. I know it."

A tiny sob escaped Róisín. "We will. Somehow, some way, we will."

Matthew pulled back and kissed her forehead. "Be careful. Stay out of her reach. Don't hesitate or question anything. Do whatever you have to do to live. She's going to play games with you. Try to trick you. Fight dirty if you have to, okay?"

She nodded, swiping at her cheeks. "If Aunellion doesn't—" She pressed her quivering lips together and took an unsteady breath. "I'll find a way to get you all home. Whatever I need to do, I'll do it."

"We'll be okay." He swept her hair from her face. "Go."

She glanced at the doorway, hesitating. Shasta. She needed to say goodbye to her. Tell her one last time how much she loved her.

"She'll understand," Matthew said thickly. "We only get one chance. Timing matters."

She took his hand and Lily's hand, giving them both a light squeeze before shifting away to Legianne.

🐇

RÓISÍN STOOD IN THE MIDDLE OF THE NIANTI FIELDS. THE glowing insect the field was named for scurried up and away from her as she turned in a circle, taking it all in. It was late summer, the fields in full bloom with cosmos and hollyhock. Their scent surrounded her as they waved their greeting in the gentle wind.

The last time she had been there, a dusting of snow had blanketed most of the field.

The Nianti returned to the blooms nearest her once she stilled.

"She's going to play games with you..."

What Matthew hadn't known is that Róisín excelled at games. Especially what she called the game of reverse Cat and Mouse. Róisín often finding herself the mouse with cats hungry for her death magic snapping their teeth at her neck.

She had Madigan to thank for it all. The first time she killed him, she had played small, meek. *Weak.* Róisín had taken down Madigan, the Cat, when she had been a much weaker mouse. Now, she'd had plenty of practice. Had time to become stronger. Learn her magic. Her *freed* magic.

"Just don't let her get too close," Róisín whispered.

Róisín knew what happened when a siphon got too close. That night would haunt her forever. This time, she was alone.

"My daughter," a voice called across the field. "It fills me with such relief to see you."

Show time.

"Wh-what's going on? Why am I here?" Róisín spun in a circle. She released her magic, low, pushing it into the ground at her feet. Then, she sent it out, searching. "Hello?"

"You have accomplished much in your time," the voice drew closer. "You make me proud."

There. Her magic pinned Gea's location just to Róisín's right.

"I'm afraid that I've failed. The Covens..." Róisín flexed her hands at her sides. She couldn't make the first move. Inside, everything was gathering, pooling in all her empty spaces. It would build and build until she released it. She grit her teeth against the feeling, eyes scanning for Gea.

"The Covens are nearly united, daughter." Gea's figure came into view near a cluster of cosmos. "You have just one remaining." The blooms leaned away from her as she moved through them.

As she neared, Róisín saw why. The once glowing, ethereal appearance of Gea had faded, like a piece of glass being tossed among the rocks at the sea's edge until it had lost its shine.

"But Shianshani is in chaos."

Gea waved a hand. "Once your task is complete, Shianshani will heal."

When Gea was only ten steps away, Róisín stepped back. She let her shoulders round and bit her lip.

"So beautiful, just like your mother," Gea said. Her lips curved into a smile that didn't reach her eyes.

"You knew my mother?"

She swept an arm out and turned. "I know all of my daughters and sons."

Bullshit.

"Which coven is left?" Róisín asked. She knew the answer, but she wanted to hear Gea said it. Unsure why, but her heart wouldn't let her not ask.

"Hm?" Gea turned back to her.

"You said that I have one more left. If Shianshani will heal, that means they're all united."

"Oh, my daughter, it's so easy to forget, isn't it? Without a seat at the council table for so long, it is understandable." She took a step closer to Róisín. "We need to bring Earth's realm back to us. Home, where it belongs. We can rebuild it. Our people can live and thrive there just as they had once before."

Something deep inside Róisín snapped, and her magic rioted. The wind kicked up around them, whipping her hair behind her. "No."

Gea's brows flicked up. "Excuse me?"

"I said no." Her magic grew hotter, heavier. "I'm not playing this fucking game with you." In an exhale, she released her magic. The sound of it was a loud boom across the field. The Nianti shot up into the sky. The wildflowers flattened. Gea was rocked off her feet, sent sailing in the air. Before she could land, Róisín released it once more.

She stood with her hands fisted, eyes trained on where Gea's body had fallen. After a moment, Gea struggled to her feet.

"Oh, Róisín, you have no idea what you've just done," she called over to Róisín.

"No, Hydrangea de Oro." There was venom in the way she snarled Gea's name. "I absolutely do. *You* have no idea who I've become." She reached beneath the earth, her magic pulling for the roots of the decimated flowers. Gathering them, she shot them toward Gea.

"Just who is that?" There was a wry amusement to Gea's tone.

"Exactly who you made me to be." Flames erupted from the ground between them.

EIGHTY-NINE

"**H**AVE YOU come to gloat?"

Shasta groaned inwardly at Nanette's greeting. At least she didn't smell of alcohol or look as though she had just rolled out from beneath a rock this time. Her salt and pepper hair was in a neat bun atop her head. Her golden eyes were clear, focused.

"No. We need to talk." Instead of waiting for an invitation, Shasta pushed past her and into the house. "Close the door."

Nanette scoffed. "Well. Lead the way." She motioned with a hand toward the kitchen. "I hope you're not here to ask me to take in more refugees. Just the ones that have arrived in the last week and a half have raised suspicion among the humans."

"With a little bit of hope, those refugees will return home soon."

Nanette turned to her with two empty glasses in her hand. "Is Anthony...?"

She shook her head slowly, then told her everything.

"Why did no one come to me for help?" Nanette asked.

Shasta's brows shot up. When Nanette stared at her, clearly waiting for an answer, she said, "Oh. Oh, you're being completely serious. Nanette, you drew that line when the girls left. When I came to talk to you, you made your choice clear."

Her face fell. "I am not proud of who I was all those years ago."

"It's not too late." She reached across to cover Nanette's hands with hers.

"I don't..." She swallowed and shook her head. "When they came, it spiraled into an argument. I don't know how to... make it right."

"You start by being honest with them. They need to know the truth. Why you closed out Ione. Why you sheltered Lily." She gave her hands a light squeeze. "You need to deal with the fear you have for them. You can't stop things from happening, Nanette."

"I don't want them to hurt Ione. I don't want—" A sob broke free. "Lily is so much like Moira. I can't lose her, too."

"Those feelings are very valid. You know how easily it can all shift and our loved ones can be lost. If you keep casting yourself as the villain, you won't even get the chance to love them for whatever time fate may have left for them."

Nanette gave her a small smile. She used the back of her hand to wipe away tears. "This is quite a turn of the table, isn't it? You've grown into an amazing woman, Shasta. I'm so sorry for the ugly things I said to you. I know you and Evelyn wanted a family of your own. The things I said, I was so cruel."

"I knew you were hurting and lashing out. That eventually you would see I wasn't trying to take the girls from you." Memories of all the times Caid and Lina had called her mom flooded her, making her smile.

"What?" Nanette straightened and eyed her.

"Stick around long enough and you'll see."

She hummed, but kept her eyes on Shasta. "What happens now? If what you say is true... we'll really be free of it all?"

"I don't know what will happen in our realms. It's been so much different from Earth. There will be growing pains. That is a given. But yes, we'll be free."

"Even with the rough road, that sounds like a dream." She propped her chin on her hands. "I only hope I'm given the chance to make it right with Ione and Lily. Bring our family back together again, no matter how that looks."

Shasta wouldn't put words to the worry that was trying to eat her alive. Caid hadn't returned before everyone scattered. She didn't even know where he and Tura had gone. Time hadn't worked in their favor when Róisín had been pulled to Legianne. Her goodbyes to Matthew and Lily had been hasty, leaving her heart even more broken.

She wasn't sure that she could survive losing them all. If they didn't make it, nothing would stop the darkness from consuming her.

NINETY

MATTHEW SHIFTED his weight from one foot to the other. The moment they had arrived in Aunellion, a weight had settled in his chest. Each breath he managed felt like a miracle.

"This is…" Jackson turned in a circle next to him.

"Creepy," Lily whispered.

Memories of his time there pushed in against him on all sides, forcing Matthew to squeeze his eyes closed. He swallowed deeply. "What do we do next?"

Wordlessly, the Seer began to walk away from them.

Jackson looked over at him, his face pale, eyes wide. "We follow?"

"I guess." Matthew reached for Lily's hand.

"How do we know if it worked?" Lily asked.

Jackson's footsteps scuffed along the pavement next to them. "What did the one with wild, curly hair say again?"

"Ten. She said that Cronan's curse stated *the restoration of his beloved to the realm*," Lily said.

Matthew stopped walking, jolting Lily.

"What?"

"But we're *here*. The Seer is *here*." He squinted at the fading figure of the Seer. Further away from the trio, until they were swallowed by the fog.

"So," Jackson drew out the word, bringing his arms out wide. "Did it work? That's the question."

"Nothing feels different." Lily stepped in front of Matthew. "What are you thinking?"

He dropped his gaze down to her. "You don't want to know," he said quietly. Panic had grown legs and raced along his skin, burrowing, scattering around his insides at the thought of watching Lily go through what he had when he had been trapped there.

Before he could say or do anything, the Seer reappeared. They looked at each of them, expectant.

"You cannot just stand there. Come," they moved their hands in a sweeping motion.

Lily stiffened and sucked in a sharp breath. "They know. They know what to do."

Matthew's jaw flexed. "They've always known."

"This is it," the Seer said. "Help me up." They waved Matthew and Jackson closer and held out their hands.

An eternity later, they were greeted by the heavy steel doors of the Castle Aunellion, the Milsenett seat. Matthew shoved the door open and Jackson led the Seer inside. Lily stepped in behind him.

Then it felt like the entire realm exhaled.

The fog that had crept into the castle over the centuries edged out of the room they stood in. As it receded, it revealed walls lined with paintings. Looming stone statues of soldiers stood in each of the corners. At the center of the room was a large, woolen beast. The Traujus, a large, horned animal that was native to the realm.

"Home at last," the Seer said.

Something about their tone had Matthew spinning quickly away from the Traujus to face them. Gone was the withered, frail witch that walked slightly hunched over with a limp. In their place stood a witch that looked nearly a millennium younger with smooth, milk-white skin. Their eyes were gray. Hair darker than night spilled down their shoulders.

Jackson gasped next to him. "Holy fuck."

"How?" Lily asked.

"That you ask that shows how little you truly know of Gea," they said. "My husband was cruel, as were many of the Aunellion witches, but there has never been one as cunning and dark as Gea de Oro."

"Has what you've seen for Róisín changed?" Matthew asked, almost immediately regretting it. He wasn't sure he was ready for the answer.

The Seer stilled, their eyes closing. "I'm afraid no. I still see two paths for her. Kincaid will free the sisters and destroy The Gray. The realms will find peace again, but I cannot see clearly the rest."

Matthew's stomach sank like an anchor. If the realms found peace, that meant Gea would be destroyed. That Róisín still had two paths could only mean that she lived, or she died with Gea. When the Seer approached him, lifting their hands, he flinched.

"It's alright, child." They placed their hands on his cheeks. "Three-ninety-nine Tillson Lane is what you seek here." The air around them became hot and heavy, faint with a metallic scent. Magic rippling out and across the space.

"Excuse me?" He wrinkled his nose.

They pat his cheek, smiled, then turned away, walking deeper into the castle.

"I think that's our cue to go," Jackson said.

It was then that Matthew realized he had inched toward the door, dragging Lily with him, leaving Matthew to stand alone in the middle of the room.

When they stepped outside, they immediately lifted their hands to shield their eyes.

"It's beautiful," Lily said.

Jackson snorted. "If you like dead things."

The fog had been pushed clear of the courtyard and city beyond the castle, revealing brick buildings lining the streets. Jackson had been right. Everything that was once living was black and withered. But Matthew could see it as Lily was, in full bloom, people milling around shopping, in the park on walks or playing with their children. The water fountain drew his attention, and without a word, he moved toward it.

"Matthew?" Lily's voice followed him.

"Tillson Lane." He pointed to a street sign at the end of a road that exited into the center of the town, where the fountain stood dormant.

"It's an address then?" Jackson fell into step next to him.

"I think so." Matthew kept his eyes moving from one side of the road to the other, noting that the odd numbers were to his left. "This side."

"Two-fifteen," Lily said. "With the pattern, the house would be at the end of the road."

Five minutes later, they stood on the sidewalk in front of a two-story home. Its brick facade was a deep red. White shutters hung weathered and fading next to each of the windows. The door was chipped, revealing grayed wood beneath the green paint.

His heart thundered in his ears. The hammering overwhelmed him. For a moment, he struggled to catch his breath.

Lily slipped her hand into his and moved to stand before him. "Matthew, breathe." She squeezed his hand tightly. "We'll wait here."

He could only nod, putting everything he had into making his legs carry him to the door.

Once he gripped the door handle, the sound of everything around him, within him, fell away. He sucked in a breath, holding it. Then, pushed the door open. The moment he stepped inside, he knew. His instinct had been right. This had been his mother's home. Jackson's father's home. He had just turned to call for Jackson to come inside, but something out of the corner of his eye made him hesitate.

Closing the door, he moved from the foyer to a room at the side. Immediately, he broke. Crashing down to his knees, the tears came quickly, hot down his cheeks. Sobs ripped free from his chest as grief swamped him anew.

He looked as though he had sat in the chair and fallen asleep for an afternoon nap. So peaceful that as Matthew wiped furiously at his eyes to clear the tears, he stared at Lucius's chest, waiting to see it rise and fall with a sleepy breath. He struggled to his feet, then forward. Closer to the chair where Lucius's body rested.

How? It had been years.

Then it hit him. The magic he had felt the Seer release after they gave him the address. It had been their way of showing their gratitude.

Giving Lucius to Matthew to bring home, to place in his eternal rest beside where they had buried Clarissa all those decades before.

His chest heaving with his cries, Matthew dropped before Lucius. "You're coming home, dad. You and mom will be together again. I promise."

Lily's quiet sob made his chest tighten even more.

"I just wanted to... I'm sorry, Matthew. It had been a few minutes. I wanted to make sure you were okay," she said.

He glanced over his shoulder and saw that Jackson had also come into the house. He stood with shoulders high, tears in his eyes, lips pressed into a tight line behind Lily.

Matthew rose to his feet. Then he slid an arm under Lucius's legs, another behind his back, lifting him against his chest. Turning to Lily and Jackson, he said, "Let's go home."

Lily came to his side and brought an arm around his back, her show of support.

Jackson rested a hand at his shoulder. His voice breaking as he spoke. "Maybe we can go fishing when we get back. In honor of Uncle Lucius."

He nodded. "He'd like that. Just... just promise to not bark like a dog this time."

Jackson's grin came quick. His chuckle was gruff. "I'll do my best."

Matthew exhaled a heavy breath and shifted them all to Ely.

NINETY-ONE

CAID TRAILED behind Tura. Each step feeling heavier than the last when they didn't lead him back to the kitchen where everyone had been gathered. It hadn't been a shift that had brought them to this place. Tura had simply stepped from the kitchen, into the gray. He assumed it would happen the same way, but in reverse, at any moment.

Any moment.

Any. Moment.

He would hold Róisín in his arms. Kiss her one last time. Draw in her scent once more. Profess his love to her just once more.

Something exploded inside him. It was hot, sharp. It dug into his guts, his lungs. Stabbed at his heart. His magic flared, ready, angry, as he doubled over gasping for breath.

"No." Tura had stopped in front of him. "No."

"Tura," he ground out, clutching his middle.

She spun back to him. "We have to go back."

"I thought that's where we were going?" He clenched his jaw as another wave of heat thrashed him. "Back."

"We were going to the others. But we have to..." her eyes lifted from his face, to beyond him.

This wasn't happening. This *couldn't* be happening.

Róisín wasn't in Legianne already. He wasn't here, going back to that little cottage.

No.

The anger that pulsed from his magic shifted into something darker.

Tura reached her hand out for his. "We have to—"

The gray around them rippled. A shockwave knocked them off their feet. She scrambled to her hands and knees, her hand extending again.

"Now!" She shouted at him.

He rolled to his side and gripped her hand tightly. A weightless sensation fell over him and, once again, he was standing before the storybook home.

Stepping forward, he felt the vibration of whatever kept the cottage shielded from trespassers. A gnawing sensation, akin to hunger, began in the pit of his stomach.

"Trust?" His magic said the word like a question.

Caid had no choice but to trust his magic. He couldn't hesitate. Their window was small, the chain of events beyond this space giving them a limited opportunity. Rolling his neck, he handed over the reins of his body to his magic.

It made him feel larger. Stronger. He pushed his hands through the barrier, his muscles burning in protest as he gripped and pulled, creating an opening. When he stepped through, Tura followed quietly.

"You should stay back," he told her, not recognizing his own voice. It was darker, almost guttural, as he spoke. "It's not safe for you."

"I can't leave them again," she said.

The door reached out for them. Invisible hands pushed at him, trying to hold him away. The way Tura shot forward, he knew the house was trying to drag her in.

"Tura."

"No," she said through clenched teeth.

His magic seeped into the air around them. The shrubs along the front of the cottage withered, then turned to dust. Ink-like vines snaked from the ground along the home. Hissing as they went. They slipped around the window edges, disappearing into the house.

Something pushed back against the magic as it began to pull apart the cottage piece by piece. It only made his magic multiply, press deeper. Burn hotter.

Drenched in sweat, he lifted his booted foot to kick in the door. Tura rushed in ahead of him before he could stop her.

"Tura?" A voice cracked in the room's darkness as he entered.

"I am here, sisters," Tura's voice was thick. "I am here. We are free."

"What do you—Who are you?" The voice demanded.

Fire pulsed from Caid's left hand, lighting the room. Two women were huddled together in front of a large wooden loom. Their eyes were wide, darting from Tura to him and back.

"He's here to help us," Tura began.

"We have to go, Tura. It's..." His magic cut off the rest of his words. Something had reached for it, tried to grasp it. In response, his magic had grown teeth and hands, slashing and gnawing back.

"Sisters, please. I can tell you everything when we get to safety," Tura's tone was pleading.

Whatever it was existing inside the home grew larger when the sisters moved closer to Tura. There was an underlying panic in it. That was all his magic needed. The opening to pounce. Tura gripped her sisters' hands, fleeing as Caid's magic intercepted the hands grasping to stop them from getting out.

A bitter taste hit his mouth the moment he realized his magic was *consuming* it. Mouthful after mouthful, his magic ate. As he took it within himself, it kicked and thrashed in protest.

Exhaustion pulled at him as he kept his body from being thrashed around by it.

Then his magic released a satisfied sigh and settled itself. Unable to stand any longer, he dropped to his knees at the threshold of the cottage, panting.

"That was delicious," his magic hummed in delight.

"What the fuck *was* that?" He fell forward onto his hands. Nausea rolled through him, and his vision swam.

"Vengeance."

Caid dredged deep to find the strength to stand. Tura stood between her sisters, who clung to her, faces pale and soaked with tears.

"How do I destroy this place?" He asked Tura.

"Your magic will know how." Her arms came around her sisters' waists and she pulled them closer. "There's still time."

"Time?"

"Leave nothing behind, Kincaid," she said.

"What do you mean, there's still time?" He took a step toward her.

She stepped back with her sisters. "Fate will never forgive me, but I will welcome the consequences of my actions. I cannot take from her anymore than we already have. Nor you. The others. This is my burden to bear."

"Tura—"

"It is my burden to bear," she repeated, her tone was dark, venomous.

As her words sunk in, a sense of urgency rose, sending his magic rioting again. A fresh wave of adrenaline washed over him. He clenched his hands at his side to hold it at bay for just one second longer.

"Leave nothing behind and go to her."

Then the sisters were gone, and his magic was screaming with power.

NINETY-TWO

M ARCELO PROPPED his sketchpad on his knee. His heart squeezed as he took in the quartet of half-sketches of Nolani's face. He had been drawing her as though he were desperate to commit her features to memory. Yet, he knew he would never forget.

Across the room, Anthony threw his pencil at the door.

"That is *not* relaxing," he bit out. "I can't even put into words the rage that I feel right now."

Marcelo lifted an eyebrow. "Do you want to play a game of chess, then?"

"So you can kick my ass?" He brought a fist to his mouth, trying to cover a hacking cough. "I'd rather not spend my last days being tromped by my big brother. Thank you very much." He struggled forward in his chair.

Marcelo watched him struggle to stand, then shuffle his way back over to the window. "Watching the city is better?"

"No. Not even close."

"Then, why?"

Anthony looked over his shoulder. "It keeps the monster inside quieter than your silly drawing."

The door handle turning stopped both brothers from saying more. When Aja stepped into the room, Marcelo jumped to his feet.

"Nolani? Is she?"

Aja lifted a hand. "She's alright. She's with Cicile in Molennius right now."

Marcelo watched the way Aja's red eyes took in Anthony's figure. "Why are you here?"

"Let's sit." He motioned toward the chair that Marcelo had just vacated.

"I-I'd like to stand," Anthony said roughly.

Aja dipped his head in a slight nod. "Do you think you can hold on for just one more day?"

Anthony's brows came together. "I can try."

Aja licked his bottom lip before pressing them together. His eyes blinked rapidly before he turned his attention to Marcelo. "It's happening. You missed a lot after you left, but..." He rubbed a hand over the top of his head. "Róisín's found the Seer."

"What do they have to do with any of this?"

"That's why I suggested sitting down." He rounded the chair next to Marcelo and lowered his large frame into it. "As I said, you missed a lot."

AJA HAD BEEN RIGHT. MARCELO HAD MISSED A LOT. IT FELT like he had missed *everything*.

Could his brother be saved? If they could rid themselves of the monsters within... Marcelo's heart reached out with hesitant hands to grab hold of his own hope.

"What do we do now?" Marcelo asked.

As Aja had spoken about what Hecate and Tura had said, what Róisín believed, Anthony had inched closer to them until he too was sitting. Marcelo studied him now. He held his arms wrapped around his middle and leaned forward slightly toward Aja. It had been the first time in the days he had been with Anthony that Marcelo saw any semblance of light in his brother's eyes.

This had to work. He couldn't let Anthony down.

"I don't know how it will all work, but if Róisín succeeds and what Ten, Cicile, and Ione said about the Seer is right, I believe we'll feel something. The humans won't, of course. But the witches—" He nodded. "And you two."

"We'll be free of," Anthony began, but halted. He moaned and doubled over, his head falling to his knees.

Aja moved to rise, but Marcelo stopped him.

"His monster is still strong. Let me." Marcelo rose to go to his brother, and he immediately fell back into the chair. His legs too weak to hold him upright.

Aja gasped, one of his hands flying to his chest.

"Celo." Anthony let out a sob. "Celo."

Marcelo slid from his chair and crawled over to him. "I'm here, Ant. I'm—" He grit his teeth as everything inside of him went taut, then stretched. "I'm here."

With his head still on his knees, his body quaking, he reached out for Marcelo. "Don't leave me. Please don't leave me. I don't want to die alone."

A snarl burst out of Aja. Marcelo struggled to shift around to see him. The veins in Aja's neck and arms were raised. His jaw fluttered and his nostrils flared wide with his harsh breaths.

If they were all...

"Is it?" Was all Marcelo managed of his question before his lungs clutched in his chest.

"Fuck." Aja's eyes flew open, and they were a dance of reds, black, and deep green. "Anelle."

Marcelo felt Anthony's fingers flex on his forearm. He was here with his brother, but Aja was realms apart from his sister. His twin.

Another sob slipped from Anthony. "Celo, I..."

Something settled inside of Marcelo. A lightness that was new and welcomed by his entire being.

All at once, his body relaxed. Anthony's grip released him, and Marcelo felt his body slump in the chair.

"Ant?" He took him by the shoulders. "Ant?"

"I'm so tired," Anthony said softly. "And hungry. Those orange cakes the cook used to make. I'd love for one of those. Do you think they'll make some?"

The tone of Anthony's voice, the boyishness of it that Marcelo remembered from the days, the years *before*. Marcelo felt a burning begin at the bridge of his nose.

Marcelo gave Anthony's knee a squeeze. "I think we can figure something out. Aja?" He turned to him.

Aja's chest was rising and falling rapidly. His eyes were still a swarm of colors from his magic. "Are you okay?"

"I think so. I feel"—he licked his lips—"different." He had been born cursed, so he didn't know life without it. Even if his monster had never woken, what he felt at that moment was far different from what he had felt before. It was as though a light had been turned on inside of him. "Does that mean it worked?"

"It has to. Not just that bringing the Seer to Aunellion worked." His head bobbed, and he swallowed. "That she did it. Roisin did it."

Marcelo let the unspoken question he could see in Aja's eyes, and felt inside of himself, linger.

Róisín destroyed the Goddess, but had she survived it?

NINETY-THREE

Róisín's magic sang loudly inside her. Twenty paces away, Gea was climbing to her feet. Her laughter echoing over the decimated field to Róisín. As they had battled, Gea had tossed out comments meant to dig beneath Róisín's skin. To get inside her head. Make her fumble and stumble.

As the well source thrummed at her feet, Róisín could only smile.

"Do you know what I still cannot work out?" Gea asked.

"I don't really care. I'm sure since you enjoy hearing yourself talk, you'll tell me," Róisín said, more to herself than Gea. She flicked her magic outward. The ground at Gea's feet spread, sending the woman plummeting out of sight.

She didn't want to admit it, but Gea's last blow of magic had stung. She was toying with her now as a chance to catch her breath. Matthew and Lily must not have made it to Aunellion yet, because Gea was still barreling forward at her full strength.

Róisín had handled it so far. She had yet to bottom out her magic since it had been returned to her. An added benefit was that she was at the heart of her realm's magic. Except she knew she couldn't trust any of it. She knew how quickly everything could change.

Gea floated out of the hole and Róisín could see the fire burning in her eyes from where she stood.

"How your mother arrived at the veil with her magic already gone."

Róisín stilled. Her magic that had been dancing freely, openly, next to her, paused. Quieted.

"Something told me that day to be there. I hadn't been sure why. Everyone coming into the afterworld that day had been so... bland." She smoothed a hand over her knotted hair. Then the tatters of her dress. "Your mother, though. I could *feel* it in Brenna McKenna when she arrived. You can imagine my surprise when I learned that somehow her magic had already been inherited, given *that* isn't supposed to happen until they move through the gate of the afterworld."

Róisín's heart thudded heavily against her ribs. Her mother's magic had been sealed into a stone because the council had deemed Róisín not ready to inherit the magic that she had left behind. She felt the click of understanding. Tura was the Goddess of the Hells. The sister with future sight. She had known. Brenna's magic had to have been placed in the stone by Tura so that when Brenna arrived at the veil, Gea wouldn't have any magic to take.

"I was even further surprised to learn about this little rock that apparently held her magic." She wiped a smudge of dirt from her cheek.

"That's why you put her in the in-between," Róisín said quietly enough that her words didn't carry.

"I locked her in the in-between," Gea continued. "Then set out in search of that rock. I call that time period a surprise party. Do you want to know why?"

Róisín rolled her eyes. *Hells, she really likes to hear herself talk, doesn't she?*

"Because every time I turned around, *surprise*—" Gea's eyes went wide. Her head quickly looked this way and that. "No. That's impossible."

Bingo.

"Surprise." Róisín grinned. The air around them became fragrant with the smells of magic. Floral, earthy, metallic, every scent she had ever known their magic to smell like, filled her senses to the brim.

Bubbles rose inside of her. They tickled her gut, her lungs, her heart, as they worked their way higher. From her throat, they burst from her mouth in a fit of laughter. She had just bent forward, placing her hands on her knees, when something burst through the air, rolling over them in a heavy wave.

Gea stumbled, falling to her knees. But only for a moment. Recovering quickly, she got to her feet again. The venom in her voice was potent. "*What have you done?*"

Róisín couldn't stop the grin that split her face. "Did you think you could take it all away from me and I wouldn't figure it out?"

"And do you think you can really beat *me?*"

Róisín flexed her fingers outward, her elemental magic coming together, creating two Katanas much like the ones she had in Lucius's training room. "I don't know, but I'm going to fucking try." She flipped one of the blades. "For my mother." Magic surged down her arms, filling the weapons in her hands. "My father." She lowered into her fighting stance. "My family. And everything else you've taken from me. From my people."

She drew in a breath and charged. Gea quickly threw up a wall of dirt, pressing it forward to block her. Her magic shot ahead of her, creating a hole for her to leap through.

"You're the one that sent the darkness demon for my father." Róisín slashed a Katana out.

"Human rats do not belong in our world." Gea released a magic-fueled bolt as she spun away from her. "Your mother belongs where *I* put her. Order will be restored to my realms."

Róisín leapt into the air, clearing another bolt. "Hecate's realms."

"You foolish *child*! That woman is only out to ruin us all." Gea swung a sword of stone up to block her incoming blow.

She lifted the ground at Gea's feet, making the woman stumble. Using the momentum to her advantage, Róisín advanced forward, swinging at the same time. Gea lifted her sword to block, but she had misjudged Róisín's swing. The Katana landed at Gea's forearm, severing it. Gea released a howl of pain as the arm and sword fell to the ground.

"You messed with Fate, Gea." Róisín moved back a step, knowing all it would take was one touch from Gea and it would be over. "You stole magic from families. Bound the magic you couldn't reach. Then, you pulled a thread from a loom of fate." Her laughter was heavy and dark. "Fate sent me to collect."

Gea's mouth fell open, and it took a moment for her words to come. "What have you done with my daughter?" She surged to her feet. "Where is Tura?"

Róisín shifted away from her.

"Where is Tura?!" Gea let out a guttural scream that made Róisín's ears ring. "You will pay!"

"She is safe. You will not lay a hand on her."

Róisín's vow garnered another scream from Gea.

"You will no longer use her power to bend the Hells or its demons to your wishes." She felt her magic building, building inside of her again. She nudged it harder, encouraging it. She needed it to be more than ever before. More than in that back storeroom. The house. The alleyway. More than the times she had spent practicing on the small, deserted island she had found off the coast of Maine. *More.* Even if it took her with it.

"None of you would survive without me."

"Once upon a time, I believed that. But,"—She dropped her voice— "not anymore."

"You'll never win against me."

The pain of holding her magic in made her eyes water. The heat that surged through her made her skin break into a sweat. Her T-shirt clung to her body, soaked through. Just a little longer. A little more. "The Seer is back in Aunellion."

"That's impossible." Gea inched closer. "They've been missing since you destroyed their home."

"Anything is possible." So close, just a little... she grit her teeth, pulling the magic from the well source now. Her skin felt ready to split. "Don't tell me you can't feel that. That ripple from breaking Cronan's curse. Undoing your binds to them."

Gea stopped in mid-step.

"You fucked with the wrong witches." There. That was it. It would be enough. It had to be.

Róisín dropped her Katanas and let her magic explode just as arms came around her from the side.

NINETY-FOUR

Róisín's body hit the ground so hard, everything inside her rattled. Every muscle screamed in protest. Her chest was on fire. Each breath a shout for mercy. Her heart a faint thud in her chest.

She was alive, but fading. Breaths became harder to draw in. Her heart slowed just a little more, the empty spaces between beats growing.

The weight on top of her shifted. Then she was moving.

No, she was being moved.

Her magic kicked out, pushing at whatever it was in defense. It sent her body plummeting. She hit something hard. Fresh pain lanced through her. She wanted to scream, to cry.

Had Gea lived? No. *No*, she couldn't have failed.

Her body moved again. Gea. It had to be Gea. She was the only one there with her, and now she was taking her. She was going to siphon her magic and go after Hecate.

Fury struggled to explode free from inside her. It punched and pushed. She was too weak. Could she pull from the well source before Gea could complete her task?

As she wondered, a tingle began along her spine. The pulse of her Life magic throbbing deep inside her core.

"Róisín." Her name was a breath against her cheek before the touch of soft, warm lips. "Róisín, baby, wake up."

Caid.

She tried to push her eyes open, but they wouldn't obey her command. Instead, she tried to speak. Fingers pressed against her throat. Then she was moving again.

Caid's tone turned desperate. "Róisín."

She released a moan. Her body painfully and slowly coming back together as her magic worked to heal her.

When his lips brushed her cheek, her lips, her forehead, she felt a tear slip from her eyes and roll down her temple.

"You're okay." Her body swayed slightly. "You did it, baby. We did it. All of us."

Another tear rolled into her hair. She fought at the weakness still tugging her down. Lifting her hand, she moved it until she felt his face.

"I'm here. I've got you." His hand was warm over hers. "I've got you," he whispered.

"Caid." Her voice was rough and thick. "How?"

"I couldn't let you fall apart," he said into her hair. "I promised."

The arms she felt band around her before she had released her magic. This time, when she tried to pry her eyes open, her eyelids lifted. All she could see at first was Caid's neck and the fabric of his shirt. The faded green and gray flannel he had been wearing before Tura had whisked him away. She pressed her other hand to his chest. The heavy beat of his heart pounded against her palm.

She swallowed, then licked her lips. "Is she...?"

He sat up and peered down at her. His eyes were a sea of green, gold, and brown as they danced over her face. "There's a leg there." He pointed to the left. "A bit of her... upper body, maybe? *Something* anyway, over there." He moved his hand to point to a spot behind her. "I'd say she's toast."

Róisín's eyes fell closed. She let relief bathe her healing body. "Where did Tura take you?"

"To bust her sisters out and destroy this space between realms that Gea made to hold them." He threaded his fingers into her hair. "It had to be Hecate, me, or Lina. Hecate was too risky, Lina was a flat-out no. So, it was me."

The more her magic worked to heal her, the colder she felt. A shiver racked her body. She shifted closer to him. "The others?"

He hugged her to him. "I don't know yet. Tura said I had time to finish what I needed to and get here for you. I didn't hesitate." His voice trembled. "I got here and — I got here just in time."

She wrapped her arms around his neck and pressed a kiss to his jaw. "I can't believe I did it."

"I can. I know what Tura and the Seer said, but I knew. You would never let Gea walk away, even if it meant you were left in pieces across this field, too."

The pain in his voice cut her straight to the core. She tipped her head back. His mouth was slightly curved down. Brows lowered over his eyes. Lines bracketing both eyes and lips. She pulled him down until his lips met hers. One of his hands cupped the back of her head. She nipped his bottom lip before opening her mouth to welcome his tongue. She wiggled so that she was more upright, using the momentum to nudge him backward. It was enough to break the kiss, and she sprawled over his chest.

"What next?" He asked.

"We make sure everyone else is okay." She nuzzled his neck. "Then we go home and start trying to make some babies."

He coughed. "What?"

When she lifted her head, he had lifted his and was looking down at her, his eyebrows high on his forehead. "We just discussed this, Mr. McGrath. Right after you broke our towel stand."

Beneath her, his body shook with laughter. "I seem to recall it was you that broke it by trying to sit on it."

"Mm." She stroked a hand over his chest. Leaning forward, she gently bit his chin. "But who put me on the stand?"

The magic had calmed in his eyes. The hazel was shining under the Legianne sun as he studied her.

"I can always find someone else if you're not ready." She made to pull away, but he gripped her tighter. "Caid, too tight. Can't breathe."

"Róisín, there's nothing I've wanted more than *peace* for us so that we can have a life and a family of our own." He took her face in his hands. "One, two, hell, five or six kids, whatever our family looks like, I want that." He kissed her softly. "With you and only you. If you want to start now? We start now."

"Can we get a dog, too?" She asked, tearily.

"Are we talking about a small dog, or a big dog?"

Now it was she who laughed. "A rescued mutt from the shelter. Preferably medium sized."

"I can get behind that." He nodded. "I love you, Róisín."

She smiled down at him. "I love you, too." She peppered his face with kisses. With a giggle, she nipped his bottom lip, then said, "Let's go home." She brushed her nose along his jaw. "Celebrate with everyone. See my mother and father again." Her heart began to race. "Lucius. Clarissa." As her heart danced, butterflies exploded to life inside her stomach. "Make sure Marcelo and Anthony are okay." She rested her forehead against his shoulder and whispered, "Really meet my grandfather. Know him."

Caid moved her so that she was completely sprawled over him, then wrapped his arms around her. "Let's do it." He kissed the top of her head. "Ready?"

Closing her eyes, she rested her head against his chest. "As I'll ever be."

AFTERWORD

~~Dearest Reader~~, No. That doesn't fit here in this story or the realms.

I had flirted with the idea of an Epilogue for the end. However, that quickly became an entire novel in itself. Or at least, close to one. A lengthy novella more like.

I had wanted to give deeper closer on the key characters to this story.

I wanted everyone to know that Róisín and Caid finally got their peace. Had their family. Their sweet little girl, Brielle and a baby on the way. Something that we'd get a glimpse of at Abigail and Parker's wedding thirty some-odd years down the road (that's right, the McGrath/Burke family coming together for full circle).

How Róisín passed on the estates in Wurbray to Abigail, who deeply loved and adored Legianne in a way that Róisín knew she never would.

Matthew and Lily starting their own family. His accepting that even way back when he dreamt of Madigan at the Seer's home - it was actually his Sight coming into being.

Marcelo's story getting an unexpected, unexplainable extension that Hecate would only smile about when asked. A secret between she and fate. A gift to Celo and Nolani.

Shasta and Evelyn reuniting.

Brenna and Stephen bearing witness to the lives of their grand-children.

Lucius and Clarissa.

But then it came to Thomas. To Wyatt. How their lives always came with a period. A definitive ending. And I didn't like that. I didn't like that Wyatt and Caid's banter and horsing around would come to an end. Or that Thomas's endless love (and hots) for his wife would become a thing of memory. It hit a little too close to home, and made old hurts for real losses float back to the surface.

So this is where we end. And this is where I close the book on these characters and this world (or rather, these realms).

With everyone still together, be it through the veil, or in the realms. Alive. Happy. Finally at peace.

ACKNOWLEDGMENTS

To be honest, I don't even know where to start. This series has been a massive undertaking mentally and spiritually. It has helped move me forward on my path to healing in a way that I wasn't sure I would ever be able to. Even *with* therapy (which, how many other others out there take full sessions to work out why your own books have hurt you? Just me? No? Eep).

A massive thank you to the incredible group of women who gathered over texts and group calls to help me strip this book down and rebuild it in a way that best suits the stories told within and the overall story of the series. I know you didn't want to be named specifically, but I know that you all know this is you. I love you and I'm so grateful to have you in my life and that I get to work in the industry alongside such amazing women.

This is how I know I could never win an award in which I need to give a thank you speech. Writing this, I'm still a stuttering, forgetful mess of words. I know I'll forget someone that has been key to this book!

Thank you to my husband who has cheered me on from the background of this whole journey.

My kiddo for being the best publicist anyone could ever ask for. To see how proud he is of his momma, and hear how he talks about my books to any adult with willing ears has been the most heartwarming experience. He doesn't even know what they're about, but he's the biggest champion of them.

And lastly, thank you to every single reader that has stepped into this world alongside me. It has been an honor to get to share bits and pieces of these characters who are based upon people who were once here with us, but have moved on.

About the Author

H.S. Sullivan comes from a long line of storytellers and poets, so it is of no surprise she has been scratching down stories of her own since she was a small child.

She holds a B.A. in Journalism and is an award winning journalist for feature writing and photography. Writing professionally for 16 years, she often moonlights as a ghost writer for fitness blogs and magazines.

Sullivan was born and raised on the northern New England coast, where she currently lives with her husband, son, and their rescued heeler mix. When she's not writing or reading, she is training for her next Masters weightlifting meet, tending to her gardens, or swimming in the Atlantic.

The Forgotten Realm is Sullivan's third novel. Her previous titles are Daughters of Legianne, and The Unraveling of Covens from the Realms of Covens series.

To stay up-to-date on the Realms of Covens series and other upcoming works, visit hssullivan.com or follow on Instagram at @themothermermaid.

www.ingramcontent.com/pod-product-compliance
Lightning Source LLC
Chambersburg PA
CBHW050913030726
47503CB00007BB/2274